RISE OF
KALI

DURYODHANA'S MAHABHARATA

Yudhishtra to Drupada:
Dharma is subtle and we do not understand it. We faithfully
follow the path tread by our predecessors. My voice does not
speak untruth, nor does my mind dwell in *adharma*.

Duryodhana to Krishna (*Sabha Parva*):
I know what (your) *dharma* is. I know what you call *adharma*
is. Yet I follow my heart. If you are Janardhana, it is you who
dwell in my heart and make me do what I feel. Is it not my
Kshatriya *dharma* to protect what is mine?

Krishna to Arjuna in the *Bhagavad Gita*:
O Partha, that intelligence which is covered by darkness,
believes that *adharma* is *dharma* and gets all meanings
backwards. That is ignorant intelligence.

Bhishma to Yudhishtra (*Anusashana Parva*):
But it is not always easy for mere mortals to arrive at
dharma-vinischaya (definition of *dharma*). Only kala (time or
Yama, the God of Time or *Yamam*), knows what is *dharma* and
adharma.

Krishna in the *Bhagavad Gita*:
I AM TIME.

***

RISE OF KALI

DURYODHANA'S MAHABHARATA

AJAYA

Epic of the Kaurava Clan

BOOK II

ANAND NEELAKANTAN

PLATINUM PRESS

ISBN 978-93-81576-04-5
© Anand Neelakantan, 2015
Layouts: Chandravadan R. Shiroorkar - Leadstart Design
Cover: Kunal Kundu
Printing: Thomson Press (India) Limited

Published in India 2015 by
PLATINUM PRESS
An imprint of
LEADSTART PUBLISHING PVT LTD
Unit 25-26, Building A/1, Near Wadala RTO,
Wadala (E), Mumbai – 400 037, INDIA
T + 91 22 2404 6887
W www.leadstartcorp.com

To the loving memory
of my beloved mother,
D. Chellammal Neelakantan,
who left us on Thiruvonam day.

ABOUT THE AUTHOR

 I WAS BORN IN A QUAINT little village called Thripunithura, on the outskirts of Cochin, Kerala. Located east of mainland Ernakulam, across Vembanad Lake, this village had the distinction of being the seat of the Cochin royal family. However, it was once more famous for its hundred-odd temples, the various classical artists it produced, and its music school. I remember many an evening listening to the faint rhythm of *chenda*s from the temples and the notes of the flute escaping over the rugged walls of the school of music. However, in recent times, Gulf money and the rapidly expanding city of Cochin have wiped away all remaining vestiges of that old world charm. The village has evolved into the usual, unremarkable, suburban hellhole, clones of which dot India.

Growing up in a village with more temples than was necessary, it was little wonder that mythology fascinated me. Ironically, I was drawn to the anti-heroes. Life went on...I became an engineer, joined the Indian Oil Corporation, moved to Bangalore, married Aparna, and welcomed my daughter Ananya, and son, Abhinav. But the voices of yore refused to be silenced. I felt impelled to narrate the stories of the vanquished and the dammed, and give life to those silent heroes we have overlooked in our uncritical acceptance of the conventional renderings of our epics.

This is Anand's third book and follows the outstanding success of his #1 bestsellers, ASURA Tale Of The Vanquished *and* AJAYA Book I, Roll Of The Dice. *Anand can be reached at: mail@asura.co.in*

Contents

AUTHOR'S NOTE

WHY WRITE ABOUT THE DEFEATED?

In the first volume of *Ajaya*, I elaborated on my reasons for choosing to write the *Mahabharata* story from Duryodhana's perspective. Since its publication, I have received numerous e-mails from my readers – some critical, others adulatory or analytical of the perspective I brought to the age-old epic. There were readers who were unhappy that I had cast Krishna in an unflattering light and portrayed the Pandavas in a negative way. Hence, a short note about my portrayal of Krishna and the Pandavas is perhaps merited here.

I have written *Ajaya* from the perspective of the vanquished side – the Kauravas. For them, Krishna was a rival, if not an enemy. If the Kauravas had accepted Krishna's divinity and agreed to whatever he ordained, the Mahabharata war would not have taken place. It would thus be unrealistic, even ridiculous, for the Kauravas to be seen worshipping Krishna. There would have been no story left to tell. The great sage, Vedavyasa, never portrayed Krishna as God or an *avatar* in his original version, *Jaya*. It was only later, in the *Mahabhagawatam*, that he is seen as an *avatar* of Vishnu. There were many criticisms voiced about Krishna in the *Mahabharata*. Characters like Shishupala, Suyodhana, Gandhari, and even Balarama, his brother, sometimes made scathing verbal attacks on Krishna. Vyasa effectively used these opposing viewpoints to create a rounded story.

The *Mahabharata*, in essence, is a narrative without a hero. Rather, every character is a hero. I suspect the sage Vyasa adopted the title *Jaya* for his great epic in order to point out the irony of violence and a war in which no one wins. For me, *Jaya* is an anti-war story. I have condensed the *Gita* and placed it slightly ahead in the conventional storyline, as a conversation between Balarama and Krishna. The two brothers, though they loved each other, had many disagreements over the Kauravas and Pandavas. While

Krishna favoured Arjuna, Suyodhana was Balarama's favourite.
In this rendering, Balarama denounces Krishna before the war
for the violence he is trying to unleash. But for Krishna, it is the
call of duty and *dharma*. I have used this space to imagine how
the conversation between Balarama and Krishna might have
gone. Here, as in the original, Krishna is unable to convince
Balarama about the necessity for a war; this would have been an
argument between two great intellects. I have used this space to
voice Balarama's doubts as he speaks to Krishna. Rather, they
are my own doubts on reading the *Gita*. I plead guilty to putting
my words into Balarama's mouth, and occasionally Arjuna's.
Vedvyasa just says Krishna and Balarama disagreed about
the war and that Balarama went on a pilgrimage when it took
place. I have included the *Gita* in its conventional space, though
some of the doubts Arjuna airs are my own. The original *Gita*
is a conversation between a mentor and mentee, when Krishna
convinces Arjuna to fight the war.

As I have stated in the many interviews I have given and articles
I have written, I am a seeker; my stories are more about questions
than answers. I claim neither the intellect nor the scholarship to
make a critical analysis of the *Gita*, words which have inspired
countless men and women over the centuries. My questions are
mundane and ordinary, like the doubts that gnaw at a child's
mind when an adult tells him wonderful stories. The child
knows the stories are fascinating but curiosity still makes him
ask questions for a better understanding.

Recently, on the auspicious occasion of Thiruvonam, the day the
great Asura emperor, Mahabali (Lord Vishnu, in his Vamana
avatar had banished Mahabali to *patala*, the underworld), comes
to visit his people on earth, I suffered a shattering personal loss
when my mother passed away. I sought solace in Krishna's
message in the *Gita*, but the analogy of the *atma* (soul) departing
the body as being nothing but a change of clothes, did not give
me any comfort. Death is real and devastating and no intellectual

circus can take away the pain of the people who are left behind. When the rituals were over and my mother's ashes sent to Kashi for immersion in the Ganga, I was left feeling bitter and bereft. I asked the chief priest of my village, who had conducted the rituals, whether there was any meaning in such customs. In response, he told me this story:

Mandana Misra was a great scholar and authority on the *Vedas* and *Mimasa*. He led a householder's life (*grihastha*), with his scholar-philosopher wife, Ubhaya Bharati, in the town of Mahishi, in what is present-day northern Bihar. Husband and wife would have great debates on the veracity of the *Vedas*, the *Upanishads*, the *Gita* and other philosophical works. Scholars from all over Bharatavarsha came to debate and understand the *Shastras* with them. It is said that even the parrots in Mandana's home debated the divinity, or its lack, in the *Vedas* and *Upanishads*.

Mandana was a staunch believer in rituals. One day, while he was performing *Pitru Karma* (rituals for deceased ancestors), Adi Shankaracharya arrived at his home and demanded a debate on *Advaita*. Mandana was angry at the rude intrusion and asked the Acharya whether he was not aware, as a Brahmin, that it was inauspicious to come to another Brahmin's home uninvited when *Pitru Karma* was being done? In reply, Adi Shankara asked Mandana whether he was sure of the value of such rituals. This enraged Mandana and the other Brahmins present. Thus began one of the most celebrated debates in Hindu thought. It raged for weeks between the two great scholars. As the only other person of equal intellect to Shankara and Mandana was Mandana's wife, Ubhaya Bharati, she was appointed the adjudicator. Among other things, Shankara convinced Mandana that the rituals for the dead had little value to the dead. Mandana became Adi Shankara's disciple (and later the first Shankaracharya of the Sringeri Math in Karnataka).

When the priest related this story to me, I was shocked. He was not giving me the answer I had expected. Annoyed, I asked him what he meant by the story if Adi Shankara himself said such rituals were no use to the dead. The priest replied, "Son, the story has not ended." And he continued... A few years later, Adi Shankara was compiling the rituals for the dead, to standardize them for people across Bharatavarsha. Mandana, upset with his Guru's action, asked Adi Shankara why he was involved with such a useless thing. After all, the Guru had convinced him of the uselessness of such rituals. (Lord Krishna also mentions the inferiority of Vedic sacrifice to other paths, in the *Gita*. *Pitru karma* has no vedic base either.) Why then was the Jagad Guru taking such a retrograde step? Adi Shankaracharya smiled at his disciple and answered, "The rituals are not for the dead but for the loved ones left behind."

This demonstrates how critical thinking is the basis of all our philosophy. We have no concept of blasphemy. This openness to criticism is what makes the Hindu religion and its traditions unique. Vyasa did not hide Krishna's faults, nor did Valmiki remain silent on Rama's shortcomings. This openness to debate and discussion has helped us evolve over time and withstand thousands of years of foreign rule, reforming as the times demanded. Otherwise, Hinduism would long have been dead, like the ancient religions of Greece and Egypt. It is said that for every village there is a *Ramayana* and for every person there is a *Gita*. In chapter 18:63, Lord Krishna says:

iti te jñānam ākhyātam
guhyād guhyataram mayā
vimriśyaitad aśeshena
yathecchasi tathā kuru
[I have given you the most confidential of all knowledge.
Analyze it critically and act as per your wish and understanding.]

Krishna does not ask Arjuna to follow blindly, nor threaten him with hell if he disobeys. In voicing my own doubts, I too have followed Krishna's advice by critically analyzing the *Mahabharata*. I hope that those who possess a deeper understanding and knowledge of the epic will aid me in finding answers to the questions which have troubled me. I believe I am not alone in my occasional puzzlement. Some of my readers certainly share my doubts. I request you to bear in mind that this is a work of fiction, in the best Indian tradition of *Vada-Prathivada*. The Gurus of yesteryear opined that the best way to understand something is to debate it. I have rolled my dice with the prayer:

vimriśyaitad aśeshena
yathecchasi tathā kuru

[Analyze it critically and act as per your wish and understanding.]

*****

Select Cast of Characters

Aswathama: Suyodhana's close friend and son of Guru Drona, this Brahmin youth refuses to blindly follow tradition. He believes Suyodhana's cause is just and is willing to fight even his illustrious father. He views Arjuna as his arch foe.

Balarama: Leader of the Yadava clan, an idealistic dreamer who wishes to bring prosperity to his people and belives in the equality of all men. He sees the path to progress as lying in farming and trade. A pacifist at heart, he builds an ideal city on the west coast of Bharatavarsha, where he puts his ideas into practice. He longs to prove one can rule without compromising one's principles. Krishna and Subhadra's elder brother, he is also Suyodhana's Guru-mentor, and inspires men like Karna to reach beyond the limitations of caste.

Bhishma: Grand Regent of the Kuru clan and granduncle to both the Pandavas and Kauravas. Also known as Gangadatta Devavrata. Referred to here as the Grand Regent or Bhishma, a name acquired after he took a vow of celibacy and relinquished his claim to the throne, as a precondition to his father marrying Satyavathi, a fisherwoman (who had another son, Krishna Dwaipayana Vedavyasa, prior to this marriage).

Dhaumya: An ambitious and unscrupulous Priest, he is Parashurama's eyes, ears and arm in Hastinapura. His aim is a perfect society where Priests will decree and the rest follow. He is Kunti and Yudhishtra's chief advisor.

Dhritarashtra: Son of Vedavyasa, he is the legitimate, though blind, King of Hastinapura, and father of the Kauravas. Denied the Kingship due to his blindness, Pandu (his albino younger brother), reigns instead; on his death, Dhritarashtra assumes the Kingship nominally, with Bhishma as Grand Regent.

Draupadi: The wife shared by the five Pandava brothers. Dhristadyumna is her brother, and Shikandi (a eunuch), is an adopted sibling. She is spirited and does not take insults quietly. Fiercely determined, she is perhaps the real 'man' in the Pandava camp.

Durjaya: A man of the gutters, he rules the dark underworld of Hastinapura. A crime lord, he engineers riots and is in the pay of the Gandhara Prince, Shakuni.

Ekalavya: A tribal youth who desperately wants to become a warrior, he is ready to give his life to achieve some dignity for his people.

Gandhari: Princess of Gandhara, Bhishma forcibly carries her off to marry his blind nephew, Dhritarashtra. She voluntary chooses to bind her eyes to share her husband's blindness. She is the mother of Crown Prince Suyodhana and his brothers, the Kauravas. Her brother is Shakuni.

General Hiranyadhanus: Father of Ekalavya and Commander-in-Chief of Jarasandha's army, he has risen from the lowliest Nishada caste by dint of his own merit and the friendship of King Jarasandha.

Guru Drona: Teacher to both the Pandavas and Kauravas; and Aswathama's father, he will do anything to make Arjuna the greatest warrior in the world. His love for his disciple is legendary, exceeded only by his love for his son. Orthodox to the core, he believes in the superiority of his caste and that no low castes should have the privilege of knowledge. The poverty of his early life haunts him.

Indra: The last king of the Deva Empire, he lives in penury in the forest. He wishes to make a secret weapon for Arjuna, without which he fears his son is doomed.

Iravan: Son of Arjuna and the Naga princess Uloopi. In the north Indian versions of the *Mahabharata*, Iravan is a minor character who dies a heroic death on the 18th day of the war. In the south Indian versions of the epic, Iravan is the epitome of sacrifice, who gives his life before the war to aid victory for the Pandavas. He is worshipped as a major village deity in the South.

Jarasandha: The King of Magadha. In his kingdom, merit rules instead of caste.

Jayadratha: King of Sindh, he is Suyodhana's brother-in-law.

Karna: A low-caste Suta and son of a charioteer, he is willing to travel to the Deep South to become a warrior par excellence. Generous, charitable, exceptionally gifted, he is Suyodhana's answer to Arjuna's challenge. He is spurned for his low birth and insulted by Draupadi, but Suyodhana staunchly stands by him.

The Kauravas: The legitimate scions of the Kuru clan that holds suzerainty over all the kingdoms north of the Vindhya ranges. Crown Prince Suyodhana and his siblings are determined to hold on to what is rightfully theirs.

◉ Suyodhana: Meaning 'one who cannot be easily conquered', the eldest Kaurava (Dhritarashtra and Gandhari's firstborn), is the legitimate Crown Prince of Hastinapura. This book narrates his fight to claim his birthright. Perhaps the most celebrated villain in Indian mythology after Ravana of the Ramayana, we see him here as loyal, generous, brash and arrogant, his mindset against the taboos and convoluted arguments of orthodoxy.

◉ Sushasana: Suyodhana's next sibling, more famous as Dushasana.

◉ Sushala: The only girl child among the Kauravas, she is known as Dushala in popular lore, she is also the loving wife of Jayadratha, King of Sindh.

Khatotkacha: Son of Bhima and Rakshasi Hidumbi.

Kripa: A maverick genius as well as a learned Brahmin warrior, he does not believe in caste. He is Drona's brother-in-law (his opposite), and Aswathama's uncle. He believes Suyodhana has a point. A carefree soul without boundaries, he is outspoken to the point of arrogance but kind-hearted beneath his rough exterior. He believes knowledge ought to be shared freely.

Krishna: A Yadava Prince who many consider an *avatar* of Vishnu – one of the Hindu Trinity. He believes he has come to save the world from evil.

He is also Arjuna's brother-in-law and mentor. He sees the Great War as an inevitable conflict for *dharma* to be reinstated. His greatest challenges come from men like Jarasandha, Suyodhana, Karna, Ekalavya and Carvaka.

Krishna [black] **Dwaipayana** [born on an island] **Vedavyasa** [chronicler of the *Veda*s]: The great scholar-author of the *Mahabharata,* the *Mahabhagavatha* (the longest epic in the world), and 18 *Puranas*. He codified and edited the *Veda*s and is considered the patron saint of all writers. Son of Satyavathi, a fisherwoman and Parashara, a Brahmin saint, he is the Grand Regent's stepbrother. He is also the biological father of Pandu, Dhritarashtra and Vidhura, and hence the grandfather of all the main protagonists of the *Mahabharata.*

Kunti: First wife of Pandu and collective mother of the Pandavas, she has an illegitimate son as well. Ambitious, ruthless, and self-righteous, she is determined to ensure Yudhishtra succeeds to the throne of Hastinapura.

Mayasura: A great architect and a low-caste Asura.

Pandu: Dhritarashtra's younger brother and briefly King of Hastinapura until his premature death. Cursed never to have marital relations, his two wives, Kunti and Madri, are impregnated by sages and Gods. There are, however, enough hints in the *Mahabharata* that their five sons were not, in fact, of divine origin. The sons, called the Pandavas, are recognized as Pandu's sons though he did not father them. He dies attempting sexual union with Madri, who commits *sati*, leaving Kunti to care for all five boys.

The Pandavas (Five Sons of Pandu):

Ⓞ Yudhishtra (Dharmaputra): The eldest, was born to Kunti, fathered by Dharma or Yama, the God of Death. His claim to the throne of Hastinapura rests on the fact that he is considered Pandu's son, has divine lineage, and is older than Crown Prince Suyodhana by a day. The whole *Mahabharata* hinges on this accident of birth.

Ⓞ Bhima: Kunti's next divine progeny is the Crown Prince's archenemy. Renowned for his brute strength, he is ever ready to use it on his brothers' behalf.

Ⓞ Arjuna: Youngest of Kunti's three divine sons, he is a great archer and warrior, and Yudhishtra's only hope of winning against the Kauravas.

Ⓞ Nakula & Sahadeva: Madri's twins, also of divine lineage, play minor roles in the epic as sidekicks to their three older siblings.

Parashurama: Drona, Kripa and Karna's Guru, friend-turned-foe of the Grand Regent, and the supreme spiritual leader of the Southern Confederate. A fanatical Brahmin and the greatest living warrior of his time, he curses Karna for duping him about his caste. He yearns to defeat Hastinapura and bring all of Bharatavarsha under his sway. He rues the peace treaty he signed with the Grand Regent years ago and awaits the opportunity to ignite a great war.

Parshavi: Vidhura's wife.

Purochana: A corrupt but efficient bureaucrat in league with Shakuni.

Samba: Son of Krishna and the Vanara woman, Jambavati, he is credited with starting the civil war that destroyed the Yadavas, and is often portrayed as irresponsible and impulsive.

Shakuni: Prince of Gandhara, Queen Gandhari's younger sibling and maternal uncle to the Kauravas, his only ambition is the destruction of the kingdoms of Bharatavarsha, in order to avenge himself against Bhishma for sacking Gandhara, killing his father and brothers, and abducting his sister. Skilled at dice and intrigue, he always carries the loaded dice made from the thighbones of his slain father.

Subhadra: Suyodhana's first love, and later wife of his greatest foe, Arjuna.

Takshaka: Leader of the rebel Nagas, who wishes for a revolution whereby the Shudras and Untouchables will become the rulers and the high castes their slaves. He is a fierce warrior and a megalomaniac dictator in the making.

Uluka: Son of Shakuni

Vasuki: Deposed Naga king, he is old and frail, but desperately wants the leadership back. He believes Takshaka is leading his people to destruction.

Vidhura: Youngest of Bhishma's three nephews, he was born of a lowly *dasi* and the sage Vedavyasa. A renowned scholar and gentleman, but of low caste, he is the Prime Minister of Hastinapura, and the conscience-keeper of the Grand Regent.

Yuyutsu: The son of Dhritarashtra and the Vaishya woman, Sugadha. He is older than both Yudhishtra and Suyodhana, but never lays claim to the throne. The merchant-warrior is a master strategist and one of the survivors of the Great Mahabharata war.

And finally, the most important of them all:

Jara and his blind dog, Dharma: A deformed beggar, Jara lives on the dusty streets of Hastinapura, and sometimes Dwaraka, accompanied by his blind dog, Dharma. Illiterate, ignorant, frail and dirt poor, he is one of the many who believe in the divinity of Krishna. He is a fervent devotee of the *avatar*. An Untouchable, rejected by all and spurned by most, yet Jara rejoices in the blessings of his beloved God and celebrates life.

*****

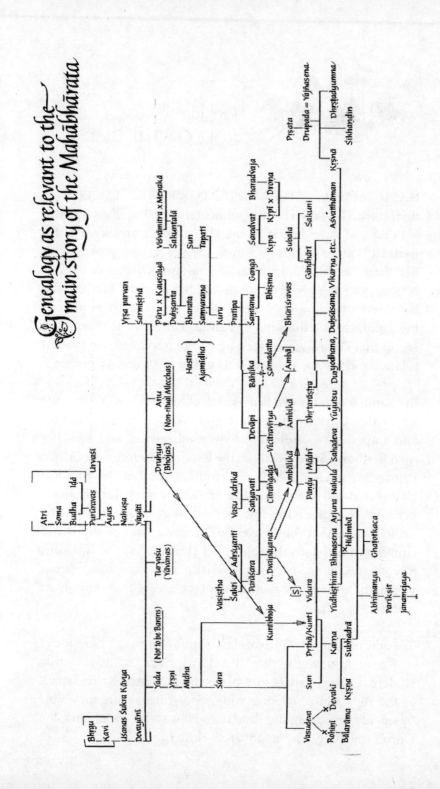

Genealogy as relevant to the
main story of the Mahābhārata

Prelude
ROLL O F THE DICE

HASTINAPURA, THE MOST POWERFUL EMPIRE in Bharatavarsha, is faced with political strife. King Dhritarashtra is blind and rules but in name. His younger brother, Pandu, is dead. Pandu's widow, Kunti, arrives at the palace with her three sons – Yudhishtra, Bhima and Arjuna, as well as Nakula and Sahadeva – the sons of her co-wife, Madri, who has committed *sati*. Together, the five brothers are known as the Pandavas, or the sons of Pandu. However, it is an open secret that Pandu was cursed by a sage never to have marital relations. The Pandavas are thus not his biological children.

But Kunti is determined to make her eldest son, Yudhishtra, the next King. Dhritarashtra's foreign-born Queen, the beautiful and imperious Gandhari, believes otherwise, and sees her own firstborn, Suyodhana, as the legitimate successor. Crown Prince Suyodhana and his 99 brothers, scoff at the Pandava claims and call them bastards. In desperation, Kunti claims her sons are of divine lineage and aligns herself with the orthodox elements of the clergy. Dhaumya, an ambitious and cunning priest, dons the role of her chief advisor. Meanwhile, Suyodhana, a headstrong, idealistic and generous-hearted youth, disregards the caste system, believing that only merit matters.

The new martial arts Guru of Hastinapura, Drona, is a supporter of Kunti; Arjuna, the third Pandava prince, is his favourite student. Drona arrives to replace the maverick Kripacharya, as the royal Guru, making young Suyodhana's life miserable by openly favouring the Pandavas. However, Aswathama, the Guru's son, becomes Suyodhana's close friend.

18

As rivalry between the cousins escalates, there are attempted murders, allegations and counter allegations. The air is thick with intrigue. Civil war looms. Holding the empire together is the noble patriarch, the Grand Regent of the Kurus – Bhishma Pitamaha. He rules the country with an iron hand, with the help of his scholarly and able Prime Minister, Vidhura, who is also step-brother to Dhritarashtra and Pandu, but born of a palace maid, hence considered of lowly birth.

When Bhishma attacked Gandhara years ago and forced Gandhari to marry his blind nephew, Dhritarashtra, the patriarch, had committed a grave error in sparing the life of the young Gandharan prince, Shakuni – Gandhari's brother. Shakuni has vowed to destroy Bharatavarsha (India, as he calls it). He is a foreigner, despised by many, but works his way through the politics of the Hastinapura court, moving his pieces dexterously to foment trouble.

As the orthodox elements impose a crushing caste system on the populace, a revolution brews in the forests of Bharatavarsha under the charismatic leadership of the Naga leader, Takshaka. Shakuni secretly helps the elements of destabilization, bringing the crime lord, Durjaya, back into action.

Ekalavya and Jara are untouchable Nishadas. Ekalavya yearns to become an ace archer, but Guru Drona rejects him as a pupil because of his caste. He learns archery by secretly watching the Guru teaching the Hastinapura princes. In time, his skill excels even that of Arjuna, Drona's favourite. When Ekalavya finally musters the courage to demonstrate his archery to the Guru, Drona asks him to cut off his bow thumb as his *gurudakshina*, so that Arjuna remains unchallenged. Ekalavya burns with hatred and vows to become the better archer despite his handicap.

Jara becomes an accomplice of the crime lord, Durjaya. His life would have ended in the gutters but for a chance encounter with a pious Brahmin, when Jara arrives to loot his house. Jara has a change of heart when he discovers that the Brahmin and his family have been mercilessly killed by Durjaya's men. He becomes a staunch devotee of the Yadava Prince, Krishna, whom many believe to be an *avatar* of Lord Vishnu. Thereafter, Jara roams the streets of Hastinapura with his blind dog Dharma, singing paeans to Lord Krishna.

Krishna himself wants a stable society and believes Suyodhana is dangerous. Though he does not promote caste hierarchy, Krishna believes each person should follow his *kula dharma*, which has been predetermined. Only then can society be peaceful, happy and prosperous. He is a charismatic leader, loved by many.
Krishna's elder brother, Balarama, is the supreme leader of the Yadavas, as well as Prince Suyodhana's Guru. He wishes to expand cultivation, agriculture and establish new trade routes. He builds a model city, Dwaraka, on the west coast of Bharatavarsha. A pacifist, he is deeply fond of Suyodhana and wishes him to marry his sister, Subhadra as the two are in love.

The Yadava clan has migrated from the northern plains to the west coast to avoid further confrontation with the monarch of Magadha, Jarasandha, a sworn enemy of the Yadavas. He runs a tight empire based on merit. The untouchable Nishada, Hiranyadhanus, Ekalavya's alienated father, is the Commander of his armies.

Meanwhile, Karna, son of the low-caste charioteer, Adiratha, wishes to study archery and become a warrior. Guru Drona and many other high-caste individuals of the court and clergy spurn him. However, Karna is determined. He travels on foot to the South to learn the warrior's art under Parashurama, the supreme leader of the Southern Confederate. The Confederate, eyeing a takeover of Hastinapura, views Bhishma as a liberal who is negating caste values. Karna learns archery from Parashurama by posing as a Brahmin. He gains the supreme accolade of becoming the *Dharmaveera* but narrowly escapes with his life when his secret is blown, leaving Guru Parashurama prostrate and unconscious with shock.

Karna arrives in Hastinapura on the day the Kuru princes are set to display their prowess in arms. He enters the arena and outdoes Arjuna in every feat of archery, but is still ostracised by Drona and the other Brahmins because of his low caste. Prince Suyodhana steps in. Defying orthodoxy, he elevates Karna to become King of Anga on the spot, thereby earning the wrath of the Brahmins and Karna's lifelong friendship and loyalty.

Suyodhana pays the price for his rash act when Subhadra rejects him and elopes with Arjuna, persuaded and aided by Krishna, leaving him devastated and deepening the enmity between him and Krishna.

Guru Drona demands that his students defeat and drag to Hastinapura in chains, his friend-turned-foe, King Drupada of Panchala, as his *gurudakshina*. Prince Suyodhana and his friends thus arrive in Panchala. To their surprise, King Drupada gracefully accepts his wrongdoing in humiliating Drona when the latter had approached him as a supplicant. In Panchala, Karna meets Princess Draupadi, the King's beautiful daughter, and they fall in love. Suyodhana returns to Hastinapura bearing King Drupada's apology to Drona as well as gifts from him. But the Guru remains adamant. He orders his favourite disciple, Prince Arjuna, to defeat Drupada. Arjuna's men descend on an unsuspecting Panchala and wreak havoc. King Drupada and his sons, Shikandi and Dhristadyumna, are dragged to Hastinapura in chains. Bhishma intervenes to free them, but Dhristadyumna believes that Suyodhana cheated them by offering peace and then sending his cousins to destroy Panchala. He also warns Aswathama that one day he will murder Drona.

To avoid further family friction, Bhishma asks Kunti and her sons to move to Varanavata, where a new palace is built to house them. Shakuni bribes Purochana, the officer-in-charge of the project, to use inflammable materials in the construction. Shakuni leaks this secret to Kunti through a spy. The Pandavas thus believe that Suyodhana has conspired to kill them. Kunti determines to outwit Suyodhana and entices a Nishada woman and her five children into the palace, which is then set on fire. The Pandavas escape but the rumour spreads like wildfire that Kunti and her five sons have perished in the fire. The Nishada woman and her sons who are the true victims of the fire, are related to Ekalavya, causing him to vow revenge. Ekalavya believes that Krishna is the reason for all his miseries.

On the day of Princess Draupadi's *swayamvara*, Karna is insulted once again for his caste when Krishna persuades Draupadi to reject him, even though he has won her fairly in the competition held for the suitors. Draupadi marries Arjuna instead. However, Kunti decides, in interests of family unity, that all the Pandavas will share Draupadi. Thus Draupadi becomes the common wife of all five brothers, and Yudhishtra, as the eldest, gains the first right to live with her for a year, followed by the others, in order of seniority.

To avoid any clash among the brothers over the beautiful Draupadi, Krishna persuades Bhima and Arjuna to travel to Magadha with him. In a duel that follows, Bhima kills Jarasandha and his general Hiranyadhanus, Ekalavya's father.

Meanwhile, Suyodhana marries Princess Bhanumati, daughter of Chitrangada, King of Kalinga, and sires a son and daughter – Lakshmana Kumara and Lakshmana. Karna too, marries Vrishali, a charioteer's daughter. Arjuna and Subhadra have a son, Abhimanyu, who grows up to be close to his uncle, Suyodhana.

To avoid war, Bhishma persuades King Dhritarashtra to hand over the forests of Khandivaprastha to the Pandavas, where they can build a new city. Krishna advises Arjuna to burn the forest and purge every living thing in it in order to enable a new city to be built there to rival Hastinapura. Arjuna and his soldiers kill thousands of Naga men and women but spare the life of the young architect, Mayasura, who bargains for the life of a few women and his foster father – Indra, the fallen Deva King. Maya builds a splendid palace and city but is then banished from his creation, being an untouchable. Indra, Arjuna's biological father, refuses his son's offer to live in the palace and follows Maya into exile. However, Indra decides to build a deadly new weapon with Maya's help, to gift to his son. He believes that without it, his son is doomed.

The Nagas are incensed by the pogrom that killed their people. Shakuni fans the flame of hatred. Ekalavya is welcomed by Krishna's foes, such as Shishupala and Shalva, and they decide to capture Krishna during the *Rajasuya* sacrifice being done by Yudhishtra to inaugurate his new palace. Suyodhana too, receives Yudhishtra's invitation to attend the *Rajasuya*.

At the *Rajasuya*, Shishupala defies the Brahmins by seating Ekalavya near the holy fire. But when the Pandavas elect Krishna as their honoured guest for the *Rajasuya*, Shishupala stands up to accuse Krishna of many wrongdoings. Krishna kills Shishupala on the spot. In the tussle that follows, Ekalavya escapes. He and Shalva rush to Dwaraka with their army, intent on pounding Krishna's city to dust. Krishna is forced to leave the *Rajasuya* to save his city. Unknown to him, Takshaka and his army of Nagas, have planned to ambush him on the way to Dwaraka.

Suyodhana reaches the Indraprastha palace angered by the treatment meted out to Mayasura and the other common folk of low caste. In the course of an argument with the Pandavas, he accidentally falls into a fountain. The entire Sabha bursts into laughter and Draupadi mocks his soaked nakedness. Suyodhana vows revenge for the insult and storms back to Hastinapura.

Unknown to them, Parashurama, the Supreme Leader of the Southern Confederate, has recovered from his coma and the southern armies are on the move towards Hastinapura to capture Karna.

Shakuni moves his pieces carefully. He persuades Suyodhana that defeating Yudhishtra in a game of dice is an easier way to take revenge than to fight him. At Suyodhana's invitation, Yudhishtra arrives in Hastinapura for the game. One by one, Yudhishtra pledges his possessions, city-state, brothers, and even his wife, against the wily Gandharan, and loses them all. Suyodhana orders his brother Sushasana to bring Draupadi, who dared to mock and humiliate him, to the Sabha – to be stripped like a whore before all.

The story continues...

1 SHAME

DRAUPADI KNEW HE WOULD BE BACK. She had merely bought time by cowing the messenger sent to fetch her with an imperious glare. She had sent him back with a question for the elders in the Sabha: Had her husband pawned her before he himself had become a slave or after? A slave belonged to his master, he had no rights, no possessions and could not have staked her. The messenger had bowed in confusion and rushed back to convey her words. The door had slammed shut but the enormity of what Yudhishtra had done began to overwhelm Draupadi's mind. She could sense the stunned silence in the Sabha when her question was repeated.

Draupadi forgot to breathe when she heard heavy footsteps hurrying up the stairs. They were coming for her. Her words had not deterred them. She stood with her back to the wall, her heart thudding in her chest as fear crept insidiously up her body from her toes. She desperately clutched the single sari that custom dictated women don during menstruation. As the other women in the chamber watched in aghast silence, the door was kicked open. Prince Sushasana stood with his feet planted on either side of the threshold, a lopsided grin on his flushed face. He rushed towards Draupadi but Subhadra threw herself between them. Sushasana roughly shoved Subhadra away and grabbed Draupadi by her long, lustrous hair and pulled viciously. She fell to her knees in pain.

'Why is he doing this to me? Where are my husbands?' Frantic thoughts flooded Draupadi's mind. She could bear the pain but not the shame. She clung to the bedpost, the door, the handrails – anything that would stop Sushasana from dragging her half-clad to the Sabha. But she was no match

25

for the burly Kaurava, drunk with soma and lust. The women of the royal household watched the brutish display in wide-eyed horror. Not a word was uttered; the only sounds were Draupadi's pitiful appeals to the Prince and his loud laughter echoing down the stairway...

Murmurs ran across the Sabha like a wind though a field of wheat. Every eye was on Sushasana and the woman he was dragging into the marbled hall, one hand at her breast, the other grasping at anything that could stop her being dragged away. The bruises on her arms and face marked her torturous and resisting journey. She sensed the men staring at her but did not raise her head. She noticed every petal and frond of the design inlaid into the marble at her feet. She could smell the incense in the air and the odours of the crowded Sabha. She could feel the lustful gaze of hundreds of men on her bowed, scantily-clad form. She could sense their thoughts.

Suddenly, raucous laughter echoed around the vast hall. Unbidden, her father's parting words rose to Draupadi's mind: 'Whatever the destinies may have in store, my daughter, always remember that you are of royal blood, the daughter of a King, a Princess. Act in accordance with that knowledge, which no one can take from you.' Unable to bear the thought of her proud father hearing of her humiliation, Draupadi raised her head defiantly. Karna's blazing eyes stared back at her, contempt and pity mingled in their glowing depths, his fine lips set in silent condemnation.

Sushasana pulled Draupadi forward by one arm. Trembling with anger and fear, she clutched at the flimsy sari covering her breasts.

"This is ignoble! This is no way to treat a woman! Cousin Yudhishtra is my brother Suyodhana's slave. How can a slave stake anything?" The lone voice of Prince Vikarna, Suyodhana's young brother, rang out, extinguishing the laughter and chatter. There was pindrop silence in the Sabha. Draupadi closed her eyes in relief. Someone to protect her at last.

"Prince Vikarna, this is a matter between a master and his slave. It does not concern anyone else." Karna was standing up, pointing a finger at the young Kuru prince.

Draupadi felt breathless as she waited for her lone supporter to answer. But all she heard was defeated silence. It was the law.

Finally, Vidhura pleaded in a soft voice, "She is a Kuru wife and daughter-in-law..."

"Sir, you are a scholar. Is it for me to remind you that our laws consider a woman who shares the bed of more than four men a prostitute? This woman serves five men. She was pledged in the dice game by her husband. Prince Suyodhana won her fairly with all of us as witnesses. He is entitled to decide what is to be done with her."

'Karna, how can you be a party to this? How can you do this to *me*?' Draupadi stared at Karna, the silent words beating in her heart before she hissed at him, "Enough, you Suta!"

Before Karna could retort she turned towards her husbands, standing beside the dais where the fateful game had been played out. "Am I your chattel to pawn when you wish, share when you want, and sell when you fancy?" She looked at Yudhishtra's stooped shoulders, trembling fingers and bent head with contempt. "Speak! Do something! Can you not see what is happening? How could you pledge me when you were already a slave?"

When the erstwhile Prince of Indraprastha, considered a font of knowledge, remained mute with his eyes downcast, Draupadi closed her own eyes in despair. Was this the same man who had braved his warrior-brother's wrath to share her?

Jayadratha, King of Sind, his eyes flickering over Draupadi's slim form gave a mirthless laugh and said, "They are slaves now, lady. They cannot speak without permission from their master." Shakuni chuckled in glee.

"Arjuna, do you not hear these taunts?" Draupadi whispered. But all five of her warrior husbands remained silent, their eyes fixed to the floor. "Are you Kshatriyas? Are you even men?" Draupadi's chest heaved in agitation as laughter resounded round the Sabha.

"Draupadi, be patient, they are consulting the holy books," Jayadratha said to fresh roars of laughter.

Draupadi dropped to her knees and covered her flaming face with her hands. No, she would not weep because her five brave husbands had forsaken her when she needed them the most. She was still the daughter of a King. She looked up at Suyodhana and asked in bewilderment, her throat burning, "Prince, why are you doing this?"

"Did you really think you would go unpunished after insulting me? Did you think you could get away with abusing a man like Karna? You are a slave now and must do as you are told, like your valorous husbands over there," Suyodhana snapped, his eyes blazing. He slapped his thigh and commanded, "Come and sit here, Draupadi or you will be stripped naked in front of the entire Sabha."

The laughter ceased. An uneasy silence reigned.

Shakuni leaned forward and spoke. "Perhaps Devi Draupadi is ignorant of the law of *karma*. She should seek instruction from her first husband. For every action there will be a..."

"Shut up, you Mlecha!" Draupadi yelled in fury. But Shakuni merely grinned and ran his fingers through his greying beard.

"Pitamaha..." Draupadi's lips trembled as she turned to the Grand Regent. Bhishma sat rigid, his gaze fixed on an invisible spot on the ceiling.

Draupadi turned to the King, her hands joined in supplication. "I am your daughter-in-law, Sire."

Dhritarashtra turned to his scribe and asked in a low whisper, "Sanjaya, where is Gandhari?"

"Acharya Drona..." Draupadi pleaded, turning to the Guru, who looked in embarrassment at Dhaumya for support.

"Guru Dhaumya..." Draupadi cried. The High Priest vanished behind a group of clergy.

"Acharya Kripa?" Draupadi asked with a sinking heart, hoping the maverick would do something to save her. He had championed the most unlikely people in the past.

An ironic laugh was his answer as got up to walk out. She gazed at him incredulously as he stopped in front of her. "Daughter, it is for you to ask your husband why he gambled you away. Ask the gamblers on both sides whether they realised they were gambling with destiny."

"Devi Draupadi, may we get on with the business at hand without further delay?" Shakuni's words got a few laughs from some of the Kaurava princes. "Prince Sushasana, what are you waiting for? Strip her!" he ordered, caressing the dice between his palms.

Draupadi shrieked and turned to run, but Sushasana quickly grabbed hold of the end of her sari. Her five husbands stood staring at their hands, not looking at her – puppets controlled by priests and obscure texts. 'Krishna! You were the one who told me to marry these cowards.' With anger scathing her heart, she cried aloud, "Krishna... Krishna..."

Sushasana tugged hard at Draupadi's sari while she struggled to preserve her modesty. Finally, drunk and bemused, he tripped over the unending cloth and fell. Draupadi crouched on the floor, her head on her knees, yards of sari spread around her, unable to face the Sabha. Oh shame! Was there not a man in this Sabha who would raise his voice in protest of this atrocity against a woman?

As if reminded by some higher powers, murmurs rose in the assembly, condemning Suyodhana and his loyalists. When the great priests and noble Kshatriyas remained silent, Vidhura moved to the centre of the Sabha and stood near Draupadi. For the first time in his life, the son of a *dasi* stood before the Kshatriyas and pious priests with his head raised high and addressed them in a contemptuous voice, "A question has been raised in this Sabha of noble men, by a helpless woman, about *dharma*, and all you answer her with is your silence?" His eyes blazing, Vidhura turned to his master, Lord Bhishma. "Sir, Prince Vikarna tried to answer Draupadi's question with whatever knowledge he has. You are the Grand Regent of the Kurus, the most noble of the Kshatriyas, why do you then remain silent in the face of *adharma*? Answer this daughter-in-law of the Kurus. How could he pawn what he did not own in the first place?"

Bhishma glared at his longtime and loyal aide, who had put him in such a difficult position now. All eyes were on him. He cleared his throat and said in a voice devoid of its usual commanding timbre, "I am unclear about this point of *dharma*. It is true that Yudhishtra had already become a slave when he pawned his wife, but some Shastras say a wife is the property of her husband, so when he becomes a slave, she too is a slave. I leave it to the King's wisdom to decide."

Karna sprang up from his seat. "Suyodhana! These three men, Vidhura Mahasaya, Bhishma Pitamaha and Guru Drona, will always side with the sons of Pandu. You have all the rights here to do whatever we please with these slaves."

A sudden tussle broke out among Pandavas. The normally silent Bhima shouted at Arjuna, who was trying to restrain him, "Let me go Arjuna, unhand me! Bring me some embers of fire and let me burn Yudhishtra's hands which itch to gamble. How dare he make the purest of all women suffer like this? It is not Duryodhana who has brought misery upon us but he who always speaks of *dharma*."

At these impassioned words Suyodhana and his friends burst into laughter. The man who was considered the epitome of *dharma* was exposed for what he was, thought Suyodhana. Yudhishtra continued to stand with his head bowed.

Vidhura turned to the Crown Prince, his face flushed with anger. "Suyodhana, are you not ashamed of what is happening here? You are the man who speaks of noble conduct and the blood of the great Bharata flowing in your veins. Yet now you behave like a boor. Where are your principles and famed generosity of heart now?"

Suyodhana winced at his uncle's words. He had never thought things would go this far. He had won his cousin's kingdom and reduced the Pandavas to slavery. He could afford to be generous. But when he looked at his cousin Yudhishtra, standing before him, resentment rose in him like bile. When he had been shamed in Yudhishtra's Sabha, there had been neither Vidhura nor the other learned men to support him. There had been no debate about *dharma* and *adharma*. Shaking away Shakuni's restraining hand, Suyodhana stood up.

"Draupadi, I see your point. Yudhishtra had no right to pledge you as he had already become my slave. Neither had he any right to pledge his brothers. Let him say aloud in the Sabha of the Kurus that it was *adharma* to pledge you and his brothers. Let him say that he uttered a lie when he gleefully pledged all of you when he did not own you. Let him say he did it in the hope of winning what he does not deserve – the inheritance of Hastinapura – from me. And all of you shall denounce him and declare you do not belong to him. I shall then restore all he has lost and even consider giving my cousin Indraprastha back, as a vassal state. This is the promise of a Kshatriya. Speak! You can regain everything you have lost."

There was an embarrassed silence in the Sabha. Even Bhima, who had been agitated a few moments before, remained silent. Suyodhana's generous offer put Yudhishtra in a fix. His four brothers looked at him. Draupadi's eyes glowed like jewels in her face. Surely if there was one man who had the humility to admit a grievous fault, that one was Yudhishtra?

"Tell him you were wrong, brother. Once we have Indraprastha back we can declare war against evil Duryodhana and punish him for what he has done to Draupadi," Bhima hissed into his brother's ear.

But Yudhishtra shook his head. He was a gambler who longed to win the throne of Hastinapura, but he would not go back on his word. "My brothers and my wife will not deny that, as eldest, I have the right to decide for us all. I committed no *adharma*, nor do I question destiny. If it is my destiny to suffer at the hands of my cousin's injustice, I shall do so with dignity, as will my brothers and wife." Yudhishtra's voice was quiet but firm. An animal cry rose from Bhima's throat. Draupadi's shoulders drooped in despair.

"Duryodhana, you are trapping my brother with vile words and low tricks. Come and fight me like a man," Bhima shouted.

"Loud words, Bhima," Shakuni intervened. "As loud as an empty drum and as hollow. Masters do not fight slaves. Ask your brother."

"I beg the forgiveness of the Sabha for my brother's outburst," Yudhishtra said, ignoring the burning condemnation in Bhima's eyes.

There was a stir at the door and Gandhari stormed into the Sabha with Subhadra and Bhanumati hurrying behind her. The Queen found her way to Suyodhana and touched his face to ensure it was indeed her eldest son. He attempted to rise but before he could do so, his mother slapped him hard across his astonished face, leaving her palm print emblazoned on his cheek.-

There was a collective gasp in the Sabha and then utter silence. Bhanumati rushed to Draupadi, trying to cover her, but she pushed her back angrily.

Turning to where Sushasana lay in a drunken stupor, Draupadi kicked him with her bare foot. He did not stir. Clutching her dishevelled hair, she said in a voice that shook with emotion, "Each one of you hear me now...I will not tie my hair, touched by this swine at my feet, until my husbands are men enough to kill him. Then I will wash my hair with the blood of those four evil men – Duryodhana, Dushasana, Karna and Jayadratha."

Bhima took a step forward. "I will kill them for you, Draupadi."
She snorted and flicked her hands as if he was an annoying fly.

"I am ashamed." Gandhari's voice silenced the Sabha which
had begun to hum with voices. "Where were the Acharyas and
Gurus when a woman was being humiliated in our own Sabha?"

Draupadi glared at the courtiers, refusing to cry, refusing to be
pitied. She was a Princess; she would not bow her head. She
had done no wrong. The roomful of warriors, nobles, courtiers
and high-caste clergy, stood with their heads bent. The silence
damned them all. The Grand Regent sat as if carved from stone.

Gandhari turned towards her sightless husband. "Perhaps
arrogance and pride made them blind, but you, my Lord, our
King? Draupadi is but a woman. She begged for your mercy.
Why were you silent?"

Vidhura walked up to the Queen and guided her to a chair
beside Dhritarashtra. When she touched his arm, the King's eyes
shone with unshed tears. There were no words. He had done an
ignoble thing. He had tarnished the crown he wore.

A haunting howl rose from the palace gardens. The courtiers
looked at each other, some in fear, many in confusion. Gandhari
turned to her husband. "Prabhu, our son has shamed us by
his ignoble actions. Do you not hear the ill omens? Jackals
have dared come near the palace in broad daylight. They are
the harbingers of a dark future. I see war and death. The Kuru
dynasty is cursed with the tears of its women, and now we have
added Draupadi's name to that inglorious list. My Lord, I know
you will be just and follow *dharma*."

The King felt bitter and angry at his Queen's words. His son had
won the game of dice fair and square. Suyodhana had even offered
them their kingdom back. All his brother's high-principled son
had to do was admit he had acted against *dharma* in pledging his
wife and brothers; but he refused to do so. No one had forced
him into the game. And now he, Dhritarashtra, was being blamed
for permitting it to happen in the Sabha. Where had the priests,

who were ever eager with unwanted advice, gone? Everyone remained silent and he was to take the blame. Even his son was acting mighty and generous after shaming him and making him look a fool – a blind, good-for-nothing fool. No, the Dhritarashtra who had fought elephants bare-handed and could crush rocks with his palms, was second to none when it came to nobility and generosity. He was the greatest Kshatriya and would be generous to the sons of his cursed brother, Pandu, who had taken the throne citing his blindness. Dhritarashtra would shame his dead brother's soul with his generosity and greatness.

The murmuring which had begun in the hall subsided as the King stood up and said in a voice hoarse with emotion, "Something has taken place here which should never have happened. Draupadi, my daughter, no words of remorse can undo what was done to you. Yet I ask you to find it in your heart to forgive us all."

Suyodhana sat stunned by the turn of events. He was proud of the ethical stand he had always taken, often going against the established norms. No longer could he claim the moral high ground. He had committed a grave error of judgment. But as he listened to his father, he felt anger stir within him like a hooded cobra.

"Daughter, you may ask me for three boons and as King of the Bharata clan, I promise to bestow whatever you seek. Ask. Allow a blind man to try and right the wrong that has been done to you."

Draupadi looked up in surprise when she heard the King's words. Shakuni's fingers wrapped around the dice, his knuckles turning white. His sister had spoilt everything. Now that fool Dhritarashtra would act high and mighty and undo the good work he had done. But when he looked at Suyodhana's stern face, his smile returned. He could work this out. He would wait.

"Oh King, the greatest of all Kurus!" Draupadi exclaimed with folded hands. Dhritarashtra's lips broke into a satisfied smile. "Free my husbands from your son's slavery."

"Daughter, your wish is granted," Dhritarashtra said. There were murmurs of approval from the Sabha. They would be singing his praises in the streets of Hastinapura. His fame would travel far and wide and history would judge him as the greatest of all Kings.

"Restore my husbands' kingdom and all that we have lost," Draupadi said, eyeing her husband with contempt. Yudhishtra looked up and gazed at his wife in amazement.

"I restore to the Pandavas all they lost in the game. I also give to my nephew, Yudhishtra, half my kingdom, to rule independently."

Murmurs of approbation rose on all sides as Dhritarashtra sat down. Yudhishtra's face lightened. Suyodhana's eyes burned with fury. How could his father give back Indraprastha to the Pandavas? The kingdom, the wealth, the power, it was all his by right. How could some bastards take it away?

"The Pandavas receive their kingdom from the hands of a woman and they dare to call themselves Kshatriyas? Devi Draupadi, you are more than equal to all five of them put together," Karna said, his eyes mocking the men who had always insulted him for his caste.

Arjuna sprang up in a fury. "Suta! I am no longer a slave. Come forward and fight me like a man."

"Why would I fight you, Arjuna? If you lose, you will go to your wife, who will beg the King to rescue you."

Yudhishtra restrained Arjuna, holding onto his wrist. Before things could get uglier, Bhishma rose and all eyes turned to him. "The Sabha is closed. Let arrangements be made for King Yudhishtra to travel to Indraprastha."

Shakuni panicked. He had been on the verge of success when his sister arrived and destroyed everything. Something needed to be done quickly. Wiping all doubt from his face, he moved to Yudhishtra, who was picking up his discarded clothing. "Your Highness, why be indebted to Suyodhana's charity and a woman's mercy like this? Would you care to try one more throw for a chance to win back everything, like a true Kshatriya?"

"Shakuni, I know what you are up to..." Gandhari cried when she heard her brother's words.

"Sister, this is the accepted protocol between dice players," answered Shakuni suavely, his customary smile back on his face. "It is my duty to give my opponent a fair chance to win back his losses. It is the code of the dice. Of course, if the King of Indraprastha does not care to take up the challenge, that is another matter."

"I will play." Yudhishtra once again climbed onto the dais, still laid with the dicing cloth. Cupping his palms, he accepted the dice Shakuni held out to him.

'Some people never learn,' the courtiers whispered to each other.

"What is the wager, Your Highness?" Shakuni asked with elaborate courtesy.

Before Yudhishtra could answer, the Grand Regent stood up. There was complete silence. "The Princes Suyodhana and Yudhishtra have both chosen to prove before this assembly that neither has attained the maturity or wisdom to rule a country. A ruler is but the custodian of the land he rules, he does not own it. Similarly, a husband is an equal partner in the marital relationship; he does not own his wife. It remains their shame and our sorrow, that these noble Princes of the Kuru clan have forgotten the tenets which mark civilized men." Lord Bhishma paused, his eyes fixed not on the assembly but the glistening river beyond the windows. The Sabha waited.

"Since my grand-nephews have decided to gamble again, despite what has happened today, I will decide the wager. The person who loses will surrender his kingdom to the winner and face banishment to the forest for twelve years. In the thirteenth year of exile, the loser will remain incognito. Should the winner find him during that period, the loser will repeat the cycle of twelve years in the forest and one year in hiding."

There was appalled silence in the Sabha. Twelve years and another in hiding, hunted by one's foes? Was it even possible to win free?

"I agree to the terms," Yudhishtra said immediately.

Gasps of disbelief sounded through the assembly but the Pandava Prince merely looked straight at the Grand Regent, calm and assured. He was sure he would win this time. In one throw he would regain Hastinapura and banish Duryodhana and his evil cronies forever.

Draupadi stood frozen. What was Yudhishtra doing? Could he not see her anguish? Had she not suffered enough? Bhima turned to walk out, telling Arjuna to inform him when it was time to go into exile. Arjuna held on to his arm, begging him to stay.

Gripped by gambling fever and overcome by his public humiliation, Yudhishtra's years of intellectual training deserted him. Touching his lucky amulet, he mumbled, "This time the charm will protect me. I have always followed *dharma*. *Dharma* will protect me from evil. Trust me, my brothers, our luck will turn. We will all witness the auspicious event of Duryodhana losing everything."

Shakuni merely smiled and threw the dice. Once again the bones rolled. A lucky talisman, crafted by a superstitious country clashed with the skill of a master strategist. "Aha! I win." Shakuni said, raising one hand in victory.

Yudhishtra sat in shocked silence. He had lost everything. Again. A crow cawed from the garden, seeming to mock him. The crow was considered to be the vehicle of Shaneeswara; the God of Misfortune was calling him. It was his destiny to bear this with a calm mind. He felt bitter thinking of the countless hours he had spent in prayer, in fasting, for the hours spent in studying the scriptures. In the moment it mattered, the Gods had forsaken him. *Dharmo rakshithi rakshitaha* (*Dharma* will protect he who protects *dharma*) – his Guru's words echoed in his ears. He could feel the heat of Draupadi's accusation and contempt searing his skin; he could hear Bhima's anger in his laboured breathing. He, son of *dharma*, had lost everything to a foreigner. The Suta was laughing at him; men were ogling his wife; and his brothers were standing with heads bowed. 'Lords of heaven, why are you punishing me like this?'

After a few moments of utter disbelief, Yudhishtra stood up and shook out the folds of his *dhoti* – the only possession left to him. Bhima, almost blue with rage, shouted across the Sabha that once they returned he would personally rip apart Duryodhana and his brothers with his bare hands.

Arjuna ignored all the others and pointed a finger at Karna. "Suta, you have won for now, but do not doubt that we will meet in battle, when we will finish this."

Karna bowed low. "Arjuna, rest assured I will be waiting for you."

At the massive doors of the Sabha, which towered over him like a tomb, Yudhishtra hesitated for a moment. He waited with the forlorn hope that Bhishma would call him back, or perhaps the King would ask Draupadi to seek the third boon he had promised, or that Guru Drona would speak. He heard Draupadi's voice, as cold as the ice on the Himalayas, hiss in his ear, "Walk!" With bent head, Yudhishtra walked into the afternoon sun. The guards standing on either side remained upright. Somewhere in the distance, thunder rolled, sounding like frenzied war drums.

Draupadi followed her husbands out of the Sabha, wrapped only in her sari, her head held proudly erect, her hair flying wildly in the playful breeze. She glared at Duryodhana and Karna as she passed them. The hatred burning in those fiery black eyes sent a chill down their spines.

Shakuni breathed a sigh of relief. The Sabha had ended but the courtiers refused to disperse. They clustered in groups and discussed the rights and wrongs of what had happened. Shakuni looked at them with disdain. It had not gone as perfectly as he had planned, but nevertheless it was a victory, considering everything. It had been touch and go with Gandhari interfering and making a mess of his plans. Fortunately, the fool Yudhishtra fell into the trap he had set. He could still hear the faint sounds of the procession accompanying the Pandavas out of the city. Gandhari was speaking to Suyodhana, but Shakuni did not want to stand and listen to his sister's harsh words. Lazily, he walked through the massive archway that separated the Sabha from the wide veranda which ran around the hall. He paused to admire the intricate carvings on the ceiling. Though it was late afternoon, the air was hot and dust swirled outside the fort, creating a haze all around.

Effeminate Indians! Which husband sat and watched someone strip his wife? Which husband wagered his wife in dice? In his country, men died to protect the honour of women. His fellow Gandharans would never believe such things could happen. The audacity of these Indians to call themselves the greatest culture in the world! It was time to get out, time to visit the motherland. He needed to take care of a few things and then he would go back to Gandhara. It would be the start of winter there and all would be painted white – the colour of purity, of God – unlike the dust and grime of India.

Suddenly, Shakuni's hard eyes caught sight of a stranger talking to Jayadratha. He looked travel worn and agitated. What was he saying to the King of Sindh? When the man turned, his gaze froze on Shakuni's face and his jaw dropped. Jayadratha followed his companion's gaze and frowned. Shakuni saw Aswathama join Jayadratha and they all stood staring at him. Something was wrong.

*****

2 ESCAPE

SHAKUNI'S HEART POUNDED LIKE THAT of a cornered beast. He had to get to Gandhara quickly. He needed a horse. He hurried towards the stables, weaving through the men grouped outside the Sabha discussing the day's events. He could hear someone following him and his walk became a trot. He could sense danger behind him but did not dare to look back as he hurried to the stables.

The smell of horse dung and urine assaulted his senses. The man in charge of the royal stables was sitting with his head hung, as if in shame, his hands supporting his forehead. Worry creased the face already lined by the sun. In the slanting afternoon light the tired eyes glistened with tears but Athiratha did not move even when Shakuni reached him and impatiently shook his shoulder. The charioteer sprang up with a start, shocked that a noble had touched him. When he saw who it was, Athiratha relaxed.

"What has happened to you?" Shakuni asked Karna's father.

"My son died today, Swami. What is the use of education and learning if you cannot use them? How will I tell his mother how her Karna behaved today? How could he behave like that to a woman? He was never my son... and never will be."

As Athiratha rambled on about his son's fall from grace, Shakuni's eyes scanned the area for danger. His heart skipped a beat when he saw Aswathama running towards them. "Athiratha, get me a horse quickly." Shakuni threw his gold bracelet to the amazed charioteer.

Athiratha caught it by reflex and then looked down at it as if he had hold of a live snake in his hand. "Swami, are you joking with me? I have many faults but I have never stooped to taking bribes. I have lived an honest life..."

"Athiratha, hurry!" Shakuni smashed both his fists on the stable wall.

Karna's father flinched at the uncharacteristic display of anger by this usually cool and controlled foreigner. "You are the Queen's brother, Swami. Please take whichever horse you wish," Athiratha said in a flat tone.

Aswathama shouted at Shakuni to stop. He was so close. Shakuni jumped into the saddle of the nearest horse as Aswathama leapt over the fence and lurched at Shakuni, making a grab for the reins. Shakuni kicked off his hands as the horse jumped the gate and shot forward. Aswathama ran after him for a few yards, coughing in the cloud of dust thrown up by the galloping horse.

"Where was he going?" Aswathama asked Athiratha, panting.

"I don't talk to scoundrels who misbehave with women." Athiratha slammed the stable door shut in Aswathama's face.

The Brahmin kicked the stable door with all the force he could muster, battering it with both fists, but the door remained closed. Defeated, he turned and shook his fist at Shakuni, now a black dot on the horizon.

***

The two guards bowed and backed out silently. They knew when to leave the Grand Regent alone. They closed the massive doors and stood outside, their spears crossed over the door to prevent anyone entering the chamber.

Bhishma wanted to be alone. The lone six foot oil lamp that stood in the corner, threw gigantic shadows, making the huge chairs, upholstered diwans and decorated pillars look like crouching beasts. Bhishma paced the room, shaking his head forlornly. However hard he tried, the image of a pleading Draupadi refused to leave his mind. Had he lowered the prestige of the

Kurus? Why had he not put a stop to the shame? He could have ordered it done and even arrested the two fools who were gambling with what did not belong to them. The country belonged to him, Devavrata Gangadatta Bhishma. Dhritarashtra and his sons merely enjoyed what he had gifted them.

When had the Kshatriyas of the Kuru clan started thinking partially? A woman was shamed and it did not matter *who* had shamed her. He should have punished the culprits. Perhaps Suyodhana had been justified in doing what he had done. The Pandavas were his grand-nephews too, but there was a difference. Unlike Suyodhana, they did not have the blue blood of the Kurus flowing in their veins. The shame of five Pandava brothers sharing the same woman still rankled. He had never understood it. Years of forced bachelorhood and self-willed celibacy had made him bitter, though he was always a thorough gentleman in his demeanour. No one showed more respect to women in public, no one was more decorous in his courtesies nor so polite in his speech than him. In public, he always supported women taking an active role in the administration of the country.

But in his heart he despised all women, especially women like Kunti and Gandhari, who were not content to live in the *antapura* and played politics. His heart had hardened after what Kunti and Gandhari's internal strife and intrigues had done to the country. He still rued the day he had permitted them to attend the Sabha. Gandhari had even had the audacity to chide the King today. That it had taken a woman to speak the words he should have uttered, made him all the more bitter. Dhritarashtra had surprised him with his generosity, by giving back all that Yudhishtra had lost. Had not the young fool fallen for Shakuni's tricks, the entire world would have now been praising the greatness of the blind King – a King who had taken the right decision when a great man like Bhishma remained silent, a King who had the grace to ask for forgiveness of a woman who had been wronged. Bhishma had never known Dhritarashtra to act so decisively and that too, angered him. He was losing his grip on the King. Things were getting out of his control. Bhishma hated Draupadi for having made him into a man who did not do the right thing when it mattered. He was terrified that history would stand in judgement because of his silence. That woman had no business sharing five men.

With a shock he realised he was thinking like the Suta, that Draupadi was immoral because she had five husbands. He could bear anything but the laughter of the Suta. How dare Karna come to his palace and mock his granddaughter-in-law? In his rage, Bhishma forgot that Karna was not the reason why his beloved Suyodhana had behaved like a street ruffian. 'Uncultured boor, son of a charioteer,' he fumed.

Suddenly, Bhishma remembered something and rushed to his table. He ruffled through various messages and threw down the scrolls of birch and palm leaves after a quick glance at each. Where was that message? When he had received the message from the Southern Confederate that morning, he had not given it much thought. It was written in the bombastic language typical to the South, with couched threats hidden in oblique praise. He had dismissed the usual banter about the South invading Hastinapura and not given a second thought to their demand to hand over Karna. He had not even thought it worth discussing in the Sabha. Now, an idea started forming in his mind. He could do something that would save his face. He would sacrifice the Suta and become a hero again. Bhishma was afraid that one day the rivalry between his grand-nephews would flare up to destroy his beloved country. And that Suta upstart was a danger to both sides.

For a moment, Karna's handsome face came to mind; the Suta who had had the courage to challenge the Kshatriyas. A grudging respect for the underdog who has fought his way up made Bhishma hesitate in his decision. Then he slammed the message on the table and drew to his full height. He had to do it for the sake of the country. The thought gave him courage and helped him push away considerations of fairness. The Suta had to be finished. Without Karna, he could control Suyodhana and remain kingmaker. No, he was not hungry for power; Bhishma hastily corrected the insidious thought. His life was a sacrifice – for his father in his youth, for his nephews in his middle age, and for his grand-nephews in the twilight of his life; a life lived for others. He smiled at the thought, pleased with himself.

Bhishma called the guards and asked for Senanayak Mahaveera. Without turning to look at the bewildered Captain, he said in a voice from which all emotion had been banished, "Arrest the King of Anga and hand him over to the Southern Confederate."

As the Captain bowed and went out, the guards closed the door, leaving the Grand Regent to his solitary state.

*****

3 ARREST

SUYODHANA WAS STARTLED TO SEE Aswathama and Jayadratha emerge from the darkness. He looked at them in surprise as they brushed past him and entered Shakuni's chamber. The bells over the door jangled in protest. A moth whizzed past and dived into a flaming torch, filling the air with an acerbic odour.

"Shakuni has escaped," Aswathama said, challenging Suyodhana to contradict him.

"He may have gone for a walk," Suyodhana suggested, avoiding looking at the infuriated Brahmin.

"A long walk indeed! He may have even got halfway to Gandhara by now," retorted Aswathama.

The mouldy smell of the room mixed with the distinctive perfume Shakuni always wore. Suyodhana pulled the burning torch from the wall. Night withdrew wherever the circle of light touched it and rushed back as soon as it was turned away. Insects scurried to hide in the crevices of the walls.

"No! No!" exclaimed Suyodhana, his voice hoarse with repressed anger and denial. "Uncle Shakuni..." His hands shook, making the circle of light vibrate. The curtains moved restlessly in the breeze and shadows danced around the room.

Aswathama put a hand on his friend's shoulder. "He betrayed and tricked us."

Suyodhana knocked off his friend's hand and began rummaging in the cupboards. He overturned the bed, emptied the drawers and then smashed them shut. If he did not do something he would go crazy. Beads of sweat formed on his creased forehead.

Jayadratha stood at the window, watching. He had been surprised by Suyodhana's behaviour today. He had made a bad bargain in marrying Sushala, Suyodhana's sister. He had expected to grow his kingdom with the help of the imperial Hastinapura army and had counted on Suyodhana to support his expansion plans. The new city of Dwaraka and the riches of Krishna's land were inviting. But Suyodhana was too preoccupied with the rivalry with his cousins to pay attention to his brother-in-law. Nor did Sushala make things easier for Jayadratha with her constant comparisons of him to her brother. They had a son now, whom Sushala desired to raise to be like Suyodhana. He could hardly wait to tell her how her high-minded, perfect, Kshatriya brother had behaved in the Sabha today. And the way Suyodhana pampered a low-caste like Karna made his blood boil with rage. He spat out a stream of red betel nut juice, watching it clear the veranda and land in the flowerbed below. There was a pale moon playing hide-and-seek with the clouds and the palace was eerily still. In the distance he could hear the sound of marching feet and a frown creased his forehead.

"Remember this?" Aswathama held up something in one hand. Suyodhana did not want to look. It would make everything final. He wiped his forehead, a lump forming in his throat. Aswathama moved towards the light and held out a white shawl. It was the same one which had almost indicted him in Bhima's murder trial years before.

The torch fell from Suyodhana's hand and lay smoking at his feet, making their eyes sting. "I did a despicable thing today." Suyodhana's voice and body shook with emotion. "How will I face Bhanumati or my mother? How will I face the people of my country?"

"Shakuni made us do it, we were stupid," Jayadratha snapped, secretly enjoying Suyodhana's predicament. He wanted to see his wife's face when he narrated the incident to her. Her noble brother and his great acts. Jayadratha wanted to laugh.

Aswathama was digging through the Gandharan Prince's possessions. "Look at this...and this...and this..." He threw down

46

some palm leaves. They lay on the floor mocking Suyodhana's naivety. "Do you understand what they are? Documents about the arms smuggled into our country, cryptic replies from Durjaya. Everything is falling into place. Ask Jayadratha! Ask him what his spy told him. Evil Mlecha!"

"Suyodhana, Durjaya and his men are being trained in Gandhara. They will wreak havoc in our cities soon. Your Uncle..." Jayadratha's voice trailed off when he looked into Suyodhana's face.

"Enough!" Suyodhana shook his head. Red heat was rising behind his eyelids. He closed them. No, his uncle would never do it, but...

"I almost caught him but he managed to escape. I would have chased after him but at that crucial moment I didn't have a horse. Athiratha slammed the stable doors on my face saying he would not speak to women abusers," said Aswathama bitterly.

"Where is Karna?" Suyodhana asked.

"With Vrishali. She is giving him hell for his act today."

Suyodhana rushed out and his friends followed. They were surprised to see a troop of guards marching down the corridor. Suyodhana broke into a run and commanded them to halt but they ignored him and continued to march in cadence. Aswathama and Jayadratha raced through the gardens and reached Karna's room just before the soldiers and Suyodhana.

The troop halted and the Captain stepped out and addressed the Crown Prince. "Sir, pray, move aside. We are here to arrest His Highness Vasusena Karna, as per the orders of the Grand Regent."

"Just try it," Aswathama suggested belligerently, pointing at the young Captain's chest.

To his enduring credit, the Captain stood his ground. "Sir, pray, allow us to do our duty. We would not like to use force."

"Tell the Grand Regent that Karna is not available," Aswathama said and shoved the Captain back.

The scene was becoming uglier by the minute as the soldiers got ready to charge.

"What is going on here?" Suyodhana was relieved to hear Vidhura's voice. The Prime Minister came hurrying towards them and the soldiers bowed low.

"Sir, what is all this?" Aswathama enquired of Vidhura.

***

Karna knew the very air of this palace was oppressive to Vrishali. She had boiled with rage when her maid told her what had occurred in the Sabha. How could a man like Karna stoop to this level, she had asked. He had no answer. "You are not the Karna I know," she finally said. He had behaved like a common lout, ordering a woman to be stripped in public. He had tried to justify himself saying Draupadi had insulted him and she was just a whore who shared her bed with five men. But Vrishali had lifted an eyebrow in disdain and asked whether it was his bitterness towards Draupadi for spurning him as a suitor that made him hate her. He had looked away knowing it was true but unable to admit it even to himself. Deep in the recesses of his troubled heart, Karna still loved Draupadi.

Karna's justifications grew weaker as time went by. When he said he had done it for his friend, something snapped inside. Was it fair to blame Suyodhana for what he had done?

"Let us leave all this, Karna, and go far from here, where no one knows who we are," Vrishali begged earnestly.

Before he could answer, there was an urgent banging on the door. Karna quickly strode over to open it, glad of the reprieve it gave him from answering his wife. Aswathama's face stared up at him. In the dim light he saw armed soldiers behind his friend.

"Karna, run! I'll hold these scoundrels," Aswathama shouted, pushing back the Captain. The soldiers clanged their swords against their shields in warning.

"Run?" Karna asked, jerking back his head. "But why?"

Karna saw Suyodhana's worried face appear. He looked back at Vrishali and flinched at the look of hatred those eyes bore towards his friend. 'No, Vrishali, Suyodhana is not to blame,' he wanted to say. There was so much to explain to her. Karna looked at her heavily pregnant body, wanting to protect her from all harm, but Suyodhana grasped his arm.

"You are not running anywhere; let us see the Grand Regent."

As the tall form of Karna stepped forward to walk beside his friends, behind them the soldiers of Hastinapura stood ready to arrest him at the slightest nod from the Grand Regent and hand him over to the Confederate.

*****

4 THE CHALLENGE

BHISHMA ORDERED THE GUARDS TO OPEN the door to his chambers. Prince Suyodhana entered. "My apologies for disturbing your rest, Pitamaha, but Karna, King of Anga, wishes to speak with you urgently."

Bhishma frowned, undecided. His mind was in turmoil. He knew he was being unfair to the Suta. When he took his decision, he had acted to save face. Now, the prospective of having to face Karna made the Grand Regent uneasy. The last thing he wanted was to see Suyodhana or his cronies. 'Scoundrels! Shameless creatures!' he told himself, trying to recapture the rage he had felt scorching him that afternoon.

Karna entered and bowed. What was this Suta doing in his chambers? He had to be bundled off to the South without delay. He could not look into Karna glowing eyes. What strange eyes the Suta had, Bhishma thought irrelevantly for a moment. He was about to order them out when Vidhura entered.

"Yes, honourable Prince? Who is your next victim? Are even your mother and sister safe?" Bhishma asked testily, unwilling to acknowledge Karna even by a stare. A guard came in and lighted the lamps in the room. Bhishma's eyes caught the glitter of diamond ear studs in Karna's ears and felt irrational rage. Karna was making him look small. "Yes?" Bhishma's eyebrows arched, a distasteful frown wrinkling his brow.

Suyodhana was taken aback by his grandsire's icy tone. "I...I deeply regret what has happened, but why arrest Karna?"

"And you have nothing more to say than you deeply regret...?" Bhishma moved closer to the Crown Prince.

"Pitamaha, that woman insulted me. You know what happened at Indraprastha. I am a Kshatriya. You cannot expect me to take such an insult lying down. I stood naked in their court. I was ridiculed and shamed. How do you want me to take it?" Suyodhana's anger rose. Why was everyone blaming only him? Was it his fault Yudhishtra had gambled and lost?

"You are destroying this country." Bhishma's nostrils flared. His eyes were cold and hard.

"Destroying this country? I didn't see this anger when the Pandavas destroyed Khandivaprastha. I didn't see you take action when my Aunt Kunti had six Nishadas murdered." Enough! He was not going to take these accusations lying down anymore. They were all partial to his cousins – Pitamaha, Guru Drona, everyone. Only his friends had stood by him.

"How dare you talk to an elder in this fashion, Suyodhana?"

"Pitamaha, I am not a child. I won this country."

"Won this country? Has this Suta given you such silly ideas? He is going to be your ruin, young man."

"What has happened to make you so angry, Pitamaha? We only threatened to strip her, we did not..."

"You arrogant fool! How dare you try to justify your behaviour?"

"Sir, I did not touch the woman."

"Leave this room, *now!*"

"If you wish. But tell me why you are arresting Karna."

"Because the Southern Confederate wants his head. Because he cheated his Guru. They have declared war on Hastinapura. If I do not hand over this Suta, they will ransack Hastinapura."

"Sir, what is my crime?" Karna asked, lifting his eyes to the Grandsire's face.

Bhishma covered his hesitation in a bout of coughing. He did not have an answer. The Suta's eyes pierced his conscience. "I will not spill my soldiers' blood over a Suta."

"Sir, I am a low-caste but am I not a warrior too? I have fought for Hastinapura. I have protected her whenever she has been threatened. Allow me a warrior's death, not that of a criminal. I request this from one warrior to another," Karna said.

"Warrior? A man who condones the stripping of a woman in public cannot call himself a warrior."

"Yes, it was a grave mistake. Will you forever hold it against us? Is there no place for forgiveness in your eyes, Sir?" Karna asked, desperation in his voice.

"You know that woman got what she deserved." Suyodhana glared back defiantly at his great-uncle.

Karna quickly moved to the fore, pushing back his angry friend. He bowed low before Bhishma. "Sir, please accept my apologies. I beg your pardon for our dishonourable conduct. Allow me a chance to fight my enemies."

"Fight? You think you can fight Parashurama?"

"Jayadratha has three thousand men and complete trust in Karna's abilities. Karna can lead the soldiers of Sindh to take on the Southern Confederate. We just need your permission," said Suyodhana.

Jayadratha, standing in a corner of the chamber with Aswathama, was shocked to hear it. Why should he lend his soldiers to the Suta? How could his brother-in-law promise his friend what was not his? He mulled over the proposal in his mind and decided to wait till he knew what came of this interesting conversation. Maybe he could make a bargain with Suyodhana, for the favour he was doing.

Bhishma gave a snort. "Three thousand men and this Suta to lead them? To face an army numbering a lakh of men? Led by none other than Parashurama himself. Do you not know I fought him for six hard months, with the entire might of Hastinapura behind me? Did I claim victory? All I got was a disadvantageous truce! Do you young hotheads even know what you are saying?"

Suyodhana looked at the Grand Regent and said clearly, "Sir, Karna has done nothing wrong."

"Vidhura, are they crazy or just plain stupid? Fools! Now listen to me. If you want to fight this war, fight it far from Hastinapura. Suta, your ego and arrogance are galling, but I will not stop you. Just stay away from my city."

"Sir, we will take..." Suyodhana stopped short when Bhishma raised his hand.

"We? Who is this 'we'? You are not going anywhere, Suyodhana. I cannot, in all conscience, send you on such a suicidal mission. You will stay here in Hastinapura and learn to rule. You have done a shameful thing today. You will have to learn to face your subjects. You cannot run from your responsibilities. Let this Suta fight and die at the hands of the Southern Confederate. I will not stop him."

"I do not expect Prince Suyodhana to come with me," Karna said.

Bhishma stared at them and then said to Suyodhana, his face expressionless, "At least the Suta has some sense."

"Sir, you are insulting me," retorted Suyodhana, his eyes ablaze.

"It was meant to be so. Neither you nor your cousin Yudhishtra are fit to rule. You have demonstrated that to the whole world today."

"Pitamaha! Do you not yourself cling to power? How can you then accuse everyone else of being fools?"

Bhishma remained standing, his face devoid of expression. Vidhura rushed to Bhishma. Still staring at Suyodhana, the Grand Regent slowly sat, his head bent, not wanting these young men to catch him in a moment of weakness. After all the sacrifices he had made, after all the wars he had fought, after all the hard work, this is what he got; he bit his lips in bitterness. Power! When had he ever been hungry for power? He had always carried it as a burden. He could have been King, yet he had remained true to his vow, and this is what he got for his sacrifice. And that too from the boy he had loved the most. This ungrateful land! Was this Suta so important that Suyodhana would speak to him so? The Crown Prince had to be saved from Karna. Hastinapura had to be saved from this arrogant low-caste upstart.

Only the white-knuckled grip on the armrests betrayed the Grand Regent's emotions. 'Three decades of selfless service and I have to live to see this day,' he thought bitterly. Bhishma could feel Vidhura's comforting presence. Who knew, perhaps even Vidhura would turn against him one day.

With sudden energy, he pushed away Vidhura and stood erect. Although his eyes glistened with unshed tears, he was the Grand Regent of the Kurus once again. He turned to Suyodhana and the Crown Prince took a step back. But Karna stood his ground, putting himself between Suyodhana and the Grand Regent.

"Move away, Suta, I have something to say to my grand-nephew."

Karna and Bhishma stared at each other. It was Karna who looked away and stepped back to stand behind Suyodhana.

"Suyodhana, foolish son, you think you can make me feel guilty and I will toe the line? You think this Suta can fight and win against Parashurama? Ha! I am still the only man equal to Parashurama."

"Karna will fight Parashurama and he will win," Suyodhana stated calmly.

Bhishma stared at him and then broke into bitter laughter, his body shaking with contemptuous mirth. "You say a Suta is going to win where I failed? Suyodhana, I have never gambled in my life but today I will. Let this Suta come back alive, I do not even say he has to win, just let him return alive, and I promise I will step down as Grand Regent."

Suyodhana bowed to Bhishma and walked out of the chamber. Karna looked at the mighty warrior before him, then kneeled and touched the floor at his feet. Raising his hand to his head in obeisance, he rose gracefully and walked away. The door closed. Vidhura withdrew with quiet steps.

The Grand Regent of the Kurus collapsed on his spartan bed. Why had he not stopped Shakuni? His eyes became misty when he remembered the blood-soaked five-year-old he had carried from Gandhara so many years before. There was no end to man's selfishness. Suyodhana, Yudhishtra, Shakuni, everyone had betrayed him. He had always tried to act with noble resolve, never allowing selfishness to cloud his judgement even for a minute.

A strange fear gripped him. Would he stand ruined by a Suta? He tried to ignore it. It was not the fear of his country disintegrating but the Suta winning, where he, the illustrious warrior of the Kurus, the Kshatriya of Kshatriyas, had failed, which filled his heart now.

Below his windows he could hear Karna's army getting ready to march South. The Grand Regent sighed. Disaster loomed over Hastinapura; the country he had built with his blood and sweat would disintegrate. From where had that accursed Suta come into Suyodhana's life? As slumber refused to close his eyes, the prayer that lay like a barb in his heart was, 'May the Suta die...'

Suddenly Bhishma remembered Krishna. Had the wily Yadava been with Yudhishtra, the boy would not have committed such blunders. He might not even have accepted the invitation to the game of dice. As sleep finlly spread its mantle over him, Bhishma wondered where the Yadava had vanished.

***

55

Unknown to Bhishma, Krishna was facing grave danger in the unforgiving desert, on his way to Dwaraka. He had halted a few feet from where Takshaka lay in wait. Every instinct in his body cried out to him not to proceed further. He pulled at the reins of his horse and barked at his followers to halt. The cavalry ranks rippled like a whip at the sudden stoppage as the soldiers tried deperately to control their whining and stamping mounts. The smell of horse dung and urine soon filled the air. Krishna dismounted and examined the sand. There were many footprints, more than there should have been in this desolate place of shifting sand dunes and bushy shrubs. He could see a cluster of boulders in the distance. How many men could hide there? Whoever had selected it as an ambush spot, knew his job. Could it be Takshaka or Vasuki?

From behind the rocks, the eyes of the Nagas watched the Yadava army, their arrows ready in their bows.

*****

5 Gandhara Beckons

THE FRIENDS STOOD HUDDLED TOGETHER in the final moment of parting. Their pain was too great to be allayed by words. Karna hugged each one in turn. Aswathama watched quietly as his friend stood in silent prayer, facing east, though it was too early for the sky to have lost her cloak of darkness.

Mounting his horse, Karna blew his conch as a signal to move out. The ranks of armed men jerked like a giant reptile awakening from sleep. They soon broke into a trot and in a few moments vanished in a cloud of dust, leaving only the odour of horse and elephant dung.

A vast emptiness filled Aswathama's mind and heart. 'Karna, will I ever see you again?' he wondered as he swished his sword at a bush. Leaves fell around him, mutilated. He turned towards Suyodhana, a question on his lips, but stopped when he saw the expression on his friend's face. In the pale moonlight he could see tears glistening in Suyodhana's eyes, their usual burning intensity quenched. 'Karna, if you do not return, how will we bear it? How will Suyodhana go on?' Aswathama felt tears fill his own eyes. No, it was not jealousy. 'I cannot be jealous of my best friend going to war.' He swished his sword again, lacerating a shrub, but the feeling remained.

Jayadratha had moved his pieces carefully. He had not bothered to ask his men whether they were ready to face the might of the Confederate. They were on his payroll and it was their *dharma* to die for him. But he had asked Suyodhana for one thing in return for his men – the promise that in the event of Suyodhana leaving Hastinapura for any reason, he would be made Regent Crown Prince for the period. He had mitigated the absurdity of his demand by saying it was his sister Sushala's wish. When Aswathama had protested, Suyodhana had dismissed his fears and promised Jayadratha that his sister's whim would be satisfied if the occasion arose. Satisfied with the bargain, Jayadratha had stood away from the three friends, watching their sentimental parting with contemptuous amusement. Now, as the night grew gray with age, Jayadratha, standing lost in his own thoughts, felt weary. "My men have marched off to face their destinies, yet I remain standing here. But the time will come, my friends, when we too, must march." So saying, he walked off, the first hint of day touching his shadowy form.

Birds had started their hurried chatter in the bushes and the blades of grass were turning saffron at their tips. A myna fluttered its little wings and landed nearby, looked at them and flew away. A single myna, an ill omen; Suyodhana tried to push away thoughts of death and prayed Karna would return victorious. The two friends stood in silence, their emotions too deep for words.

"I wish to go to Gandhara and bring back that son of a bitch," Aswathama finally said, and waited for Suyodhana's response. But the Prince continued gazing in the direction Karna had vanished. "Suyodhana? I am going to Gandhara. I need an army right away." Silence greeted his words. 'Doesn't he even care? I was his childhood friend long before he met Karna.' Heart sore, Aswathama turned to leave.

Suyodhana grabbed his friend's hand. "You too want to leave me alone, Aswathama?"

The Brahmin swallowed hard and licked his dry lips. After a long pause, he said, "I want to get that devil, Suyodhana. I must go to Gandhara. Allow me to do so. Give me some men so I can flush out Shakuni and Durjaya from their caves."

"There are no men for Suyodhana, Aswathama. I am the pariah, the untouchable. If Karna loses, I will remain so and the kingdom will go to that self-righteous Yudhishtra. The Grand Regent will see to it. The alternative is even worse. If by some miracle Karna wins, I will be known as the ingrate who forced the Pitamaha to resign."

Aswathama remained silent. 'What am I in the larger order of things? The court jester? The affable and witty Brahmin who appears in stories and folk tales? The funny clown, the side-kick of the hero? All my life my father has stifled my growth, and now my friend is doing the same thing. I am a better warrior than either Arjuna or Karna. Karna the hero was born the day the princes graduated. They showed their prowess and the crowd adored them all. My father basked in the glory of his students, until Karna came and spoilt everything. They are all part of the legend now, but no one remembers Aswathama. I was just the priest who mumbled the *mantras* at a Suta's coronation.' Aswathama kicked a pebble in disgust. He turned his back, lest the Prince read his mind.

"Aswathama? You too want to leave me and go in search of danger?" Suyodhana asked, placing a hand on Aswathama's shoulder. "Why can we not go together in search of my uncle?"

Aswathama shook his head.

"I wish you all success, my friend, but I have no men to spare. Nor can I go with you to share in the glory. It is your journey. Go, Aswathama, if you want to, though it breaks my heart to say so. Who else will I lose today?" Suyodhana looked up at the fingers of dawn stretching across the sky.

"I am sorry, Prince, but I have to go to prove myself," Aswathama managed to say.

Suyodhana looked around. The Captain and his group of soldiers, who had come to arrest Karna a few hours ago, were huddled near the fort gate. He called to them and the Captain immediately ran up and bowed to the Crown Prince. His soldiers ran up behind him. There were about sixty men. When Suyodhana asked for volunteers, they hesitated. But when the Prince appealed to their duty to the motherland, thirty-five of them, and Captain Mahaveera, volunteered to accompany Aswathama on his dangerous mission.

Aswathama felt a pang of guilt. Why was he doing this? Why was he taking these men to their certain deaths? For what? Ego?

As though reading his mind, Suyodhana said, "Aswathama, I have done what I can. Some, or perhaps all of them, will die, but they are going with you because they love their country more than their lives. I am sure you will be a worthy leader."

"Suyodhana, among all your friends, I am the only one who has not earned your friendship. Allow me to do so."

"You talk nonsense, my friend," Suyodhana said, embracing Aswathama one last time. "Aswathama, I should not ask this of you, yet I must. If you see my Uncle Shakuni, spare his life. I want to look into his face and ask him some questions before I decide what to do with him."

'What the...' Aswathama pulled away from Suyodhana, shocked at the request. It would take all his self-control not to kill that Mlecha if he chanced upon him.

The Crown Prince had already started walking towards the palace. Aswathama did not have the heart to tell him what he thought of Shakuni. Instead, he turned to the Captain. "We will assemble here in an hour. Let the men say their farewells to their families."

"Sir."

Aswathama hurried home, ignoring the comments of some of the soldiers that their families lived in distant villages. He hated to hear about their poor relations, who waited for the small amounts the soldiers sent back once a year. He could not bear to hear the stories of the young wives, old mothers, little girls and boys, who would be waiting for them to come home. He did not want to hear about their peasant fathers who hid their fears by boasting about their sons. If he listened, he was afraid he would never be able to take them to Gandhara with him.

When he reached home it was already dawn. He went to the well, drew water, and poured it over his head, enjoying the slithering cold as the water rushed down his body. A breeze caressed him with its ticklish fingers and he shivered with joy. It was going to be very cold in Gandhara, so cold that it snowed. Snow! How would it look and feel? He had never seen such a cold country. How did people survive there? He smiled to himself, trying not to think of the fate of the soldiers waiting for him. No, it would be a grand adventure. "Shakuni, I am coming for you, Mlecha!" he said aloud as he ran towards his room to dress.

His mother was drawing *rangoli* patterns in the courtyard, her fingertips white with rice powder. He could hear the tinkle of a bell from the prayer room – his father would be at his *puja*. Aswathama stopped near his mother, the water dripping from his body making patterns on the cow dung floor. His mother looked up. Her lips were set together and he could sense her anger. He knew she was angered by what had happened in the Sabha. He felt ashamed and shifted his feet, bracing to face her words. But she said nothing, merely looked at him and pushed away the strand of hair that had fallen onto her forehead with the back of her hand. He wanted to reach out and dust the white rice powder from her hair – or was it age that had made her hair grey?

"Ma, I am going to Gandhara."

The bowl of rice powder fell from his mother's hand, covering the beautiful patterns on the floor. The *rangoli* blurred as Aswathama felt tears sting his eyes and his chest tighten with a pain that had no name. He fell at his mother's feet, not wanting to face her. "Ma, give me your blessing before I go."

He could feel her hands on his hair. Her shaking fingers ran over his face and a few tears fell on his shoulder. But he did not answer her frantic questions, afraid of his answers. He ran to his room and gathered his weapons. Swords, bows, quiver of arrows, dagger – he bundled them with some clothes. Then he donned his armour and walked out.

His father was still in the *puja* room; his mother sat beside him, her eyes closed. Aswathama dropped his bundle on the floor and walked up to them. The dancing figure of Shiva stared back at him, magnificent in its poise and grace. Aswathama fell to the floor in obeisance, his hands folded over his head. The familiar aroma of incense and camphor almost made him cry. It was the smell of his childhood. He had sat with his father and learned the *mantras* from him. How he had resented it then, wanting only to dash out to play with his friends. Now he yearned for those days to return. His mother had not spoken a word after her first flood of questions. He touched her feet in *pranaam*, but she did not stir. His father sat cross-legged in meditation, his face serene and calm. Aswathama touched his father's feet. 'Bless me, father. I am going to Gandhara,' he said in his mind. Surely, his father would say something to him, bless him and wish him success? Would he have behaved this way if he were Arjuna?

But Drona did not move. 'Enough of this!' Aswathama thought sternly as he picked up his bundle and left the room. He lingered at the threshold, running his fingers over the doorframe. He might never see his home again. The swords in his bundle rattled.

His mother came rushing out. Her muffled sobs pierced his heart. But it was his father's voice that almost made him turn back. "Stop crying, woman. Nothing will happen to him. He is the greatest warrior I have ever known. He is Drona's son."

Aswathama wanted to throw down his bundle and rush to hug his father as he had done as a child. 'Father, do you truly mean it? Am I better than your Arjuna?' He wanted to feel his father's hands on his head in blessing. Suddenly the wish to go anywhere vanished. He wanted to remain in Hastinapura as his father's son. But the smiling face of Shakuni rose before his eyes and the young Brahmin raised his bowed head. 'Father, if I return alive, I hope I will have the courage to tell you what I feel – that no son has ever loved his father more than Aswathama. But for now... Gandhara is waiting.'

***

Though Shakuni had travelled many *yojanas*, he could still feel the burning eyes of the Brahmin boring into his back. The wind was howling in his ears and the horse frothing at the mouth, yet he kept urging greater speed. He knew Aswathama would come after him. He could feel it in his bones. His heart thudded louder than the sound of his horse's hooves.

When his mount finally jumped over some bushes and flew into Gandhara, Shakuni punched his chest. 'Aswathama, we will arrange a welcome feast for you. Welcome to Gandhara, Brahmin!'

*****

6 DARKNESS

"BHANU!" THE VOICE SOUNDED OVERWROUGHT, like that of a tired man recovering from sickness.

Bhanumati pulled the quilt over her sleeping daughter. 'Why did he do it? Suyodhana, I cannot look at you.' How she despised him for what he had done. The breeze carried in the sweet scent of *parijat* flowers. 'Why doesn't he just come in, instead of calling out like a dying man?' she thought. Had he gone away? How could he go leaving her like this?

Silence surrounded her. Unable to bear it a moment longer, Bhanumati tread on noiseless feet to the door and yanked it open. She saw a shadow in the gloom of the corridor. She approached him, afraid her determination to hate him all her life would melt if she looked into his eyes. His shallow breathing stopped altogether as he sensed her presence. She wanted to touch him but withdrew her hand at the last moment.

"Bhanu, I did nothing wrong," he said beseechingly.

Bhanumati withdrew in horror. 'Nothing wrong? What are you saying, my husband?'

"She deserved it. That woman deserved every bit of it." The low whisper scorched her ears. Forgetting to breathe, she stood still, waiting for him to say something that would make her believe in his remorse.

"Why do you stare at me like that, Bhanu? Tell me you understand. Was it so wrong to pay her back in her own coin? It was her husband, not I, who pledged her in the game of dice." Suyodhana punched his fist into a pillar. Bhanumati flinched, that must have hurt. She stood in silence.

"Tell me something, woman. Why do you gape at me like an idiot? I will teach them a lesson – those five villains and their arrogant wife. Bastards!" Suyodhana spoke rapidly.

Bhanumati had heard enough. There was really no point talking to him anymore.

"Bhanu, where are you going?" Suyodhana grabbed her arm and jerked her back, peering into her eyes. She stared back, willing her tears to remain unshed. "Am I so evil, Bhanu?"

She heard his voice crack. When his arms embraced her she forgot every retort she had planned, the words she had rehearsed. She lifted his chin and looked into his eyes. Moonlight glistened in their tormented depths. 'Perhaps the rest of the world sees him as evil but for me there is no one nobler,' she thought.

He pressed his lips to hers and she tasted the saltiness of his tears on her lips. It did not last. The threatening face of Draupadi grew to fill the sky! The voice of the shamed woman filled the palace. Bhanumati pulled away from Suyodhana's embrace and ran to her bed, hands over her ears to block out the sound.

Suyodhana came to her and cradled her head on his shoulder. His arms enfolded her as he spoke soothingly. Soon she was soaked in the fuzzy happiness of having her head on his shoulder. She wanted to remain thus until *pralaya* claimed the world. In the east, the sky blossomed like a hibiscus flower.

Her husband shattered the moment by reopening the wound. She looked at him in fear as he told her how he had stood up to Bhishma for Karna's sake. 'Why did he do that?' she wondered as her heart beat like the drums of war.

"Now my friends have all gone, Bhanu. I feel alone. Perhaps I should have gone with Karna to meet the fanatics of the Confederate or with Aswathama to Gandhara. Why do I feel like a coward? Why am I so miserable, Bhanu?"

"It is their duty to protect the country, Suyodhana." She hated herself for the envy bubbling inside her against her husband's friends. The first rays of the sun had started sneaking in through the silk curtains and she could hear the sounds of servants cleaning the corridors and gardeners raking leaves in the garden. The world went on, not caring a damn about who died and who lived, who was shamed and who was honoured. The silence in her room was stifling. He had not answered her.

"Bhanu, have I failed Karna? Have I sacrificed Aswathama?"

'Karna! He is the one who has changed my husband!' Bhanumati clenched her fists. Why was he so important to him? More than Pitamaha, more than her. Something jarred in her mind whenever she thought of the Suta, noble and righteous though he was. 'Perhaps it is Karna's almost inhuman righteousness and generosity that frightens me,' she thought.

As if reading her mind, Suyodhana stood up. He drew aside the silk curtains and stood with his hands gripping the window frame. The sun was rising over the Ganga, turning her waters into a sheet of gold. The fresh morning breeze carried the smell of blossoms, the chirping of birds and the faint shouts of the boatmen. "Bhanu, see the sun in his divine glory. I can see the face of Karna there." He turned back to Bhanumati, his hair fluttering in the breeze. "It is a new day, the dawn of a golden future."

She did not reply but her hands felt stiff. If Karna died in the war with the Confederate, she would get her husband back, for herself. She shuddered at the thought that singed her soul. 'Oh God, it is a sin to even think like that. Karna, of all people! Forgive me, oh Shiva!'

"I am sure, they will return, Bhanu. Both of them will be back. I have thirteen years to prove myself. Do not let this foolish incident with Draupadi and her husbands stand in the way of our happiness. I have no regrets. That woman and her husbands deserved it. May they never return. I am determined to create a world where no one is miserable, where a ruler can rule without discriminating; create a country where nobody goes hungry to bed and the law is equal for men and women, rich and poor alike.

I need my friends with me and they know it. They will return and we will prove all this to the world. Bhanu, our kingdom will not deny men like Karna what is due to them because of caste, or be cruel to Nishadas and untouchables. I want to get into the cause of the Naga problem and resolve it. I want to do a hundred thousand things. I want the whole world to love me for my fairness; I want to be known as a righteous man who did not care for caste, who gave Karna, the noblest man of all, his life. I want my people to think there is no one better than Suyodhana. They will not hate me for what I did to that woman. There is no one who deserves the throne more than I. It is a new day, a new beginning."

Bhanumati looked at him in surprise. He had spoken of his dreams many times before but something was different now. Something was unfamiliar, as if the window to the darkest place in Suyodhana's mind had opened and light was falling on the dust in the corners. She felt she understood him now but wished she did not. Even his love for Karna was a reflection of his love for himself, his love for glory and fame. How then was he different from the Pandavas he hated? Was there a Yudhishtra hidden inside Suyodhana and vice versa? Was Duryodhana taking over Suyodhana?

"You are no different from Yudhishtra," she said. Her hands flew to her mouth as if to stop the spoken words.

Suyodhana's head snapped towards her in shock and anger. She wanted to look away but knew this was a decisive moment in her life. He walked to the door. "I cannot forgive or forget that," he said.

"You cannot forgive me?" Bhanumati said, her voice choking with sobs. "It is you who should be asking forgiveness, Suyodhana, for the way you treated Draupadi, not me."

"Enough, woman! You are my wife. Do not forget your place. I have done nothing wrong. I am a Kshatriya."

"Kshatriya! When has disrobing women become a Kshatriya trait? You talk about a caste-free society, yet stand on Kshatriya pride."

"She insulted Karna!" thundered Suyodhana.

"Oh, forget Karna. You and your friends! May the Suta never return from his war with the Southern Confederate! May the Brahmin die in Gandhara!"

Suyodhana rushed towards Bhanumati. Grabbing her hair, he pulled back her head. She saw murder in his eyes.

With a calm voice that made Suyodhana weak in the knees, she said, "Do it Suyodhana. Kill me. It will not change the fact that what you did was wrong."

The grip on her hair loosened. He turned away from her. She folded her hands and pleaded, "Natha, please. Ask for her forgiveness. Give your cousins their due. Be the husband I knew. Please..."

Suyodhana stood towering over her, the white shawl over his shoulder flapping in the breeze. The small lamp in the corner flickered, throwing light and shadow over his face in crazy patterns. A sudden gust snuffed it out and the smell of the burning wick filled the room. In the golden light of the rising sun seeping into the room, Bhanumati saw his face and all hope died.

***

Far away in Dwaraka, Ekalavya's army had surrounded Krishna's city. As the Nishada looked at the domes and spires of Dwaraka shining golden in the sunshine, he clenched his teeth in seething anger. The prosperity of Dwaraka was a sore sight when millions of Nishadas and Nagas lived no better than animals.

When the fort gates opened and Balarama's army rushed out to confront the Nagas, Balarama was a worried man. He could feel the energy of Nishada's army and sense their bloodlust. If only he could reach Ekalavya before too many people died in the pointless war, he might be able to convince him about the futility of all this violence. He could not capitulate or it would be nothing short of shameful surrender. As the King of the Yadavas, he had a duty to lead his people to victory, to protect them. Fight he would, but if there was a way to achieve a truce and avoid bloodshed, he would find that way.

A cruel smile played on Ekalavya's lips as the sight of Balarama's army. Victory was finally going to be his. He could see it in the way Balarama held his bow, the way he looked at his men, the lack of enthusiasm in the Yadava war cries. Without Krishna for protection, Dwaraka was going to succumb easily. He turned to his companions. "If Balarama offers a truce, we will seem to accept and then kill him once we enter the city. We will burn the city, kill all the men and take all the women. Their treasury brims with the wealth they have grabbed by exploiting the downtrodden. We will distribute it among our people. "

Balarama was walking into a trap.

*****

7 SERPENT HUNT

TAKSHAKA WAS GETTING IMPATIENT. Why had Krishna's army slowed down? Why had the wily Yadava dismounted? Had he sensed the trap or was it just a coincidence? His men were getting restless. A gray moon shone reluctantly in the sky. He cocked his ear to listen to what Krishna was saying to one of his men. The breeze was unfavourable and he could not hear what was being said. One of the Nagas coughed and Takshaka's heart skipped a beat. Had it alerted Krishna? Had he heard? He hissed at his men to be silent.

***

"What has happened?" asked Kritavarma, sitting proudly erect on his horse. He was the Commander of the Narayana Sena, the famed elite corps of Yadava warriors trained personally by Krishna. Kritavarma had once been a close friend, but the carnage at Indraprastha had caused them to drift apart.

"Let us halt here."

"Krishna, are you mad?" Kritavarma asked, surprised.

"I am tired and the boys too, need a rest." Krishna's eyes never left the boulders in the distance. 'I should never have spared Vasuki when we caught him in Indraprastha,' he thought.

"So you would rather halt here and see Dwaraka reduced to rubble? Why are we wasting time?" Kritavarma asked, raising his voice.

"What can a few Nishadas do to us?" Krishna's heart was pounding in his chest. If only he could provoke the Commander, he might be able to pull off something. "I have seen many

Nishadas in Khandiva; they ran like mice before a cat when Arjuna and I..."

"Krishna! I do not wish to hear anything more concerning your disgraceful conduct in Khandiva."

"The Nagas are cowards. Why should a Nishada scare you, Kritavarma? We should have stayed in Indraprastha and enjoyed the evening instead."

"Don't get me started on your amoral Pandava friends!"

"Kritavarma, you only say that because my brother, Balarama, has an inexplicable fondness for Duryodhana."

"I get it now, Krishna, why you want to halt in this wilderness. You are aiming at the throne of Dwaraka. You do not wish to save our Dwaraka at all!"

"My brother is a wonderful man but not the leader the Yadavas need now. It is better that he be defeated. The Yadavas can then elect a fit person as King, someone who can..."

Krishna felt the cold tip of Kritavarma's sword on his neck. "Another word about Balarama and you are dead."

Krishna tried hard to suppress a smile. Kritavarma had taken the bait. Krishna tugged at the reins of Kritavarma's horse and it plunged forward in pain, throwing Kritavarma to the ground. Krishna laughed, hoping to provoke him further.

Had a head popped up in the distance? It was dark, with only a few sorry stars staring down from a bleak sky. When Kritavarma tried to get up, Krishna kicked him and laughed again. No warrior worth his salt could swallow such an insult. Kicking a fallen man! That too, a reputed warrior like Kritavarma!

"Draw your sword, you...you..." Kritavarma stood up, stuttering in rage, unable to spell out the insult that frothed in his mouth.

Krishna walked up to his own horse and took down his sword. He took his time removing it from its sheath and then began polishing it with deliberate strokes, as if he had all the time in the world. His eyes never left the boulders in the distance. Another head popped up and vanished in the dark. Krishna slipped his barbed discus into his waistcloth and then walked towards Kritavarma. By the time he reached his Commander, the Narayana Sena had split into two factions and most had dismounted from their horses. One group bowed to him and he acknowledged them. The other group stood behind Kritavarma, watching the proceedings with hostility.

"Let us decide the rules of the duel..." Kritavarma did not finish.

"Attack!" barked Krishna to his supporters.

Kritavarma's mouth opened in surprise. They had not even agreed on the rules of combat, yet Krishna had ordered an attack on him! Before he could react, men were running towards him with drawn swords.

"Kill those unscrupulous Yadavas," Kritavarma shouted, parrying a deadly sword swipe with his own blade.

His followers attacked Krishna's men. Soon, what should have been a civilized duel, turned into a full-fledged battle. Krishna kept himself to the periphery of the fighting men, far from the enraged Yadava Commander. He kept taunting Kritavarma about his lineage to fan his outrage. Men began dropping dead on both sides. Limbs were severed and faces gored. There was blood everywhere. The Yadavas were hacking each other to death. Over the din and fierce cries of battle, Krishna's eyes kept searching for any movement from the hidden enemy. Nothing stirred. His men were dying in a battle he had started. Had he lost the gamble?

***

"Don't move!" Vasuki hissed to Takshaka, but the Naga leader was getting restless. The Yadavas were fighting each other to the death and this was the most opportune moment to finish off the notorious Narayana Sena, as well as Krishna himself. "That cunning Yadava and his tricks!" Vasuki hissed again.

'Perhaps he is and perhaps he is not,' mused Takshaka. The Yadavas had always been notorious for their in-fighting and drinking.

"We only have to delay them enough for Ekalavya to take Dwaraka. Don't bat an eyelid. Be still." Desperation sounded in Vasuki's voice.

'Why is he using that tone with me, the cranky old man?' Like a thunderbolt, the answer struck Takshaka. 'Wily old rascal! He knows that his own plan of making Ekalavya leader of the Nagas will fail if I get Krishna.'

"Krishna is faking it. Stay here!" Vasuki cried as Takshaka rose from his hiding place.

'If the cunning Yadava was faking the battle, would he allow his own elite soldiers to die like this?' Takshaka wondered. No, it was real.

Vasuki grabbed Takshaka's wrist in a last ditch attempt to stop him. The revolutionary leader pulled his hand away with contemptuous ease. "Attack!" he shouted.

Screaming and yelling, the Nagas ran towards the Yadavas. They did not see Vasuki get up and run through the scrub and desert as fast as his tired old legs could carry him. Neither did they see Krishna was no longer among the group of fighters hacking each other to death.

***

At last! Krishna heaved a sigh of relief when he saw the Nagas leave their hiding place and rush towards them. He crouched behind the carcass of one of the slain horses. The smell of death hung in the air. Twenty of his elite soldiers were dead and many others wounded in the in-fighting.

Takshaka was only a few feet from Kritavarma when Krishna rushed from his hiding place towards them. Holding his *Sudharshana chakra* in one hand, he hacked his way through

the melée with his sword in his other hand, not bothering to
see whether it was a Naga or Yadava he was cutting down.
Takshaka and Kritavarma were engaged in deadly swordplay.
Krishna hurled himself on the Naga leader. They fell to the
ground, rolling over. In a trice Krishna had prised Takshaka's
sword from his hand. When the dust settled, Takshaka was on
his knees with Krishna standing behind him. The sharp edge
of the *Sudharshana* gleamed against the dark skin of Takshaka's
throat. There was an angry roar from the Nagas and they rushed
to save their leader, swords and lances at the ready.

"Ask your men to drop their arms." Krishna's voice was calm. A
smile played on his lips.

"Kill him!" Takshaka barked and a few Nagas stepped out,
ready to strike Krishna.

"Don't tempt me, Takshaka," Krishna said and yanked the Naga
leader's head up by the hair. He pressed his *Sudharshana* harder
and a fine red line appeared on Takshaka's throat. Drops of blood
dripped onto the earth, making dark blotches where Takshaka
knelt. One by one, the Nagas dropped their arms.

"Now you die," Krishna said without emotion.

But before he could slit Takshaka's throat, Kritavarma grabbed
his hand and tried to prise away the *Sudharshana*. "Krishna, this
is ignoble and unfair. You gave your word."

"Kritavarma, you fool... let me do my duty."

Takshaka seized his opportunity as the Yadavas argued. He
scooped up some sand and threw it in Krishna's face. The split
second during which Krishna loosened his grip was enough for
Takshaka, who wrenched out of Krishna's grasp and fled for his
life.

"Catch him!" Krishna yelled in frustration. His eyes were still
itching from the sand and he was unable to see clearly, but he
knew the Nagas were escaping. By the time his sight cleared, all
the important Naga rebels had gone.

"Satisfied now?" Krishna asked the still fuming Kritavarma, shaking his head in exasperation.

"Krishna, what you did was both dishonourable and deceitful. This is not the warrior's way…"

"My friend, an ambush was waiting for us. They would have slaughtered us had we walked into it. I had no other choice but to provoke you…"

"You are a genius, Sir," one of the older soldiers cried. "We did not realise it was part of your plan."

His men lauded his wisdom as Krishna stood basking in their praise. The night grew old and streaks of grey appeared in the east. If only Kritavarma had not stopped him from doing his duty. Why did he not understand this was war and there was nothing unfair about winning? But the Commander burned with anger and humiliation.

"Come, let us forget this and go on, Kritavarma," Krishna said, extending his hand.

"Forget what, Krishna? The death of twenty of my finest boys? What will I say to their families when I return to Dwaraka? You feel smug that you have saved the majority. That is poor consolation for the families of the dead, killed by their own comrades in arms. How will I face their widows? What a dishonourable victory!"

Krishna sighed as he looked at the smoke rising from the funeral pyres built for the dead soldiers. Then he turned and yelled at the top of his voice, "Let us rush to Dwaraka, my friends. There is no time to lose."

The elite cavalry rapidly fell into formation. Krishna's horse shot forward like an arrow and the Narayana Sena galloped behind him. They rode for the better part of that day, stopping only to rest their horses and have a quick meal. Krishna tried to make amends to Kritavarma, but the Commander refused to speak. By evening, they had reached the outskirts of Dwaraka.

"Oh my God!" Krishna cried in anguish. A huge army of Nishadas were engaged in a pitched battle with Balarama's men.

"For our motherland, for Dwaraka, and for Balarama..." Kritavarma raised his sword high in the air and rushed into battle. His men rode behind him with daredevil bravery.

Krishna shook his head in dismay. When would his people learn? There was no point in being chivalrous towards enemies who attacked an undefended city or waited in ambush. It was neither cruelty nor cowardice to beat them with cunning and skill. In this game, there were no rules or laws; only winning mattered. The man who was fighting so nobly would have been the first person to break the rules had he known what lay in store for him. Krishna felt pity stir for Kritavarma, but he did not have the luxury to stand and watch them get butchered by the Nagas. Dwaraka had to be saved at any cost. His brother would see goodness even in his enemies and walk into a trap. Krishna would have to do something daring again, something distasteful to people who forgot to look at the whole picture. He had to do what he felt was right without worrying about the results and what others would say about his methods. He had to perform his *karma*.

Krishna took out his *Sudharshana* and began moving towards the enemy. His form merged with the shadows. He had to find Ekalavya before his brother met the Nishada.

*****

8 Refuge

"SISTER, WHY ARE YOU LEAVING THE PALACE?" Gandhari asked.

Kunti ignored her, seething with rage. She ordered the maids to pack only two saris and no ornaments. She would not take anything that belonged to that hated Duryodhana or his blind father. She would leave the palace with only the possessions she had brought when she came with her sons. Kunti did not want anyone's charity, not when she had five warrior sons.

Gandhari found her way to her sister-in-law and took her trembling hands in her own. "Do not leave. What will the people say about the King? About me?"

"You are worried about appearances, Gandhari. I have suffered enough, living in your palace. Can you say no one poisoned me or arranged to stab me in my sleep? I have had enough. I will not stay a moment longer in this cursed place."

Gandhari withdrew her hands and steadied herself, trying hard to control the sharp words that rose to her tongue. What right had Kunti to accuse her? She was the daughter of the great Gandharan King, Suvala, the *pativrata* who had refused the light denied to her blind husband; no, she did not have to listen to accusations and abuse from a woman who had conceived children with men other than her husband. Gandhari's lips curled in disdain. "Sister, it is your choice to leave. Let these servants be witness that the daughter of Gandhara has not failed in her *dharma*."

Before Kunti could answer, Gandhari had turned and left the room. When she reached the door of the royal chambers, she flinched at the sickening noise coming from within. Dhritarashtra was hammering the iron replica of Bhima with his mace. She walked in softly, not wishing to start a conversation. She wanted to be alone. She felt triumphant, afraid and angry at the same time. In her heart, she had hated the stiff formalities of the Hastinapura court from the day she had set foot in the city of elephants. Though she had learned to love her husband and her adopted land, she yearned for Gandhara in the quiet moments when she was alone. The vivid memories of the day her father and all her brothers except Shakuni, died in Bhishma's invasion, still haunted her in her dreams. Even after all these years she woke moaning from her sleep, mourning her father and brothers. Her husband no longer stirred in his slumber, nor did the palace maids rush to enquire about her troubled dreams.

But she was not the only one who had nightmares. Some nights, the shouts of Dhritarashtra challenging his long dead brother, Pandu, to a duel, would echo through the dark corridors. He would boast how his strong hands had stopped an elephant from trampling his brother in childhood, and how much better he was with the mace, despite his blindness. In the oppressive loneliness of the crowded palace, in the royal chamber fragrant with exotic perfumes, Gandhari would sit watching her sleeping husband – pity, revulsion and love filling her heart.

She hated Kunti with a vehemence that was matched only by Kunti's hatred of her. Her sharp intelligence allowed her to see how meaningless their hatred was, when they were both equal sufferers in a man's world where women were stolen, pawned or deified, but never treated as equals. Yet they both fought like trapped cats, not against the trap but each other, maiming and scratching, fiercely protective of their kittens; yet showing faces of gentility and loveliness to the world watching them.

In a way, Gandhari was relieved Kunti was leaving, but cold logic told her that it was better to suffer Kunti in the palace than turn her out. She knew what Kunti was trying to do and hated her for her deviousness, while admiring her intelligence.

Kunti was trying to turn public opinion against Duryodhana by playing the martyr. In the eyes of the public, Kunti was now a helpless widow, who had been thrown into the streets by the evil Duryodhana. Her son was now the demon who had tried to humiliate Kunti's daughter-in-law and sent his cousins into exile after grabbing all their possessions.

Dhritarashtra gave a bitter laugh when he felt Gandhari's presence in the room. He turned to her saying, "Let her go, Gandhari. The sons of Pandu have gone to where they belong. Those begotten slyly in the forest belong in the forest. The palace is not for bastards."

What did this man know of the beast their son had unleashed? There was no point answering him. He would not understand. Yet she could not help saying, "You should not have allowed it to continue after the first game of dice."

"Ah, my dear, I gave them back everything after the first game. I was more generous than necessary to people with whom I share no blood. I did not ask the son of *dharma* to play again. Besides, Pitamaha did not object," Dhritarashtra chuckled.

"Do you know why Pitamaha did not object? Had the game ended there, you would have outwitted everyone with your act of noble generosity. We would have proved Yudhishtra to be an incompetent ruler who could keep neither his kingdom nor his wife safe, and they would have been beholden to us. That would have made Pitamaha irrelevant; you know he does not like you to take any decision without first consulting him. But now, everyone has forgotten your noble act, your humility in asking Draupadi's forgiveness, and your good heart."

"Pitamaha has always disliked me, Gandhari. He denied me the crown until my brother died. Is it my fault I am sightless? In Pitamaha's *dharma*, an impotent man like my dead brother, Pandu, could be King, but not the blind Dhritarashtra, who could defeat a hundred men in combat. He never did anything for me."

'Except invade a friendly neighbouring country, butcher the King and his sons and steal the Princess to marry him to you,' Gandhari thought bitterly. "What is done cannot be undone," she said calmly, touching her husband's strong hands. "Call for Suyodhana. He needs to be told to stay quiet for some time. The public will lynch him if he moves out. The Magadhans and Sutas have spread exaggerated stories of his bad behaviour. I wish Kunti had stayed in the palace."

***

Yudhishtra walked with his gaze fixed to the ground. 'I have lost everything. I have always followed *dharma* and given gifts to the Brahmins. I have never uttered a lie in my life, I have done all the ritual sacrifices, yet why has fortune forsaken me? Mother has left, saying she does not trust me, that I might gamble her away too, one day. Oh the shame! The shame of walking barefoot on the streets where my golden chariot raced along, the shame of so many eyes staring at my wife's desolate face. Oh, the shame of losing to Duryodhana!'

A blind dog came up to him and wagged its tail. A mellifluous voice rose, singing of Krishna's love for the unfortunates of the world.

"Bhima, I wait for the day you will bring me Dushasana's blood. I will drink it with relish."

Yudhishtra shuddered at Draupadi's words. The song faded away. The sound of rushing hooves passed them. Yudhishtra heard Arjuna exclaim between clenched teeth that it was Shakuni, Prince of Gandhara. He heard Sahadeva vow to crush the bastard's skull one day. Yudhishtra did not speak a word. As they turned a bend on the royal highway, he paused to look back at the palace for the last time.

"Why look back now? You gambled and lost everything." Draupadi's words furrowed his heart. "Never forget, Yudhishtra, never forget my shame, now or ever," Draupadi said clearly as she walked past. His brothers followed her.

The crowd that had tagged after them at first had long dispersed to their mundane routines. Yudhishtra stooped to gather a fistful of earth. He caught the eye of the beggar who had been singing, sitting under a tree close by. He felt embarrassed by his action. Did the beggar shake his head in disapproval? Yudhishtra could not be sure. When he looked back, both the beggar and the dog had vanished.

***

Vidhura coughed, masking his hesitation. "Devi, I will send the priests to perform the ritual cleansing of this house." He knew the rituals were essential to make a Shudra home fit for a Kshatriya lady. Kunti nodded silently.

As Vidhura began walking away, Kunti said softly," I do not know how to thank you, brother, but when my son Yudhishtra becomes King, I will ensure you are sufficiently rewarded."

Until that moment, Vidhura had not known that so much frustration lay dormant within him. He turned back, suppressing the retort that rose unbidden to his lips. "I am always at your service. I but do my duty."

Vidhura gritted his teeth, trying to suppress the anger he felt. When he had returned home from the Sabha, he had found Kunti waiting for him. She did not wish to live in the palace, she said. He knew what she wanted. Without a word he had ordered his wife to pack up. They would move to their unfinished home in the woods. He had not even allowed his wife to voice her dissent.

"God bless you," Kunti said again.

Vidhura felt pity for her, mingled with contempt. He did not wish to embarrass her further. The pride in the sacrifice he was making was exhilarating. His family were already far ahead on the road and he hurried to join them. As he walked, dry leaves cartwheeled in the breeze, dancing in the dust that swirled around him. A blush tinted the eastern sky. The birds had begun stirring in their nests. The street was deserted, though he could hear the sounds of cooking from a few homes. Vidhura felt overwhelmed by the events of the day. He had tried his utmost to stop the shaming of the Princess Draupadi. Why had even Bhishma remained silent, and why had he reacted so violently to Suyodhana once the event was over? There had been no need to sacrifice Karna. Was he seeing another side of Bhishma, a ruthless streak which Bhishma had kept hidden from him? The more he thought of the incident in the Sabha, the angrier he became. No one had listened to him, and no one would be spared.

More than the incident itself, it was the fact that he had been ignored, that upset Vidhura's normally calm mind. All his self-consciousness about being the son of a *dasi*, all the insults, big and small, that he had faced from childhood, and all his fears of becoming irrelevant in the coming age, added to his frustration. What right had men like Bhishma, Drona, Kripa or Dhaumya to rule over him, when they behaved in such a cavalier fashion when a woman was insulted in public? They were proud to be Brahmins and Kshatriyas, yet they had not had the courage to speak out against *adharma*. Only the son of a *dasi* had spoken out against Suyodhana, there had been no dissent, except for the meek voice of young Prince Vikarna.

Vidhura now felt a rising contempt for all the men he had held in high esteem before. He, a Shudra, would observe *dharma* more perfectly than all those highborn men, he vowed. He had even given up his home for Kunti to live in. He would show the world nobility lay in one's thoughts and deeds and not in belonging to a particular caste. He would show them by his deeds who was superior – the Kshatriyas who gambled and fought, or the Brahmins who debated endlessly about the nuances of scriptures, or he, the son of a *dasi*. Suddenly he remembered Kunti's words about Yudhishtra becoming King and stopped in his tracks. A deep sense of foreboding gripped him. There would be a war; he was sure of it. All that Bhishma and he had worked for would be futile.

A small contingent of cavalry was approaching fast, their bobbing forms obscuring the rising sun. A few elephants and some rickety war chariots followed. When Karna passed by, Vidhura remembered Bhishma's vow. Karna's victory would end the Grand Regent's time at the helm of affairs. Would he himself be able to work under Suyodhana? Could he work under anyone other than the gruff old man? He was afraid to think of the beasts that lay crouched in the dark folds of time. Perhaps Karna would not return.

As he was nearing the forest, Vidhura saw another contingent of cavalry rushing north, with Aswathama riding in the lead. Where were they going? Why did these young men so desperately seek danger? From whom were they running? Vidhura could almost hear Shakuni's laughter and the dice rolling on the floor. Someone was moving his pieces dexterously. They were all mere pawns in the deadly game of dice. He looked in the direction Aswathama's cavalry had vanished and said softly, "Son of Drona, do you know what awaits you in the snow-clad heights of Gandhara? Why are you so naively rushing to your death?" An owl that was perched on a branch above him hooted as if in reply.

Vidhura wiped his perspiring face and hurried to catch up with his wife and sons.

*****

9 Trapped

KARNA LOOKED AT THE VAST ARMY spread before him. His steady gaze betrayed none of the desperation he felt within. How long could he hold out? His own army looked puny compared to the ocean of men, horses and war elephants that waited on the other bank of the Narmada. He dismounted, abandoning his horse for a chariot. It meant putting his trust in an unknown charioteer of Sindh, but it was the only way he could use his stockpile of weapons.

The first arrow struck perilously close to where Karna stood, spraying splinters of wood around him. From a distance, King Uthayan raised his bow in challenge. Karna answered with an arrow that took down the flag of the Chera King, smiling at the rage his shot produced. "Flame-throwers to the front," he barked and three dozen men arrived in response to his command.

The Confederate army answered with its own volley of flame-tipped arrows. Shrieks of men on fire, the neighing of frightened horses and the trumpeting of crazed elephants filled the air. What was that moving in the Confederate ranks? The ripple travelled quickly through the enemy lines. A major faction of the Southern Confederate army broke ranks and began crossing the river. To Karna's surprise, they were not shooting at the Hastinapura army but at their own soldiers.

"Stop firing! Wait!" Karna yelled. Immediately, runners dashed off in all directions to convey his order.

A huge column of the Confederate army was advancing in a wide arc towards him. Was it a ruse? Why then were they holding white flags? As the first horse climbed out of water, their faces became clearer. Karna looked up at the sun, murmuring a prayer of thankfulness.

The King of Kalinga dismounted from his horse and bowed low. Karna felt weak at the knees. He had been lucky, again. "Sir, we crave your pardon. You are the chosen warrior of the Sun God. We cannot fight against you."

The game had changed. The odds no longer seemed impossible. 'How can I thank this man, this venerable old King of Kalinga, whose belief in his God is stronger than caste prejudices?' wondered Karna.

"Get the traitor first and leave the Suta to me."

Karna was shocked by Uthayan's voice so near him. An arrow zipped past the King of Kalinga. Before Karna could think, the rushing cavalry of the Confederate descended on them like a tidal wave.

"In the name of Surya," Karna yelled over the din of metal clashing on metal, horses neighing and men crying in pain. He jumped into his chariot and drew his bow. His first arrow broke Uthayan's bow. The next wounded the Chera King's forearm.

The waters of the Narmada turned red with the blood of men and beasts. The doubts that had plagued Karna that morning gave way to reckless enthusiasm. He lost count of the men he killed with his precise volley of arrows. Nevertheless, the Confederate forces pressed on.

"Your Highness, with your permission..." In the mad melée, Karna did not hear what the Brahmin warrior near him was trying to say. Before he could answer, the man had gone, his horse jumping over obstacles and dodging arrows. 'Where have I seen him?' wondered Karna for a split moment. As the daredevil equestrian disappeared among the Confederate armies, the answer came to him in a flash. He was the Brahmin warrior from Kalinga, who had come first in horse racing so long ago in Muzaris. But what was he up to now?

An arrow from the King of Vatapi, a Confederate General, struck Karna's breastplate and fell to the chariot floor with a clang. It lay vibrating as if alive. Karna returned fire in one fluid movement. Using the catapult attached to his chariot, he propelled a mud pot of oil, hitting the Vatapi King's chariot, drenching it in oil. He picked up the arrows wrapped in oilcloth, held them to the pot of fire and shot off the flaming missile. The Vatapi chariot burst into flames, causing the panicked horses to plunge in their harness and run wild. Some soldiers attempted to extract their King but the chariot collapsed in a burning heap. As his men watched in horror, their King was charred to death along with the horses.

Karna immediately realized his error of judgement. The Confederate armies had resisted using unconventional weapons thus far. Till then the battle had been fought using *Hastamuktha* arrows and manual weapons. Now that he had broken the unwritten code of warriors by using a *Yantramuktha* missile, launched from a mechanical contraption, there was nothing to stop them pounding the Hastinapura army with their own missiles. It had been a trap and he had fallen into it. Karna berated himself for being an unthinking fool.

Smoking arrows carrying poisonous herbs started descending on his forces. *Nagastras!* They were notorious for leaving a trail of smoke that carried death with every breath. Karna's men started falling as the smoke spread among the ranks. He desperately searched for the antidote. His Guru had taught him about the herbs capable of neutralizing the *Nagastras*. Where was the damned cache? Choking and coughing, Karna rummaged through his weapons. A fire-tipped arrow lodged itself in the canopy above his head and the material burst into flames. Through the haze and smoke he saw a pot of oil flying towards him and the smile on Uthayan's face. Time was running out. Karna quickly mixed the herb powders, praying he had got it right. He did not even wish to imagine the terrible consequences, should the mixture go wrong. Thanking God for the body armour that protected him from the arrows that struck him. He put the mixture into a pot of oil and loaded it in the catapult. The pot began smoking, emitting a noxious smell.

An arrow struck one of Karna's horses. Something exploded near him, bursting into flames. It was only a matter of time before an oil pot exploded inside the chariot, which stood tilted at a crazy angle. The charioteer lay dead, an arrow sticking out of his neck. The wounded horse whinnied in agony, making the chariot rattle.

As if possessed, Karna mixed ingredients and hurled pots among his men. Those who had survived the first blast of the *Nagastras* began recovering with his antidote. The time had come to pay back the Confederate armies, but before that, he had to release the horse from its agony. To do so, he had to get down from the chariot – a dangerous step which would make him vulnerable. Karna jumped down. Instantly, the shower of arrows harassing him stopped. He turned to look and read the impatience in Uthayan's eyes to slay him but the Chera King held fire until Karna got back into position.

The moment Karna once again stepped into the chariot, an arrow struck his thigh and fell off. He shot back in anger, pinning Uthayan's hand to the shaft of the canopy above him. Karna could see blood spurting from the wound as the Asura King tried to free his hand. He toyed with the idea of sending an arrow into the throat of his foe, but remembered Uthayan had not shot him when he was out of his chariot. Instead, Karna's next arrow pinned Uthayan's other hand, causing him to close his eyes in pain. The Confederate forces rushed forward to prevent Karna from killing one of their Kings. Even in his pinned position, Uthayan barked commands and the army closed in. The warriors of Kalinga surrounded Karna. He attempted to keep them at bay, but the circle was shrinking fast.

When all seemed lost, Karna saw the Brahmin warrior from Kalinga, the man who had plunged into the enemy ranks. He had managed to stay alive and reach the rear of the enemy lines. Karna saw a flame-tipped arrow rise high into the sky and fall deep into the Confederate elephant corps. For a moment nothing happened, then the first elephant ran amok, smashing into the one ahead of it. The second elephant turned back, enraged, breaking rank and starting a stampede. The panicked elephants charged, trampling friend and foe alike. The smell of poisonous herbs and powders pervaded the air. There were explosions everywhere. Oil pots burst and catapults discharged, creating ever more panic and rage in the elephants.

The horses, struggling to get free, dragged Karna's chariot hither and thither. An elephant smashed into Uthayan's chariot, toppling it. The mammoth gored the horses with its iron-capped tusks and crushed the Chera King's chariot into rubble. There was no way Uthayan could have survived that, thought Karna. But before he could indulge in a sense of relief, he was thrown from his own chariot by a stampeding elephant. The wooden box hung perilously above him for a second, as if hesitating to fall over him. Then, with a sickening crash, the chariot came down on him, trapping him inside its dark confines.

Karna tried to lift the chariot, pushing with his powerful shoulders. His whole body ached. What was that low rumbling outside? The whinnying of the horses and the trumpeting of elephants filtered through the cracks of his coffin. The Southern Confederate elephants were running amok, his upturned chariot in their path, with him trapped inside like a bauble in a baby's rattle.

The lid of the cache containing the poisonous weapons flew open and powders began raining on him. A skin-burning itching and throat-choking blackness descended on Karna.

***** *

10 AHIMSA

"KRISHNA, WHY DID YOU DO IT?" Balarama knelt beside the lifeless bodies of Dhantavakra and Shalva.

"They were trying to kill us all, you, me, Balarama..."

"No, Krishna, they were not; we had already defeated them. They were on the verge of surrender. They had put down their arms. Balarama had proposed an honourable surrender, but you..." Kritavarma stood glaring at Krishna, puzzlement and contempt fighting their own battle over the lined terrain of his face.

"Kritavarma, they were going to sack out city. They were killed in battle. Does it matter how? Yes, I used my *Sudharshana* from behind to cut their undeserving throats. An enemy slain is an enemy less. The methods are mere details. My city and people are safe and that is the only thing that counts. Why is there an argument over it? Instead of wasting time, we should be looking for their leader, ah...Ekalavya. Where has he vanished to?"

Balarama stood up wearily and began walking through the battlefield, wet with blood and excreta. The battle was over; the Yadavas had won; but the weight of victory caused his shoulders to stoop. He did not want to stand there and listen to his brother and his Commander argue over the rights and wrongs of the war. All war was wrong. The wailing widows walking from the city gates in procession to search for the bodies of their loved ones was proof enough for him. For a child who had lost his father, what did it matter whether they had won or not? 'Oh, Rama, what have I done?' His heart heavy with sorrow, Balarama walked on. As he stopped to look at each body with equal pain, unmindful whether the dead one was Yadava or Naga, the vultures fluttered their wings angrily, waiting for access to the pickings.

Balarama stopped near a Naga who, at death's door, was trying to say something. Balarama put his ear close to his mouth. "Water," the feeble voice said. Something inside Balarama's mind gave way with the simple request of the dying man. He ran about, frantically searching for water. He yelled to some guards to fetch water. Krishna and Kritavarma stopped their argument to stare. Krishna ran towards his brother, trying to mask his concern.

"Krishna, get some water. The poor man is dying. Hurry..."

"Brother, he is beyond help. It was war. Let the man die like a warrior. What has happened to you?" Krishna turned to order a soldier to fetch water for the dying man.

A guard came running with a pot of water and Balarama snatched it from his hands. But when he turned, the Naga had no need of the water. His lifeless eyes stared at Balarama. The pot fell from his hands and broke, water drenching the blood-soaked earth. The leader of the Yadavas stood staring at the little bubbles that lingered on the surface for a few moments before popping. Balarama turned and walked towards the palace, dragging his mace over the ground, trying to shut out the images of the dead and dying. He walked past the wailing widows and did not even pause to acknowledge the bows of his soldiers.

"Where had the Nishada vanished? We should have taken him, dead or alive."

Balarama paused a moment when he heard his brother chastise the soldiers. He knew where Ekalavya had vanished to but he did not wish to tell Krishna. He had seen Ekalavya running along the fort walls when Krishna was slaying Shalva. For a moment Balarama had considered shooting the Nishada down with an arrow. He knew he could do it, yet he did not. Ekalavya had vanished. He may have jumped into the sea. It was a steep drop from the ramparts and it was doubtful that he had made it alive. If he had survived, he deserved to live. But let his path never cross that of his brother.

Balarama walked on, his head bent low. He felt like a criminal. 'Why did I kill so many people? Who am I to take the life of another living being?' Violence and bloodshed, he was sick of it. He did not hear the cheers of the people who thronged the road. Krishna's chariot stopped near him. Balarama looked at his brother standing in all his divine glory. When he shook his head, Krishna's chariot moved forward with a jerk. From both sides of the road, people threw garlands and coins. Victory cries rent the air. Balarama remained deaf to the cheering. 'Rama, Rama, what have I done?' he mumbled to himself as he walked, his feet crushing the flowers his people were throwing at him.

Krishna's eyes searched for Ekalavya. Where had the Nishada vanished? He was dangerous. Krishna admired the man who had fought his way up from the bottom of the caste hierarchy and turned himself into a fearsome warrior. But the Nishada was filled with bitterness, and that made him a danger to society. He had to be made to see reason. A man who was so determined could be utilised for the benefit of society, provided he knew his position. He was born a Nishada; instead of trying to be a Kshatriya, why he did not concentrate on making the lives of his fellow Nishadas better? Why he was so bent on beating Arjuna and proving himself the better warrior? What if every Nishada started feeling that way? No, for peace, everyone had to strive to be better within his *kuladharma*. If he wanted respect, why did he not become a sanyasi? The path of spirituality had no *varna*, or *jati*. Valmiki had been a dacoit before he became a hermit and wrote the *Ramayana*; Vyasa was a fisherman's son; Viswamitra a Kshatriya; yet they were all respected irrespective of their caste in their *purvashrama*. But when people aspired to what was not destined for them, they created havoc. Parashurama was an example. The Brahmin had caused so much bloodshed trying to act like a Kshatriya. Aswathama was another danger; he could bring disaster trying to act like a Kshatriya. But Karna's audacity was the most intolerable. Society was in shambles. If only his brother had captured Ekalavya, he could have made the Nishada see reason. Who knew, with his intelligence he could have become another great poet who would chronicle the story of Gods and *avatars*. Where had the man gone?

Unknown to Krishna, Ekalavya was fighting a grim battle for survival just a few *yojanas* away from the Dwaraka fort. In this, neither his superlative skills with the bow nor his prowess with the sword were of any help. All alone in the roaring, frothing darkness, under a dark and uncaring sky, the waves exploded with mirth as they pounded him senseless.

*****

11 THE CHASE

"BEWARE!" THE YOUNG CAPTAIN SHOUTED.

Aswathama yanked on his horse's reins, bringing the steed to a plunging halt in the very nick of time. A massive boulder missed him by inches and crashed onto the narrow path behind him with a thud. It then bounced down the cliff face and disappeared into the river deep below, felling a few trees on its way. The splash of the boulder hitting the water sounded unusually loud.

When the dust cleared, Aswathama was still trying to steady his panicked horse. One missed step and he knew he would follow the path made by the boulder and splatter like an eggshell a thousand feet below. His heart pounded in his chest. Had the boulder been an accident or was someone following them? He looked around; the place looked desolate and forlorn. Nothing stirred. Far below, the Deodar trees in the valley had turned white with their burden of snow. The eerie silence when the wind stopped howling was frightening. The mountain crouched like a wounded beast. He had undertaken this mission thinking it would be an adventure. He had always longed to see the ivory-tipped peaks of the Himalayas. It had been so inviting and he had jumped at the opportunity. In the distance, he could see the mountain ranges dissolving into the sky. He wanted to rub his hands to get the circulation back but was afraid to let go of the reins. It was freezing cold. The chill pierced his skin and gnawed at his bones. But more than the elements, it was the inaction and boredom that was killing him.

"Where are the bastards hiding?" Aswathama asked, more to himself than of the Captain.

"Sir, I think we have lost our way again."

Aswathama heard the pain and frustration in the Captain's voice and his anger returned in a flood. "No, we have not!" He watched the words escape his mouth in white puffs. An argument would have been welcome, but his Captain refused to oblige.

As silence crawled back, Aswathama loosened the reins and the horse sauntered forward. His army of thirty-six men dragged itself behind him along the treacherous mountain path. It had started to snow again.

Boom! A scream followed the crash. Aswathama almost fell from his saddle. They had been hit. In that instant he knew the first boulder had been no coincidence and that more were on their way. The second one hit the rear of the column and carried away two men, along with their horses. Aswathama knew that all his skill as a great archer was futile in this battle. He was not fighting on the vast and dusty plains of India. Gandhara had the reputation of teaching reigning superpowers and invaders hard and unforgettable lessons.

The next boulder crashed down just behind Aswathama, hitting the Captain and his horse. He saw them topple over the cliff and vanish into the depths below. The agonized screams of the man and his beast echoed around them, making the survivors edgy. He could sense the fear of his companions. What was that moving there? Rather, who was it? Aswathama peered up towards the top of the mountain, shading his red-rimmed eyes with his hand. He had seen someone moving. Or was the snow playing its usual games of illusion? As he gazed at the point high above, a silent scream began to rise from his belly. The warrior in him sensed it long before his eyes could see. The enemy had waited until they reached this narrow path – the cliff face towered on one side and the deep abyss plunged into darkness on the other. It was the perfect spot for an ambush.

Aswathama's right hand inched towards his sword. At that moment, the entire mountain began to reverberate as mounted warriors began descending on them at great speed. "Advance!" he shouted, galloping like a man possessed. He had to get off the narrow path. It was now or never. The mountainside began exploding behind them.

The Brahmin warrior and his daredevil companions rushed across the gravel-strewn goat trail. Boulders rolled down, frightening the horses and threatening to dash them all into the waters far below. Behind them, men with faces masked with the ends of their turbans, chased them towards their deaths.

"Either we will get that bastard today or we will all perish. We owe ourselves warrior's deaths in the service of Prince Suyodhana and our country," Aswathama shouted over the din, trying to motivate his companions. He could not be sure they heard him.

But his next action inspired them to follow suit. It was one of reckless courage, yet the very insanity of it made his small band of men delirious. Aswathama let go the reins of his horse and stood up in his saddle, facing the Gandharans, his back to his galloping horse's head. Balancing perilously, he drew his bow and arrow. His men did the same. His first arrow pierced the throat of the man leading the attack; those of his companions caused many others to fall.

"Shoot only to kill...shoot...shoot!" Aswathama kept screaming as he showered lethal arrows on his foes.

Although they had managed to slow down their pursuers, Aswathama knew they could not continue holding them off. A single missed step by one of the horses or a hit by any of the boulders falling around them, would finish everything.

Then Aswathama saw him and almost slipped from his saddle. The cloth covering the face of one of the pursuers fluttered back in the wind. There was no mistaking that face... He had never expected Shakuni to lead from the front. Though it was said he was a great warrior, trained by Bhishma himself, it was difficult to imagine the conniving bastard doing well under fire.

'One direct hit, is all I need,' thought Aswathama desperately. His next arrow shaved Shakuni's neck but the Gandharan did not wince. Those burning eyes did not even flicker when an arrow hit the man riding behind him. He kept staring at Aswathama and the Brahmin shuddered at the hatred emanating from the depths of those eyes.

There was just a couple of hundred feet to go to escape the narrow path. "Hold on! Hold on!" Aswathama urged his men as another boulder rolled by so close that it showered them with powdery ice. Despite the men Aswathama had taken down, Shakuni had dodged the arrows with an ease that bordered on magical, the glint of madness in his blue eyes. Another shot and another miss. The man had nine lives.

Aswathama heard a huge crash behind him and looked back. A huge ice-covered boulder had fallen onto the path, cutting off their retreat.

"Good bye, Brahmin!" Shakuni's laughter echoed around them.

Trapped! Aswathama felt panic-stricken, but he could not let down the dozen surviving men with him, nor his country or Suyodhana. 'Father!' he prayed in silent despair. The smiling face of Karna, who might already be lying dead on some battlefield in the South, flashed before his eyes. 'Suyodhana, I have earned your friendship, perhaps even more than Karna, for I chose this battle, unlike Karna, whom it was thrust upon,' muttered Aswathama, trying to rally his thoughts. If he had to die, it should not be in vain. Something had to be done to finish the bastard who had ruined the country.

Time stood still as another arrow struck the Brahmin warrior. He scowled in pain as he removed the two arrows from his shoulder. Blood gushed from the wounds, bright against the pure white snow. What was the lesson his father had taught him about snowy mountains? It was something that had captured his imagination as a child. Aswathama's hands went to the sealed clay pot that contained powdered sulphur rock. "*Gandhakastra!*" he bellowed, ignoring the look of horror among his followers. The men immediately pulled out the small clay pots they all carried.

"It won't be enough to take them out," a soldier near him whispered.

"Not all of them," Aswathama agreed, as he pulled the arrow that would carry the small clay pot to its destination, from his quiver. He scanned the mountain for a visible crack in the ice. He found one, unsure whether the small explosion would trigger what he wanted. "Fire the *Gandhakastra*," he shouted as his arrow arched high over the mountain. It was followed by a dozen more from his men.

"*No!* Are you crazy, you bastard?"

It was good to hear the panic in Shakuni's voice as his men scrambled back, trying to retreat along the slippery trail. They were men of the mountains and knew what was coming as the mountain rumbled under their feet and the horses panicked. They knew nothing would survive in the path of the avalanche the mad Brahmin had triggered with his explosive arrows.

The mountain of snow started at a glacial pace at first, but soon gathered frightening momentum. The air was rent with the sounds of panicked neighing of horses and the terrified cries of men.

"*Har Har Mahadeva!*" Aswathama screamed as the mountain vibrated in anger.

His men answered in full throat. They waited for the embrace of Shiva as the mountain came rushing towards them.

*****

12 Digvijaya

KARNA OPENED HIS EYES TO DARKNESS. 'Have I gone blind?' he wondered. Pungent powders burnt his throat and he tried to cough out the bitterness. Everything was silent. 'My life cannot end like this. Oh Lord Surya, have you forsaken me at my death?'

From a small crack, water came trickling in. Water! From where could it have come? The river was some distance away, as Karna remembered; no water could flow in. He used all his strength to break through the crack. The chariot wobbled. Had it become lighter? Water was seeping in from the ground below. There was the faint sound of rain splattering on water. 'Surya! The river is flooding.' The water was making the chariot buoyant but it was also rising fast, threatening to drown him.

Karna put an injured hand to the crack and tried to lift the heavy chariot. It rose a little and then crashed back, splashing water all over him. He could hear the river fighting to push in. With all his might he pushed again and finally the chariot toppled over with a huge splash. River water rushed to embrace him. He kicked hard and came up to the roaring surface of the Narmada, spluttering and coughing. When he climbed to the shore, the devastation caused by the war elephants was a shocking sight. Limbs were strewn everywhere, some mashed to pulp. Carcasses of horses and men lay rotting, half-eaten by wolves and crows. A few men stood shivering in the drizzle. Who had won the battle?

Some of the men who had seen Karna climbing out of the river, now walked towards him. The river was gobbling up the shore at an alarming rate and Karna waded in through knee-deep water. It had been dry just a few moments before. From their attire, Karna could see the men were Kalinga soldiers. What had happened to the soldiers he had taken on loan from Jayadratha? How many had died?

A movement near him caught Karna's attention. A half-broken chariot lay buried in the slushy earth. A crow, pecking on the carcass of a horse, tilted its head and peered at Karna for a second before hopping away. Was there someone pinned to the ground? As he moved closer, he could hear the wheezing sound of a dying man. Karna looked down and a familiar face stared back.

"Suta, if you value your life, use your sword to end my agony.... If you do not, it will be the biggest mistake of your life..."

Uthayan lay under the rubble. Even at death's door he remained defiant and proud. Such brave men should not be allowed to die. Karna put his shoulders to the toppled chariot and tried to move the weight crushing Uthayan. A few soldiers watching him from a distance, ran to lend their support. Together, they extricated the Chera King. Uthayan's hands were still pinned to the shaft of the chariot. Karna extricated his arrows from Uthayan's palms, feeling the pain of his foe. He stole a glance at Uthayan's grim face, a small hope in his mind craved gratitude from his old foe but all he saw in the eyes of the man he was saving was the glint of unadulterated hatred. Uthayan collapsed on the earth as soon as his hands were freed and lay in a heap, wheezing with pain and exhaustion at Karna's feet.

Soldiers on both sides whispered to each other about the valour of the Suta. Awareness of his magnificent victory began sinking into Karna's mind. He could feel the rays of the rising sun on his shoulders, warming his tired muscles like a caress, almost like a blessing. He was the chosen one of the Sun God. He smiled at the thought. 'Suyodhana, I have done it! It will be fun to watch Lord Bhishma's face when this Suta enters the Sabha. Arjuna, are you watching? A Suta, the son of a charioteer, has done the impossible. Krishna, where are you?'

Karna looked at the carnage around him and then up at the heavens. 'This is not enough. Like the warriors of yore, I must conquer the whole earth – a *digvijaya* – winning victories in all directions. Suyodhana, my friend, you gave me a tiny kingdom to rule but this Suta will repay you by giving you all of Bharatavarsha. Our friendship will no longer be based on your charity.'

The men around Karna bowed deeply in homage. He felt powerful, invincible, and immortal.

That evening, after cremating the dead, the Suta's quest for *digvijaya* commenced. Karna raced south, ignoring the proud King of an ancient race sitting behind him. Nor was there any thought in the Suta's mind about the outstanding valour shown by a Brahmin warrior from Kalinga. The fine equestrian who had made his victory possible lay burnt to ashes on the cremation pyre. Such things did not matter to Karna now. He was chasing his destiny.

The news of their rout at the hands of the Suta reached Parashurama much before Karna did. When his aides asked him whether they should prepare to defend the city, Parashurama answered, "No, invite Karna to my chamber. We will offer no resistance."

As his surprised subordinates withdrew, murmuring to each other, Parashurama sat wondering whether his gamble would work. If it did, it would be the greatest victory of his life. The North would be conquered without spilling a drop of blood.

The temple outside was closing after the night prayers. Parashurama folded his hands in prayer as the last bell and prayer sounded as the doors of the *garbagriha* closed with a screech. Let the Suta come. He did not know what lay in store for him. Parashurama smiled grimly to himself.

*****

13 THE FEAST

ASWATHAMA AWOKE SCREAMING IN PAIN. He could not open his eyes. He panicked, thinking he had gone blind. He could not recollect where he was or why. It took him a while to realize that ropes bound his hands to a pole high above his head. A fire burned nearby, throwing grotesque shadows all around. It was bone-chillingly cold despite the flames. A bearded man walked up to him and threw scalding water onto his face. Aswathama groaned. The group of men around him laughed. Where were his men, those brave souls who had trusted him on this suicidal mission? He strained to see his companions.

"Where are my men?" Aswathama whispered, swallowing the scathing pain in his throat; his face felt on fire.

"You want to know where your men are, Brahmin? Don't you want to know how many of our brethren were killed in the avalanche?"

Aswathama smiled. The bearded man slapped him across his face, cutting his lip. Aswathama cocked his head to one side, spat out some blood and asked, "Is the Mlecha dead?"

Instantly men sprang up with swords drawn. The bearded man kicked Aswathama viciously. "You filthy pig! You dare call our King Mlecha?" His companions joined in kicking their prisoner.

"Enough!" a familiar voice commanded. Immediately the torment ceased. Aswathama raised his bloodied face to see Shakuni standing a few feet away, supporting himself on a long stick. His gaze dropped to Shakuni's knees and he smiled again. The Gandharan limped towards the Brahmin. On either side men stood respectfully with bowed heads. In a voice more frightening for its calm, the Gandhara Prince said, "You have killed more than 3000 Gandharans. You have made me lame for life."

"I am sorry I couldn't do more," Aswathama replied.

Shakuni began to laugh. "I have killed all your men. I could have killed you too, like a fly." His face was inches away as he traced a line across Aswathama's throat with his finger. "Do you know why I spared you, Brahmin? I wanted you to see how I am going to destroy your country."

"Stop blabbering, Mlecha. You cannot even take one step beyond the Indus. You are a wanted man. I will die with the satisfaction that Suyodhana will hunt you down one day."

"Spare your breath, Aswathama. The dice has just started to roll. The game is not over. Not yet, not so quickly, not so easily."

"It will be, when the Hastinapura imperial army marches in. Have you forgotten what Lord Bhishma did to your precious country? When Suyodhana comes, you will wish Bhishma had come instead."

Shakuni's face darkened at the mention of Bhishma. "Hmm, let my nephew come. I want him to come. I want his friends to come too. I want all of India to come." Turning to his companions, the Gandharan said, "Kill the goats. My nephew will be visiting us soon. Bring the *soma*. Let us celebrate."

While his men ran to fetch the goats and threw more wood into the fire, Shakuni moved back to Aswathama. He spoke in a voice as cold as it was soft. "Don't gloat over the few victories your countrymen have won. You breed like pigs and have a bigger army, but ultimately victory will be ours. The day is not far when *we* will rule *you*. Do you want to know why, son of a cursed Brahmin?" Aswathama glared back at the foreigner, furious at his own impotence. Soon, the smell of roasted meat filled the air. The Brahmin crinkled his nose in disgust. Someone began playing a string instrument and drums kept beat to the strange music. Some of the men began dancing, embracing and kissing each other's cheeks. *Soma* flowed freely. Women who had become widows just a few days before, and mothers who had lost their sons in the avalanche, now danced with reckless abandon. Aswathama watched the strange customs of the Gandharans with distaste. What sort of society was this that celebrated even in death? It was the antithesis of everything his father had taught him. The Gandharans lived in the moment, without bothering about the afterlife or the eternal soul. For them, there was no *moksha*, *sanyas* or *brahmacharya*. There were no seekers or philosophers in their midst. Life was now.

When the meat had cooked, they dropped the roasted chunks into a big bowl and mixed it with rice. They devoured the food, dippping their hands in the large bowl as they ate together. There was no difference between rich and poor, prince and pauper. They were one; eating, drinking, dancing, thinking and acting as one. The Mlecha had said they would rule Bharata one day. As Aswathama watched the Gandharans up close, the Mlecha's words held a ring of truth. Bharatavarsha, despite its great warriors, its ancient civilization and refined culture, its accomplishments in art, science and architecture, would collapse like a house of cards before the onslaught of something as primeval as the force he was witnessing. A country obsessed with who was touchable and who was not, who could eat with whom, who could love whom, who could stand how many feet from whom, and who could learn what, did not stand a chance before a people who ate from the same bowl.

As the temperature dropped further and the icy wind from the Hindu Kush shrieked around them, the dancing grew ever more frenzied and wild.

Shakuni approached Aswathama with a chunk of goat meat and thrust it in his face. "Eat!" he commanded, his eyes challenging the Brahmin. Aswathama turned his face away. Shakuni howled with laughter. "What a luxury your people have. You can choose what to eat and what to avoid. Your land is fertile. Here, if we are lucky we get to eat sometimes. We cannot afford customs about who can eat what. What we get, we eat together." Shakuni tore off a chunk of meat with his teeth. The cultivated manners that he had exhibited in Hastinapura had vanished. He laughed at Aswathama's expression of distaste. "Ours is a war-ravaged country; it has been raped and pillaged. Gandhara! We are the children of a lesser God. Just wait and watch what I am going to do to you and yours, Brahmin."

"Dream on, Mlecha. The imperial army is five lakh strong."

"You are amusing, Aswathama. Are you thinking I will fight my nephew? Oh, no. I want him to win." Shakuni fished out a gem from the folds of his clothing. It shone brilliantly in the firelight. It was the most beautiful gemstone Aswathama had ever seen. "Do you know what this is, Brahmin? This is my gift to Suyodhana." Shakuni held it close to Aswathama's eyes. The lustre of the gem was blinding. "For all its beauty, this stone is said to bring misfortune and disaster. I am going to bestow it upon my nephew as a reward for sparing my life. Perhaps you think it is all superstition? You are free to think what you wish, but know this, not two months after my father got this stone from a Yavana, Bhishma invaded our land. See what it did to our country. Now watch what it will do to yours." Shakuni laughed.

"You talk nonsense. Stones do not decide destiny. We do."

"Wait and see, young man. Just wait and see." Leaning on his stick, Shakuni limped back to watch the dancing.

Aswathama wondered what the conniving Mlecha had implied. He wanted Suyodhana to win. He wanted to gift him one of the most precious gems in the world. Why? The bastard! If Suyodhana took it, it would mean he had forgiven his uncle and Shakuni could worm his way back. The gem was worth the entire treasury of Hastinapura. Perhaps there was also some truth about it bringing disaster. That was no doubt the reason why Bhishma had not taken it when he invaded Gandhara all those years ago. Such a possession would have made the kingdom vulnerable.

Shakuni was gambling again. The stone was tempting enough to be stolen but would make its possessor insecure enough to be paranoid. It would beckon invaders and plunderers to his land. Aswathama fervently wished Suyodhana would not come in search of him. Knowing his friend, he was sure that one day or the other, the Prince would come. That would be the worst thing that could happen to his country. For the first time since his capture, Aswathama wept.

*****

14 GURU AND DISCIPLE

KARNA'S ARMY SMASHED THE LAST Confederate defences and rushed deep into the South. In his chariot, the Chera King sat bound in chains, as Karna conquered the kingdoms one by one. Like the sun dispelling darkness, Karna aimed to carry the torch of progress to the Southern Confederate, which slept in the shadows of orthodoxy and caste. The Suta's mission was to remind an ancient culture about the equality of all men, which emperors like Mahabali and Ravana had proclaimed at the dawn of civilization. The juggernaut of Karna's army rolled on, deeper and deeper into the Confederate, conquering kingdoms, toppling empires, and destroying the plague of inequality and caste hatred. Karna's mammoth army rushed to Muzaris after sacking Kanchipuram and Madurai. The last remnants of the terrified Chera army awaited the great Suta warrior's march into their ancient city with their king bound in chains.

"Suta, kill me but do not keep me chained like an animal."

Karna ignored Uthayan's plea. He had no time to pander to the sensibilities of his vanquished foe. He had spared his life and that was a great thing. As his army crossed the hills and marched towards Muzaris, his heart leapt with joy. He suddenly remembered how he had first arrived in this city, a terrified young boy. How it had changed over the years! On either side of the road, people silently watched him ride past them. No one waved. He could see the glistening spire of Parashurama's palace and the silver sheet of sea beyond. The sight unleashed long-suppressed emotions in his heart. Karna's felt salty tears in his throat as he stared ahead, his gaze unwavering. 'My Guru, have you forgiven this seeker of knowledge?'

"Suta, your deceit almost took our revered Guru to the gates of *Yamaloka*. He is just recovering. Don't you dare play with his life again, you son of a low-caste," Uthayan threatened through gritted teeth, rattling his chains in anger.

Karna looked back at Uthayan and smiled. "No one knows my Guru better than I do, Your Highness." He jumped down before the chariot had come to a halt and ran up the Palace steps. He could hear his soldiers dragging out the vanquished Chera King, but he did not pause to watch. Such things could wait. He saw the priests move away as he walked in. Karna was pleased that he could instil so much respect in them. The fruits of victory were sweet.

"Suta, stop! Do not pollute the holy abode of the Guru!" Uthayan shouted from where he stood, a King held captive in his own palace.

It struck Karna like a blow from a *gadha* that the priests had not moved away from him out of respect, but in fear of the pollution a low-caste like him could cause their high-caste souls. Karna felt helplessness wash over him. All his insecurities about being born the son of a charioteer raised their heads once again. He had vanquished the Southern Confederate, yet he remained a mere Suta?

A group of priests stood at the door chanting *mantra*s, daring the Suta to cut off their heads before they allowed him to enter his Guru's presence. Karna knew all his valour did not matter in these dark rooms. How could he use force against these unarmed men? He was a Kshatriya by *karma*. He swallowed the lump lodged like a stone in his throat. How long could he resist the pressures of society?

"I wish to ask my Guru's forgiveness, respected Brahmins. Kindly make way." Karna sank to his knees and bowed low.

The murmuring stopped for a moment and then started again, this time the priests vigorously debating among themselves. 'He is a cheat, do not believe the Suta. The Guru's holy presence should not be defiled.'

Karna heard the chained Chera King command the priests not to let him through, but he remained on his knees. He was tempted to get up and behave like the victor he was. He could have pushed these chattering men to one side with laughable ease and walked into his Guru's room. Within, Parashurama coughed and Karna's heart skipped a beat. One of the priests went in. The Suta remained kneeling like a supplicant before the Brahmins.

It took an eternity for the priest to return but when he did, he indicated the Suta was to enter. Karna remained in the same position, his head bowed in silent prayer. Through his shut eyes, a few tears fell to the floor. He did not wish them to see how vulnerable he was. A priest remarked that the Guru did not have all day. Uthayan protested loudly, insisting that he be taken to the Guru first. Wearily, Karna stood up and walked into the room where his Guru lay. The priests scrambled away lest he pollute them.

The room was in darkness and it took Karna a moment to locate the frail figure on the cot. He was shocked to see Guru Parashurama. He wished he had not come. The broad-shouldered warrior with long muscular limbs had vanished, leaving a frail imitation in his place. 'What have I done to him?' Karna thought in silent horror as Parashurama's frail form was racked by coughing. Finally the Guru gestured for Karna to approach. Parashurama raised a hand to touch Karna and then hesitated a moment, remembering that his favourite disciple was nothing more than a Suta and his fingers would be defiled by touching him. Karna felt like a knife had been stabbed into his heart. He was about to turn away bitterly, when Guru Parashurama's shivering palm came to rest on his bowed head.

Karna closed his eyes, his heart full. Like a child seeking his father's forgiveness for a transgression, Karna wept, his head on the Guru's chest. The old man's fingers caressed his head affectionately. In that moment, they were not a Suta and his exalted Brahmin warrior-Guru, but father and son. Boundaries of caste and prejudice did not matter. Karna wished the moment would never end. He could hear the soft beating of his Guru's heart. 'Has he forgiven me?' the son of the charioteer wondered. Slowly he raised his head and saw the tears in his Guru's eyes.

"Karna, the path you have chosen is the wrong one," Parashurama whispered.

Karna stood up, his hands shivering with emotion. "Guru, I ..."

"No, I am not referring to you lying to me about your caste. Had you not lied and become my disciple, I would never have known you, my son. I forgave you long ago." Parashurama paused, trying to catch his breath. Then he said hoarsely, "I speak of the company you are keeping. You are the *Dharmaveera*. Why then have you befriended Duryodhana?"

Karna's heart skipped a beat. He prayed fervently that his Guru would not demand he leave his friend. He knew he had to defend Suyodhana but somehow the words deserted his tongue.

"Karna, he is evil. He does not respect tradition and he will pay the price for it. You are not what you think you are. Your destiny is different. I am bound by a promise, else I would have told you."

Karna was perplexed, but he knew he would never betray Suyodhana. 'He was the only one who supported me when the whole world was making fun of a Suta who dared to dream of being a warrior,' he wanted to say, but the words were trapped in his throat.

"Your destiny lies with the Pandavas. Go, ask Yudhishtra for forgiveness."

"No!" Karna stood up abruptly. This longed-for meeting had turned bitter. How could his Guru even suggest such a thing? He, Karna, befriend that arrogant Arjuna? "Guru, forgive me, but I could never forsake Suyodhana..."

"Karna, my son, you will regret it later."

"I would rather be known as evil, than ungrateful."

Parashurama sighed. Silence filled the room like a thick fog. Karna yearned to leave the room and get away from the old man who was asking him to befriend his arch rival and betray his best friend. How could he even think such a thing? 'It would have been better that he did not forgive me, and chased me away calling me a Suta,' Karna thought sadly.

"Karna, will you promise this old man something?"

"Anything, Guru, anything except betraying Suyodhana."

"You have destroyed the Southern Confederate and all these kingdoms are now vassal states of Hastinapura. The people of these lands follow an ancient culture and traditions. Your friend may try to impose his newfound ideas here too. I fear that renegade Brahmin, Kripa, will assist him in doing so. In these lands, learning is respected, the Vedas are followed, and Brahmins are considered God's people. Everyone knows their place. Society is stable. Keep your evil friend away from here." Another bout of coughing cut short the Guru's words. Karna stood in silence, his heart and mind in turmoil.

"The way to earn the respect of the Brahmins is not by brute force, but by being righteous. As a King, you should know how to respect learning. It is not your caste that is standing in the way of you gaining people's respect, but your rebellious attitude. There are enough examples of men from various *varnas* becoming King, but they all respected our traditions. Even now, it is not too late. Promise me that you will never deny a Brahmin anything he asks, that you will treat our traditions with respect, and promise me that you will keep your friend away from these holy lands..."

'But Guru, I will still be treated as a Suta all my life." Karna regretted the words as soon as he spoke them.

A smile flickered on Parashurama's lips. "My blessing will always be with you. My blessings still go a long way across Bharatavarsha. Remember my words and see how you will be treated. You can earn respect in two ways – by force or by deeds. The choice is yours. Either way, you will be remembered."

Doubt started gnawing at Karna's mind. Was this a blessing or a bargain? Did it really matter whether a few priests respected him? His duty was toward his friend. Then why was the Guru's offer so tempting? Throughout his life, he had faced scorn for being a Suta, and now... "I promise I will never deny a Brahmin what he asks. I will respect our traditions and culture. I...I am a Kshatriya..."

"You are, my son, whether the world knows it or not. I know there is no one more Kshatriya than you. It would have been better for you to join the Pandavas. Perhaps you will when the time comes and you know the truth. Come, let me embrace you."

Karna moved towards the old man, bending gracefully over the supine figure in the bed. The Guru affectionately ran his fingers over Karna's thick hair for a long time. "I cursed you that day. I must make amends, Karna." Parashurama said, trying to sit up. He fell back in exhaustion as someone tapped on the door. "Open the door," he said to Karna, short of breath. A few Brahmins came in, eyeing the Suta suspiciously. "Where is Uthayan?" Parashurama asked.

The Brahmins looked at each other, embarrassed. Uthayan walked in, his hands in chains, but his head erect and proud, even in defeat.

"You tied him like a slave, Karna?" Parashurama asked and then began to laugh, but his laughter quickly turned into coughing.

Karna saw Uthayan's shoulders slump and he felt compassion for the Chera King stir in his heart.

"Free him," Parashurama ordered.

Karna moved to unchain the King. Uthayan hissed in his ear, "You will pay for this!" Karna ignored him. The chains fell in heaps and Uthayan stepped free. "Luck was with the Suta." He bowed to the Guru.

"Suta he may be to you, but to me he is the best Kshatriya in all of Bharatavarsha." Uthayan and the group of priests gasped in surprise. "Why look so surprised? Here is my order, ensure that it is carried the entire length and breadth of Bharatavarsha: as long as Karna keeps his *dharma* and his promise of never denying anything asked by a Brahmin, as long as he worships the *smritis* and Vedas, he is to be accorded the respect due to a Kshatriya. To mark this pledge, I gift him the *bhargava astra* and my bow, Vijaya."

"No!" Uthayan shouted. "But Guru, why?"

Karna himself was shocked by the gesture. Did the weapon really exist? He had heard rumours about the weapon, a missile of tremendous explosive power. It was said to be a *yantra muktha*, to be released from a chariot. As a student of Parashurama, he had asked him about the weapon many times but the Guru had never given him an answer.

"I forged the weapon with my own hands. Scores of master craftsmen have worked on it for more than a dozen years. There is nothing more beautiful and fearsome as this *astra*," Parashurama said with pride.

"Guru, you cannot give it to this Suta. You are our mentor, our Guru. We have always been loyal to you. Why are you giving the most prized possession to this low-caste impostor from the North?" Uthayan's voice was shrill with agitation.

Parashurama tried to answer, but a bout of coughing caught him unawares. Karna could see the look of shock in the eyes of the Brahmins. The *bhargava astra*, the most feared weapon in the entire country! He could hardly believe he was to possess it. Unbidden, Arjuna's face came to his mind. Karna smiled despite himself.

"Have you forgotten the vow of your ancestors, Guru? Have you forgotten that for twenty-four generations, your clan has killed Kshatriyas? Parashurama brought the wisdom of Brahminical rule to the country and now you are supporting a low-caste who lied to you, cheated, and insulted the Southern Kings. The entire Asura country has bowed to your wisdom, treating you like a

God. Guru, this is unjust. You are giving the best to this Suta."

"King Uthayan, a man who has failed in battle has no right to speak. Had you won against Karna, I would have considered you more worthy. But you lost and surrendered Bharatavarsha to Karna. I have forgiven his sin against me. As a man of honour, he has promised to uphold *dharma*."

"I will not deny a Brahmin whatever he asks," Karna repeated quietly.

Parashurama asked one of the priests to take Karna to the secret place where the *astra* was kept. Karna bowed deeply to the Guru. He saw the hatred in Uthayan's eyes. How bitter-sweet was this victory! Despite their enmity, he admired and respected Uthayan's qualities as a proud King and fearless warrior. Silently, Karna turned and followed the priest.

***

When the door had closed, Uthayan said to the Guru. "I have failed. Allow me to end my worthless life, Guru."

Parashurama remained silent for a long time, staring far away through the window. Uthayan bowed and was about to leave, when the Guru called him softly.

"Son, only the battle is lost, not the war. *Astras* do not win wars, strategy does. We are fighting for a bigger cause. Have you not understood what I have done? No, I was not being a hypocrite. Karna is like a son to me, dearer than anyone else in the world. Nevertheless, my gift to him has nothing to do with that love. It is an act of war. Think and you will understand."

"Guru..." Uthayan protested; then a wide smile appeared on his dark, war-scarred face. "Guru, my respects! It is brilliant. "

Parashurama's laugh brought on another bout of coughing. When it subsided, Parashurama looked out of the window and smiled. The auspicious sound of conch shell reverberated in the air. He could almost smell the incense and his heart leapt with joy when he heard the pealing of the temple bells. Outside, under a shining sun, his dear disciple was paying his obeisance to the priests by prostrating himself on the ground. The priests stood a few feet away from the Suta, who was still not allowed inside the temple, yet it was a start. Times were changing and one could not always expect the same people to rule always. If an idea was to survive, it had to adapt with the times – bend but not break, show it was changing, yet never really change. Sometimes even Kripa's philosophy made sense. The accident of birth could not stand in the way of anyone becoming King or kingmaker. Even a Suta could be King, especially when he had defeated an entire army. The only thing was to ensure that, irrespective of the lineage of the ruler, he paid obeisance to tradition and caste. Then he could be elevated as a Kshatriya. Was that not *dharma*?

'Poor fool,' Parashurama thought, looking at Uthayan's dark face. 'Once, your ancestors fought us, and see what happened. A few Asuras like Ravana and Mahabali had to be killed or banished, and now you are ready to die for us. What is a mere Suta compared to giants like them? But we must ensure that the audacious son of the blind King stays away from the emancipated lands of the South. The promise extracted from the ambitious Suta will come in handy one day, when the life and death of a civilisation will hang in the balance. Karna conquered the Confederate physically, but who won the spiritual victory? Look at who is lying prostrate at whose feet? Who is the victor and who the vanquished? Karna, my son, you are just beginning to know what is *dharma* and *adharma*. Dharmaveera Karna, when the time comes, have the courage and conviction to renounce your evil friend Duryodhana and join Dharmaputra Yudhishtra in his great cause. After all, Pandavas are your brothers in faith.'

Rebels like Karna could be managed and manipulated, but for his victory to be complete, rebels like the Nishadas and Nagas, who were fighting against the *varna* system, had to be eliminated. For that, Parashurama required divine intervention. As King Uthayan sat massaging his tired feet, Parashurama closed his eyes in meditation and prayed for the victory of *dharma* over evil forces like the Nishadas, who, as the news which had reached him said, had dared attack the holy city of Dwaraka.

***

And far away, in the northern seas near Dwaraka, the Gods were doing everything in their power to sink a rickety fishing boat. Precariously perched in the swaying boat was the Nishada who had dared to attack Dwaraka. A huge wave crashed over Ekalavya and he gasped for breath. He did not know how many hours he had been floating along, battered by wave upon wave. The sea was a dark beast that roared and hissed around him. He grimaced as pain shot through him. Every time the sea licked his wounds with its salty tongue, his entire body throbbed in pain. 'I should have been dead long ago', he thought as another wave rocked his puny boat, almost toppling it. Fortunately, the frail craft steadied and he wiped the salt water from his red-rimmed eyes. The skies cracked open with lightning and the sea roared back.

They had almost won the war, notwithstanding the valour of the Yadava leader. All the tales of Balarama being frail and a pushover were gross untruths; the wounds on his body were proof enough of that. With Krishna away, he had thought it would be an easy matter to take Dwaraka. Shalva and Dhantavakra had paid the price with their heads. 'But I could have still pulled it off,' Ekalavya thought wistfully. Balarama had taken the ruse of his truce offer at face value. Ekalavya had planned to slay Balarama and kept his dagger ready. Then he would have taken over Dwaraka; the Naga revolution would have become reality, overthrowing both Hastinapura and the Confederate eventually. But Krishna had arrived and foiled the plan. Who would have thought he would sneak up from behind and cut down Shalva and Dhantavakra like a thief in the night? And why had Takshaka failed to finish Krishna in the ambush they had planned?

'Oh Shiva!' Ekalavya gasped in horror as a wave, more than twenty feet high, raised the boat like a straw. It rode the crest for a few moments and then plunged into the trough. Another wave pressed it down as the rain fell in sheets. It was cold, bitterly cold. Ekalavya found himself struggling under tons of water. Which way to swim; which was up and which down? He felt his lungs would burst. 'Do not drink the water, hold on, hold on,' he told himself as the sea pulled him down into its watery embrace. He struggled up, coughing and choking, salt water burning his nostrils as another wave pinned him down. When he came up again, he took a deep breath before the next wave hit. Where had the boat gone?

Ekalavya had not given up when life cheated him at birth or when his Guru tried to end his dreams. He would not give up now. The Nishada battled on. 'I cannot die now, I refuse to die now! It needs greater forces than this to stop me,' Ekalavya screamed. The sea roared in laughter, foaming and frothing, pounding and dragging, but the Nishada held on to life. For another hour, the son of forest and the sea played a deadly game, testing the Nishada's will to survive. Finally, the sea gave up with a hiss, the sky stopped pelting rain, leaving a few streaks of lightning to die flashy deaths behind the breaking clouds.

Ekalavya floated on his back for a while. Where had his boat gone? He knew he could not float like this forever, but he did not have the courage to look around. A lone star appeared in the sky, vanished behind a dark cloud, and then returned. 'You and I are alone in this black world,' Ekalavya thought as the star twinkled above him. Determination seeped back into his battered body and he turned, scanning the horizon for his boat. There was no sign of it anywhere. When he had almost given up, brilliant lightning lit up the sky and he saw something far away. Was it the boat? If it turned out to be something else, the sea would win. He began to swim towards the smudge on the horizon, ignoring the pain in his limbs.

It was his boat. It took him the better part of an hour to reach it and climb in. He collapsed into it, unmindful of the water bobbing inside. He did not know how he had survived thus far, nor did he know whether he would survive hereafter. It had been perilous to jump from the ramparts of the fort. Why had Balarama not shot him down when he had the chance, Ekalavya wondered. For a fraction of a second, his gaze had locked with that of Balarama. Ekalavya had stood poised to jump. Balarama had raised his bow, aiming at him. Then the Yadava leader had looked away and his bow had dropped to the floor of his chariot. At the time Ekalavya had felt only relief as he jumped into the raging sea, preferring to take his chance with the elements rather than with men. Later, he realised bitterly that he owed his life to the very man he had planned to assassinate. Having jumped into the crashing sea, Ekalavya had hidden in a half-submerged cave as the Yadava soldiers searched for him. Late that night he had pushed a small fishing boat into the water and paddled away without direction.

Now, after his tortuous battle with the sea, as he lay limp in the rickety boat, the Nishada thanked the Gods for saving his life. But gradually, like the first mists of winter creeping over the rushes, bitterness shrouded his mind. His indebtedness to Balarama sat like a stone in his heart. Ekalavya stood up, rocking the boat. He had to find a way to reach land and resume battle. Where had the paddle gone? He searched desperately, knowing that the sea had snatched it away. The boat drifted on. Helpless, he felt powerless to control his life and destiny. He tried to stay awake, recalling the anger he felt towards Krishna, the Pandavas, and all those self-righteous men who treated his people like dirt; but nothing could stop the cold feel of death creeping up from the dirty water at his feet. The boat drifted where it pleased. By the next day, sleep had overcome the Nishada.

When he woke, his mouth was gagged and he was bound in chains.

*****

15 SON OF A RAKSHASI

"I DO NOT UNDERSTAND, DHARMAPUTRA. Why do you refuse to fight?"

Yudhishtra heard the impatience in Dhaumya's voice. He could almost feel Draupadi's mocking smile behind him. Why did she always judge him so harshly? Why did this Brahmin not leave him alone?

"I am a fool. I have gambled away everything. Perhaps I deserved it. Let Duryodhana rule. He deserves the crown. What are we after all?"

"Arjuna, speak to your brother." Dhaumya's face turned red with anger. A chattering squirrel ran among the trees, as if mocking them.

"I have nothing to say," Arjuna said and continued to polish his bow.

"It is such a long period of exile and you can argue there are special circumstances. Yudhishtra, your mother is suffering. She now lives in a Shudra's house."

"That is her fate. This is mine," Yudhishtra said quietly. He knew what would come next.

Draupadi gave a mocking laugh. "Fate! Fate indeed!"

"Draupadi, is it necessary for you to torture me like this every moment? Yes, I made a mistake..."

"I was stripped in public by that evil Duryodhana."

"Draupadi, enough!"

"Enough? You did not even raise a little finger, my brave and truthful husband."

"It was not *dharma*. I had already lost, you were Duryodhana's slave. I had no voice."

"It is better we stop talking of this, brother," Arjuna interjected before Draupadi could retort.

"So, you will not fight? Is that your final decision?" Dhaumya asked with barely concealed anger.

Yudhishtra looked around. His brothers were looking at him curiously. He could order them to fight but he was not sure how much support he would get. There was no denying he wished to rule, but something kept nagging at him. The look of that beggar when he had picked up a handful of dust troubled him. Was a handful of earth worth fighting a war over? Was the throne worth it? Until that fateful game of dice, his political moves had been dictated by his Guru and his mother; it had been a game. But power was a great addiction. Now, having spent barely a few months on the road, he was seeing life in a completely different light. Nothing made sense. All that grand talk about *dharma*, all the speculation about soul, *karma*, hell, heaven, and rebirth – it all sounded hollow.

Even glorious Indraprastha, which he had surrendered to Duryodhana in the game of dice, had lost its appeal. He had met a few Naga women who had toiled to build the palace and then been banished from the city. Yet they had come to his aid when he and his brothers entered the forest, bringing fruit for the Pandavas to eat, always standing at a respectful distance. He had given them no space in his city, yet they shared what they had with him. It was all very confusing.

'War! Whom should I fight against?' he wondered. It had always been Arjuna who had the doubts, who questioned everything. He had always been so sure of his own divine right to rule, what *dharma* was. Now the roles had been reversed. His brothers thirsted for revenge against Duryodhana. They felt their honour could only be restored by killing Duryodhana and his friends, who had insulted their wife and made them beggars. As Guru Dhaumya said, he should lead the fighting, yet...

"I will not go back on my word, We will suffer the exile. After the stipulated period, if we still feel the same way, we will fight. Until then, let the son of the King rule," Yudhishtra said, gazing into the distance.

He heard a crash behind him and turned back. Bhima was hitting a tree with his huge mace, his face grim, his muscles taut. Arjuna sat beside Draupadi, consoling her. It distressed him to see their strong-minded wife weeping. It was more painful than her spirited rebellion and mocking words. The twins had wandered away and Dhaumya followed them. Yudhishtra knew the Guru would try to persuade him again later. The Guru would say all the right things, such as taking revenge against Duryodhana for disrobing Draupadi. He would try to incite their anger. Why did he not feel any rage? As a man wronged, anger should have festered within him like a sore; every living moment he should have felt burning pain, yet all he felt was numbness. 'Is it because there is very little Kshatriya blood in me?' he wondered. Who had been his father? How much credence could be given to his mother's stories about his divine birth as a gift from the God of Death? Yama? Did such a God even exist? Yama was nothing but time, *kala*, dark time. 'Am I then the son of Time?' Yudhishtra wanted to laugh. Perhaps this exile was a catharsis, a journey of self-discovery in search of the real meaning of *dharma*. Not the *dharma* spoken of by Dhaumya or even the silver-tongued Krishna.

Yudhishtra's thoughts were interrupted by Bhima. His huge brother stood reverently before him. "Brother, I wish to see my son. I saw him and his mother from a distance today. The forest dwellers say Hidumbi and my little one live in this forest."

Yudhishtra stared at Bhima without comprehending what he was saying. Son? Which son? Then he remembered – the son of that untouchable Rakshasi, the Asura woman, Hidumbi. He did not know what to say.

"Yudhishtra, that son was a youthful mistake by your brother. I have been trying to make Bhima see reason, but nothing seems to change his mind. It is accepted that Kshatriyas seek honey in different flowers, like a bee, but the fruit belongs to the plant, not the bee." Dhaumya rushed to speak, afraid Yudhishtra would weaken and forget his *dharma*.

"Brother, I saw my son today. Just once, I want to hold his hand. He refuses to leave my mind." Bhima pleaded.

Yudhishtra looked at Dhaumya. A few days before, he would have categorically refused such a request. How could his brother associate with untouchables? Kshatriya boys were permitted such exploits, though he had never indulged in them. However, looking into Bhima's eyes, he could not bring himself to deny his brother. He looked at Dhaumya for a way out.

"Bhima, they are untouchables, Rakshasas," Dhaumya said, shaking his head vigorously.

"Hidumbi is my wife and Khatotkacha is my son," Bhima stated flatly, almost choking in his effort to speak.

Yudhishtra was surprised by Bhima's sudden display of emotion. He had rarely seen his brother with anything but a scowl on his face and had often wondered whether he felt any emotion other than anger. Life in the forest was changing them all. He was about to give his permission when Yudhishtra caught Dhaumya's eye. He had angered his Guru enough for one day.

"Bhima, my brother, it is not good to have attachment towards anything in life. Attachment leads to grief. Bhima, stop!" Yudhishtra watched Bhima walking away without waiting to hear more. Bhima picked up his mace again and began raining violent blows on a tree. He saw Draupadi move towards Bhima and felt a pang of jealousy. He was aware of Dhaumya's eyes watching him and he hoped his emotions were not reflected in his face. He could hear Draupadi's voice clearly, telling Bhima more loudly than necessary, to imagine that the tree was Duryodhana. The tree shook in rhythm to the thudding of Bhima's mace, shedding leaves and splintering inch by inch in groaning protest. The violence in the air was frightening and Yudhishtra shuddered when he heard his Guru laughing.

Dhaumya turned to Yudhishtra and said, "Prince, do not let the anger die. That evil son of the King has to be killed one day. He and his friends are destroying our *dharma*."

"Let my brother Bhima take care of Duryodhana," Arjuna said as he whisked his bow from his shoulder and in one fluid movement, shot an arrow at a distant tree. Another arrow followed, piercing the first with unnerving accuracy. A third followed and split the second. Then Arjuna turned to his brother. "It is not Duryodhana's head I yearn for. When all is said and done, he is of our blood, our cousin. What I cannot stand is the arrogance of that low caste Suta. One day, my arrow will pierce Karna's heart."

Guru Dhaumya retired to his hut with a smile. He was leaving the next morning but had promised to return with Krishna. Yudhishtra was sure that even Krishna could not persuade him to break his resolve to not fight till their term of exile was finished. The sun was sinking behind the trees and the forest was alive with the chatter of monkeys and birds.

As Yudhishtra stood watching him aiming arrow after arrow in anger, an uncomfortable thought entered his mind. Perhaps it was the angle of the setting sun or perhaps it was just a delusion induced by hunger.

Arjuna looked at Yudhishtra and smiled. "Why are you staring like that, brother?" Arjuna shot another arrow. There was that thought again! Arjuna turned and chuckled. "Brother, your expression resembles our evil cousin, Duryodhana."

Yudhishtra looked at Arjuna in silence and then sauntered back to his hut. It was time for his evening ablutions. He had been shocked by Arjuna's words. Expressions mirrored the thoughts of the mind. He had often laughed at the confused face Duryodhana sometimes had. Then he had been sure about right and wrong and had mocked his cousin for not knowing what *dharma* was. Now he was not sure who was right and who was wrong. He should have felt the same anger Arjuna or Bhima felt for the wrongs done to them. That he did not, surprised and confused him. He needed to ponder over it.

As Yudhishtra washed his feet before entering his hut, he looked back at Arjuna once more. In a flash, the same thought that had flashed through his mind earlier, returned with blinding force. His brother resembled that low-caste impostor, Karna! How could a Prince of the Kuru dynasty resemble a Suta? In the final reckoning, was there no difference between him and Duryodhana, or Arjuna and Karna? Night had descended from the heavens and the forest was silent except for the sound of crickets. Yudhishtra placed a reed mat on the mud veranda and sat down to meditate. But his mind refused to be tamed. Right, wrong, *dharma*, *adharma*, duty, devotion, evil, good, princes, beggars, Nagas, Krishna, everything jumbled together in a confused melee.

A few feet away, Draupadi was urging Bhima to hit the tree harder. He should have allowed Bhima to see the Rakshasi woman and her son. Perhaps the next time he asked, he would let his brother go to see Khatotkacha. But Yudhishtra knew Bhima would never ask again. With a crash, the huge tree fell, frightening the night birds. Yudhishtra looked up from his disturbed meditations. Draupadi's laughter filled the silence of the night and Yudhishtra felt a shiver of fear. 'Duryodhana, may this exile never end. Then, perhaps, we may both escape facing the inevitable,' Yudhishtra murmured softly. When he looked up, Guru Dhaumya was standing beside him, a deep frown on his face, his arms crossed over his chest. With head bent like a child caught stealing, Yudhishtra went into his hut without a word and closed the door.

But late into the night, Yudhishtra kept wondering about the strange resemblance between the Suta and his brother, Arjuna. When he remembered Karna, his jeering laugh in the Sabha echoed in his mind. The Suta was enjoying the royal life of Hastinapura with his friends while he, the son of *dharma*, the man who had followed every religious vow, performed every ritual without fail, respected Brahmins and cows, done all that was proper, and never uttered a lie, languished in the forest wearing a single cloth. Life had been unfair to him by showering blessings on the undeserving, like Karna. But he would not be bitter; he would accept his destiny. He would grow beyond hatred and find meaning in such ironies, the eldest Pandava vowed to himself. But, like an aftertaste of unpalatable medicine, Karna's laughter when Draupadi had stood shamed, refused to leave him. How lucky men like Karna were! He struggled to concentrate his mind on meditation, but the Suta's laughter continued to ring in his ears.

***

Which of those men was his father? From a distance Khatotkacha thought he recognised him. His mother had pointed out a giant of a man who stood at least a foot taller than the other Pandavas. As a child, he had fantasised about this moment, when his famous father would visit him in their tribal village, shower him with presents and embrace him. The adults treated him with respect, saying he was lucky to be the son of the famed Pandava, Bhima. But among the boys of his own age, he was the subject of ridicule. His small frame did not help and when one of the older boys had called him a bastard, he had fought him and lost. He had rushed to his mother with a bleeding nose and a black eye. Holding back his tears he had asked her what 'bastard' meant. His mother had cried for a long time that day but she had not told him what the word meant.

Later, when the last lamp in the village had gone out, and they were lying together in the courtyard, his mother had told him the story of his father and his uncle Hidumba, whom his father had slain. She told him of Bhima's exploits and heroism, how he always defeated his evil cousin, Duryodhana. Little Khatotkacha's heart filled with pride. If bastard meant being the son of such a great man, he could handle the taunts of his friends. He asked innocently when his father would come to see them and waited a long time for a reply, staring at the distant stars that blinked at him from afar. There was no answer that night, nor any night that followed. But in his dreams, his father took him upon his lap and played with him. That was enough.

"Shhh, Khatotkacha, you promised you would not make a sound," Hidumbi said, tightening her grip on his little wrist.

"But he is my father. You said he would come to see me with lots of presents..." The boy pressed his lips together, excited and tense. His mother had warned him not to make a sound. They were perched on a little hillock and had been waiting since dawn. At last, he could see five men and a woman walking along the forest path. He tried to wriggle free from his mother's grip but she held him firmly. When the strangers were about to vanish from view, he managed to escape and run towards them.

Hidumbi choked on a sob and called out, "Khatotkacha, wait!"

The boy crashed through the thick undergrowth, startling the tall man in the lead. Khatotkacha suddenly wished he was back with his mother, but his legs refused to move. His heart thudded against his ribs and his throat felt dry. One of the men had taken out his sword.

"Bhima, this urchin looks familiar," the first man said to the giant behind him.

Khatotkacha's shoulders relaxed. He was sure his father would come forward and lift him up. At that moment, his mother's work-worn hands pressed against his shoulders. She was staring at his father. Why did he not even smile at her?

"Father..." Khatotkacha muttered. Bhima took a hesitant step forward.

"Rakshasas! Do not pollute yourself, Bhima," Yudhishtra urged.

Bhima froze. Hidumbi's grip tightened on Khatotkacha's shoulder. He saw the pain in his father's eyes as the woman with them said with a jeer, "Don't touch them? How did Bhima father this boy? Another divine birth?"

Yudhishtra turned to Draupadi. "Do not concern yourself with them. The marriage was due to my mother's misguided pity. Bhima killed Hidumba, this woman's brother, so our mother made Bhima marry this Rakshasi. Today we are paying for that sin."

Bhima stood with his gaze fixed on his giant toes.

Pointing at Khatotkacha, Draupadi asked, "Sin? This small boy is a sin to you?" Draupadi's mirthless laugh echoed the bitterness in Hidumbi's heart.

"Draupadi, when woman mocks, misfortune follows," Yudhishtra said sternly.

Draupadi laughed again, startling the birds in the trees. "Of course, of course, it was my laughter that ruined us, Yudhishtra, not your gambling. We all know that."

Khatotkacha saw the trace of a smile on the lips of the man standing near Bhima, but then Yudhishtra said to him, "Arjuna, let us not waste time in frivolous chatter. Ask this Rakshasi and her son to move out of our path so that we can proceed."

Without a word Hidumbi moved to one side, dragging Khatotkacha with her. A teardrop fell on his head and he looked up. His mother was wiping her eyes. Was she crying because he had not behaved well? Should he have touched his father's feet and asked for his blessing?

"Father!" Khatotkacha called out.

Bhima stopped. His companions turned to look. Khatotkacha gulped in embarrassment. His father was staring at him. He tried to keep his chin from trembling. "Father, I heard that Prince Duryodhana cheated you of your palace. When you fight that evil man, call me, I will come to help you."

"Now that was the only insult left – street urchins and untouchables offering to help the Pandavas," Arjuna said. The others laughed at the irony. Even Bhima laughed.

That hurt Khatotkacha the most. His mother dragged him away. He was so small, with such puny little hands and dark skin. Which father would not be ashamed of such a son? Perhaps a bastard was someone whose father was ashamed to admit you were his son. Khatotkacha silently vowed to become a great warrior one day. He would never let down his tall, handsome father. He wanted to scream his determination to Bhima's retreating form. He burrowed his heels into the earth to make his mother stop and turned to look at his father one last time. The sun leaked through the jungle canopy and leaves rustled in the breeze. His father and uncles had vanished, but their laughter lingered in the air.

*****

16 Lesser Men

VIDHURA HAD BEEN STANDING without saying a word. He shifted his weight from one leg to the other, desperately wishing he could sit down. Today he was feeling his years. Bhishma had not spoken since evening. He kept staring through the window, his hands clasped behind him, deep in thought. Outside, the city of Hastinapura was decorated with oil lamps and colourful festoons. The mood inside the chamber of the Grand Regent was more suited to a funeral than a festival. Outside, drums beat in a frenzied rhythm. The clopping of horseshoes, the clanging of bells and the waxing and waning of thousands of cheering voices could be heard, sometimes clearly, sometimes from a distance. A reluctant breeze entered, making the lone torch in the chamber flicker, and played gently with the long flowing beard of the Grand Regent. The beard was now completely white. They were both ageing. Vidhura sighed at the thought.

How did the Suta achieve it, Vidhura?" Bhishma finally asked.

Vidhura wished he had not heard the hint of jealousy. He had no answer. He focused his eyes on the pool of darkness in the corner of the room. He could not look at the pain in Bhishma's eyes. Applause sounded outside and the beating of drums grew louder. The Suta's victory procession had entered the fort. Karna, the son of a charioteer, had achieved what generations of Kuru princes could not. He had defeated the powerful Southern Confederate and was returning with immeasurable wealth from the South. The cheers of 'Dhanaveera', 'Dharmaveera', and 'Digvijayi Karna', echoed around the fort, making the silence in the chamber unbearable to the two men.

"I never imagined the South could be conquered, and that too, by a mere Suta." Bhishma gripped the bars of the window. "I think there is more here than the eye can see. Do you think Parashurama would have bestowed his *bhargava astra* on this Suta without thinking? The Suta must have used deceit. I cannot believe he would otherwise have subdued the South so easily. The most I could gain was a worthless truce."

Vidhura did not reply. Bhishma began pacing up and down. Vidhura focussed on the Regent's shadow, which grew into a giant one moment and then turned into a dwarf the next, when he turned.

"There could be a trap, Vidhura. The fool Suyodhana thinks the South is an ally. They are the people who never forget a slight. And a mere Suta has conquered them. All the loot the Suta has brought with him is going to be of no use to us. The South will turn against us when it would matter most, I am sure of it."

Outside, the cheering rose to a crescendo and Bhishma paused to listen. "I must warn Suyodhana. It will be difficult for me to face that Suta. I never expected to see him again. But I must swallow my pride, must I not, Vidhura? Nobody will say the son of Ganga did not respect a great warrior. Yes, that boy is good, too good for his own well-being. Karna! What a son you fathered, Athiratha."

Vidhura sneaked a glance at the Grand Regent and saw a small smile lift his lips. He relaxed.

"How did he win when I could not?" Bhishma asked again. "To face everyone after what I said to that Suta will be difficult, Vidhura, but I must. I have never run from a battlefield and I will not run from embarrassment." Suddenly, Bhishma put his hand on his Prime Minister's shoulders and said, "If I falter in my courtesies to the Suta, Vidhura, stand beside me and remind me of my duty."

Vidhura turned away, unable to look at those greying eyes. His heart felt as heavy as a stone. At that moment Vidhura hated the Suta and his victory more than anything in life.

Bhishma went to his chair, sat down, and gestured to Vidhura to sit near him. Relieved, Vidhura eased himself onto the chair. Bhishma began going through the pile of palm leaves on the table but it was evident his mind was not on the task. The victory procession had moved into the palace and the faint sounds of cheering and clapping floated into the Grand Regent's chamber. Each time they heard footsteps outside, the men looked at each other and then at the door, expectantly. After what seemed like an unendurably long wait, they heard a knock.

Bhishma sat back in his chair, the expression on his rugged face was stern and cold. "It must be Suyodhana and his friends come to tell us of the victory."

Vidhura walked to the door. It opened to admit a servant, who bowed deeply and placed a silver tray with a glass of milk and a bowl of dried fruit and nuts on the table and then left without a word. The two most important men in the empire looked at each other silently.

Bhishma beckoned to Vidhura and they began poring over the various administrative matters of State. Time dragged by. The party ended in the palace but no invitation came for the Grand Regent. Finally, when the sky had grown grey in the east, Bhishma stood up wearily.

Vidhura did not look up. He knew what was coming. When the Royal Insignia of the Kuru empire was gently placed before him, the Prime Minister turned away, tears in his eyes. "No Swami, no. Do not do this..."

"Vidhura, my time has ended. Prince Suyodhana is being kind. Remember my words, Vidhura? I said I would hand over the reins of empire to him if the Suta came back alive. Well, he has not only come back alive, but victorious. Hastinapura no longer needs the services of this old man. The Prince has subtly reminded me of my own insignificance."

"No, Swami, no." Vidhura stood up angrily. "I will talk sense into that young fool. He cannot treat you like this. I will not allow anyone to treat you like this."

"Vidhura, no man is indispensable – neither you, nor me. If someone thinks otherwise, he is a fool. The world existed before us, and will do so after we are gone. My time has ended, that is all. I am no longer young. I have borne the burden of ruling this country for a very long time. For the last three generations, I have nurtured this kingdom, without in-fighting, palace feuds or coups. Before me, the corridors of power were paved with the flesh of kin fighting kin for the throne. The flowers in the garden drank more blood than water. For three generations, I have preserved this land. Now the Princes have grown up. My duty is done. The time has come for this old man to rest."

"Sir, the throne for which all these fools are fighting, belongs to you. It is only because of your renunciation..."

"I did it voluntarily, Vidhura. This also I do voluntarily. I must keep my word. Let Suyodhana rule. Let him learn how easy or difficult it is to rule a country, a people. Let me sit back and watch. It is already a new day. The past was buried yesterday. The sun is now shining on a new generation. The Sun God has showered his blessings on the Suta. So be it. Who am I to question destiny?"

"Swami, they are young and heedless, they may have forgotten... "

"Vidhura, the past is meant to be forgotten. We are the past. I am not bitter, why are you? Hand over the Insignia to the Crown Prince and announce my retirement. Do not wake him now. They will be tired after their celebrations. You, too, go home and get some sleep. I can now sleep with a clear conscience and a free heart. Ah! The sweetness of freedom is exhilarating. I should have done this long ago."

With a sinking heart, Vidhura took the Insignia from the Grand Regent's outstretched hand and walked to the door.

"Vidhura." The call was soft and tender and Vidhura felt he would collapse right there and die. "Son, do not do anything rash. You have a family to feed. Your children are still young. Do not resign your post. The younger generation needs your wise counsel."

"Suyodhana can search for a new Prime Minister from today. If poverty awaits me, so be it, but I will not bow my head to any man other than you."

For the first time in his life Vidhura defied the Grand Regent and walked out. He did not know how he was going to feed his family and bring up his children, but he was determined never to enter the palace again.

It was a glorious day outside.

*****

17 DARK PRINCE

A LONG TRAIN OF SERVANTS CARRIED in the ransom and loot from the Southern Confederate and piled it in the Sabha. Karna walked to the centre of the great hall and pulled out a fistful of precious stones. He turned towards the group of Brahmins standing huddled in the corner with sullen faces. "Revered ones, these are the humble offerings of a Suta," he said, placing the stones on the floor and walking back a few steps so as not to pollute them. He stood humbly, his head bowed.

The Brahmin priests looked at each other. One of them quickly moved forward to pick up the stones. Seeing that the Suta's respect appeared to be genuine, they broke into animated conversation. Finally, one of them cried out, "*Dhanaveera* Karna! *Dharmaveera* Karna!"

An uneasy silence followed. Karna stood upright and tense. Then the group of priests shouted the accolades in chorus, their voices reverberating through the palace. Karna's handsome face lit up like the rising sun. At last, he was getting his due. The people who mattered were accepting him as a hero.

"What is all this, Karna?" Suyodhana whispered in his friend's ear, but Karna ignored him. He was terrified that his friend would say something rash.

Bhanumati appeared with her twins, saving the situation. Lakshmana Kumara ran towards Karna, followed by his sister. They jumped into Karna's arms as Bhanumati looked on with a smile. But when her eyes met Karna's, she pressed her lips together and tears filled her eyes. Suyodhana stood apart. Karna sensed that something was wrong between his friend and his wife. What had happened?

"Where is Aswathama?" Karna asked.

Suyodhana stared out of the window. Karna's eyes searched for the impish Brahmin in the crowd. Had he not returned from Gandhara?

"He has not come back," Bhanumati whispered.

"Not come back! And you are sitting here doing nothing?" Karna turned to Suyodhana but his friend refused to look at him.

"Lord Bhishma has a vice-like grip over everything. He and Uncle Vidhura would not hear of a rescue mission to Gandhara. Why blame Suyodhana?" Sushasana said, moving closer to his brother.

"Suyodhana, we must save him," Karna said, his eyes glittering dangerously.

A soldier entered and announced the King of Sindh.

"Jayadratha! We had no prior intimation of your coming!" Suyodhana walked towards the proud King, hands outstretched.

Jayadratha looked at the bounty piled in the hall, the group of Brahmins standing with their presents clutched to their chests, and laughed mirthlessly. A flush crept into Karna's cheeks.

"Congratulations, my friend. You have become *Dhanaveera Digvijayi* Karna," Jayadratha said, the sarcasm barely concealed.

"With the help of your men, Your Highness. It is all thanks to the bravery of the soldiers you lent me," Karna said with cold civility, bowing low. The soldiers of Sindh had been the first to turn tail when they faced the assault of the Confederate troops.

"I have a gift for you, Suyodhana. I have captured the leader of the Nagas – Takshaka himself," Jayadratha announced.

An awed hush fell in the Sabha.

"Bring him in!" Jayadratha commanded, his cold eyes never leaving the proud Suta's face. He was not the only man who could perform wondrous feats .

As the Sabha waited anxiously, a group of soldiers pushed and shoved a tall, dark man in chains into the hall. His muscles rippled as he tried to free himself.

"Behold Takshaka!" Jayadratha turned to Suyodhana, awaiting his words of appreciation.

The Sabha reverberated with applause. When the din died down, Suyodhana moved towards the captive man. His gaze rested on the man's right hand. It had four fingers. The captive looked him straight in the eyes, the hint of a smile on his lips.

"Ekalavya! Welcome to the Sabha of the Dark Prince, Duryodhana," said Suyodhana.

*****

18 NISHADA'S DAUGHTER

EKALAVYA EYED THE CROWN PRINCE HAUGHTILY. He knew it was a futile statement but he could not help rattling the chains that bound him. 'They are amused, these privileged, highborn rascals; amused to see me like this. They make me stand in their Sabha like a performing monkey in a market.' Rancour welled in his heart like bitter bile. 'Where is Drona's son? Why did the Suta laugh? They will no doubt purify the marble floors with cow dung after sending me to the gallows. They should have killed me instead of subjecting me to such humiliation.'

"Untie him."

Ekalavya could not believe his ears. A soldier struggled to free him of his chains. A little girl, standing near the throne, giggled. Ekalavya stared at her, anger burning in his eyes. 'Even the little ones of these high-castes make fun of us,' he thought. But the little girl smiled at him, dimples leaping into her cheeks. With the chains removed, the thought of fleeing flashed though Ekalavya's mind. No, he was exhausted. Months of imprisonment had sapped his strength. His body could not follow his mind as quickly as he wanted it to. He would have to bear the humiliation for some time.

"I have been trying to trace you for a long time, Ekalavya, in fact, from the day you gave Drona your *Gurudakshina*." Suyodhana said.

Ekalavya quickly covered his mutilated hand with his other one. "So you have not finished having fun with us, eh?" Ekalavya smiled at the gasps in the Sabha. It felt good talking back to the mighty Crown Prince. Perhaps he only had a few minutes to live but he was determined to go down with his head held high. "You think you have defeated us? Krishna thinks he has escaped. You may kill me, but one day my people will rise and sweep you into the Ganga. You can kill me now, but how many Ekalavyas will you kill, Duryodhana? The forests of this country are pregnant with revolution. There are thousands of Ekalavyas rising."

"Ekalavya, I wish to stop the revolution."

"The entire army of Hastinapura and all the great warriors here will not be able to stop it, Prince."

"I do not wish to stop it by force. I know I cannot do that. I wish to stop it by..."

"By acting nice and throwing us some tidbits? Ha, I would rather face your cousin Arjuna's arrows than your patronising acts."

"You feel proud to be rude, Nishada? I am merely extending my hand in friendship."

"Are you so desperate to prove yourself a good man, Prince? You think I will fall for such petty tricks? You are preparing for a war against your cousins. You think one more warrior, even without a thumb, will be useful against Arjuna? Do you want to know what we think about your fight with your cousins? We think that it is a sham. Whoever wins, our plight will remain the same."

"I am the only person who has stood up for your people."

Ekalavya watched Suyodhana flush with anger. His ghost thumb itched savagely. "Where were you, Prince, when my aunt and cousins were burned like chickens in the trap you set for your cousins? What did you do when Arjuna murdered thousands of helpless women and children to build Indraprastha? Had your nobility gone into hiding then? Where were all the mighty warriors – the righteous Bhishma, the great Guru Dronacharya, the noble Suyodhana, the wise Vidhura, and *Dhanaveera Dharmaveera* Karna? Where were all of you when our people were dying in the forest fire or being shot by Arjuna's arrows? Not a man raised his voice to say it was *adharma*, not one woman of this noble land shed a tear!"

"I have tried to make amends. The Pandavas have been exiled."

"Ha, you tricked them, not because you felt sorry for our people but because a woman laughed at you. Do not make your battle with cousins to be some cosmic fight between *dharma* and *adharma*. Do you think the common people cannot see through it? These are cheap political ploys for power to crush the weak and oppress the common people. The Pandavas bow to the Brahmins because they think they will get their support in their war against you. You have already lost the support of the priestly class, so you have come to us, thinking we will shed our worthless blood for you. Do you think you can sit on the throne and claim you are our saviour? Think again, Prince; we live in different worlds."

"Another word from your uncouth mouth and you are dead, Nishada." Karna's sword was pressed against Ekalavya's throat, his eyes glittering. He looked at Suyodhana for permission to plunge in the sword and silence the Nishada, but Suyodhana was looking away, his eyes clouded with shame.

"Go ahead, Suta, show your loyalty," said Ekalavya, facing Karna calmly. The sword pressed into the Nishada's skin and a drop of blood appeared.

"Karna, drop your sword! He has the right to speak in this Sabha. If I do not listen to the voice of my own people, what kind of King will I be? Free him!" Suyodhana waited until Karna reluctantly returned his sword to its scabbard and then turned to Ekalavya. "I do not know what force prompts me to act the way I do. Perhaps I am a selfish man, who has done many things wrong to gain power. But power is my birthright. I am the firstborn of the King and no one can take that right from me. I was wrong to disrobe Draupadi, I admit it to my eternal shame. But I will not accept being called evil by my cousins and their sycophants. I do not have the blood of innocent people on my hands as they do. Your aunt and cousins, the thousands that were slain in Khandivaprastha, the blood of King Jarasandha and your father Hiranyadhanus, the list is endless, yet I am called the evil one, not my cousins Pandavas. Ironic, is it not?"

"Have you dragged me here to listen to your justifications, Prince? We have suffered enough because of the power struggle between you Kuru cousins. Our people are desperate and many among us think Takshaka is the answer to our problems. I know Takshaka, and I know what will happen if his revolution wins. We are caught between you."

"I will make amends, not only for my silence when my cousins razed Khandivaprastha, but also for the wrongs done to your people. I will make you King of all the forest lands in Hastinapura's domain."

The assembly broke into an uproar. Even Karna looked shocked. Ekalavya watched Karna's reaction before replying. Perhaps the Suta was thinking he was not as special as he had thought. Suyodhana had gone one step further than he had done with the Suta, and dared to offer kingship to a Nishada. 'But I am no Suta to wag my tail before the master,' Ekalavya thought to himself. He rubbed his chin with his mutilated right hand and smiled when he saw Suyodhana wince. The thumbless hand had that effect on most people.

"Are you trying to buy me off, Prince? Who are you to make me King of my own lands? Your writ does not run in the deep forests of this country. The only power you have over me is to kill me now. I have faced death and far greater humiliation than you can subject me to. You hold no power over me. You can bestow nothing on me."

"Suyodhana, will you allow this arrogant Nishada to insult you like this?" Karna's hand was once again on his sword. Jayadratha and Sushasana also moved closer to the Nishada, ready to pounce on him at the slightest nod from Suyodhana.

"Karna, we can silence one Nishada here. Can we silence the entire country? We have thirteen years until my cousins return and stake a claim to my throne. I know war will come, but I do not intend to allow them to take what is not theirs. Meanwhile,

I am determined to prove I am fit to rule this land. I will not be bound by mindless rules and traditions. I will listen to the voice of the people. He is that voice. I will not silence him. Yes, I want power. I am no God, nor claim to be the son of one. My parents are mortals, blind at that. Ekalavya's words have made me realise I was more concerned about the insult from Draupadi than the mass murder Arjuna committed in Khandiva; more concerned about clearing my name in the house of lac incident than about the lives of the Nishada woman and her children who perished in it. Does that make me evil? Perhaps it does. Does it make me more evil than the ones who actually committed those acts? That is for posterity to decide.

All my acts are selfish, including our friendship, Karna. Every act of love is selfish. I believe that when the time comes, you will stand by my side. So will Jayadratha, Aswathama and Sushasana. I believe that all my brothers will stand by me, not because I am righteous or the epitome of *dharma*, which I am not, but because you love me as a man and a friend. I offer the same friendship to you, Ekalavya. It is for you to accept or reject it. Whatever your decision, you will leave here a free man. I cannot promise what will happen tomorrow; perhaps as a ruler I may order your death or capture, but today you have a choice."

Ekalavya was thrown into confusion. Was this a trap? Was the offer of friendship nothing but a bait by the Prince, the usual one set by the elite to trap the poor? Ekalavya tried to hide his emotions but found it difficult to mask his happiness. Was this not what he had always yearned for, to be accepted like Karna by the same society that had made him toil to put together his shattered ambition? Yet, in a corner of his mind, something nagged at him; his primeval instincts told him it was a big mistake to align himself with the Crown Prince.

"I will accept your offer on my own terms – you will not interfere in our affairs; there will be no killing of Nagas, Nishadas, Kiratas or any forest dwellers; you will grant me freedom to rule as I deem fit; and in the areas I rule, no *varna* or *jati* system will be accepted."

"I agree, but on one condition. When required, you and your people will support me."

"You will have to earn it, Prince. You are acting in your selfish interests and I in mine."

"Suyodhana," Karna said in a horrified voice, "do not accept such terms from this man. He is our captive. You cannot go against all the accepted norms of our society. I have given my word to Guru Parashurama that we will make amends and try to win back the acceptance of the Brahmins. We have become villains to many people by disrobing Draupadi and sending the Pandavas into exile."

"What are you afraid of, Karna? Is not my friendship enough? Why do you yearn so much for universal acceptance? I find your tone since returning from the South quite disheartening. I do not fear society. We must make new norms. I did wrong by Draupadi, but let no one use that as a tool to brand me as evil. I have no regrets. I did it for you. I did it for my bruised ego. Yudhishtra was a fool who gambled everything, including his wife, and lost. I prefer being called evil to being known as a fool."

"Did I suggest you disrobe Draupadi?" Karna asked indignantly.

"Stop this and decide what to do with this Nishada," Sushasana said, moving to stand between Karna and Suyodhana.

"I accept your terms. I will crown you a vassal King for all the forest lands and their inhabitants. We will have the coronation here, today." Ignoring the murmurs that rose in the Sabha, Suyodhana turned to a guard. "Summon Acharya Kripa. Tell him Suyodhana is making a Nishada a King. Request him to conduct the ceremony as per the Vedic rites."

"Brother, we are forgetting that one of us has not come back from Gandhara. When are we going to do something about it?" Sushasana asked and the Sabha fell silent.

"Karna has returned and the Confederate has been crushed. Pitamaha will keep his word to me. So we will leave for Gandhara soon.More than Aswathama, I wish to meet my Uncle Shakuni. I have a few questions for him."

The arrival of the Prime Minister cut off Suyodhana. Vidhura stood under the massive arch of the door, his eyes red with fatigue and anger. Ekalavya could see the Prime Minister was seething inside. He walked in and eyed the Sabha with distaste. Suyodhana bowed low. Taking their cue from him, the entire Sabha bowed to the Prime Minister.

Vidhura deposited the cloth bag he was carrying on a table. "Your Highness, here are the official seals of the empire."

"What is the meaning of all this, Uncle?"

"Your Highness, these are the Royal Insignia of the Grand Regent of Hastinapura and the Prime Minister. May God be with you." Vidhura walked out of the stunned assembly, his head held high.

For a moment there was pindrop silence, then Suyodhana pushed Ekalavya away and called out to the fast vanishing form of the ex-Prime Minister. But Vidhura hurried away, neither answering, nor turning back.

"Where is Pitamaha?" Visibly agitated, Suyodhana rushed out.

The Sabha rapidly emptied, leaving Ekalavya standing alone, feeling ignored and unimportant. He wondered about the strange relationship Karna had with Suyodhana. Did Karna ever feel equal to the blue-blooded Prince? Did Suyodhana cultivate the Suta merely for his own selfish ends? It had shaken Ekalavya that the Prince had agreed to his allegations of selfishness. Suyodhana's frank acceptance of his self-interest made him somehow more likeable. But he would never be a slave to Suyodhana, like Karna. They were emotional fools.

Ekalavya was shaken from his reverie by a sharp punch to his stomach. "My father is a good man." A little girl was standing waist-high before him with clenched fists. She dared him to contradict her, ready to throw another punch. Ekalavya burst out laughing. The girl punched him with all her strength.

"Who are you, young lady? Why are you punching me? Ouch! That hurt; you are a strong woman," Ekalavya said, trying to hide his amusement by clutching the belly the little hands had pummelled.

"You will get more if you fight with my father. You will become chutney. Why do you call my father names, you black monster? *Bhuta*, that is what you are, a black *bhuta*."

"Who is your father, little one?"

"Suyodhana, Crown Prince of Hastinapura. I am Princess Lakshmana. And you are not supposed to address me in that way. Also, you must bow to me."

"My apologies, Princess Lakshmana." Ekalavya knelt on both knees and bowed low. "I do not bow to anyone, not even to the King or your father, but I will make an exception. I will bow to you."

"Hmm, I forgive you. Next time bow when we meet. Why did you call my father an evil man?"

"Princess, I did not call him that."

"Are you really a *bhuta*?"

"Yes. I am a *bhuta* of the dark forests."

"Do you belong to the *bhutaganas* of Lord Shiva?"

"Princess, I *am* Lord Shiva."

Lakshmana peered at him intently and Ekalavya bit his lips to control his laughter. A little boy who was playing with a toy cart nearby looked up at hearing the name of Shiva and walked towards them.

"No, you are lying. You are not wearing the snake necklace," pointed out Lakshmana.

"Oh, I left it in the forest. It has gone to visit other Nagas."

Lakshmana's gaze travelled down and stopped at Ekalavya's mutilated hand. The Nishada quickly tried to hide it, embarrassed by his imperfection. Suddenly he became aware of his position. He was a low-caste untouchable, chatting with the Princess of the empire, in the Sabha. In earlier times, they would have purified the place he had stepped on with cow dung. Now he stood free inside the most important building in all of Bharatavarsha.

"You do not have a thumb. Show me, show me."

"No."

"Please show me." Lakshmana grabbed Ekalavya's hand.

Reluctantly the Nishada opened his palm. He felt annoyed; the Princess was making fun of him. He wanted to run from this sickening place.

"It must have hurt you so much!"

More than you could ever imagine, Princess. More than any one of you will every feel. Ekalavya tried to pull his hand away, but the little girl held it tight between her own. He looked around, embarrassed. He was an untouchable and the Princess was holding his hand. That hand... If anyone came in and said something to him now, he would kill him, the Nishada vowed. For a moment he thought of shoving the little girl away and running off. The ghost thumb itched.

Shocking him, Lakshmana kissed his hand. Despite himself, tears welled in the Nishada's eyes. "That should make you fine. That is what my mother does when I get hurt."

"I will never let you get hurt, my Princess," Ekalavya said hoarsely. He looked away, not wanting her to see his tears. He smiled bitterly. All those years of hard struggle and fighting, and now a little girl had broken all his defences with her dimpled smile.

"How did it happen?" Lakshmana asked innocently.

"It is a long story and you will fall asleep."

"Oh, but I love stories. Please tell me the story."

"It is a sad story and you do not want to hear it."

"Oh yes, I do," she insisted, trying to shove aside the little boy who had sidled up to her, his eyes wide in anticipation of a story.

"Oh do not mind him, he is my brother, Lakshmana Kumara. Please tell me the story." Lakshmana sat down and her brother followed her example. The children looked at the Nishada eagerly. Reluctantly, Ekalavya sat down. The children smiled at each other, clapping their hands in glee.

While Suyodhana faced Bhishma in another wing of the palace, the Nishada sat with the Prince and Princess in the centre of the Sabha and started his story. "Once there was a Nishada boy who wanted to be an archer, but he was so poor that he starved on most days. One day, when he thought he would die of hunger, he entered the palace grounds to steal some mangoes. There he met a Prince, an evil Prince..."

*****

19 The Merchant

SUYODHANA DID HIS UTMOST to persuade Bhishma and Vidhura to change their stand, but they remained adamant about resigning from their respective positions. Bhishma then advised Suyodhana to forget about Aswathama in Gandhara and get on with ruling the country. This resulted in yet another argument between the Patriarch and the hot-blooded Crown Prince.

Finally, when Bhishma realised that Suyodhana would not heed his advice, he sighed wearily and said, "If you see Shakuni, do not stop to ask questions; cut off his head and bring it to me. This is the only thing I ask for the long years I have served this country."

Suyodhana was surprised by Bhishma's anger. But he understood the pain of betrayal; Shakuni had done it to himself. There was no time to waste, he had to see his father and get his permission to mount an attack on Gandhara. Suyodhana bowed to the Patriach and hurried towards his father's chamber. When he thought about Bhishma's words, he began to feel doubt gnawing at him. Would he have the courage to cut off the head of the man he had once trusted and loved? Perhaps, if Aswathama was dead, he would be able to do it. But if Aswathama was still alive? Suyodhana had no answer.

***

"No one would dare touch my son. He is the Crown Prince, Gandhari. I will not allow him to suffer my fate. No one with a sweet tongue and poisoned heart will steal his birthright, like they did mine. Have you heard, the Suta conquered all of Bharatavarsha? My son did well by choosing him for a friend, without bothering about his caste and lineage. Karna has returned victorious, and I am now Emperor of a land stretching from the snow-capped Himalayas to the sea-kissed Kumari."

"I wish Suyodhana had not befriended that Suta. It has made him unacceptable to many powerful men. And now he has made a Nishada King of the forest lands."

"Bah, Gandhari! Who cares for the opinion of a few priests who know nothing about warfare? Such matters concern only Kshatriyas. I admire the Suta's pluck in challenging Arjuna. I can sympathise with him, for I see myself in him. I have told you before but I shall tell you again now, they would keep me away from arms; hiding the swords, maces, bows and arrows from me when I was a little boy. I would sit in a corner of the practice grounds, beside the idol of Kali Ma, nibbling on the sweets the servants gave me to keep me amused so that I would not disturb the practice of my brother Pandu. I was blind and could get hurt, they told me. So I was kept away, while my brother was trained by none other than Bhishma Pitamaha."

Dhritarashtra stood up and walked to the iron replica of Bhima. Caressing it, he allowed his fingers to linger on the dents his mace had made in the iron body. "Whenever Pitamaha left us alone, Pandu would challenge me, making fun of my clumsiness. He was not cruel, he was just being a boy, but at the time, it hurt. It still does. I had my pride and was not one to back away from a challenge. The same blood of the great emperor Bharata flowed in my veins, as it did in Pandu's. For the first few years, he would lick me in every fight and scream with joy, sitting on my chest. The servants would watch with amusement, commenting on my handsome brother and expressing sympathy for my blindness. More than anything else, the sympathy hurt. Unknown to anyone, I began practising by myself. When the mace fell on my foot, when swords and daggers cut my fingers, or the strings of bows snapped and lashed my face, I refused to cry. I was a Kshatriya! I am not a learned man but I was determined to beat my brother, my handicap notwithstanding. After all, I was to be the next King and kings were the best warriors of all."

Gandhari did not speak. She had heard it all many times before. The tale never failed to move her to tears. If not for such stories, she would have gone back to Gandhara long ago.

"I got better and better. Five years later, built like an ox, I could shoot better than him, fight better with a mace, and defeat him in hand-to-hand combat. What I lacked in eyesight, I made up with iron will and my other senses. On the day of our graduation, I demonstrated my skill in front of all the citizens of Hastinapura. An elephant had run amok that day, trampling men and horses. I was in the middle of the arena, a blind man with a mace. Even now I can hear the terrified screams of the spectators. To his credit, Pandu ran to stand between the charging elephant and me. I heard the crowd groan as his arrows missed the elephant's head. The beast was so close that I could smell it. I jumped onto my brother's shoulders and crashed my mace on the beast's head. The elephant collapsed. I waited for the crowd to cheer. They did, but it was for Pandu. In the split second between my blow and the elephant falling, he had pierced his sword into the elephant's mouth. Pitamaha declared that Pandu's sword had killed the beast, and that he had saved his blind, helpless brother. The Magadhas and Sutas sang of Pandu's bravery, when anyone with some knowledge of elephants knew a beast that size could not die with a sword thrust, certainly not immediately. It was my mace that killed it."

Dhritarashtra took a deep breath. He did not speak for some time. Then, with a sudden show of anger, he slammed his fist on the wall. "I saved my brother but there were no songs about my courage. He was the hero. And that was just the beginning. I was cursed with blindness, so I did not deserve the throne, even though I was the firstborn, they said. How could a blind man lead the country in a war, they asked. My brother edged past me, making me a figure of pity. I was cheated at birth, but it did not stop me from eventually becoming King. Fate and destiny interfered in mysterious ways."

A wicked smile played on Dhritarashtra lips, "God has a way of looking after people like me, Gandhari, men who are shunned by all for no fault of theirs. Men like Karna cannot die unless they are broken from within. We do not need the crutch of scriptures to prop us up. I am proud of Suyodhana for standing by Karna. I know that many, including Pitamaha, wish Karna dead. Why did you turn your head when I said that? Do not deny you turned your head, for I can sense your movements, my dear. You are surprised, Gandhari? I know many things, I who act like a fool and act as if I were helpless without Pitamaha and the other nobles. They all imagine I am as helpless as a calf gone astray, and would never survive alone in this cruel world, nor win. But I have my own spies and I keep a close watch on things happening around me. Don't laugh, there are ways to watch without eyes."

Dhritarashtra leaned towards his wife, his face inches from hers. "Do you know why I act like a weakling? The moment I show I can stand on my own without their support, they will conspire against me. I play a part so they can imagine it is they who are running the kingdom. I know Bhishma, and I know he rues the day he relinquished the kingdom. I humour him by saying foolish things and posing as if I cannot take decisions, so that he feels powerful and important. In this way I keep the courtiers at bay, so they do not replace me with someone else. Who knows, they could even appoint Vidhura King if they found out what I really thought of them. After all, we share the same father. They would find some scriptures to justify even that. Of course, I know Vidhura would not be happy with such a decision. He is truly pious. Our scriptures can be interpreted to suit what a few priests want, so I do not take any risks, at least not till Suyodhana can take over. Now call him and give him the benefit of your valuable advice and let me play the affable fool."

Dhritarashtra took up the mace and began hitting the iron sculpture again. For the first time Gandhari realised she had not married a fool, but it did not make her feel happy. It made things more difficult. She called out to a guard to fetch the Crown Prince to her chamber. When Suyodhana arrived, an intense argument ensued between mother and son.

The more Dhritarashtra heard, the more worried he became. His son was not practical. He was an idealistic fool who valued friendships, relationships and such abstract things over strategy and practicality. He loved his son, but his shrewd mind told him that people who used the concept of *dharma* as a weapon would find a way to trick his son. They would paint him black, citing his foolish act in the Sabha by shaming his cousins' wife, and make killing him an act of *dharma* against *adharma*.

The same people had once cheated him of his crown, quoting obsolete scriptures, and they would do it again to his son. Because of the loyalty he inspired, and his clean heart, his foolish eldest son would drag all his brothers and friends towards disaster. Then they would invite Pandu's son to sit on the throne, his throne. No! He would not place all his bets on his idealistic son. He had to make his moves carefully. None but his own blood would rule Hastinapura. The bastard sons of Pandu would not inherit at any cost. If they did not allow Suyodhana to inherit, Dhritarashtra would outmanoeuver them. He knew that he himself would appear ridiculous by doing what he planned to do, but he had played the helpless fool for long enough to get away with it. The game was getting deadly with his and his brother's sons sharpening their swords. They would fight like lions. He needed to bring in a vulture.

There were Brahmins, Kshatriya and Shudras on both sides. It was time to bring a Vaishya into the game, and who better than the greatest of them all, the merchant par excellence – Yuyutsu? In fact, he had already written to his son by a Vaishya woman. He had heard that Yuyutsu's ships had reached Prabhasa and that his caravan was on its way to Hastinapura. This was not the first time Yuyutsu had visited him, but it would be the first time Dhritarashtra acknowledged him as his son. It was certain to create problems with Gandhari when she realised he had another son, by the Vaishya maid who had once come to help her. But Dhritarashtra knew he could ride the storm. Gandhari had too much at stake. Moreover, the best of it was that Yuyutsu was older than both Suyodhana and Yudhishtra. In other words, he could stake a claim to the throne of Hastinapura. Dhritarashtra chuckled. And this blind fool would sit and watch the Gurus deal with his ace move. 'Pandu, let us see who wins the final round and whose sons inherit Hastinapura.' Dhritarashtra began to laugh.

Gandhari and Suyodhana stopped their argument and turned towards him in surprise. "Gandhari, my son will inherit the throne," he said chuckling.

***

"Father, it is imperative that we go to Gandhara," Suyodhana said, eyeing his mother sitting nearby. The little twitching of her lips was the only indication that Gandhari had heard her country of birth mentioned.

"Yes! Karna has won us Bharatavarsha. Go to Gandhara, and then Cheenadesa and Yavana, filled with those yellow-haired Mlechas, and capture them all. We can rule the world. I will request Bhishma Pitamaha to lead the armies," Dhritarashtra said extravagantly.

"Father..." Suyodhana faltered. "The Grand Regent has resigned his position, as has Uncle Vidhura."

"Resigned! How is it I know nothing of this?" Dhritarashtra turned to Gandhari, agitated and nervous. "Why has he resigned? No, I do not believe it." He paused and bent his head in thought. 'The old man is jealous. He thought he would always rule this country in my stead. He always sided with Pandu. Everyone sided with impotent Pandu. He could not even father sons and yet they sided with him and his bastard children! Pandavas! They are nothing but the sons of Kunti and Madri. I will show them what my sons are capable of!" Raising his head, Dhritarashtra tapped his cane on the floor and commanded imperiously, "Call Yuyutsu!"

'Yuyutsu? Who was he?' wondered Suyodhana. Puzzled, he looked at his mother. Her fingers had curled into fists but her face remained impassive.

Dhritarashtra walked up and down, leaning on his stick. He paused when he heard footsteps, sensing the newcomer's presence even before he entered the room quietly. Suyodhana watched in surprise. The man was plump, had a prosperous paunch, and the hair on his head had started receding, giving a broad look to his forehead.

"Strange thing, but his face resembles yours, Suyodhana," Karna whispered to his friend.

Dhritarashtra turned to his sons. "Suyodhana, Sushasana, this is your half-brother, Yuyutsu. He is my son. His mother is a Vaishya woman. I have kept this a secret, even from your mother. Now he has come here. Do you know how many ships he owns, how many camels and elephants make up his caravans, how many countries he has visited? I have fathered the greatest of Kshatriya sons and the best Vaishya son as well. I do not need divine intervention to have great sons." Dhritarashtra laughed aloud.

Yuyutsu bent to touch Gandhari's feet. She reached out her hand and blessed him with an instinctive gesture.

How many terrible secrets did his father hold, wondered Suyodhana as he watched the scene. Was this yet another rival for the throne?

"Prince, I am the eldest son of the family, older than even Yudhishtra," Yuyutsu said with a sly smile.

Suyodhana's eyes glittered with cold dislike. He did not trust the merchant's easy familiarity, shifting eyes and hollow smile.

"I am just a humble merchant, a Vaishya, trying to make a living," Yuyutsu continued unctuously.

"Well said, Yuyutsu," Dhritarashtra said. "He could have had the throne for the asking, for he is my eldest son. If I place him at the fore, what argument would the supporters of the Pandavas have? But Yuyutsu knows his *kula dharma* and he will not claim the throne."

"Father, I request permission to use the imperial army to attack Gandhara," Suyodhana said, completely ignoring Yuyutsu.

"Go, my son. If you require it, seek Yuyutsu's help. He has his own army to protect his merchant caravans, which are often five or six *yojanas* long. He has a lakh of men and a large cavalry at his disposal."

Suyodhana looked away. The pangs of jealousy were unbearable. Another son! The eldest! A possible challenger… No! The throne was rightfully his, he would not surrender it to any merchant, or even to Yudhishtra. But a man with his own standing army, possessed of immense wealth, was dangerous, Suyodhana thought warily.

Yuyutsu smiled, as if reading the Kaurava Prince's thoughts. Suyodhana bowed his head for his father's blessings.

"When you conquer Gandhara, do not harm your uncle, no matter what he has done. Bring Shakuni here. He may be in the wrong, but he is the only man who has ever understood my pain. All the others conspired to aid Pandu's sons," Dhritarashtra said quietly.

Suyodhana moved to seek Gandhari's blessing. He whispered to her, "Mother, why do you accept this sly merchant as your step-son?"

"As long as I live, no one but you, my son, will sit on Hastinapura's throne after your father," Gandhari murmured in his ear. Suyodhana kissed her on the forehead and turned, almost bumping into Yuyutsu close behind him. Had he heard Gandhari's words?

The merchant smiled affably at the Prince. "If you require my support with money, men or arms, do not hesitate to approach me. I will do all I can to help."

Had the wretched man stressed that last word, Suyodhana wondered for a fleeting moment. Without acknowledging the merchant's words, he rushed out of the chamber, barking commands to his soldiers to have the imperial army assembled quickly.

Karna hurried home to inform his wife but was soon back, beaming with joy. He had become the father of a son. The Gods were smiling on him. He was impatient to go, excited at the thought of battle.

Ekalavya stood nearby, caressing the best horse in the stable and observing the flurry of activity.

The next morning, they were joined by Jayadratha and his men. The imperial army began its journey towards Gandhara. As Suyodhana sat on his horse, supervising the activity, a wayward thought nagged at him – he had not bid farewell to his wife and children. He had been too busy preparing for battle. It was painful talking to Bhanumati these days, her unceasing advice...

An immense caravan was seen approaching Hastinapura from the desert, stretching as far as the eye could see. It carried more wealth than anyone could imagine. For hours it kept marching past the army in the opposite direction. Yuyutsu's merchant caravan finally entered the capital. As he rushed onwards, Suyodhana wondered whether he would even have a country to rule when he returned from the bleak heights of Gandhara.

*****

20 FISSURES

EKALAVYA'S DAGGER WAS INCHES from Shakuni's eyes. It had not been easy but the wily Gandharan had finally succeeded in convincing his people to surrender to the imperial army after a sham resistance. Everything had gone according to plan. The deceit was complete, except for the man now waving his dagger before his eyes. Shakuni had not counted on the Nishada being in Suyodhana's army.

"*Dhanaveera* Karna, please ask your friend..."

"Shut up, Mlecha!" Ekalavya pressed the tip of the dagger to Shakuni's eyelid, drawing blood.

Where had this merciless Nishada sprouted from, wondered the master strategist.

"Kill him, Nishada, kill him!" Aswathama shouted.

"I won the Pandava country for you. I won you Indraprastha. I made them your slaves, Suyodhana," Shakuni pleaded, his voice quavering in fear as part of his act.

"He will talk his way out of this," Aswathama said bitterly. "Ask him where he has hidden Durjaya."

"My dear nephew, please..." Shakuni bent over and screamed in real pain as Ekalavya kicked him in the groin. 'Just wait till I get back at you, you untouchable vermin,' he thought viciously.

"Ekalavya, leave him alone," Karna commanded. Shakuni closed his eyes in relief.

"Suyodhana, ask him about Varanavata, about Durjaya," Aswathama insisted.

155

"Nephew, hear me out," Shakuni gasped. "I had nothing to do with Varanavata. It was Purochana."

Aswathama darted forward and knocked Shakuni down. Karna stepped in and dragged the screaming Brahmin off the Gandharan. Shakuni hoped his people would keep calm and not react rashly. How long would they be able to stand by and watch their Prince grovelling before these cow-worshippers?

"King of Anga," cried Shakuni, grabbing Karna's feet, "have mercy! You won the South, you won Gandhara, there is no one your equal. Suyodhana will listen to what you say, please..."

Ekalavya knelt, his knees pressed on Shakuni's spine. He pulled back Shakuni's head by the hair, his dagger at the Gandhara Prince's throat. Shakuni gulped in terror, clutching at Karna's feet.

"Let him go, Nishada," Karna barked.

"Are you ordering me?" Ekalavya glared at the Suta, pressing his dagger deeper.

"Let him go," Suyodhana said.

Shakuni remained tense. The way the dagger was pressed to his throat, it seemed the Nishada might even defy the Crown Prince. Then the tension on his hair eased and the dagger moved away from his throat. Shakuni touched his forehead to Karna's feet. Karna lifted him up but turned away; he had never cared for the man.

Nevertheless, Shakuni folded his hands in seeming gratitude as Suyodhana came up to him. "Forgive your uncle, Suyodhana. I have always had your welfare in mind. I want you to sit on the throne of Hastinapura. I won the kingdom for you in the dice game and you repay me by sending your armies to ravish my land? Is that fair?"

"Don't fall for it, Suyodhana," Aswathama shouted from a distance.

'The bloody Brahmin! If not for the ten warriors holding him back, he would strangled me,' thought Shakuni angrily. Any moment Suyodhana could change his mind. He should have killed Aswathama when he had had the chance.

Suyodhana wavered. Shakuni spoke his next piece. "Nephew, remember what your uncle has done for you. As soon as the game of dice was over, I thought the biggest threat to you was Durjaya – the devil was trying to destroy the country. I received information he had moved to Gandhara and I wanted to capture him for you. There was no time for goodbyes. I was in a hurry, and Athiratha, the respected father of His Highness Karna, was kind enough to saddle me a horse. I rushed here. But your impulsive Brahmin friend here followed me, thinking me to be a traitor. Can you imagine how painful that is for me after all that I have done for you, nephew?"

"Lying bastard!" Aswathama wriggled free from the men holding him and rushed towards Shakuni. He tried to punch the tall Gandharan but Suyodhana threw out an arm to stop his friend.

"It seems Aswathama is still angry with me. Poor Brahmin. I can understand his frustration. He was rotting in Hastinapura as an unimportant man and wanted to prove that he too is a warrior. He decided to attack my poor country and I had to save him from an avalanche. Why can he not accept there is no better warrior than Karna? Even this Nishada here would have become a great archer, had not Aswathama's father cheated him of his destiny." Shakuni paused and surveyed the effect of his words on the group of men. For the first time, Ekalavya looked shaken. Aswathama stood in stricken silence and Karna looked as if he wished he were somewhere else.

Shakuni was ready with his next move. "Gambling is a Kshatriya *dharma*. My only sin is that I loved my nephew more than myself. Suyodhana, do you not wish to ride back to Hastinapura with Durjaya in chains? Remember the death and destruction he wrought in Hastinapura. Do you not want him to pay for what he has done to your people?"

"Where is Durjaya?" Suyodhana said at last, weary to the bone.

Shakuni hurried off. He was no longer a supplicant begging for his life, he was the Prince of his people again. As he walked past, his soldiers stood with their heads bowed respectfully. Shakuni did not forget to pat each one as a gesture of gratitude.

The little group soon reached a cave where two soldiers stood guard. Shakuni gestured to them to bring out Durjaya. The guards emerged, dragging out the struggling man.

"Shakuni, you cheat! You betrayed me!" Durjaya screamed.

Suyodhana stepped forward, looking down in disgust at the grovelling man at his feet. He punched and kicked Durjaya till the thug lost consciousness. Shakuni smiled at his nephew's unusual fury. When Suyodhana finally moved away, Shakuni followed, urging him to sit down on a nearby boulder. He took the precious stone he had shown Aswathama from the folds of his clothing and held it up for his nephew to see. The lustre of it startled Suyodhana and his eyes opened wide. Shakuni smiled.

"What is it?" Suyodhana asked in surprise.

"This is a small gift from your uncle for all the trouble he has caused – inadvertently of course!"

"I have no fancy for precious stones," Suyodhana said, averting his eyes from the tempting beauty of the gem.

"I know, nephew, but you can always gift it to someone dear to you. Perhaps Karna, who has won you an empire, or to acknowledge the Nishada's grit."

"This stone is too precious."

"I give it to you gladly, nephew."

Suyodhana reluctantly took the stone in the palm of his hand. He could feel it burning his skin. He looked at Karna standing nearby. He knew Karna did not covet the stone, only his appreciation and friendship. The Nishada too, sat a little distance away with a derisive smile, chewing a blade of grass. He spat when Suyodhana looked at him in the face. He had no need of gems, only justice. Suyodhana knew he had rewarded them both. He had made Karna King of Anga and the Nishada King of the forest lands. The one person who had always stood by him without expecting anything in return, had been Aswathama. Suyodhana walked over to the Brahmin and took his hand in his own. Then he pressed the shining stone into the hard and calloused palm.

Shakuni looked at Karna, and then at the Nishada, and smiled.

*****

21 VICTORS AND THE VANQUISHED

IT WAS A SECOND HOMECOMING for the Suta as the victorious army entered the capital city. People thronged to see the Kaurava army drag Durjaya through the streets in chains. Suyodhana and Karna threw fistfuls of coins into the crowd crazed with adulation. The streets shook with cries of *Har Har Mahadeva!* Yuyutsu, the richest man in the world, stood at the entrance of the palace, ready to welcome the victorious Prince and his warrior-friend. The merchant showered the heroes with exotic perfumes and flowers.

Bhishma waited for Suyodhana to come to see him, but as the day and then the night passed, he was once again reminded of the bitter truth that he was no longer needed. He yearned for Vidhura's company. He knew an era had ended and a new one had begun. He would have liked to advise Suyodhana to kill Durjaya, but the proud patriarch was unsure whether the Prince would respect his advice. He was no longer the Grand Regent, just a forgotten old man. Bhishma heard Karna's voice in the palace garden and a pang of jealousy stabbed his heart. The more he fought it, the stronger it became. How did the Suta succeed in whatever he did?

***

Bhanumati waited in her chamber for her husband to come. She yearned for his touch, his comforting embrace, his smell, and for the serenity she had always felt when he held her close. Those were fading memories now, yet she cherished them. She had been hurt and angry when he had not even taken leave of her before departing for Gandhara, but anxiety had soon pushed back her anger. She had feared for his life. Whenever she heard the galloping of a horse on the Royal Highway, cold hands clutched at her heart. Praise be he had returned without injury.

Bhanumati rushed to the balcony, hoping to catch Suyodhana's eye. She saw him riding in on a magnificent horse. He looked so happy in his own world – laughing, waving, throwing coins to the crowd and basking in the glory of victory. He did not look up. A smile would have been enough, even a tilt of the head, but it seemed that in Suyodhana's world, no one existed except Karna and himself. Bhanumati gripped the railings of the balcony as her children jumped up and down in excitement at seeing their father. 'Suyodhana, at least look at your children and give them a smile,' she begged in her heart.

As if in answer to her prayers, a man in the Prince's entourage waved to the children, his teeth a brilliant white against his dark face. It was Ekalavya, the Nishada whom her unpredictable husband had made a King. He was waving at her and the children. The audacity of the Nishada was galling. Who else would her husband befriend? Did he not care about the tongues wagging about his actions? She dragged the protesting children inside and closed the balcony door. She wanted to be alone.

Bhanumati did not know when she finally dozed off. She woke with a start and stretched out her hand, hoping to feel him near her. Already it was morning and she could hear the servants moving about outside. Why had he not come? Lakshmana stirred in her sleep and Bhanumati pulled up the coverlet her daughter had thrown off.

Had someone coughed outside? Bhanumati ran to open the door, her eyes alight with joyful expectation. A dark face stared back at her. She wanted to scream. How dared the Nishada come to pollute her space? How dared he come near the chambers of the Crown Prince?

But Ekalavya smiled and stepped back. Bhanumati stood beside the open door, uneasily aware of the man's presence outside her bedchamber. She was still searching for a suitable snub when Lakshmana woke, saw Ekalavya, and came running. The Nishada bowed low before the little Princess. To Bhanumati's horror, her little daughter shrieked with joy and jumped into the dark man's arms. Hearing the commotion, Lakshmana Kumara also awoke and joined in. Soon the three of them were rolling on the floor, laughing. Bhanumati wanted to prise them apart, call the guards and have the untouchable whipped, but she stood frozen, unable to move. She had suddenly seen a third eye burning like a coal in the centre of Ekalavya's forehead. It was there and then it was gone, like an illusion. Yet she was certain she had seen it. The dark man was running with her children to the garden. Had she witnessed something beyond her understanding? Who was the Nishada, really?

***

In Drona's home, Aswathama sat sulking. His father had not spoken a word to him since his return. It was almost as if Aswathama did not exist. Drona sat in meditation in his *puja* room. Aswathama whirled the copper tumbler his mother had placed near him with shaking hands, and a few drops of water from it splashed onto the floor.

Aswathama could not bear his father's indifference a moment longer. "I have returned from Gandhara," he said loudly and waited.

"Ask him where he got the precious stone he is wearing on his head headcloth," Drona said to Kripi. "Ask him why he has brought a stone of sin into this Brahmin's home."

Aswathama glared at his father. "It is a gift from my friend."

Not looking at his son, Drona said to his wife, "Kripi, tell your son that it is loot from Gandhara. Tell him that a Brahmin should not soil his hands with such possessions. Any possession is sin for a Brahmin. Tell him that any attachment will lead to disaster and heartbreak."

"Suyodhana gifted me the stone for my services."

After what seemed like an eternity, Drona replied, "Kripi, did you know that it needed a Suta's skill to save your son in Gandhara? Now, had it been Arjuna..."

Aswathama knocked over the tumbler, spilling water everywhere. Even the food in his father's house seemed noxious and poisonous now. Aswathama was about to kick away the plantain leaf his mother had placed before him when he heard her call to him softly. He paused, expecting her to speak in his support.

"Food is Goddess Annapurna, son. We have starved enough in our life. Do not disrespect the Goddess," Kripi said in a low voice.

Aswathama could not believe his ears. Was that all his mother had to say? He rolled up the plantain leaf, careful not to spill the food, and walked out, heading towards the river. At the riverbank he saw the beggar Jara sitting under a tree, humming to himself. Aswathama placed the leaf full of food before him. The beggar's face lit up. A pang of guilt stabbed the Brahmin.

"Krishna, you have come with food."

"Krishna! Don't you have eyes, man? I am Aswathama, not the cowherd."

"Everyone is Krishna, everything is Krishna," the beggar said serenely, first feeding his dog.

Aswathama felt irritation stir in his troubled mind. "Jara, you keep singing and praying. But have you done even a single day's hard labour? Why shame yourself by begging from others? Why not work and live on your own earnings? Does not your Krishna say that work is the greatest worship?"

"My life is an act of devotion to my Lord. I sing because my soul overflows with his praise. I take only what is required to sustain me, until my Lord gives me merciful *moksha*. I do not save for tomorrow, I do not have a house to live in, a yard to tend to, a wife to clothe or a child to feed. My dog and I eat once a day. I have clothing to cover my nakedness. I lack nothing. I do not beg for myself, I beg so that men do not forget kindness and compassion. There are different kinds of work. Work for the sake of result is not worship. Work unaffected by result is true worship."

Aswathama watched the beggar with distaste. 'Crazy' was the first word that came to his mind. Suddenly an image came to his mind, and he shook his head to erase it. He was hallucinating, he needed to sleep. But he did not want to go home to where his father lived. The image flashed again – the beggar was feeding him, Aswathama, the dog by his side. Aswathama trembled. Before the image could reappear, he jumped into the river. Jealousy of Karna and a sense of inferiority assaulted the son of Drona. He had gone to Gandhara with high expectations and failed. The few words of affection his father had spoken before he left were now a distant memory. 'Oh God, why are you so cruel to me?' the Brahmin asked in anguish. He took some water in his palms and prayed, "Ma Ganga, wash away my sins... "

Aswathama struggled to shrug off his petty thoughts about Karna. Were they all just puppets in the hands of an all-knowing God? Was life but a farce to entertain a cruel God? The beggar's song caressed his bruised soul but did not soothe his mind. The precious stone glistened on his headcloth. Jealousy rose again like bile from his stomach and Aswathama dunked his head into the cold waters of the Ganga and prayed, 'Karna, my friend, may you always be victorious! Bless my friend with glory every time, Ma Ganga!'

But even the holy waters of the Ganga could not quench the burning jealousy inside him.

***

22 RETURN OF THE MLECHA

TWELVE LONG YEARS HAD GONE BY. It had been a difficult task to win back Suyodhana's confidence. Shakuni did not visit Hastinapura for eight years following Aswathama's attack on Gandhara. Instead, he used the time to bring prosperity back to his people. His popularity stood at an all-time high in the country. His people adored him for his fairness and sense of justice. He had grown old with grace, his flowing beard now almost white. His sons had grown up. Life had been good to the Gandharan.

Shakuni could afford to turn back to the affairs of his most hated enemy. Once he had crossed the Indus, he became a different man. The last four years had been a relentless struggle to retrieve his position in Hastinapura politics. By abasing himself, pampering to the egos of pretentious men, and by using charm, bribes and intrigue, Shakuni had worked his way back into the palace. The Pandavas' term of exile was nearing its end. In another four months they would have to go incognito for a year. That would be the time to strike.

Shakuni's brain was in a whirl, planning and plotting. Yuyutsu's tightening grip over the economy and the festering resentment against the merchant was a fault line he could use to instigate a bloody civil war. The current drought was helping, too. But Indians were so passive, they preferred to die on the streets starving rather than rise up against their rulers.

Takshaka had become almost useless. The fool had moved south of the Vindhyas and founded a city for the Nagas, which he named Nagapura. All he did was harass Brahmins and non-Nagas. But the backlash against him was not quick enough in coming. He had managed to get a few followers. Nagapura was located in the centre of India but it was nothing more than an overgrown village for the dispossessed. The majority of Nagas preferred to follow Ekalavya rather than Takshaka. The forest people were either content or afraid of their King.

Shakuni knew he had to split the unity of the Nagas. Every caste and community had to be made to fight each other. Sitting in distant Gandhara, he had only been able to engineer some minor riots. Nothing seemed to work and India seemed blessed with infernal luck. But his time was coming. Shakuni flung his dice onto the table. They clattered, spun and rolled under his chair. Cursing, he bent to retrieve them. All of a sudden, he remembered Durjaya. Shakuni wished the crime lord was a free man. Though he had befriended other criminals, none had displayed the ingenuity and ruthlessness of Durjaya. It was fortunate that Suyodhana had not killed the thug. Had he gone mad in prison or fallen into despondency? There was no way of knowing without visiting him in the dungeon where he was held under tight security. It was too risky.

What would make the Kuru cousins fight each other? If the shameless Pandavas refused to fight even for the honour of their common wife, what would they battle for? Perhaps he could involve Krishna in some way, then things would change. But instigating Krishna to do something rash was not going to be easy. The Yadava Prince was the only one Shakuni considered a worthy rival in terms of astuteness and acumen. But even great men had some weakness. What was Krishna's? The man could charm a tiger to shed its teeth, he could slay an army. No, he would have to pull the rug from under Krishna's feet without him knowing it. He would need to deepen the animosity between Krishna and Suyodhana by making them both think they were fighting for a greater cause. The bloodiest wars were when both sides thought they were the righteous ones. He had to create a war where individual definitions of *dharma* clashed in self-righteous rage and destroyed each other.

No plan came to Shakuni's mind, but after an hour in a trance, peace descended on him like a gentle balm. He would have to persuade Suyodhana to visit the South. Once the Crown Prince was removed from Hastinapura and Jayadratha made Regent, he could work out something. Perhaps Suyodhana would do something rash on his visit to the conservative South. But the key lay in the rivalry between Krishna and Suyodhana. With shaking hands, Shakuni fumbled for his dice and tossed them to the floor, whispering, "Twelve". They rolled and came to rest at a perfect twelve.

"Krishna!" he cried with a crooked smile. No devotee of the charming Yadava could have uttered the name with more passion. Something big was coming his way.

***

Ekalavya sat polishing his bow when Khatotkacha approached him, accompanied by a slim boy in his late teens. Mildly irritated, the King of the forest lands asked Bhima's son, "What does he want?"

"Guru, he wants to learn the art of using weapons."

Ekalavya continued with his work. He could sense the apprehension of the two teenagers. He had come to like the hefty Rakshasa, Khatotkacha, in the twelve years he had known him. He could still remember the day Hidumbi had come to him after he had taken charge of the forest lands. She had a boy of five or six with her and she had wanted him to teach her son. Curious, he had asked about the boy's father. When he heard the boy was Bhima's son, he had declined to have anything to do with them. But the boy refused to give up. Every morning, for six months, the first thing Ekalavya saw was Khatotkacha's face. Finally, convinced that Khatotkacha's thirst for knowledge rivalled his own, he relented. Twelve years later, Ekalavya did not have any regrets.

"Who is he?" asked Ekalavya curtly. Where had he seen that face?

"Iravan, a Naga," Khatotkacha replied shortly. Ekalavya's gaze never left the boy's face.

"Who is this young man, Ekalavya?" Vasuki's voice broke into his thoughts.

The boy turned to Vasuki, bowed and said, "I am Iravan."

"That is your name. But who are your parents? Which clan or tribe do you belong to? Where are you from?" Vasuki leaned on his staff, scrutinizing Iravan's face.

"My mother is Naga. Her name is Uloopi."

"And your father?"

Iravan did not reply. His eyes fell and he stared at his feet.

Ekalavya took Iravan shoulders in a grip of iron and said coldly, "Tell me!"

"My father is the Pandava, Arjuna." Iravan's voice was almost a whisper, as if uttering his father's name was a shameful thing.

Ekalavya let go of the boy. The odd familiarity now made sense. "How dare you come to me seeking knowledge? Is it my duty to teach all the bastard sons the Pandavas leave behind in every village on their trail? First Khatotkacha, and now you! Do you know what your father did?" Ekalavya shoved his thumbless hand in Iravan's face.

"I have no one else." Iravan's eyes flashed. He refused to look at the missing thumb on Ekalavya's hand and raised his chin defiantly. "I thought you would be a person to whom skill, knowledge and ability have no barriers. I was wrong. I will go." He bowed and began to walk away.

The boy's words were like a slap on Ekalavya's face. Something in Iravan reminded him of himself – the same thirst for knowledge, the same willpower to learn and succeed. "Son!" Ekalavya's voice was hoarse, his throat dry, as Iravan stopped. Looking into the distance, the Nishada King said, "Show me what you know."

The boy lifted the crude bow he was carrying and took aim. Vasuki stood near Ekalavya, leaning on his stick. The arrow whizzed past them both, finding the narrow gap between their heads and pierced a tree behind them. The two stood frozen as Iravan pulled another arrow from his quiver and took aim. The second arrow traced the same path and bisected the first with unnerving accuracy.

"*Shabash!*" Vasuki cried and limped over to Iravan as fast as his old legs could carry him.

Ekalavya stood stunned by what he had seen. What could he possibly teach this boy? The ugly snake of jealousy raised its head. Did Iravan being Arjuna's son have something to do with his unbelievable talent?

"Accept me as your disciple, Guru. Make me a worthy warrior like my cousin, Khatotkacha."

Before he could say anything, Iravan bent and touched Ekalavya's feet. His ghost thumb itched as memories of a boy falling at the feet of a great Guru came flooding back to his mind. Was fate mocking him by reversing roles? 'Oh, Shiva, give me the courage to forget and forgive,' he prayed. Ekalavya lifted Arjuna's son. What could be more fitting revenge than making the bastard sons of blue-blooded Kshatriyas better warriors than them? What more could a Nishada ask for as retribution?

Vasuki tapped his stick on the ground. "All this is fine, but beware! Keep away from the affairs of the Kauravas and Pandavas." Like most of Vasuki's wise words, these too were ignored, eventually extracting a heavy price for having gone unheeded.

Who knew what the future held, thought Ekalavya. What mattered was the profound peace he felt at this moment. He almost felt like God, like Shiva.

Meanwhile, in another part of the forest, a hunting party arrived. The actions of one of them would trigger a set of catastrophic events.

*****

23 THE POET

"WHY DOES OUR SON BEHAVE IN THIS WAY, BHANU?"

Bhanumati clenched her fists, her lips closed in a thin line. She knew Suyodhana was tense and worried, but that was no excuse to behave in this way towards their son. The treasury was almost empty and the rains had failed for the second year. Everywhere there was drought and famine, yet all her husband fretted over was the return of the Pandavas to Hastinapura. The Pandavas' twelve-year exile was nearing its end and they would soon go incognito.

"Speak up, fool!" Suyodhana raised his voice to his son.

Abhimanyu, standing beside Lakshmana Kumara, suppressed a grin. His cousin was in trouble yet again. Bhanumati had tried to stop her son from being friends with Subhadra and Arjuna's gifted son, but to no avail. Kumara was devoted to his cousin. Each time Abhimanyu visited Hastinapura to pay his respects to Lord Bhishma and Guru Drona, he made it a point to visit them too. He had charmed Suyodhana with his winning ways and skills as a warrior. It did not help that Subhadra often accompanied her son. Bhanu saw the look in Suyodhana's eyes when he looked at Subhadra. No, she was not jealous, but no husband should look at another woman that way. She was not envious, Bhanu told herself, but the son, he was so cocky!

"Have you swallowed a stick?" Suyodhana asked, slapping his thigh. "Why are you slipping in weaponry practice? The Acharya says you are fit only to be a clerk. You are a Kshatriya, Kumara, grow up! What have you to say for yourself?"

Abhimanyu intervened with barely concealed glee. "Uncle, my cousin does not wish to be a warrior."

"He is never going to be one. Look at his limbs. Is he a boy or a girl?"

Bhanumati recoiled at Suyodhana's harsh words. Kumara's soft brown eyes, so like his sister's, filled with tears. How nice it would be to wipe that smug smile off Abhimanyu's face, Bhanumati thought. The young warrior stood ramrod straight, running a thumb over the sharp edge of his sword.

"What do you want in life, son?" Suyodhana finally asked. Bhanumati wanted to grab her son's hand and run from the room. She knew what was coming.

"Would you like me to tell my uncle, Kumara?" Abhimanyu asked solicitously, a mischievous smile on his fine lips. Kumara's eyes pleaded with his friend to remain silent. "Uncle, my cousin wishes to be a poet," Abhimanyu said, unable to hide the laughter in his voice.

There was an uneasy silence. Kumara eyed his father fearfully. Bhanumati wanted to rush to her son and hide him in a protective embrace. But it would have embarrassed him, he was almost fifteen and she could see the shadow of a moustache above his upper lip. How quickly children grew up!

"Perhaps it is best you go to someone I know. He changed my life; maybe he can change yours, too," Suyodhana said in a weary voice from which all mockery had fled.

"He is not going anywhere." Bhanumati stood up.

"Would you prefer your son to be called a sissy all his life, Bhanu? He is a Kshatriya; he has to rule this country one day."

"He would be fine if only you would stop badgering him like this."

"Enough! When I need your advice, I will ask for it. This is between father and son. Stay out of it, Bhanu."

"He is my son, too, Suyodhana," Bhanumati stated adamantly.

"Why do you insist on arguing about this, Bhanu? He is a wimp, a loser. People laugh behind our backs. Is that what you want? He should learn from his cousin. Just look at Abhimanyu."

"Abhimanyu is the son of a great warrior – Arjuna." The words were out before she could bite them back. She had crossed the line. She waited for Suyodhana to lash out at her with furious words, and was more pained when he ignored her and turned to his son.

"You will go to Dwaraka. I will write to Balarama today."

"My brother is going to Dwaraka!" Lakshmana said, excitement lighting up her lovely face. She had been sitting quietly behind her mother throughout this exchange.

How Suyodhana's stern expression relaxed whenever he looked at his daughter, thought Bhanumati. She was so beautiful! How was she to protect her daughter from the preying eyes of the world? Lakshmana was so impulsive and trusting. Her father adored her. She was everything her brother was not.

"I will go with *bhrata* to Dwaraka," Lakshmana said, eyeing her mother and smiling at her father.

"No, you will not. You are not a little girl any more, Lakshmana. You are almost of marriageable age, and I cannot have you roaming all over the country unattended."

"Ma, do you think I cannot take care of myself? What age were you when you were married? I am only fifteen!"

"Times are changing, Lakshmana. In my time it was acceptable for a woman to choose to remain single until her late twenties. Now, parents marry off their daughters even at the age of twelve."

Lakshmana knew she would not be able to get around her stern mother so she walked up to her father, head tilted in the way he loved, and cajoled, "Father, please let me go. I want to be with *bhrata*."

Bhanumati knew she had lost. Suyodhana could never say no to his daughter. In a last ditch attempt, she said, "The roads are infested with bandits." She did not know why but she felt extremely uneasy about the whole proposition.

"Bhanu, do you think someone would dare harm a Princess of Hastinapura?" Father and daughter laughed aloud. The very idea was ridiculous.

Bhanumati could stand it no more. "Do what you want. Has any of you ever listened to me? Do I even exist?" She stared out of the window in frustration, feeling helpless and unhappy that her husband no longer came to her when he needed solace, upset that he never talked to her about his dreams. Did he have any dreams left, other than to cling to the throne? Kumara came up and put his arms around her gently, trying to comfort her. She could feel his emotion.

"Are you a five-year-old to hold your mother and weep?" asked Suyodhana, disgusted.

Abhimanyu choked back a laugh. His cousin was so entertaining.

"Does your cousin's distress amuse you, Prince?" asked Bhanumati.

Abhimanyu looked away, embarrassed. He turned and quickly walked out of the room.

Kumara looked up at his father, his face expressionless, but he did not remove his comforting arm from around his mother's shoulders.

"Ma, Abhimanyu is the only friend Kumara has. He is more like a brother to him than a cousin," Lakshmana said.

"Abhimanyu cannot be trusted," Bhanumati replied with quiet certainty. She waited for her son to say something but Kumara stood in silence.

But Lakshmana had never taken anything in silence. "Ma, everyone loves Abhimanyu. How can do you say such things about him?"

"It does not matter what others say. I know he cannot be trusted," Bhanumati replied, looking straight into Suyodhana's eyes, daring him to contradict her.

"You hate Abhimanyu because you are jealous of Aunt Subhadra..." Lakshmana began, but her petulant words died at the stricken look on her mother's face.

How it hurt when her daughter said things she thought she had hidden from the world, Bhanumati thought as she turned away from her son, daughter and husband.

A corpulent man entered the room without being announced. His eyes had vanished into his puffy face, but the grin could not have been wider. Bhanumati hastily drew her *pallu* over her head.

"Arrange for the Prince and Princess to travel to Dwaraka, Yuyutsu," Suyodhana said and turned his back on the newcomer.

"So my little Princess is going to Dwaraka? I will arrange the best chariots for you. Will two hundred servants be enough to make you comfortable?" Yuyutsu asked, bowing.

"Hastinapura has enough chariots of its own. Why should my father need to borrow a chariot from a merchant?" Lakshmana asked imperiously.

"We are family, Princess. What is mine is your father's to command and what is his is... shared by the family," Yuyutsu said, beaming. "Why be angry with a poor merchant, my Princess? I am your uncle. Hastinapura owes me a lot of money but I care only about its progress. Though I am the eldest, I am satisfied with some small profit, as is a Vysya's *dharma*. Your father knows this."

Bhanumati looked at Suyodhana but her husband's face wore only a look of weariness. Where had his anger vanished to? The merchant smiled and walked out.

Suyodhana sighed and turned to his son. "Plan your trip to Dwaraka with Abhimanyu. I will write to Balarama. Come back a man, a warrior, not a whining dreamer. Take your sister with you. I am going to the South and I want to see you a man by the time I return."

"Oh thank you, Father!" Lakshmana rushed to hug Suyodhana. His tense face relaxed as he patted her hair.

Before Bhanumati could protest, Suyodhana walked out of the room. His harsh words hurt her but his indifference pierced her heart. She looked at her daughter, so full of life, so full of joy. Some deep maternal mother's instinct told her that something terrible was going to happen to her daughter. If only she had the power to stop her precious one from going to Dwaraka.

*****

24 DIFFERENT GODS

KARNA WENT TO VISIT GURU PARASHURAMA when they reached Muzaris but Suyodhana refused to see the Guru. Parashurama warned Karna of the dire consequences of breaching his trust and Suyodhana interfering with the beliefs of the Confederate kingdoms.

One hot and humid morning, what Karna feared most happened. Despite his best efforts, Suyodhana insisted they travel into the countryside. They galloped south, leaving the imperial army on the banks of the dry Poorna River. What he saw turned Suyodhana's mood black.

"How have you allowed such atrocities, Karna? I have never seen such a madhouse in my life. Forget human beings, they have even graded animals and trees as touchable and untouchable!"

What explanation could he possibly give to his Guru if Suyodhana acted on his own principles, wondered Karna anxiously. "I gave my word to my Guru that I would not interfere in their affairs," he said, but the excuse sounded lame even to his own ears.

"What do you need with such a Guru?" Suyodhana struck his thighs in anger.

Karna's gaze met Aswathama's eyes and he read the accusation in them, too. Karna's anger rose. Was it his fault that the people of the Confederate followed rigid caste rules? Was he himself not a victim of that prejudice? What was he supposed to do? Murder anyone who talked about caste? Perhaps he should have started that in Hastinapura, when he was publicly humiliated and ostracised. He pressed his lips together in hurt silence. The last thing he wanted to do was to argue with his friends. He wanted to be back with his family, to see his wife and sons. This place sickened him, he felt choked by the guilt of what he should have done.

By noon of the third day of their journey south, when the sun was a white blaze over their heads and they were drenched in sweat, they finally reached a decrepit-looking village. Hungry and thirsty, they seemed to have lost their way. Every village looked alike, with dried up ponds and dusty trees. The drought had sapped the life of this once evergreen land. The thatched roof huts looked as though they might fall down at any moment. Urchins playing in the mud paused to look wide-eyed at the strange men riding through their dirt lanes. Some women ran to collect the children and herd them into the huts. The men sitting in their mud verandas stood up in alarm and gaped at the warriors.

"Can we get some water?" Suyodhana asked a scrawny man, but received no response. He gestured with his hands for water and the men stepped back in horror, as if he had spoken unutterable words. "We just want some water. Can you not offer water to thirsty travellers? We have lost our way and..."

There was a murmuring among the men. Karna knew why the villagers were so afraid. He also knew his friend would wish no harm to fall on the hapless villagers, but before he could warn Suyodhana, an old woman offered the Crown Prince a mud pot. He took it gratefully and drank the contents like a dying man given a reprieve. The murmuring among the crowd grew louder.

"Swami, punish me," the woman said with trembling lips. A little girl came to stand near her, looking at them with round eyes.

"Punish? Mother, why should I punish you?" Suyodhana asked as he passed the pot to Aswathama.

The Brahmin took one look at the contents and squirmed in distaste. Karna could feel his heart beating under the armour he wore. He knew why the woman was afraid, she had given

Suyodhana toddy – the drink of outcasts and untouchables. By drinking from the hands of an untouchable tribal, the Kshatriya had lost caste. Suyodhana could regain his Kshatriya status only by killing her and doing sufficient penance. God knows how many gifts he would have to give the Brahmins and how many ritual sacrifices he would have to make to annul this sin.

"I am an untouchable, Swami. By taking toddy from me, you too have become one. Kill me if you want, but please spare the village. We have little..." The old woman's voice trailed off as she held the little girl close.

Suyodhana looked at her, trying hard to comprehend what she was saying. When Karna explained, Suyodhana jumped down from his saddle and gently took the woman's shrivelled hands in his own. He looked into her eyes and said, "Mother, why should I punish you? You placed the thirst of a weary traveller over your own life. Bless me like you would bless your son."

The woman did not understand the words, but it did not matter. She put her dark hands over Suyodhana's greying mane while the crowd looked on, shocked. "Who are you, my son? For the first time in our wretched lives, we are seeing a high-born person behave like this."

"She is asking who you are," Karna said, looking away, his mind a tangle of conflicting emotions.

"I am Suyodhana, notoriously known as Duryodhana," the Crown Prince replied.

An uneasy silence fell. A few women who had come out of their huts to see what was happening, pulled their children back inside. The men, too, hurried back to their huts, fear writ large on their faces.

The old woman looked deep into Suyodhana's eyes. She turned to the fleeing villagers and raised her voice. "They told us lies. This Kshatriya has treated us as human beings. For us, this man is *dharma*."

The villagers returned slowly to form a circle around Suyodhana and his friends. As the animated discussion and arguments grew louder around them, Suyodhana asked Karna what the ruckus was all about.

"They wish to build a temple in your honour," Karna said unsteadily, "and worship you."

"What?" Suyodhana laughed aloud. "Worship me? Are they mad?"

But Karna could see his friend was pleased. Suyodhana made a token protest and said they should build a Shiva temple instead, but it was evident he was relishing the thought of having a temple dedicated to him. Was every rebellious act by him an unconscious attempt to be known as a good man?

Aswathama offered the toddy to Karna, his eyes shining with challenge. As he lifted the pot to his mouth, Karna felt he would gag from the pungent smell. His entire struggle to be accepted as a Kshatriya would come to naught if news of this spread. What he had struggled for his whole life would mean nothing if he lost his caste and became an untouchable. What a fall... even for a Suta! Closing his eyes, he took a sip. The toddy tasted sweet in his mouth. As he traced its scorching trail to his stomach, the sound of the crowd receded into the distance. By Guru Parashurama's definition, Karna was no longer a Kshatriya, or even a Suta. He had lost his caste. Strangely, he felt free. It did not matter. The only thing that counted was the firmness of Suyodhana's hand on his shoulder.

Around him, the villagers had come to an agreement. A temple was to be built. A cool breeze wafted in from the brackish backwaters and Karna relished the caress of the setting sun. He wished Suyodhana's adventure to the South would end and he would be spared further embarrassment. As if in answer to his prayers, a messenger came rushing to meet the Crown Prince. They were summoned back to Hastinapura immediately. A disastrous event had taken place.

*****

25 THE PROPOSAL

WHEN THE CROWN PRINCE KEPT HIS WORD and made Jayadratha Grand Regent until he returned from the South, his brother-in-law had felt smug. He had brought Sushala and his son, Suratha, with him to Hastinapura. The boy was twelve but showed no talent for arms. Sushala yearned to see her son become a great warrior but Jayadratha, with a father's insight, did not harbour much hope of his son growing to be a warrior-ruler. He knew that unless he himself did something to please Suyodhana and extract a larger territory to rule than the small vassal state of Sindhudesa, his dynasty would remain insignificant among the great kingdoms of Bharatavarsha.

Jayadratha had been born after many years of prayer. But by then his father had become too world weary to undertake adventures of expansion. By the time Jayadratha attained manhood, the expanding Hastinapura empire had swallowed Sindhudesa among others and their exalted dynasty, which traced its lineage to Lord Vishnu himself, had become rulers of an insignificant vassal state under Bhishma. Jayadratha gained some importance by marrying the only Princess of the Kuru dynasty, but the feeling of unworthiness never left him. Sushala, with her constant comparison of the riches of her father to the insignificance of Sindhudesa, did nothing to help assuage his wounded pride. But if he made the right moves he might be able to persuade Suyodhana to hand over to him the neighbouring vassal kingdoms. And who knew what the future held? Perhaps his boy would have grown up to surprise him. If the war between the cousins took place one day and the empire weakened, he could perhaps turn things around. Hastinapura as a vassal state of Sindhudesa was a refreshing thought.

Despite his dreams of grandeur, Jayadratha was not a popular King among his subjects. His father, now almost eighty years old, had carefully spread the rumour of a boon he had received from Lord Shiva himself when he had relinquished the throne in favour of his son – If anyone killed Jayadratha, the moment his head touched the earth, his killer would die. The Sutas of Sindhu added spice to the story and soon the superstitious population began believing that if Jayadratha was killed and his head hit the ground, his killer's head would explode into a thousand pieces. It was one of the things that prevented a coup in Sindhudesa. Jayadratha in his turn spread the story of a boon he had obtained – that no Pandava other than Arjuna could defeat him.

It had been three days since he had taken over as Grand Regent but he had not had the inclination to visit Bhishma, who had adorned the revered position for so many years. The chamber of the Grand Regent was much grander than his own royal chambers in Sindh, thought Jayadratha bitterly as he viewed the luxurious appointments of the room – the twelve-foot-high oil lamp made of silver, with the exquisite carving of a peacock, had glistening emeralds for eyes; the visitors' chairs carved in ivory made his throne in Sindhudesa look like a child's playroom furniture; the curtains glistened with gold lace; the carpet stretched in luxurious smoothness; the fragrance of exotic oils and scents that permeated the air – it all made him mad with jealousy and anger. No wonder Sushala made unfavourable comparisons about Sindhudesa.

'All this is looted wealth,' Jayadratha told himself. How he wished it all belonged to him, but he knew he was no match for Hastinapura. However, if he could please Suyodhana, he could get lucky. He had six months to prove himself. He was a man in a hurry. He tried to think of a plan that would call on Suyodhana's famed generosity, but nothing came to his disturbed mind.

A guard came in and bowed to the new Grand Regent. He said the Prince of Gandhara sought permission to see him. Ah, Shakuni! Jayadratha's mind leapt with pride. Though he despised the

Gandharan, it fed his ego to be thus waited on by one who ruled a much vaster and richer territory than Sindhudesa. Jayadratha had Shakuni wait until the palace gong sounded the passing of the next *prahar* before permitting him to enter. He did not speak for some time, pretending to be busy reading various palm leaves and barking instructions, as Shakuni stood with head bowed in deep reverence. When he was satisfied he had shown Shakuni his place, Jayadratha offered him a seat. Shakuni declined, saying that vassal Kings never sat before the Grand Regent of Hastinapura. Pleased, Jayadratha persuaded Shakuni to sit down.

"Not that I cherish this added responsibility, Shakuni, but I have my hands full with ruling Sindh. But we must help Suyodhana."

"Oh, I know it is a great burden that you carry, revered Sindhu Raja, but no one deserves to sit in this chair more than you. It is not like olden times when vassal Kings had to beg and crawl before a mean old man. Now we have someone who understands our problems. The Kings of Magadha, Mithila and others, were expressing relief that you have taken over. It is not that Suyodhana is not generous, but the post of Grand Regent has remained vacant after Lord Bhishma relinquished it and you know my nephew is always partial to that Suta. Anga gets the best of everything."

"I will be just and impartial as long as I hold the post."

"I know that and I came to pay my respects. By the way, would your Excellency care to have me report to you on the movements of the Pandavas, if it will not burden your busy schedule? I was in charge of the espionage network of Hastinapura and…"

"Oh, certainly. What are they doing now?" Jayadratha sat forward, trying to keep his eagerness from showing on his face.

"In fact, they have gone in search of secret weapons and alliances, leaving Draupadi behind. Only Guru Dhaumya and a few of his disciples remain with her."

"What of her five sons?"

"The Pandavas have taken the boys with them."

An idea started forming in Jayadratha's head. Draupadi was alone in the forest. He had attended Draupadi's *swayamvara*, but had not even had the chance to try his skill. He was so insignificant a King that the Magadhan who had announced each of the Kings had hardly said a word about him. Karna had been in love with her. Jayadratha had joined Suyodhana and Aswathama in making fun of Karna and his feelings for Draupadi. He had thought the Suta would win her, but she had insulted him instead and a fight had broken out. Finally she had married Arjuna, and then his four brothers as well. In his heart, Jayadratha had always lusted over Draupadi's beauty. A woman who married five men could not be said to be chaste. Her audacity in her laughing at Suyodhana and insulting Karna made her even more appealing to Jayadratha. They had not insulted her enough in the Sabha on the day of the dice game.

Shakuni read the thoughts flashing over Jayadratha's face like an open book. "Your Majesty, I do not know whether I am crossing a line by saying this, but a great King like you should have married Draupadi, and not those poor and broken Pandavas. The Princess Draupadi deserved better."

Jayadratha stared at Shakuni, his eyes narrowed. His mind was in turmoil.

"I am sure she would be willing to listen to your offer."

The burning in his loins found voice in his mind. What if he asked her to satisfy him? If she resisted, he could take her somewhere, perhaps to Sindh, and keep her in his harem. It would not be the first time a King had taken the woman he wanted, nor would it be the last. Perhaps she would even agree to be his wife, or he could bargain with the Pandavas for her release. He was sure Suyodhana hated her and would support him in any scheme that shamed the Pandavas. Now that he had the imperial army under his control, the Pandavas would not dare question him.

And if Suyodhana behaved irrationally, well, it was he who had control of the imperial army.

"Can you take me to the *ashram*?" Jayadratha said, his hands quivering with nervous tension.

"Allow me the honour of making the arrangements, Maharajan."

The foreigner bowed and hurried out. Maharajan – it pleased Jayadratha to be addressed so. He ran his fingers over the rounded carvings of the handrests of his chair. Draupadi... at last.

***

Shakuni hurried to his chamber. The man waiting outside bowed. The Gandharan pulled out a small bag that jingled with coins and dropped it into the extended hands of the man.

"Hurry," Shakuni said, "search for the Pandavas and tell them at the right moment what Jayadratha did to Draupadi."

The man bowed and walked out. Shakuni watched him walk past the main gate of the palace and smiled. He had rolled the dice and could hardly wait for the result.

***

"Shall I wring his neck, brother?" Bhima asked Yudhishtra as he tightened his grip on Jayadratha's neck.

Jayadratha's eyes bulged and his fingers clawed at the mud in which he lay face downward. Bhima towered over him, his knees pressing painfully into Jayadratha's back.

Draupadi laughed scornfully. "Oh, not so quickly."

Yudhishtra stood looking at the face of the man who had dared grab Draupadi's hands while she was bathing. When a distraught tribal had told them, gasping and panting, that Jayadratha had abducted Draupadi, he had not believed it. Jayadratha was their cousin Sushala's husband; whatever their differences with Suyodhana, all the Pandavas were fond of their little sister.

Bhima had not waited for permission before rushing off with his other brothers. Yudhishtra had been forced to join them. He did not want to face Draupadi's accusations incase the tribal's story was true.

"I am sorry. Let me go now..." Jayadratha pleaded, every sign of arrogance and hauteur having long fled.

Draupadi laughed. The shrill sound frightened the birds in the trees. Why did she laugh in that way, wondered Yudhishtra, as he remembered the proud but demure Princess they had taken home to Kunti. Jayadratha groaned again as Bhima pressed on his spine.

"It is better we cut off his head." Arjuna pulled out his sword and walked over to where Jayadratha lay grovelling in the mud.

"No. Free him," Yudhishtra said quietly, knowing the others would vociferously disagree with him.

"Free him?" Draupadi's eyebrows arched in mocking surprise. "Oh, that is how the men of the Kuru dynasty deal with men who misbehave with their women. I had forgotten that it runs in the family. Pitamaha abducted women for..."

"Enough!" Yudhishtra said, his voice like iron. "Not another word from you about Pitamaha or anyone else, Draupadi!"

"Of course, I am a woman and not allowed to speak. They strip me in the Sabha and you all quote scriptures and remain silent. This villain tries to abduct me and you let him go free because he is your dear cousin's husband. But I should feel honoured to be the bride of the Kurus, who consider women Goddesses."

"I do not care what Yudhishtra says, Draupadi. If you ask me to, I will wring this man's neck." Bhima rubbed Jayadratha's face in the mud. The King of Sindh uttered a miserable cry.

"Let him go, Bhima. You are the only one who understands me. I have nothing against Sushala, she is a sweet girl. But I pity her having this creature as her husband," Draupadi said in disgust.

Her husbands looked at each other in surprise. Bhima's hands eased and Jayadratha groaned.

"It is generous of you to forgive him," said Yudhishtra.

"Forgive him? I will never forgive him or any man who dares harm a woman just because nature has furnished him with brute force. I free this man as a gift to Sushala and her son. But the world should know what he has done. If Sushala still wants him as her husband after knowing about his deed, may God bless her. I know she will eventually forgive him, as all women do. That is the greatest tragedy. I, too, have done so, as have many other women. If only we would learn that to forgive is also to encourage such acts... No, we will not let this brute go free. His son should grow up knowing his father's shame, so that every time he looks at a woman, he does not see an object of desire."

"Draupadi, he has asked forgiveness..."

Draupadi cut off Yudhishtra, her hand upraised. "Shave his head, Bhima, leaving only five hairs. Tie him up and make him sit back to front on a donkey. Then parade him through the villages, so that the whole world knows of his misdeed."

"No, we either kill him or free him. Insulting him and then letting him go will turn him into a dangerous foe," Arjuna said.

"I have five great warriors as husbands. Why should I fear a man who squirms like a worm in Bhima's hands?" Draupadi asked, her eyes blazing with contempt.

All her husbands, except Yudhishtra, laughed. He walked away, shaking his head and clutching his prayer beads.

"Let the saint go and pray. Arjuna, give me your sword. Our dear brother-in-law here will not mind if I take off some skin with his hair," Bhima said. His brothers laughed in delight.

Later, the ludicrous procession with Jayadratha tied to a donkey, his face blackened and head shaved except for five strands of hair, wound through the villages. While howling urchins danced around them, the villagers beat drums to announce the Donkey King.

**

Shakuni looked at the messenger and ran a smug hand down his grey beard. Then he sent the messenger to inform Suyodhana of how his brother-in-law had been treated by the Pandavas.

**

On the way to Gandhari's chamber, Shakuni whispered into Suyodhana's ear, "Remember, the Pandavas have taken the law into their own hands. They had no right to punish Jayadratha. They should have appealed to you or to the King."

Suyodhana had rushed back to Hastinapura, cutting short his southern journey. How could Jayadratha have committed such folly? Suyodhana only had Shakuni's version to rely on – that Jayadratha had made some lewd remarks in bad taste, about Draupadi. But that did not warrant the punishment he had received at the Pandavas' hands. Shakuni insisted that the rumours about Jayadratha trying to abduct Draupadi were part of the Pandavas' plan to malign Jayadratha and prove Suyodhana to be an incompetent ruler.

When Suyodhana entered the royal chamber, his father was standing with his back to him and Gandhari was seated at a window. Suyodhana motioned to his uncle to remain silent and Shakuni moved to a corner.

"Suyodhana, is my brother with you?" Gandhari asked

"No, mother," replied her son after an instant's hesitation.

Gandhari turned to where Shakuni stood. "Shakuni, leave us." She waited until she was sure her brother had walked out and then turned to Suyodhana. "Your lies are not convincing enough, my son. There is some hope for us still."

"Why did you summon me?" Suyodhana growled.

"Are you mad to order your Aunt Kunti out of Vidhura's old home?"

"Why is my mother so concerned about my aunt?"

"Answer me, son."

"We are evacuating all the houses in that street. Yuyutsu is building a new market there," Suyodhana replied curtly.-

Gandhari pressed her lips together. The sudden cawing of a crow at the window was irksome. "It is not wise to unnecessarily provoke, my son. You will reinstate them with an order from the King. Is it clear, my son?" Gandhari's words were as hard as rock,

"I am sick of this drama, mother. Why must I be generous to the Pandavas when they have done such heinous things to my brother-in-law?"

"Who is this honourable brother-in-law you speak of? The same one who molested a daughter-in-law of Hastinapura?" asked Gandhari, her voice like ice.

"The Pandavas cannot take the law into their own hands and do whatever they please. They should have come to me for justice. I would have punished Jayadratha. Who are they to act in such a high handed manner?"

"Yudhishtra was kind enough to spare Jayadratha's life. I am sure that somewhere in this sordid affair lurks my brother's hand. My sons, Kunti's sons, everyone has become a puppet in his hands. Send him back to Gandhara, Sire!"

"What makes you think he can manipulate me, mother? I pounded Gandhara to dust. My uncle is a changed man. But, by taking the law into their own hands, the Pandavas have thrown me a challenge. I ordered Aunt Kunti out because I decided not to show my cousins any mercy. Enough is enough!"

"But must you go out of your way to provoke them? Just find them during their period of exile and force another twelve years of roaming in the wilderness upon them."

"They get away with so much in the name of *dharma...*" Suyodhana said bitterly.

"Who are you trying to fool, Suyodhana? Neither of you is wholly right. Both of you have made grave errors of judgement."

"Mother, I am fighting for my rights. I have just returned from the South, where I made sweeping changes. My people love me because I am a just ruler," argued Suyodhana, his eyes blazing with passion.

"So you think, my son. This year is crucial. You must find the Pandavas at any cost. Keep an eye on Krishna. Shakuni is no match for him. Krishna will create deliberate provocations to throw you off their path. And you were foolish to go South and then cause mayhem there."

"I did what was right, mother. They were treating my subjects like filthy pigs."

"A great and noble act indeed! Tell me, son, which side will the Confederate armies fight on if there is war?"

"The people will stand by me."

"A good politician knows when to act noble and when to be ruthless. Politics is the art of using others to achieve your goals."

What his mother said made cold-blooded sense, yet how could he have done nothing on seeing the plight of people in the South? He missed his idealistic youth, when he had done as he had pleased. But his mother was right. Having held power for twelve years, it was now difficult to share it with his cousins.

"Son!" Dhritarashtra called. Suyodhana looked at his father in surprise. The tone of his voice was unusually stern. "Listen to what your mother says. Let Kunti remain where she is. And about Jayadratha, forget the entire episode. My spies tell me he was lucky to escape with his life. Had I known the entire story before he left Hastinapura in such a hurry with my daughter and grandson, I would have ordered him to be thrown into the dungeons. You have a lot to learn, Suyodhana. You do not know who to trust and who not to. I will give you some good advice, if you are willing to listen to this blind, old man. Get Jayadratha here and punish him in exemplary fashion. Do not worry what Sushala will think. She is my daughter and she will understand. That is the only way to redeem yourself in the eyes of the public. I could have done it while you were away, but I wanted *you* to do it and show everyone that you do the right thing without caring whether the culprit is a relative, friend, or anyone else."

"But father, I don't think he did..."

"Suyodhana, I used to regret they did not let me be King before Pandu's death. But I knew the answer on the day you tried to disrobe Draupadi so dishonourably. Your mother wanted me to order your arrest and punishment; to strip Karna of his kingship. I felt smug that I was the only man there who tried to correct a wrong. I argued with your mother that Pandu's gambling son deserved nothing better; that it was a small price for the insults I had suffered for having been born blind. She told me then that she was not speaking of *dharma* or taking a high moral stand, but pure strategy. Had I done what she suggested, I would have established my position as the most righteous king in the history of the Kuru clan. But I did not; not because she was wrong, your mother is rarely wrong; I declined because it would have been devastating for you, my son. There is no one dearer to me than you, Suyodhana, not even the throne of Hastinapura. Now I want you to achieve what I could not. My life is spent but you can be the greatest ruler in Bharatavarsha. Do what I say, son. Bring Jayadratha here."

"Father, what you say may be right. I know it is what I should do. But I cannot. Jayadratha is my friend. Even if he had done wrong, is it not my duty to stand by him? "

"You are the Crown Prince of Hastinapura, son. For a King there are no permanent friends or foes," Dhritarashtra said, tapping his stick on the floor in impatience.

"Forgive me, father. I will not seek revenge against the Pandavas for what they have done to Jayadratha, but I cannot punish him. He stood by me when it mattered. Without his three thousand men, Karna could not have conquered the South. I cannot be ungrateful."

"Your son is heedless; worse, he is an emotional fool," snapped Gandhari from her seat by the window. "His friends will be his ruin. It is now too late to act against Jayadratha while Suyodhana's entire trip to the South has been a disaster."

"Mother, I have done what no ruler before has done for the people. They adore me. They have built a temple in my name."

"You will realise your mistake one day, but I am afraid it will be too late then," Gandhari sighed. "Read this." She extended a palm leaf towards Suyodhana. It had Balarama's royal seal.

When he had finished reading, Suyodhana said, "But Kumara is a boy, just sixteen."

"What does that have to do with anything? I have heard Balarama's daughter, Valsala, is a beauty. She would be the perfect wife for our Lakshmana Kumara."

"But mother, have you thought..."

"Suyodhana, it won't hurt you to have Balarama on your side through this alliance."

"Have the children returned from Dwaraka?"

"Not yet. Your boy is not as innocent as he seems. He has succeeded in wooing Balarama's daughter and impressing the Yadavas."

"Has Krishna given his consent to the alliance? He hates me."

"As usual, you underestimate Krishna, my son. He has no permanent enemies or friends," Gandhari replied with a smile.

"Let me think it over. I must discuss it with Bhanu." Suyodhana bowed to his parents and turned to leave the chamber.

"And revoke the order to evict Kunti," Gandhari said to her son's rigid back. Suyodhana reluctantly nodded, knowing his mother would know he had agreed despite her bandaged eyes.

"Valsala and Lakshmana Kumara would make a great pair," Shakuni suggested, limping behind Suyodhana.

"How do you know about the proposal?" Suyodhana asked, irritated.

"Oh, I met the messenger in the palace garden and he told me. What has happened, nephew? It seems you do not trust your old uncle. You think I had my ear to the keyhole?"

Suyodhana said nothing. He had to talk to Bhanumati. He already knew she would agree to whatever their son wanted.

"Suyodhana, people are making fun of us. The Pandavas have insulted your brother-in-law. If we do nothing it would be like accepting Jayadratha's guilt," said Shakuni, hoping to catch the Prince's attention.

"We will hunt for them and blow their cover. Good night." Suyodhana shut the door to his chamber.

Shakuni stood staring at the closed door, his brain in turmoil. Once again his sister had outwitted him. He had expected the Jayadratha episode to flare up into a conflict, but it had fizzled out tamely. He had underestimated the King; his brother-in-law looked and acted like a fool, but it was a deceptive veneer, Shakuni thought with grudging respect. He knew the embers were still simmering; at the right time, he would blow on them. For now he had to accept defeat. But a chaotic Indian marriage offered wide possibilities, with throngs of people milling around. It would also make it easier for him to visit his old friend, Durjaya, in his dungeon. If he could do something to ignite the rivalry between the cousins, it would be a bonus. The dice would roll his way again.

*****

26 SON OF GOD

DWARAKA WAS FULL OF GAIETY. It was the first night of *Navaratri*. Krishna would hold people spellbound with his magical flute and discourse for the next nine nights. Women of all ages fought to dance with the handsome Prince. He bestowed his charm upon all, making every woman feel beautiful, each one special. He was the eternal romantic, the consummate lover. They were enchanting nights, and Princess Lakshmana felt she had arrived in a world of magic.

Subhadra arrived to inquire if Lakshmana had eaten anything. Aunt Subhadra was so beautiful, sighed the young girl. She wondered if there was any truth to the persistent rumour that her father and Subhadra had once been lovers. She could hardly blame him. Sometimes even she wished she was Subhadra's daughter instead of her own stern mother's. She knew she should quell such thoughts. Lakshmana missed her father, but even more than him she missed the one man who always treated her like the Princess she was.

Whenever she had been sad and unhappy, Ekalavya had always been there to console and cheer her. He would bow before her without caring who saw or heard him call her his Little Princess, to the point of making her blush. Their special friendship had started when she was three years old. The Nishada's presence kept many wagging tongues busy but her father had never cared about anyone's lineage, only their abilities. Lakshmana did not even know what lineage meant. Almost twelve years ago Ekalavya had given her his word that he would allow no harm to befall her, ever. She knew they were not playful words said to amuse a little girl, but a promise made with pride, honour and love.

The only thing they disagreed about was Lord Krishna. Like most girls her age, Lakshmana loved to hear the romantic stories the bards spun about the handsome Yadava's childhood. Lord Krishna was an enigma. When Aunt Subhadra had introduced Lakshmana to her brother, the first thought that struck Lakshmana was how handsome he was. His smile lit up the whole world, yet she felt he was smiling just for her. He was kind and considerate and called her 'daughter' while blessing her. Despite herself, Suyodhana's daughter felt she was falling in love with him, like so many hapless women before her. Aunt Subhadra later remarked that her brother had that effect on most women, irrespective of age.

Lakshmana's meeting with Krishna's elder brother had gone according to her expectations. Lord Balarama was just like her father had said – kind and affable. She had formed an awkward friendship with Valsala, Balarama's daughter, who was the same age as her. They chatted about everything under the sun while Abhimanyu tried teaching Kumara archery. Later, the four of them would lie in the garden and stare up at the star-filled sky. Kumara would sing the poems he had composed and Lakshmana would float to a world of romance. Abhimanyu and Valsala often giggled when the Prince sang, and that made her boil with resentment against them both.

This evening was no different. The four of them were sitting on the lawn watching the arrangements for *Navaratri*. Abhimanyu and Valsala sat together and whispered, while Kumara sang. When he finished, there was unexpected applause from near them. "*Shabash*, son!" Krishna stood beaming at them. They had not seen him coming. Valsala and Abhimanyu broke into fits of laughter. Kumara hung his head as if Krishna had caught him doing something shameful. Krishna put an arm around Kumara's shoulders and whispered something into his ear. Kumara's face lit up with joy. Then Lord Krishna pulled out his flute from his waistband and began playing. Kumara closed his eyes in rapture; his beautiful baritone voice rose above the music of the flute in an arc of melody which soared and soared.

When he finished and opened his eyes, everyone in the Dwaraka palace was standing around them, clapping. Kumara looked embarrassed by the first appreciation he had ever received for his talent.

Lord Krishna went up to him and asked softly, "What is the matter, son?"

"I do not wish to be a warrior."

There was a horrified murmuring from the crowd. Valsala giggled with her hand over her mouth. 'How dare she mock my brother?' thought Lakshmana in fury.

"Follow your heart, son. That is your *dharma*. Do not worry about what the world thinks. The world is transient, but you are eternal." Without waiting for an answer, Krishna moved into the crowd and the dancing resumed. Lakshmana had never seen her brother so happy before. Before long, Abhimanyu dragged Kumara into the party frenzy.

Later, she overheard Lord Balarama talking to his wife, Rohini, about how he hoped their Valsala would marry Kumara. When Rohini commented that the young Prince showed no Kshatriya qualities, Balarama replied sharply that the world had enough idiots running around killing each other, without Kumara adding to their number. Though Lakshmana could not help but smile when she heard it, she did not like the idea one bit. Something was obviously going on between her cousin Abhimanyu and Lord Balarama's daughter. She looked at her dreamy-eyed brother sitting near the jasmine bush, his gaze never leaving Valsala. He was hopelessly in love with a girl who scorned him and loved another. Lakshmana thought she would have to keep an eye on Kumara.

But something else was making her uneasy as well. It was as if someone was continually watching her, ravishing her with lustful eyes. She felt naked and vulnerable. She could sense an evil presence near her. Even when Abhimanyu dragged her into the crowd to dance, she could not rid herself of the feeling. For an instant she thought of telling her cousin, but was afraid he would make a joke out of it. What was there to fear among this gay and laughing crowd?

Unexpectedly, a hand reached out between the press of people and pulling down the front of her blouse, groped her breast. Lakshmana was shocked, humiliated and embarrassed. She briefly saw a leering face before the man vanished into the crowd. Lakshmana wanted to scream. How dared he? Even her lips felt frozen. She sat down, the crowd pressing around her, afraid even to cry. The music stopped. Many people had seen the incident and others were now looking at her, asking what had happened. Meaningless questions. She had done nothing wrong. Some bastard had touched her. She sat in terrified silence. 'How will I face everyone? Mother warned me about such situations, about my dress, my walk, my talk,' thought Lakshmana regretfully. She had rebelled, calling her mother old-fashioned. Who would possibly dare touch the daughter of Crown Prince Suyodhana? Her mother's words came back to her with alarming clarity now, that it did not matter whether she was a princess or a beggar, dark or fair, eight or eighty, she was a woman, and men would always be men. It was her duty to be careful. 'I failed you, mother. I am so sorry. I should have been more careful. I feel so ashamed now of my dress, my hair, my face...' Lakshmana pulled at the bodice of her dress, afraid people would gossip about her character.

Aunt Subhadra's hand lifted her chin. Lakshmana wanted to get up and run to some place where nobody knew her, but Subhadra pulled her close. Lakshmana buried her head in Subhadra's bosom and cried. She could hear Lord Balarama shouting orders and people running. She also heard whispers about the inappropriateness of her clothes. Lakshmana closed her ears. Leaning on Subhadra's shoulder, she dragged herself to her room. As she was about to enter, something made her turn back. What she saw would remain with her to her dying day. Lord Krishna was staring at someone, his eyes aflame with murderous rage. Lakshmana's heart stopped. The man who had disgraced her was none other than Lord Krishna's son, Samba. Krishna gazed at his son with disgust and then turned away. Fleetingly, his eyes met hers. They pleaded with her. The great man was begging her not to expose his son.

Lakshmana allowed herself to be pulled into her room. She had lost all interest in being in Dwaraka. Subhadra sat with her for some time, comforting her, but the gaiety outside beckoned. The dancing had resumed. The insult to a woman's modesty was an insignificant hiccup on a festive night. Finally Subhadra left, asking Lakshmana to bolt the door and try to sleep.

Lakshmana sat on the bed watching her shadow dance on the wall as the lamp flickered. The tears dried on her cheeks and she did not know when she slipped into a disturbed sleep. Unknown to her, a pair of eyes were watching her through a crack in the door.

*****

27 LUSTFUL EYES

WHEN LAKSHMANA ARRIVED IN HASTINAPURA, the city was bubbling with excitement. Kumara's marriage was a great occasion and the city streets were festooned with colourful buntings. People had come from all over the country and they broke into spontaneous singing and dancing. She still felt guilty about what had happened at Dwaraka. She would have liked to have told her mother but was unsure how she would take it. The last thing she wanted was for her mother to chaperone her everywhere. Her father seemed to be constantly busy, always with great-uncle Shakuni at his heels. But where was Ekalavya?

That evening, the bridal party arrived from Dwaraka. Krishna and his favourite wife, Rukmini, were the first to alight, followed by Balarama and Rohini. Suyodhana bent to touch Balarama's feet in reverence, as did all the Kauravas. Suyodhana and Krishna bowed politely to each other, followed by a brief, stiff hug. Shakuni, who was standing behind, also bowed to Krishna, who returned the courtesy with a smile – a challenge offered and accepted.

Bhanumati was trying to judge Valsala. No girl in the world would ever be good enough for her son. Abhimanyu tried to joke but his usual vivacity was missing. His long fingers briefly touched Valsala's hand. Lakshmana saw the look that passed between them and almost stopped breathing. Why had Valsala agreed to this match if she was so much in love with Abhimanyu, she wondered fiercely. She had to speak to someone. Her mother was busy with the reception of Krishna's many wives. Lakshmana had to warn her brother.

Suddenly she felt warm breath on the back of her neck. Who could be playing pranks? She turned back in irritation and all the stifled dread of the last few weeks came rushing back. She crossed her hands over her breasts and hurried off to find her mother. Bhanumati immediately began introducing her daughter to Krishna's many wives, all of whom smiled and said how majestic the palace was, how beautiful the gardens, how pretty the whole scene! Caught in an endless round of chatter, Lakshmana kept mumbling greetings, trying desperately to keep her smile in place. But the fear of Samba's presence close by was hard to ignore. Surely she had nothing to worry about? No one would dare touch her here, she kept telling herself. Then she saw him leaning against a pillar, ravishing her with his eyes. Samba winked and gestured obscenely. Even in her father's palace, Lakshmana felt suddenly vulnerable. She was no longer safe.

*****

28 MISSION DANGEROUS

"WHAT DO YOU MEAN, YOU LOVE EACH OTHER? Why on earth did you agree to marry Kumara then?" Krishna asked his niece.

"Father was so happy about it," Valsala said, choking down sobs.

This was getting difficult. While Krishna had never been keen on the marriage, his brother could be obstinate. Besides, Lakshmana Kumara was rather likeable, not at all arrogant like his father. With training, he could be made to understand the nuances of *dharma*. But Valsala's confession had changed everything.

"Leave it to me," Krishna said finally.

Abhimanyu and Valsala looked at each other, relieved. "You are our only hope," Valsala said to her uncle.

Krishna looked at them wryly and placed his hand on his niece's head in affection. The young lovers walked away, leaving Krishna worried. Had he committed to more than he could deliver? Years before, he had rescued his sister Subhadra from Duryodhana on the eve of their marriage. Now it was the turn of Subhadra's son. He would have to make Lakshmana Kumara look like a fool and turn Balarama against Duryodhana in order to compel Duryodhana to call off the marriage. Could he pull it off? He regretted having to do it to Duryodhana's soft-spoken son, but there was no choice. Krishna was one of the few who knew where the Pandavas were hiding. It had now become necessary to talk to Arjuna and ask for Bhima's help. His head whirling with plans, Krishna galloped off in search of the Pandavas. There was no time to lose.

***

"I know, Arjuna, it is not an ideal situation, but we must think of Abhimanyu and Valsala's happiness. Also, if the marriage takes place, it will strengthen Duryodhana's position. It is in our own interest to stop it."

"Abhimanyu should have told us this before. This is a dishonourable thing to do," Yudhishtra mumbled. In the pale moonlight, it was difficult to discern his expression.

Krishna clucked his tongue impatiently. "You want to be the eternal wanderer? Don't you want to sit on the throne of Hastinapura and rule Bharatavarsha as per the tenets of *dharma*?"

Yudhishtra remained silent but a mirthless laugh sounded nearby. Draupadi emerged from the shadows. "Dishonourable? Honour died in the Hastinapura Sabha. Duryodhana and his cronies deserve no mercy."

Krishna smiled at Draupadi. "We have to shame the poor boy but it can't be helped. People must say Lakshmana Kumara is an unworthy husband for Balarama's daughter."

"How will you do it? It's a dangerous game, Krishna," Nakula said.

"Dangerous? Cowards!" Draupadi raised her voice. Her five husbands did not dare meet her gaze. "Krishna, these men, if they can be called that, have grown soft eating nuts and berries. I will come with you instead."

"No, Draupadi," Krishna gently shook his head. "Don't forget the terms. If they recognize you, it will mean another 12 years of exile."

"Tchaw! Conditions of a rigged game of dice; unchallenged because my husbands lacked the courage to do so. Krishna, take me to the palace and I will thrust my dagger down Duryodhana's throat."

"Peace, my lady, peace," Krishna said and turned to Bhima. "I need your help."

"You have only to ask," Bhima instantly replied, bowing low.

"Good. Come with me. We have to go over the mountain to meet someone who is prepared to do anything for you."

"I do not know anyone living over that mountain, Krishna," said Bhima, puzzlement written on his broad, handsome face.

"Ah, but he knows you, Bhima," Krishna replied with a small smile.

"But that is the kingdom of the despicable Ekalavya," Arjuna cried.

"The Nishada will be on his way to attend the wedding. Bhima and I can slip in, do our work and get out fast. It is best that the rest of you proceed to my vassal kingdom of Virata, in disguise. It is the ideal place to finish your incognito period of exile."

"Duryodhana's spies are everywhere. Hiding will be difficult," Yudhishtra said, his voice tinged with weariness.

"Enter Matsya, the capital city, separately. Yudhishtra, you will present yourself as a dice expert. The Virata King is passionate about the game. It will then be simple for you to create a place for yourself as the King's adviser."

"Ah yes! Yudhishtra is indeed an expert in the game of dice," Draupadi said, her mouth twisted with mockery. Everyone laughed, and even Yudhishtra smiled.

"Arjuna can be a eunuch – a teacher of dance and the fine arts."

"Krishna, how can you suggest such a thing?" Arjuna protested as his brothers rocked with laughter and Draupadi nodded in agreement.

"Nakula and Sahadeva can work in the royal stables," Krishna said, ignoring Arjuna's indignant protests.

"And I?" Draupadi asked. In all their plans, she appeared to have been forgotten.

"My lady, you shall be chief maid to the Queen, the *sairandhri*."

"How can she be a maid? Draupadi is a Princess," Bhima protested.

"Princess!" Draupadi snorted. "I will take the position, Krishna, if it is available. At least I will have food to eat and a roof over my head."

"What of Bhima?" Yudhishtra asked quietly.

"Once we are back from our journey, he will apply for a position as a cook in the royal kitchens," Krishna said. Bhima grinned; he had a role he would love to play. "But remember, none of you must ever be seen together," Krishna cautioned. "Now you must be off immediately, before anyone suspects you were here or where you have gone."

Long after the four Pandavas and Draupadi had left, Krishna kept thinking of how to pull off the audacious plan he had in his mind. It all depended on Bhima and Ekalavya not being present.

As day broke over the eastern horizon, Krishna and Bhima rode in silence towards the looming mountain in the north, into the kingdom ruled by the Nishada, in search of a Rakshasi's son.

*****

29 SONS OF FORTUNE

SUSHALA DRAGGED HER SON TO ACHARYA KRIPA. After the shameful episode involving her husband, Jayadratha was as good as lost to her. He was abusive and spent more time in his harem with the women he collected by force or purchase. But she did not dare leave him for ear of the stigma that she had not been able to satisfy her husband. Nor did she dare tell her brother, fearing his wrath. All her hopes were pinned on her son, Suratha. Unfortunately, the boy had failed to meet his mother's great expectations of a warrior son. The boy was afraid of his demanding mother and abusive father and rarely spoke a word. He was not a dreamer like his cousin Lakshmana Kumara, but a boy who feared the world.

"Acharya Kripa, only you can help him," Sushala said, her hands folded before the maverick Brahmin Guru in supplication.

Kripa eyed the shy boy with pity and distaste. He was sitting in his usual place under the tree by the river. People going to the temple bowed to him and the Queen of Sindh as they walked by. Nearby, a cow munched on the banana leaves the priests had carelessly thrown out after distributing *prasad*.

"Are there not enough Gurus in Sindh who can instruct him?"

"None of them as good as you, Guru. They are unable to teach him well," Sushala said, praying Acharya Kripa would agreed. That would give her an excuse to remain in Hastinapura without setting tongues wagging.

Kripa leapt from his seat and punched the little boy. Sushala was shocked at the Guru's action. Suratha began to wail fearfully, clutching his mother's *pallu*. Sushala pulled her son to her, glaring at the crazy Guru.

"Princess, he cannot handle pain. You have made him too soft. It will be an uphill task to make him into a warrior. It would be better to teach him administration and mathematics. Take him to Vidhura. I shall send word to him."

"No, Guru. I wish him to be a great warrior when he grows up. I beg you to take him as your disciple. I will pay whatever you ask." Sushala hated herself for crying in front of the heartless Guru.

Kripa laughed. "Pay? You will pay me from what your husband has stolen from the people of Sindh? I would rather starve to death before I take that money. Moreover, I cannot take payment for a job which I am sure will benefit neither the teacher nor the student. My lady, your son is not destined to be warrior. Why should everyone be a warrior? I am sure the boy will grow up to be a decent man and perhaps a good king, if you let him."

"I want him to be a *Digvijayi*, to be Emperor of Bharatavarsha when the time comes," Sushala blurted, regretting it the moment the words escaped her mouth. Her son clutched her tighter, sniffling. Kripa looked at her with an amused smile and she averted her gaze.

"There are unscrupulous Gurus who will take your money and torture your poor child, badgering him to become what he is not. He is not made to be a warrior. Thank your stars that it is so. Send him to Vidhura."

"I don't want my son to learn from a Shudra. Do you wish the whole world to laugh at him? I know why you do not wish to teach him, Guru. You have always sided with the Pandavas. You think my son will grow up to be a threat to Arjuna one day and so you wish to discourage me."

"I am afraid your son will defeat Arjuna? My lady, the sun is very hot and can muddle the brain of those not used to its harshness. Please go back to the palace."

"Guru, you insult me with your condescending words."

"Pardon me, Princess, I meant no insult. it was but the advice of an old Guru to one who is like a daughter to me. Do not compel your poor son to be what he is not."

"You are not the only Guru, Acharya Kripa. I will hire the best teachers in Bharatavarsha or beyond. Mark my words, my son Suratha will defeat Arjuna one day. Pranaam, Guru. I am sorry to have wasted your valuable time." Sushala turned sharply, dragging her son behind her.

The chariot which had been waiting at a distance, rumbled towards her in a cloud of dust. Without looking back at the Guru, Sushala climbed in and pulled her son up. She asked the charioteer to take them back to the palace. Suratha's skin felt feverish and he moaned with pain. Sushala caressed the shoulder where Kripa had hit him. The bruise had turned blue and begun to swell. How dared the Guru hit a Prince? Kripa got away with everything. For generations, the Kuru Kings had allowed him to behave with no respect towards royalty. There was nothing she could do about it, but she vowed to show him and the world that her son could be a great warrior. She no longer wished to stay in Hastinapura; she would go back to Sindh and hire the best Guru. She would ensure no one called her son a coward.

The chariot jerked forward and Suratha uttered a cry. Sushala slapped him across his face. "Coward! Behave like a man. Do not let me hear you utter another cry," she said fiercely, though her heart broke when she saw Suratha moving away from her in fear. His lips trembled and a tear made its way down his cheek. "Fool! don't cry like a girl. You are a Kshatriya; behave like one."

People on the street paused to look at them but Sushala did not care. The boy had curled up like a centipede on the chariot floor and was sucking his thumb. As the chariot rushed past the palace gates, Sushala felt guilty for what she had done to her son and tried to hug and comfort him, but he wriggled away and jumped out of the moving chariot. He ran off calling for Pitamaha. Sushala snapped at the charioteer to stop and jumped out and ran behind her son. Her anger was getting the better of her.

Suratha crashed into the old man standing near a window trying to read a moth-eaten manuscript and clucking his tongue in irritation. When Bhishma saw that it was his great-grand-nephew, his expression changed to one of affection. Sobbing, Suratha tried to tell him what had happened.

Sushala came running into the room but hesitated when she saw her son clutching the Pitamaha's *dhoti*. She bowed briefly and tried to grab hold of her son.

"You hit him, Sushala?"

The Kuru Princess felt embarrassed, not knowing what to say to one she had always been taught to revere before all others. She looked away, unable to face him. Then her anger came rushing back. She raised her head, looked at Bhishma and said, "Yes, I hit him. He is a shame to the Kuru dynasty, to Chandravamsha itself."

For a moment, she reminded Bhishma forcefully of Suyodhana. The same pride, the same defiance of fate. Then he said softly, "He is not of the Kuru dynasty, Sushala, but a Prince of Sindh."

His words were like a knife in Sushala's heart. Was she not a Kuru? But Pitamaha was right, Suratha was Jayadratha's son, and she merely a visitor to her parents' home. She was no longer a Kuru Princess. Neither she nor her son had any claim on the great dynasty of Bharata. She was just the Queen of a petty vassal state, the wife of a King who abducted the wife of other men and was then paraded with his head shaved. She did not want to remain on Hastinapura soil. She would return to Sindh and ensure her son began a dynasty more illustrious than the Kurus. She grabbed her son and dragged him out of Pitamaha's room. The terrified boy paused for a moment, hoping Pitamaha would save him from his mother, but Bhishma stood like a stone statue, silent and aloof.

"Suratha, you will defeat your uncle, Arjuna, one day and rule all of Bharatavarsha. I don't want to see you crying again," Sushala said, dragging him through the palace corridors.

The boy flinched when he saw the amusement in the guards' faces even as they bowed; he blushed when the maids whispered to each other, pointing at him. He did not want to go to Sindh, he wanted to remain in Hastinapura, with Pitamaha and his grandfather, who treated him to sweets and listened to his little stories with an attention no one else gave to his words. He wanted to be with his grandmother, who made him laugh with the stories of her father's kingdom in the distant snow-clad mountains.

Sushala was still telling him how he would fight Arjuna one day. Suratha was scared. He knew his uncle was the ferocious warrior who had punished his father for something he had done. He was scared to go to Sindh, scared of facing Arjuna one day. If only his mother would listen to him.

***

"Father!" Khatotkacha could not believe his eyes. Bhima had come in search of him! How happy his mother would be! And it was all thanks to this dark and handsome man. Perhaps he was indeed what people said of him, that he was an *avatar* of Vishnu. Khatotkacha fell at Krishna's feet.

"No, my child, first seek your father's blessing," Krishna said to the young Rakshasa prostrate on the ground before him.

Khatotkacha stood up, moved to where Bhima stood in complete silence, and bent to touch his feet. His cousin, Iravan, watched from a distance. Until now, they had both been the unwanted sons of their fathers, but today everything had changed for Khatotkacha. Iravan felt hot tears sting his eyes.

Krishna quickly explained to Khatotkacha what Bhima required him to do. When he finished, Khatotkacha looked at both men in confusion. "But I have nothing against Prince Duryodhana or his son. Why should I spoil the marriage?"

"We too do not have anything against Lakshmana Kumara, son, but we have to do this for two people who love each other." Krishna hurriedly stepped in to fill Bhima's silence.

"Father, is this really what you want me to do?" Khatotkacha asked.

Bhima had not spoken a word since they had arrived, merely standing beside Krishna. Now he gave the smallest of nods.

Khatotkacha turned to Krishna. "I will do it, Swami, for my father."

"You know that if they catch you, Duryodhana will flay you alive?"

"I do it for my father. It is my *dharma*." Khatotkacha wished with all his heart that his father would look at him, but Bhima's face appeared to be set in stone, his eyes gazing into the distance.

"Do you wish to meet my mother?" Khatotkacha asked Bhima.

Krishna looked at Bhima and read the refusal there. He gently shook his head at the eager teenager. For a fleeting moment, pity touched his heart.

Khatotkacha knew he should not have asked. Before he could say anything more, Krishna and Bhima had turned away and left. 'Father, wait!' he cried silently. 'Let me show you my aim with the arrows, my power with the mace. Do not go!' The words never left his lips. Silently he watched his tall father vanish like a dream.

"You are lucky, cousin," Iravan said, trying not to sound jealous.

"We may be untouchables, Iravan, but surely one day our fathers will need us," replied Khatotkacha.

"Can I come with you?"

"It will be dangerous."

"Then I should be with you."

Khatotkacha looked at his cousin in surprise. Iravan was jealous but that was not going to stop him from risking his life. Khatotkacha nodded. His cousin's face bloomed into a smile like a wild flower.

Later, as he rode towards Hastinapura in the dead of night, a strange fear gripped Khatotkacha. Had Vasuki not warned them against interfering in the affairs of the Pandavas and Kauravas? He reminded himself that his *dharma* was not to think about the consequences of his actions, but merely to do what his father wanted. They rode in silence towards Hastinapura's brightly lit palace, trying not to think about the dangerous mission they had undertaken.

*****

30 THE BOY LOVER

SUYODHANA HURRIED TOWARDS THE SABHA. The courtiers rose as he walked in with Bhanumati and Lakshmana. The Royals bowed before the elders and then waited for the bridegroom to arrive. The sounds of a commotion arose above the murmuring of the *mantras* and every head turned towards the door. Balarama pulled Kumara into the Sabha, an iron grip on his arm. The young Prince had tears running down his face.

Bhanumati tried to rush to her son but Suyodhana held her back. "Guru Balarama, what is the meaning of this?"

"You want to know the meaning, Suyodhana? It means I have been a fool. My wife was against this marriage, my brother too, yet I went against them, thinking he was your son, that I could make amends for what happened to you years ago."

"What has my son done?" Bhanumati cried, tears in her own eyes.

"Sister, you will not wish to hear it in public. I will explain later. Regretfully, we must call off this marriage," Krishna said.

"Enough of your games, Krishna. You want to call off the marriage without giving us a reason?" Suyodhana turned and demanded of the younger Yadava.

"Suyodhana, my friend, did I not say I would tell you later, not here in public? You will regret it if you insist, believe me," Krishna replied, urging discretion.

"You insult me and then say you will explain later? Tell me now!"

"Such things are better spoken of in private," Krishna replied.

"I know my son, Krishna. What is it that he has done?"

"Remember it was you who insisted on hearing this publicly. Your son was found in bed with a boy."

"What?" Suyodhana stood in trembling disbelief before rushing towards his son, his face red with rage. Bhanumati grabbed his arm trying to stop him but he roughly pushed her away. He slapped Kumara, leaving the imprint of his fingers on his son's pale face. "Who was the boy? Bring him to me now!" Suyodhana yelled, his voice shaking with anger and humiliation. Soldiers ran out to search for the culprit.

"Suyodhana, just listen to what the boy has to say first." He heard Bhishma's voice but shook his head. No, he did not need further elaborations. Bhanu was crying, Lakshmana was pleading. Enough said and heard. All he wanted was to get his hands around the throat of his son's lover. Suyodhana clenched his fists and closed his eyes. How his vassal Kings and the Priests would laugh at his expense. It was a curse having such a son! He should have killed him long ago. No wonder Kumara was uninterested in archery, no wonder he was afraid of weapons, he was just an effeminate queer! How was he to entrust his empire to such a son when the time came? The shame of it! All Bharatavarsha would hear that Suyodhana had such a son.

The Sabha emptied quickly. Suyodhana could hear the whispers fading away. A few people came to offer their sympathies but most just turned away. Karna spoke conciliatory words and Bhishma tried to chide him. Aswathama said he would find the other boy. Bhanumati stood in silence. Suyodhana did not understand a word anyone said. He did not care.

Soon he was alone in the cavernous Sabha. He vaguely heard someone say that the other boy had escaped. They had found him in the royal kitchen. After having gagged and tied up six kitchen workers, he was devouring the wedding food with relish. It was almost as if he he had been waiting for someone to discover him. When the soldiers arrived, he wrecked the kitchen, overturning vessels, toppling stoves and setting fire to the structure. While the soldiers battled the flames, the boy climbed the fort wall like a monkey and disappeared. He had someone waiting for him with a horse. The hunt for him was on.

"Who was he?" Suyodhana asked the soldier standing before him.

"We do not know, Sir. He was dark and wild-looking, like a Rakshasa."

"Leave me!" His son preferred a Rakshasa boy to the beautiful daughter of his Guru?

The last of the torches finally died. The darkness became perfect.

*****

31 KIRATHARJUNEEYAM

EKALAVYA READ HIS GOD-DAUGHTER'S letter again. Something about the missive troubled him. It did not contain the usual banter that always brought a smile to his lips. He had decided not to attend Kumara's marriage, preferring not to open himself to insult again. But the letter made him change his mind. Lakshmana had written to say that her brother was marrying the wrong girl, who was in love with her cousin, Abhimanyu. What worried him was the footnote. She said someone was stalking her and she was afraid. He had to go.

Ekalavya started for Hastinapura early in the morning. The forest was drier than he could ever remember. He was worried as he rode over the rocky beds of the dry mountain streams. Why was his *manasaputri* Lakshmana afraid? His horse became restless. It raised its head and sniffed the air, ears pointed ahead. Something had stirred in the bush ahead, perhaps a wild boar. Nothing was more dangerous than standing in the way of a charging boar. Ekalavya prodded his horse to move sideways and alighted behind a tree.

The bush ahead shook and then fell silent again. Ekalavya cautiously took his bow from his shoulder and placed an arrow. A man suddenly appeared to his right, walking straight towards the bush. Fool! Could he not read the signs of the forest? The stranger was carrying a bow and a quiver of arrows. He wore a sword at his waist. But would he have the time to use the weapons? Perhaps he was an out-of-work soldier, thought the Nishada, fed up with fools from the cities wandering around in the forest as if the jungle was a picnic spot. It was one of the worst droughts in living memory and the beasts were desperate for food and water.

Ekalavya wanted to cry out a warning but that might have provoked the wild boar to charge. The bush stirred once more and the stranger stopped in his tracks. The boar charged with a grunt and Ekalavya let go his arrow. He was sure his arrow had found its mark from the squeal of the boar but that fool had to be pushed away from the beast's path. Wild boars were ferocious creatures. Even if he had hit his mark, the boar would still charge before succumbing. Ekalavya screamed to the stranger to move away and rushed to pull the man off the path. Then he saw the boar lying dead at the stranger's feet.

"Fool! What are you gaping at? But for my arrow, your intestines would be lying on the earth now."

The man stared at the Nishada, then knelt on the ground and turned the boar over. Ekalavya was shocked. He had expected to see his arrow embedded in the boar's throat, instead, there were two – a hair's breadth apart. Who had shot the second arrow? Who could shoot that well?

"Shooting dead beasts and then putting on airs, Kirata?" The man asked, pulling out his arrow from the still body of the beast.

Arjuna! No wonder Ekalavya had not even see him shoot. But how dared he come into his forest lands and then abuse him? "Have some gratitude, Pandava. If not for my arrow..."

"The day Arjuna has to depend on a Kirata to save him from a small beast is the day he should die," Arjuna said with disdain as he wiped the arrowhead in the grass. "Kirata, take your arrow and begone. You may even take the boar I shot as a reward for your labour."

"Apologize for those words, or die!" Ekalavya hissed, his sword pressing hard against Arjuna's neck.

With one swift movement Arjuna pierced the Nishada's foot with the arrow tip he was holding. Ekalavya yelled in pain. Arjuna stepped away, his bow gleaming in his hands, his eyes mocking the Nishada, daring him to fight.

Ekalavya gritted his teeth to ward off the pain and cursed Arjuna. His left foot was bleeding but that was not going to stop him. He would have preferred this encounter to have taken place in front of all the nobles and great men who had treated him like an irksome insect. Over two decades of rivalry had to be settled today. Arjuna had not recognized him, Ekalavya thought with a bitter smile. But he would tell him before he killed him. By Shiva, he was going to finish the arrogant Pandava today! Ekalavya put his sword down and picked up his bow. He stood poised to meet Arjuna.

Before he could blink, an arrow swished past his throat. "The next shot will not be so merciful," Arjuna told him.

Ekalavya replied with three arrows in succession. The first broke Arjuna's bow, and the other two pierced each of Arjuna's shoulders. "The next one is for your black heart," the Nishada mocked.

Arjuna pulled the arrows out and threw them to the earth. He unsheathed his sword and pointed it at the Nishada. Ekalavya flung his bow down and grabbed his sword. 'Gods of the forests, be my witness,' he whispered and charged at Arjuna.

The swords clashed with great force, each man determined to kill his opponent. Both men fought in deadly silence but the trees around them rang with agitated bird cries. Sparks flew from their swords and the parched grass beneath their feet began to smoke.

It was difficult holding the sword with four fingers. Ekalavya's ghost thumb hurt but he would not give up. Not to Arjuna. That burning smell. Ekalavya knew what was coming. Soon the dry scrub would be crackling with fire. He had to settle this quickly; a moment's loss of concentration would end his life. His horse neighed in fear as a tree fell with a loud crash. Unmindful, the two warriors fought on. The heat became unbearable. Thick smoke enveloped them and they were soon choking and coughing for breath.

In a quirk of fate, Arjuna stumbled on a dry root and fell on his back. Ekalavya kicked away Arjuna's sword and placed a foot on his chest. It was over. He raised the sword high over his head with both hands. But Arjuna needed to know who had defeated him before he died.

"Do you know who I am?" Ekalavya pressed his foot down hard, pinning Arjuna to the ground.

Arjuna was choking. "I know..."

The forest echoed with Ekalavya's laughter. It was enough. His victory was complete. Yet he wanted to hear it from Arjuna's mouth. "Tell me who I am," he said, leaning over Arjuna, his sword raised.

"You are Lord Shiva."

"Shiva! Do I look like Lord Shiva to you?" Ekalavya demanded, more amused than angry.

"No untouchable can defeat a Kshatriya. You are none other than Lord Shiva, the greatest of all Gods," Arjuna mumbled.

"Does this remind you of something?" Ekalavya said, thrusting his hand in Arjuna's face.

As Arjuna stared at the four fingers, all colour drained from his face. He turned his head away away and mumbled, "You are Shiva. You are Shiva."

There was no point in killing Arjuna in the wilderness with no witnesses. The world would never know that a Nishada had defeated the greatest of all Kshatriyas in a fair fight. Arjuna's punishment would be the knowledge that a Nishada had defeated him – a Nishada without a thumb!

"No Kirata can defeat me," Arjuna mumbled again.

Ekalavya took his foot off Arjuna's chest. "You are right. I am Shiva. Who is not Shiva? What boon shall I bestow upon you?"

Arjuna sat up, burning with shame at the insult. Fire was raging inside him as much as it was around him in the forest. "Give me your bow." His voice was barely audible.

"You think I won because there is some magic in my bow? You can accept magic but not a Nishada getting the better of you, Arjuna? Here, take it, the bow is yours. Consider it the divine bow of Shiva, *Pashupatha* itself. Take it and get out of my forest!" Ekalavya said with disdain as he threw the bow at Arjuna's feet.

He laughed as the Pandava stooped to pick it up. Ekalavya raised his hand in mock blessing. For a brief moment Arjuna's eyes lingered on the four fingers and the non-existent thumb, then he walked away through the smoke, carrying Ekalavya's bow.

As he watched Arjuna's fading figure, the elation Ekalavya felt was overwhelming. This was the moment he had lived for. He had finally beaten Arjuna, the great Pandava! Arjuna, the favourite of Guru Drona! An untouchable had achieved the impossible. Perhaps Arjuna was right and he was no ordinary mortal. He was Shiva, the God of Gods. Despite himself, his feet started moving. The forest fire raged around him. He could hear the beat of a *dumru* and feel the flames on his body. 'I am the Creator, I am the Preserver, and I am the Destroyer. I am SHIVA..' The Nishada danced the *tandav* as if the end of the world was at hand.

In the palace Lakshmana waited for Ekalavya to come, while evil eyes devoured her youth and beauty.

*****

32 THE STALKER

WHY WOULD HER FATHER NOT LISTEN? Lakshmana had tried speaking to him as he sat alone in the Sabha, but Suyodhana had ordered her away. She had run out stifling a sob. He had never behaved with her in that manner before. But he had to know the truth. Perhaps it would be better to wait until morning when his anger would have cooled. Then she would explain everything. Her brother was innocent; he was being framed.

Lakshmana and her mother had dragged Lakshmana Kumara to his room. His cheek was still bleeding from the slap he had received from their father. How could Suyodhana be so cruel? Kumara was reluctant to talk. It took a lot of cajoling for him to open up.

That evening, when everyone was at their prayers, Abhimanyu had whispered into Kumara's ear that Valsala wished to meet him. Enamoured and besotted, he had gone to the tryst. He found her in a playful mood and she had invited him into her room. Once he was inside, she had slipped out and locked the door from the outside. He had shouted out to her but had been thrown onto the bed by strong hands. A dark man had pinned him down. The next thing he remembered was Balarama standing at the door glaring at them. There were many others behind him. The man who had pinned him to the bed, grinned, planted a kiss on both his cheeks and then jumped out through the window. Despite Kumara's protests, Balarama had dragged him to the Sabha.

Abhimanyu's betrayal wounded Kumara more than anything else. Lakshmana insisted they discuss it with their father but her brother would not listen. Why did her father dislike Kumara so much? When she walked back to her chamber, the night had almost gone. She entered and threw her gold-embroidered upper garment onto a chair and got into bed. But sleep did not cast its merciful mantle over her even when her tired head touched her pillow. She tossed from side to side in her bed. Why did she suddenly feel afraid? Rising, she looked around her as she took the upper garment from the chair where she had cast it, and wrapped herself in it. Was someone watching her? She was afraid to close her eyes. She missed her godfather, Ekalavya. Why had he not come? She had written to him about her fears, yet he had not come. Neither the Nishada nor the Princess were aware how grievous would prove the cost of that delay.

***

Samba had been waiting in the shadows for hours for the sweet little thing to return to her chamber. He pressed further into the shadows as he saw her come. How beautiful she was! He heard her tossing about on her bed and waited impatiently for her to fall asleep. When the only sound he heard was that of the crickets in the garden, he tiptoed towards the door, making sure no one was around to see him enter. He had been stalking this girl from Dwaraka. When he had laid eyes on her a few months ago at the Yadava palace, he had decided he had to have her at any cost. For several days he had followed her, his fantasies running wild, his eyes roving over her beautiful body, imagining her in his arms. He had discovered that she was the daughter of the Crown Prince of a Northern territory and that her father was an evil but powerful man, according to rumours. Now, having seen the great city of Hastinapura, he realised she was a good catch as well. Samba was uninterested in politics. His father was considered to be an avatar of Vishnu. He chuckled at the thought. Who would dare challenge the son of a God?

Samba had seen Krishna entering Balarama's room. The marriage had been called off because the groom preferred boys. Samba felt like laughing. His father would even now be in his uncle's room, discussing Valsala's future. Everyone knew she was sweet on his cousin, Abhimanyu, but still they had wanted her to marry Suyodhana's queer son. Politics! Perhaps his uncle would permit Valsala to marry Abhimanyu now. Balarama had to save face. Somewhere in the whole episode was his father's hand.

Krishna had become intolerant of late. There had been no need for Krishna to slap and shout at him the night he had casually groped this cute little thing. In some corner of his mind, Samba feared his father's patience would snap one day and there would be hell to pay. But he had worked out a way to keep his father in check. His mother, Jambavati, was a Vanara woman of the Jamabavan tribe. His father felt guilty that his other wives did not treat the Vanara woman well. Samba had grown up watching his mother fight bitter battles with Krishna's other wives. They called her monkey-woman and him a monkey-child. His father tried to compensate by being more gentle and kind with them both.

Samba grew up to be wild and uncontrollable. Though just twenty, he was an alcoholic and indulged in rampant promiscuous behaviour. When charm did not work, he did not hesitate to use force. Few women dared resist him because he was as ruthless as he was vengeful. Though *soma* and excessive indulgence had started taking their toll on him, he had inherited his father's powerful physique and charm. He was generous with money and trinkets. Each time he got into trouble, his father bailed him out, hushing up the incident. Every time it ended the same way, with his father shouting and threatening. Samba would act repentant and beg his father's forgiveness. His mother would join in pleading with Krishna. If nothing else worked, his mother would use her usual weapon, saying Krishna was being cruel to them because they were Vanara. That usually ended with his helpless father forgiving him.

Samba knew he had to keep away from his Uncle Balarama. Twice, the old man had ordered him to be whipped in public.

He had escaped both times because his father had pleaded with the Yadava King. He was going to take his revenge on the old man one day. For now, he had no other thought except that he wanted this beautiful girl. Groping her mango-shaped breast had only served to inflame his lust. Though she had cried and made a scene, he was sure she had enjoyed his touch. Girls were like that, he thought, creating a fuss when someone gave them what they ached for.

Samba took out his knife and looked around again. No one was around. Perfect. Without a sound he inserted the knife into the gap between the door panels. He had to work the bolt with care but he had done it often it enough, with other women. They would act shocked at first but before long they would be enjoying it as much as he did. Which woman could resist a handsome man like him?

Her perfume maddened him. He could imagine his hands all over her. Samba tried to find the bolt with the sharp edge of his knife. To his surprise the door swung open soundlessly. Ah, there she was, lying on the bed with her eyes closed, her body so inviting. He was sure she had left the door unlocked in anticipation. He knew women. He hoped whatever darned business Krishna had with his uncle, would keep him away the whole night. Samba bolted the door. Biting his lip he walked towards Suyodhana's daughter.

*****

33 Vengeance

EKALAVYA WAS ANNOYED AT HIMSELF. He had wasted precious time indulging in self-congratulation. Enough of playing God. His horse had run away from the forest fire and he had spent half a day searching for it. The Nishada was worried about his god-daughter. By the time he reached the outskirts of Hastinapura, his horse was frothing at the mouth and on the verge of collapse. The streetlights were being lit as he entered the city gates.

Something was amiss. The colourful streamers and festoons still hung in the streets but the sense of festivity was missing. The city looked almost empty. An alarming silence prevailed. What had happened? Ekalavya could feel his heart thudding in his chest. People moved away when they saw him riding towards the palace. He tried asking a few pedestrians about the marriage of the Prince but the answers he received were vague. The marriage had been called off for some reason and the Yadavas had left for Dwaraka a few hours earlier.

As Ekalavya entered the fort, Karna's chariot rattled past with a band of soldiers following. Ekalavya called out to him but Karna did not stop. He and his soldiers disappeared in a cloud of dust. Another group of soldiers appeared, led by Aswathama. This time, Ekalavya blocked their path.

"Get out of my way," Aswathama shouted, trying to control his restive mount.

"What has happened? Why was the marriage called off?" Ekalavya asked his friend.

"You don't know? Move away. Suyodhana's daughter is missing."

"What?"

"She was last seen by her mother and brother in the early hours. We fear the worst. Perhaps the girl has eloped with her lover. Poor Suyodhana. Yesterday his son shamed him before the whole world, and today it is his daughter."

"Aswathama, don't talk such nonsense about my Princess!" Ekalavya's hands were shaking, his throat felt scorched and dry. 'Oh, Shiva! I have failed my daughter. If only I had not squandered my time playing God.' With a shaking hand he wiped the sweat from his brow. Where could she be? In her letter she had said someone was stalking her.

"I have no time to argue. Everyone is searching for her. It's a scandal."

"Why was the marriage called off?" Ekalavya wanted to know.

"Apparently Suyodhana's son prefers boys. What a shame! And now his daughter is missing."

"She has not eloped. Someone was stalking her."

"What? Why didn't she tell her father? Who could kidnap her from the palace?"

"I got a letter yesterday. She wrote it at least three or four days before but only sent it when the Yadavas arrived. Now we know where to look for her."

"If it was indeed a Yadava, then it isn't going to be easy rescuing her. She might have met him at Dwaraka and fallen in love. If we make a mistake, it will mean battle with the Yadavas," Aswathama warned.

"Battle! Brahmin, my daughter's honour is at stake. She has not absconded with anyone. You and your politics! Let me go in search of Lakshmana. If I start a war, so be it. I will hunt down the bastard who dared touch my daughter. I don't care whether he is a Yadava, a Gandharva or God."

Ekalavya did not wait to hear the Brahmin's objections. He had to drag whoever had harmed his Princess to Hastinapura and then tear him limb from limb. The Nishada galloped off along the royal highway towards Dwaraka, hoping against hope that he was not too late, that he would find Lakshmana before the devil had... no, he could not bear to even think about it.

*****

34 VANARAPUTRA

"FOOL! DO YOU EVEN KNOW what you have done?" Krishna was furious.

Samba chewed on a blade of grass nonchalantly while Jambavati stood between her angry husband and her unrepentant son.

"What is there to be so angry about, Father? I liked the girl so I took her. Have you not done the same in your youth?" Samba retorted.

"How dare you speak to me this way?"

"You have 16,008 wives and you are giving me advice?" Samba shook with laughter.

"Samba, apologize to your father. Beg for mercy," Jambavati said quickly before Krishna could react.

When Krishna had killed the Narakasura years before, he had freed 16,000 women from the harem. The priests had ordered that, as widows, the women had to commit *sati*. As an act of compassion, Krishna had brought them to Dwaraka to save them from such a horrible fate. Except for eight, the others were his wives only in the sense that he had given them protection. How dared Samba use it to justify his own loathsome actions?

"Jambavati, move away. This brute does not deserve to live." Krishna moved threateningly towards his son.

Jambavati, arms outstretched, pleaded with tears in her eyes. "Prabhu, forgive him. He is your son."

"Do you see any remorse for what he has done, Jambavati? He has no conscience or feelings of guilt. What have you done with the girl?"

"Oh, I left her in the forest. I had a good time. When I left, she was feigning sleep. Don't I know these girls…" Samba said with a leer.

"Fool! Do you think Duryodhana will remain silent? Do you think your Uncle Balarama will let you go free? If my brother decides to behead you, I will be there to cheer him on. Jambavati, stop bawling. I must kill this viper." So saying, Krishna whipped out his disc.

"You do what you must, Prabhu. Behead him with your own hands. After all, we are mere Vanaras. It is my fate that my husband is going to kill our only son. Kill me too, Prabhu," Jambavati cried.

Krishna watched helplessly as his wife beat her breasts and wailed in a loud voice. His other wives stood at the door, agog with curiosity. Krishna burned with shame at this public humiliation. His son would certainly bring death and disaster to the tribe. Samba had manipulated him again. Oh, the indignity of falling at Duryodhana's feet, thought Krishna. What had he done to deserve such a son?

"Your son has only one way to save his head," Krishna said, his voice faltering as he saw the smile on his son's lips. "He must marry Duryodhana's daughter."

"Why, when I have already enjoyed her?"

Krishna pushed away Jambavati's restraining arms and caught Samba by the neck. The youngster was no match for his father. Krishna pressed the sharp edge of his disc on his son's throat and hissed, "You are worse than any Rakshasa I have ever slain."

At last Samba's eyes went wide with fear. "Forgive me, Father. I will do as you say. I will marry her. Save me from my Uncle Balarama and Prince Duryodhana. I will obey you, Father."

His son was quaking in fear. Coward! Disgusted, Krishna threw Samba to the floor. He grabbed his father's legs, weeping. Jambavati fell at Krishna's feet, pleading for her son's life. Finally,

Krishna's clenched fist relaxed. He curtly told mother and son to rise from the floor and stop their wailing. He had no idea how he would avoid a conflict with Duryodhana. This was not the time for battle, not with the Pandavas away. He would lose face by begging Duryodhana, but there was no other way.

"Stay here. Let me talk to Balarama." With a heavy heart, Krishna left the chamber. Had he paused a moment to listen, he could perhaps have saved the Yadavas and their city from total annihilation.

The moment Krishna left, Samba said to his mother, "My father and his empty threats! Why should I marry that girl? What wrong have I done? She was asking for it... the way she dressed, the way she danced... I will stay away from him for a few days. Send me word when his anger subsides."

Samba vanished into the night without waiting for his mother's reply.

*****

35 THE WRETCHED

PAIN. SHE COULD SMELL BLOOD, smell the dryness of the earth on which she lay. She could smell him on her and gagged. It hurt where he had hit her. She bit her swollen lips and moaned. Her tears had dried up long ago. She heard the sound of hooves getting closer. Someone was coming in search of her. She wanted to crawl behind the nearest bush and die there. She tried to get up, to cover her shame with her hands, and drag herself from the world's unforgiving gaze. 'No one should see me like this,' Lakshmana whimpered. 'I want to die. I want to die before anyone gets here and sees my shame.'

Someone covered her with a shawl. She seized it, covering even her fingertips. Karna's face was set in a grim mask as he lifted up her shuddering body. 'Oh, he knows I am dirty,' Lakshmana sobbed silently as she buried her face in Karna's chest. The cold touch of his armour was somehow soothing. He lowered her onto the chariot floor and she lay there, coiled into a ball. Thankfully, he did not ask any questions. The chariot turned towards Hastinapura. How would she ever face her parents, her brother, the world?

When the chariot finally slowed and halted, Lakshmana heard a familiar voice. Uncle Ekalavya! Her heart leapt joyfully before sorrow overwhelmed her again. How could she even look at him?

There was a brief argument between Karna and Ekalavya. Lakshmana trembled when a hand touched her shoulder. "My Princess...forgive me..." Ekalavya's voice was hoarse with pain.

Lakshmana's tears broke like a summer flood. "You are too late."

Then came the question she feared the most. "Who did this to you?"

The name was cursed! But Ekalavya would not leave her alone. He put his arm around her shoulder gently and lifted her chin with his other hand. "Princess...tell me who did this to you."

Lakshmana looked away and whispered, "Samba, son of Krishna."

Ekalavya stood up and drew his sword. Through her sobs she could just hear him say, "Princess, you will have him before sunrise." And he was gone.

'Don't go! Do not leave me alone!' Her plea remained unspoken, except in her aching heart.

The chariot started moving again, travelling towards her father's palace. Lakshmana murmured a prayer. Ekalavya had gone in search of Krishna's rogue son. She was afraid to even think of the consequences, whether he succeeded or failed. She chewed on the fringe of her shawl, her hands shaking as if she were afflicted with palsy. 'Oh, Shiva, let me die!' Lakshmana shut her eyes, trying to shake off the image of the leering Samba from her mind. She tried not to imagine what awaited Ekalavya as he galloped towards Dwaraka.

Why had the chariot stopped? A blood-chilling howl filled the air. It rose and ebbed and then rose again. Terrified, Lakshmana opened her eyes. A beggar was dragging a dog from their path. Karna held the reins and waited, trying not to let the compassion he felt overcome him. But even as the chariot drove on, leaving the beggar and his dog far behind, the agonised howling refused to fade away.

*****

36 Retribution

A MAN SNEAKED OUT, LOOKED AROUND furtively, and then darted towards the shelter of the trees. Perhaps a deserter, thought Ekalavya. The man could lead him to Samba. He walked forward noiselessly and crouched behind a bush, as silent as a big cat stalking its prey. A bat whizzed past his head screeching but it did not disturb the man of the forest. Noiselessly, Ekalavya pounced on the man, pinning him to the ground. The man uttered a profanity. Ekalavya hit him across the face and waited. When the coughing and whining stopped, the man muttered something and Ekalavya bent to hear.

"You...untouchable...you do not know who you are playing with..."

This was no ordinary soldier. "Who are you?" Ekalavya hissed.

"You Nishada, you don't know who I am? I am the son of Krishna... You will pay for this."

Samba! Ekalavya punched him with all his strength, flattening his nose. He waited till Samba's screams faded to a whimper and then punched him again, knocking out a few teeth. "Father... father...help me..." Samba whined. Ekalavya waited.

Some soldiers were animatedly pointing towards the woods. Ekalavya knew he did not have much time but he was determined the scoundrel would not have the good fortune to die a quick death. First he would drag this stinking monster before the Hastinapura Sabha and show them what a Nishada could do while they, the Kshatriyas, still sat debating the rights and the wrongs. Then he would kill Samba, inch by inch.

"Help!" Samba cried as another man emerged from the Yadava camp.

Ekalavya's heart skipped a beat. Krishna! Another tall man came out and the two men began to argue. Samba tried to cry out but Ekalavya clamped his mouth shut. He tore a piece from his shawl and shoved it into Samba's mouth, gagging him. Then he kicked Samba in the ribs until he lost consciousness. Grabbing Samba's long hair, Ekalavya began dragging him towards his horse.

"Hey, you!" Krishna roared and began running towards the woods.

There was no time to lose. Ekalavya hoisted Samba upon his shoulder and staggered on. Samba was heavier than he had thought. He whistled and his horse broke through the undergrowth, almost knocking down Krishna. The Yadava was quick to roll away, getting back on his feet in one swift movement. Ekalavya dumped Samba's unconscious form on his horse and mounted. Krishna's *Sudharshana* whistled past his throat, splintering a tree behind him. Ekalavya kicked his horse and it shot off like an arrow. Krishna dived to catch the fleeing horse but could not get his hands to the reins.

Ekalavya galloped on towards Hastinapura with his quarry. It was just a matter of time before the fearsome Narayana Sena would give him chase. He kept his dagger pressed to the unconscious Samba's throat. When the Narayana Sena caught up with him, he wanted to be sure to take Samba with him to the abode of Yama.

After a while, Ekalavya wondered why no arrows were whizzing past him and why he did not hear the rumble of chasing chariots. His horse galloped but his heart raced even faster. When he finally looked back, emptiness stretched to the horizon. Where was Krishna's army? Somehow, that was even more terrifying.

*****

It was frustrating trying to reason with Kritavarma. Had it not been for the adamant General, he would have caught the Nishada and saved his son.

"Ekalavya has kidnapped my son and you stand here arguing with me? Do you not know what Duryodhana will do when he lays hands on Samba?"

"Krishna, your son is lucky to face Suyodhana and not me. He deserves a painful death," Kritavarma replied coldly.

The General was right. For a brief moment Krishna thought it would be better to let the Nishada kill his son. Loud wailing shook him from his reverie as a hysterical Jambavati came running towards him. 'Oh Lord Brahma! Save me from this woman,' Krishna prayed.

"Prabhu, you are his father, the saviour of all..."

Krishna sighed wearily. "Jambavati, he is a criminal."

"Would you say the same if it was Satyabhama's or Rukmini's son? Samba is a Vanara, so nobody cares if he dies, not even his father..."

"Enough!" Krishna snapped and turned to the General. "I know, Kritavarma, I know. He is a blot on our race, but he is still my son. I will go to Dur...Suyodhana and beg his forgiveness. I will ensure Samba marries Suyodhana's daughter to save her honour."

"You'd better talk to His Highness, Balarama. I will not spill the blood of my boys for such an unworthy cause."

Without a word Krishna walked towards his brother's camp, to have the most difficult conversation of his life.

*****

37 A DAUGHTER'S HONOUR

WHAT MORE COULD HE DO to set these Indians at each other's throats? Shakuni had hoped that an all-out war would break out between Hastinapura and Dwaraka. He had assiduously fanned the flames of revenge in Suyodhana's mind and the imperial army was getting ready to march towards Dwaraka. He had arranged for a few spies to incite trouble in the South. Even now, they were spreading rumours that Suyodhana had turned against Krishna. His mission was drawing to a glorious conclusion when that cursed Nishada had dragged in Krishna's loutish son. That had ruined everything.

'Indians sit and argue without end but do nothing, not even when their daughters are raped. Weaklings!' thought Shakuni in disgust. Bhishma had called back the army as soon as Ekalavya had arrived with Samba. Suyodhana wanted to behead Krishna's son but the timely arrival of Balarama's messenger seeking an audience had saved him. After a long debate, they had decided to throw Samba into a dungeon and Suyodhana agreed to meet Balarama.

Shakuni watched in exasperation as Balarama and Krishna begged the Crown Prince's forgiveness. Bhanumati tried to persuade her husband to make Samba marry their daughter. The chances of war faded. Ekalavya rushed out of the Sabha in protest but he was ignored. A Nishada had little voice after all. Following protracted discussions, they decided that Samba should marry Lakshmana to save her honour. Shakuni almost threw the dice he held to the floor in frustration and anger. In his homeland, no rapist would have got away by agreeing to marry the girl he had violated. The men here would not fight even when their wives were disrobed in public or their daughters raped.

Such shameless behaviour by spineless men! How was he to fulfill the oath he had taken to destroy India if her men refused to fight, even for honour? His hopes rose when Suyodhana said he would consider the marriage only if his daughter agreed. Lakshmana would never agree; he was certain of it.

When they brought Lakshmana into the Sabha, her face was covered with a veil, as if she was the one at fault and had to be hidden from the world.

Balarama clasped her hands saying, "Daughter, what we ask of you is perhaps more than any human should be asked to do, but can you find it in your heart to forgive my nephew?"

Hot tears dropped from Lakshmana's downcast lashes and traced their path over her once flawless face. She shook her head. There was a collective gasp of horror. That meant war. Shakuni would have liked to clap in approbation but kept his glee to himself.

Balarama spoke again. "Daughter, I know my nephew is unworthy of you, or indeed of any woman. I ask this as a sacrifice from you, for all those women who would inevitably be widowed by another battle, the children who would be left fatherless. Daughter, consider what your decision will mean to so many innocent people."

Lakshmana's mind seethed with anger. Was she now to be handed to that brute like a sacrificial lamb, even after all he had done? Was there no one who would take her side? Suddenly, she remembered what she had heard about Draupadi being dragged to the Sabha. These were the same men, were they not? She shook her head again.

Krishna stepped forward. He stood before Lakshmana, his hands folded in supplication. "Princess, you have the power to prevent so many from deaths."

Lakshmana finally raised her head and stared at Krishna. How handsome she had once thought him to be. Unable to look into those beautiful, tear-drenched eyes, Krishna looked away. Youth, laughter and life died in Lakshmana at that moment. 'Better one dead than thousands,' she thought. Without taking her eyes from Krishna's face she said, "I agree."

Shakuni could have killed Krishna with his bare hands. Blasted *avatar*. He turned and walked out of the Sabha. So much work, so much risk, so much planning, all for nothing. Now the only hope lay in the Pandavas returning and claiming the throne. If only Durjaya had been a free man. He saw Ekalavya sitting in a corner of the palace garden, his head buried in his hands. Perhaps the Nishada could be of some help, thought Shakuni, and went over to him.

"Nauseating. They are forcing the girl to marry that bastard."

"What?" Ekalavya gasped. His muscles had gone rigid.

"Oh, they have compelled the poor girl to marry that scoundrel. You should have heard Krishna and Balarama. It was sickening. That poor child! Well, I hope the wedding feast will be sumptuous."

"Shut up, Mlecha!" Ekalavya pushed Shakuni away and began running towards the palace.

"If you want to do something, I can help you, Nishada. I, too, am appalled by the whole affair," Shakuni shouted after him.

Ekalavya stopped. Shakuni hurried to his side. Looking at the far horizon, he whispered, "I know where the villain is being held."

"What do you mean?" asked Ekalavya, every sense alert.

"What if there was no Samba to marry Lakshmana?" suggested Shakuni smoothly.

Ekalavya's face reflected none of the mad churning in his brain. Every instinct warned him not to trust this man.

"In my country, we call it 'honour killing'. But here, people just talk. I can only sympathize with the girl."

"Where is he held?" Ekalavya asked, his voice dangerously calm.

"There are many guards. Security is tight and..."

"Where is he?"

"Come with me," Shakuni said as he hurried off.

Ekalavya followed soundlessly. Shakuni showed him the entrance and then quickly disappeared, hoping no one had seen them together. He watched Ekalavya move silently towards the first guard. 'This might just work,' he thought, but he had to find Krishna. Shakuni rushed back to the palace.

***

"This is an inspection. Where is your chief?" Ekalavya barked at the guard. The man ran off to fetch his superior.

When the Chief came, he eyed Ekalavya suspiciously. He knew the dark man to be a minor King so he bowed, but his right hand remained on the hilt of his sword as he asked, "Sir, have you any token of your authority to make this inspection?"

"I am Ekalavya, a close friend of the Crown Prince and King of his forest lands," Ekalavya answered in an officious tone, hoping the man would not prove too difficult. He would rather not have to kill him.

"My apologies, Sir. Please come to my room. Leave your weapons outside – your sword, bows, quiver, everything. It is regulation."

The Chief led Ekalavya in. As soon as they entered, Ekalavya bolted the door and hit the Chief on the head with his balled fist. The man collapsed silently onto the floor. Ekalavya waited for some time to be sure the Chief would not come around soon and then dragged him to his chair and arranged him to look like he was taking a nap. Then Ekalavya went out and closed the door, walking with a confident gait and nodding to the soldiers on duty, who bowed to him. The air was damp and musty. Large spiders lurked in the corners. Somewhere bats screeched. It grew darker as he walked on. A few torches threw more smoke than light into the dungeons. It was the most feared prison in Hastinapura and housed many of Durjaya's men. Prisoners with long dirty beards screamed when Ekalavya passed, rattling their chains and the iron bars. The guards tried to silence them by hitting the bars with long sticks.

Where was Samba? Ekalavya knew he could not ask without raising suspicion. He did not have much time. Shakuni was sure to be back. He had to find that monster and kill him before someone came to fetch the bridegroom. The word tasted like mud in his mouth – bridegroom indeed! 'Princess, I will never let him touch you again,' Ekalavya vowed as he descended further into the bowels of the earth.

The air became damper and the ground uneven, littered with pebbles and rocks. It was the deepest chamber, where hardened criminals were held. Ekalavya felt vulnerable without his weapons but his rage was as sharp as any sword. He turned another corner and in the dim light of a guttering torch, he saw Samba talking to the prisoner in the opposite cell. Durjaya! Perhaps it was the day for two murders.

In an authoritative voice he commanded the guards to move away. Samba fell silent, the blood draining from his face. In the smoky, flickering light Ekalavya walked towards Samba's cell with the finality of death.

*****

38 DEATH IN THE DARK

"WHAT DO YOU WANT NOW?" Gandhari asked her brother, her face turned away from the doorway where he stood.

"Sister, I need only a moment. I need the King's permission to free Samba. It looks awkward keeping the bridegroom in prison."

"Stay out of what does not concern you, Shakuni," said Gandhari, an edge to her voice.

"Shakuni, your sister has some fancy ideas about statecraft," said Dhritarashtra, getting up from the chair he had been sitting in. "I am delighted we now have Krishna on our side. That was a brilliant move by Suyodhana. Go, free Krishna's son. We cannot appear disrespectful. Ring the bell, Shakuni, and call for my seal."

"I have the order ready, brother." He turned to a guard and ordered the royal seal to be brought in.

Dhritarashtra asked Shakuni to read the document and then affixed his seal at the end, his face a blend of pleasure and pathos. Shakuni knew his brother-in-law was not what he appeared to be; he was unpredictable at best. Clutching the royal order, Shakuni hurried out. If things went as planned, he would trigger a war and Krishna would look like the fool who started it all.

***

"I am honoured," Krishna said to Shakuni in a flat voice, drumming his fingers on a table.

"Here is the royal order freeing your son," Shakuni responded, ignoring Krishna's tone.

"Oh, let him stay one more night in the dungeon. He deserves nothing better."

This was getting difficult. Shakuni fidgeted with the royal order. Precious time was being lost. "Sir, your son's life is in grave danger. If something happens to him in prison..."

Krishna laughed. "He is in the most secure prison in Bharatavarsha. You worry needlessly, my friend. If you will excuse me, I was getting ready to visit my Aunt Kunti."

"Sir, it would be better to get your son out of that prison before it is too late. The Nishada King who kidnapped your son is not happy with the alliance."

"Many people are not happy with the alliance. Can we afford to worry about the opinions of the whole world?" retorted Krishna with a smile.

"Ekalavya is dangerous. He hates your son. Prison is no longer safe for Samba. This order frees him."

Shakuni knew he had touched a chord by the way Krishna's posture changed. Without waiting, he turned and began walking away. Krishna's footsteps followed him. Shakuni smiled, the Yadava had taken the bait.

When they reached the prison, Shakuni presented the order to the Deputy Chief. "Where is the Chief?" Shakuni asked. The Deputy responded that the Chief was taking a nap.

"This is Lord Krishna, the Yadava Prince," Shakuni said, introducing his companion.

Hearing the name, the Deputy immediately fell at Krishna's feet saying, "Bless me, my Lord. We are blessed indeed to see the *avatar* of Lord Vishnu with our own eyes."

Shakuni rolled his eyes to the ceiling. "The Lord is in a hurry," he prompted. "He has come to fetch his son who is in this prison due to some misunderstanding. Please take us to his cell."

"With pleasure, Prabhu." The Deputy stood up.

"You can stay here. Just tell us the way," Krishna said.

The Deputy's face fell but he traced the way to Samba's cell in the sand with his baton. "Prabhu, forgive me, but no arms are allowed inside," he stammered apologetically. With great reverence, he collected Krishna's *Sudharshana* disc and Shakuni's jewelled dagger. As Krishna and Shakuni entered the dungeon, the Deputy called out, "Sirs, the Nishada King is making an inspection of the facilities also."

Shakuni and Krishna looked at each other. "You have left him alone without worrying over his safety?" Krishna asked, trying to hide the rising tension in his voice.

The Deputy looked embarrassed and said in a low voice, "Sir, no guard was willing to go with him as he is an untouchable."

"Fools... idiots..." Krishna hissed and ran into the dungeon.

Shakuni struggled to keep pace. Prisoners' screams filled the air as they moved through the underground prison. As they turned a dark corner, they could hear the rhythmic sound of a hard object hitting metal. A bloodcurdling cry rose above the din and Krishna ran towards it, stumbling over the rocky surface. Shakuni knew what the sound was and thanked his stars. They had made it just in time.

The door to the last cell stood wide open. In the opposite cell, a savage-looking man with a waist-length beard was screaming murder. He rattled the bars and tried to twist open the heavy metal lock with his hands. Durjaya! A shiver passed through Shakuni's frame. Thirteen years of incarceration in this dark dungeon had made Durjaya look devilish. When he saw Shakuni, he stopped yelling and the brief silence sent a chill down Shakuni's spine.

"Nishada!" Krishna screamed.

Shakuni looked into the cell. Ekalavya was sitting on Samba's chest, choking Krishna's son to death. Krishna tried to prise him away. In the throes of death, Samba thrashed his legs wildly. Krishna reached for his *Sudharshana* and uttered a curse. They had left their weapons at the prison gate. With all the force he could muster, Krishna hit Ekalavya, but the Nishada did not even feel it. Samba's life was ebbing away. However much he tried, Krishna could not prise Ekalavya's hands that held Samba's throat in a vice-like grip.

Shakuni searched the rough floor. If only he could find something hard, a stone perhaps. The rock Ekalavya had used to wrench open the cell door grazed his fingers. Krishna had almost given up hope when Shakuni handed him the stone. With all the pent up anger and rage he felt, Krishna brought it down with great force on Ekalavya's head. There was the sickening sound of a skull cracking and Ekalavya's grip on Samba's throat loosened. Krishna brought down the rock again and again on Ekalavya's head until he collapsed to the ground. The glassy eyes of the Nishada looked up at his murderer. For a moment Krishna thought he saw a blazing third eye in the dark forehead. He blinked and the illusion disappeared. Perhaps the flickering torchlight had played tricks with his eyes. A breeze rushed through the damp dungeon and snuffed out the struggling flame, plunging them into complete darkness.

The rock slipped from Krishna's hands and rolled away. His palm was sticky. Despite himself, he brought his hand up to his nose. It smelt of blood, of murder. 'Oh God, what have I done?' Krishna shivered. He had slain many people before, but they were his sworn enemies, evil men. For the first time in his life, he felt he had done something wrong. The laws of *karma* would not allow him to escape. He hoped his Yadava clan would not be destroyed in that lethal retribution.

"Is he dead?" Shakuni whispered.

Krishna had no answer. He did not even know whether the Gandharan was asking about Samba or the Nishada. He sat on the damp ground with his head buried in his hands, the heavy rock of guilt hammering at his heart.

"I will get a torch," Krishna heard Shakuni say.

The Gandharan's footsteps faded away. Krishna heard someone cough. Had the Nishada come back to life? He lifted his head but the dark contours of Ekalavya's body did not move. Again, he heard the coughing. When his eyes had adjusted to the shadows, he saw his son moving. Krishna felt no joy in knowing that Samba was still alive. He was beyond any emotion. He struggled to find some justification for what he had done. He knew he would carry this guilt to his funeral pyre.

When Shakuni returned, Samba was standing. He should have waited for a few more seconds before passing the rock to Krishna, the Gandharan thought with a slight grimace. In the flickering light of the torch he held, he saw Samba's eyes glittering with maniacal rage.

"Ekalavya is dead. You are safe, my son. We saved you, Samba," Shakuni cried, backing away a few steps from the scene.

Krishna woke from his stupor. "What you have made me do?" he cried, looking at his son.

"One Nishada less is one trouble less," retorted Samba.

A vein throbbed in Krishna's neck as he looked at his son.

"You saved my life, but as a father it was your duty and your *dharma* to do so. Why are you so glum?" Samba said, backing out of the cell.

"You have made me do something I will always be ashamed of," Krishna replied quietly.

"Just think of him as a Rakshasa you killed to save the world, or say that you gave him *moksha* and that he is now in Vaikunta, enjoying all the things that were denied to him in this life. Dhaumya will know how to spread the right rumours. Why worry? Let us get out of this hellhole and go back to Dwaraka. Life is too short to worry about a dead Nishada."

Krishna's eyes hardened but Samba's lips curved into a derisive smile. He knew how to control his father.

Durjaya shouted from the other cell, "Friend, friend...have you forgotten our deal? Have you forgotten our pact that whoever gets free first, will release the other?"

"Oh, never! Samba always stands by his friends," Samba said as he pushed past Krishna. He kicked Ekalavya's body, picked up the bloody rock that had killed the Nishada, and rushed towards Durjaya's cell.

"What are you doing?" Shakuni asked, trying to stop Samba, horrified at the thought of the consequences. Things had been going terrible wrong for the Gandharan in the last few moments. If Durjaya was freed on terms other than his, he knew he would never be able to control the crime lord.

Samba shoved Shakuni away. The torch rolled away from his hands and shadows danced in its haphazard light. Samba broke open the heavy lock on Durjaya's cell with powerful blows. Durjaya grabbed the rock from Samba's hands and rushed to the next cell, and the next, breaking the bolts and freeing his followers.

Krishna heard soldiers rushing in and the yells of men fighting a pitched battle. They appeared to be in the midst of a prison riot.

"Fool! What have you done?" Krishna hissed at Samba.

"Durjaya is to me what the Pandavas are to you. Is it not my *dharma* to help my friend when he is in distress?" Samba hissed back at his father. "Durjaya, throw this trash in some forest," Samba shouted over the din, pointing to Ekalavya's still body. Durjaya ran back to them with two of his men. One of them lifted Ekalavya onto his shoulder.

"A feast for the beasts of the forests," gloated Samba, punching Ekalavya's face.

Krishna was horrified by his son's words and actions. Was this beast really the flesh of his flesh? Did his blood flow through his veins?

"All the guards are dead and we have lost twenty men. No one escaped to raise an alarm," one of Durjaya's men shouted.

"Good!" Durjaya hugged Samba and bowed to Krishna. Then he turned towards Shakuni who was trying to remain inconspicuous in a corner. "Mlecha, say your last prayers!" he yelled with glee.

Two dozen men advanced towards Shakuni. The Gandharan's hand reached for his dagger; and he cursed when he did not find it. Of course, it had been taken from him at the entrance.

"Bloody foreigner! You betrayed me! Thirteen years I have rotted in this dark dungeon. That is what your friendship earned us. You will pay for it, my dear friend." Durjaya walked towards Shakuni, terrible intent clear in his eyes.

"Durjaya, wait! I can explain. Don't act in haste and regret it later." Shakuni's voice faltered. He stumbled backwards until his head hit an overhanging rock. "Don't kill me." Shakuni cursed himself for the fear he felt. He was going to die like a rat at the hands of vermin like Durjaya. He would die without having achieved his life's ambition of destroying India. 'Lords of heaven and earth, give me one more chance,' he prayed fervently, every fibre of his being beseeching his Gods above for a reprieve.

"Kill you? Why would I kill you so quickly? You are coming with us," said Durjaya, shaking him by his hair.

Men rushed to Shakuni, punching and kicking. The Gandharan knew it was useless to resist and so fell to the ground, feigning unconsciousness.

"Samba, we will meet again someday. For now, I am taking your dead Nishada and my old friend, Shakuni." Durjaya and his men rushed out of the dungeon, carrying Ekalavya's dead body and Shakuni's inert form with them.

When Krishna and Samba emerged, stepping over the bodies of the slain men, it was already dark outside. They later learnt that Durjaya had murdered the stable guards and ridden away on the stolen horses. The hunt for the fugitives would prove futile. Durjaya and his gang would come to haunt the Yadavas later, but they did not know it at the time. Survival was the greatest *dharma*, Krishna tried to convince himself. He had to get away before Duryodhana learnt the truth. It was essential his loutish son marry Suyodhana's daughter before he discovered what had happened. Once the marriage rites had been performed, Duryodhana would not do anything to harm his son-in-law. The life of a widow was the worst fate a father could inflict upon his daughter. However, for everything to go according to plan, Samba had to agree to the marriage.

"I found you lying unconscious in prison and brought you out. There was a riot... the guards had been already killed when I got there. That will be the story we will relate. We have not seen Shakuni or Ekalavya," Krishna said, his mouth tasting of ashes.

"Whatever you say, Father. But I do not fancy that girl anymore. I had her and she holds no further charm for me. Nevertheless, if it makes you happy, I will marry her. This is a good kingdom; once I take care of that boy-lover brother of hers, it will be mine. I will keep your dirty secret safe, but never lord it over me again," said Samba, a lopsided grin on his rugged face.

Krishna wished he had smashed his son's head instead of the Nishada's skull. It was too late now. Samba was his burden, the burden all fathers who sired wayward sons carried. '*Karmaphala*, the fruits of *karma*,' he sighed, as he dragged himself towards the palace where Duryodhana waited.

*****

39 SOLITARY SOUL

"SWAMI, SWAMI!" THE PANICKED VOICE woke Vidhura from a disturbed sleep. He reached out to touch his wife's forehead. It was burning hot. She looked even more frail than she had the previous day, but somehow she had survived another night. God be praised for His mercy.

"Swami!" the voice grew frantic.

Vidhura rose from his bed, opened the rickety door, and peered out.

Jara and his dog stood outside.

"Swami, come with me." Jara began running off without waiting for Vidhura's reply.

Vidhura followed as fast as his rheumatic legs would carry him. They reached a clearing where some tribals stood around something lying on the ground. The smell of putrefying flesh was like a physical blow. Vidhura willed himself to look. It bore little resemblance to a man, much less a warrior. Jara sat nearby, tears running down his face. The dog sniffed at the remains of the body, but Jara pulled the animal back. The man had been dead for a long time. Flies buzzed over the bloated face. There were open wounds all over the sagging black skin. Wild beasts had been there before them.

Fighting the bile that rose to his throat, Vidhura bent to look closer. Where has he seen this man? Then it struck him like a thunderbolt. Ekalavya! Memories of the proud boy who had sat in his home years before, refusing a second serving of food, came rushing to his mind.

"I loved him like my brother. He *was* my brother, Swami."
Jara cried. "But everything is *Maya*; Krishna is testing us. No
one ever dies, Swami. The soul is immortal. Krishna knows
everything. He sees everything. He is compassionate. He would
never let this happen without a reason. We are merely fools who
do not understand, Swami. But when I look at my brother's
face, I forget Krishna's divine teachings. I do not deserve to be a
Krishna *bhakta*, Swami."

"Get me a shovel," Vidhura said curtly to the men standing around.
He was not in a position to give Ekalavya a proper funeral. Burning
his body might attract someone's attention. Already these tribals
had seen it. He had to extract a promise from them that they would
keep quiet. One day or the other the truth would come out, but he
would delay it as long as possible. The country could not afford a
war, not when people were dying from the drought.

The men returned with some rusty implements and they began
to dig. The ground was rock hard and it took them a long time
to make a pit deep enough to bury the Nishada who had once
dreamt of challenging Arjuna. If they had fought on equal
terms, who would have won, wondered Vidhura. Could a self-
taught Nishada, who lacked a thumb, have possibly defeated
the greatest archer in Bharatavarsha? It did not matter now. The
Nishada was dead. He had deserved much more in life. Even in
death, he was denied the dignity he merited. Had he been born
in some other country, far from this holy land, bards would have
sung of his heroic deeds for thousands of years.

"Do not speak about this to anyone," Vidhura called out as Jara
began to walk away, his shoulders bent, his dog trotting behind.

"I will not, Swami. Life and death are like day and night, a part
of nature. His soul is immortal. It will have reached Vaikunta,
at the feet of Lord Vishnu. I cry because I am sad and ignorant.
May Krishna give me wisdom."

The men who had found Ekalavya soon dispersed. Vidhura
stood alone in the forest for a long time. Around him, gnarled

trees begged the sky for water. Bird cries were now just faded memories. The sun glowed like a fireball, sucking life out of the earth. When his shadow grew long, Vidhura walked back to his hut, wiping the sweat from his body with his shabby *angavastra*.

Life had not been easy for Vidhura. His wife had been sick for a long time. What he earned by teaching a few students was hardly enough to keep his family from starving. In the initial days he had taught students of all castes and found some happiness in passing on what he knew. But soon the students had dropped out, one by one. Except for the *brahmacharis* Sage Vyasa sent his way occasionally, there was no one willing to learn the Vedas from a Shudra. The upper castes detested him and the lower castes found no value in learning what he had to offer. His sons grew up wild and ignorant. They even shared the same woman, emulating the five Pandava brothers who had married Draupadi. Vidhura's heart ached for his sons.

When he opened the reed door of his hut, Vidhura saw he was now alone in the world. Parshavi looked serene in death. Vidhura sat on the mud floor looking at her still beautiful face. He had failed her as a husband. He had not even been there when she left him forever. He had gone to bury a Nishada, as though it was more important than bidding farewell to the woman who had suffered with him for twenty-five long years. He wanted to say many things to her, apologize for everything and nothing, but the words had lost all sense for her, and for him. The hut seemed destitute without her, just like his life. Vidura wept.

*****

40 Ransom

"IS THIS A BEGGAR'S RANSOM?" Durjaya asked and his companions roared with laughter. Moving towards the boy, he lifted the stubborn chin with the tip of his dagger. "Thirteen years in a dark dungeon infested by rats and scorpions is what I got for trusting your father," Durjaya spat out.

Swallowing his shame, Uluka fell at Durjaya's feet. Shakuni averted his eyes. His son, the scion of Gandhara, falling at the feet of a worthless criminal! 'Father, forgive me, but it is all for the cause. I will make India pay tenfold and its soil will be soaked in blood,' he vowed silently as he watched his son abase himself.

"Sir, have mercy. We have stripped our places of worship, emptied our treasury, begged each household in Gandhara for gold. We have pawned all our assets, including our palace, to the merchant Yuyutsu – all for my father's life."

His son was begging, kneeling at the criminal's feet. It was almost more than Shakuni could bear. Perhaps it would be better to die and spare Gandhara this shame. But that was the coward's way. His country was more important than his pride.

"Lick my feet," Durjaya ordered.

There was a moment's hushed silence and then more howling laughter. Uluka licked Durjaya's feet. Shakuni's fingers dug into his thighs. Someone cut the ropes that bound him and Durjaya yanked Uluka up from the floor.

"Mlecha, I am sparing your life for now. The Crown Prince of Gandhara has licked my feet for your life." The laughter was like molten lead poured into Shakuni's ears. Durjaya's hand tightened around Shakuni's throat. "I can reach deep into your country, Mlecha. Wag your tail again and you won't even know what hit you." Durjaya pushed Shakuni away disdainfully.

Durjaya's men shoved the treasure into sacks. Gandhara's treasures. When they had taken the last coin from the ground, someone kicked Shakuni in the face. Soon others were doing the same. Shakuni coiled into a foetal position. He was determined not to give them the pleasure of hearing him cry in pain.

Like a storm passing, Shakuni's tormentors grew tired of the sport and went away. He steadied himself, supported by his son. Uluka half-carried, half-dragged his father away. Without his son, he would have slipped on his own blood. A pariah kite was circling in the gloomy sky outside. Shakuni stared at it for a long time and found his strength creeping back. "How did you raise so much money?"

"I emptied the treasury, pawned the palace to Yuyutsu, and when that was not enough, begged the people."

"Did you use force to collect the ransom?" Shakuni asked. The kite's circles were becoming tighter.

"Not really. Most of our countrymen love you more than I ever could." His son's voice betrayed an odd sense of pride.

Shakuni suppressed the sob that threatened to break his heart. He could not fail his people's trust. The kite circled in the air.

"Father," his son's hand was gentle on his shoulders, "come home."

"What would you have done if Durjaya had killed me?"

"I would have led the Gandhara army to Hastinapura to capture and strangle him to death."

Shakuni's eyes blurred with tears. "Son, I am doing the same thing for my massacred father and brothers. This is my *dharma*. When you get home, tell our people that no King ever loved his people as much as Shakuni has. Beg their pardon for the wrongs I have done them."

Shakuni limped away. Any more words and he would have cried like a child. He saw the kite dive into the forest like an arrow. It must have found its prey. He wiped the blood from his lips. He should have said a proper goodbye to his son, embraced him one last time. He was not sure he would see Uluka again. The time had come for a final roll of the dice.

*****

41 VIRATA

SHAKUNI TOOK A DEEP BREATH before entering his nephew's chambers.

"Where have you been?" Suyodhana asked with a trace of irritation.

Karna and Aswathama looked at each other.

Shakuni bowed low. Should he tell Suyodhana about Ekalavya's death now or later? It would be better to save it for later, when the impact would be greater. "I had some urgent business in Gandhara. The Yavanas dared to attack again. I heard about the prison riots. Have you caught Durjaya? I am sorry to have missed Lakshmana's wedding. Your plan to blow the Pandavas' cover and avoid a costly war is certainly a clever one, Suyodhana." Shakuni smiled thinly at his nephew.

"We have no time to worry about Durjaya now. Our soldiers are out hunting for the Pandavas but there are only 15 days left for the end of their exile. How are we to entice them out of hiding?" Sushasana asked.

"Ah, Sushasana, I didn't even see you sitting in that dark corner. Think, my nephew, what would force them to leave Virata? What is their greatest strength? Think how we can convert it into their greatest weakness," responded his uncle.

"They claim they are the sons of Gods," suggested Sushasana.

"Their pride in their skill with arms?" Aswathama asked.

Shakuni kept pulling at his salt and pepper beard. Finally, when there were no more ideas forthcoming, he said, "Suyodhana, their greatest strength is the support they enjoy from the orthodox. Attack anything that is considered holy by the priests, and we can force Yudhishtra to come out and fight."

"Are you going to tell us or not?" Sushasana asked impatiently. He was tired of his uncle talking in riddles.

"Patience is a virtue you should practise more, nephew. The Virata King has thousands of cows. Steal them and you will have all the priests screaming for war. To them, a cow's life is more precious than that of a man. The Pandavas would have to fight to protect the cows." Shakuni sat back and waited for their reaction.

"Tchaw! The Pandavas did not even fight for their wife; do you think they will fight for a few cows?" Suyodhana said dismissively.

"Nephew, to such people, a wife's honour can be pawned but a cow's life cannot be compromised. The easiest way to conquer Bharatavarsha is to march a few cows before the invading army."

"That is not an honourable way," Karna said coldly.

"Fine then, go ahead and declare war on Virata. The Pandavas would sneak away like rats while you fought a useless war with a vassal state. Remember, you have just two weeks to blow their cover. Fail and they will come back to claim their share of the kingdom. Do you really want that?" Shakuni studied Suyodhana's face.

"Let them come. I am waiting to fight Arjuna," Karna replied.

"A war would be devastating. The rains have failed and the granaries are empty. Already half the country's assets have been pawned to Yuyutsu. I do not know how we will ever get that merchant off our backs. But we cannot have him joining the Pandavas with his enormous wealth and private army. No, my uncle is right. In this way, we avoid a disastrous war. Let us try to lure the Pandavas out of hiding," Suyodhana said thoughtfully, ignoring Karna and Aswathama's protests.

While Suyodhana and his friends debated the details, Shakuni did some mental arithmetic. Perfect! If he played the game with finesse, he could make both parties think they were right. That would be some war, where both parties fought for *dharma* – a *dharmayudh*a – a holy and righteous war which any prophet would approve. What was it that Suyodhana had said about Yuyutsu? That could be something to explore. Also, the Southern Confederate had to be dragged in somehow and the drought and famine conditions exploited. Things were certainly getting interesting.

***

"There he is!" Suyodhana exclaimed, unable to conceal his delight. He had brought a small force with him to Virata and in the dead of the night, they had overpowered the guards at the royal barns and driven out all the cows. By morning, Suyodhana's spies had spread the rumour that his army was going to feast on beef. That was sure to provoke the conservatives who valued cows over men. If the Pandavas were hiding in Virata, Yudhishtra would be forced to fight to save the cows if he wanted to retain the support of the Priests. They could murder the entire population of Khandivaprastha and still be called righteous, but they would be damned if they let a single cow die! The idea was not to fight a full-fledged battle but to smoke out the Pandavas if they were hiding in the kingdom. Shakuni's idea was perfect in its simplicity. Suyodhana made a mental note to thank his uncle for avoiding a major war that would have ruined Bharatavarsha.

The man, dressed as a woman, who was leading the Virata army could be none other than Arjuna. Suyodhana looked back at his commanders and shouted, "We have found them! Another thirteen years of exile for the Pandavas."

Suyodhana was surprised to see that neither Bhishma nor Drona shared his joy. Which side were they on? He had avoided a major conflict by finding Pandavas in the nick of time, just twelve days before their period of exile ended.

"From this distance we cannot be sure whether it is Arjuna or not. It appears that their commander is a woman. We have to categorically prove it is the Pandavas," Bhishma said, shielding his eyes from the blazing sun. Behind the Kaurava army, the stolen cows mooed piteously.

"Oh, I shall prove it," Karna said, twanging his bowstring.

"Karna, watch out!" Aswathama screamed as an arrow broke Karna's bow in two.

"It is Arjuna! No one can shoot like that," Guru Drona said with utter certainty.

Suyodhana was relieved. Drona himself had acknowledged it was Arjuna. He had achieved his goal. He turned to Shakuni to thank him for the wonderful plan. To his surprise, he found Shakuni had left his position and was near Karna. What was he saying to him? All of a sudden, Suyodhana saw Karna charging towards Arjuna recklessly.

"Karna, hold on! You will be trapped." Suyodhana heard Aswathama yell desperately.

Suyodhana's heart skipped a beat. What was Karna trying to do? Commit suicide? "Karna, come back! There is no need to fight. We have found Arjuna." Suyodhana shouted just as he was hit in the arm by another well-aimed arrow.

"Retreat!" Suyodhana heard Bhishma voice as the conch shell sounded, ordering a retreat. Bhishma had been made Supreme Commander and on the battlefield. His conch shell was the final call.

The Hastinapura forces turned back just as the Virata army, led by Arjuna, charged.

"Pitamaha, Karna will get trapped. He does not have the support of our cavalry and elephant corps," Suyodhana shouted to his Supreme Commander, desperately trying to keep his horse from turning tail.

Arrows rained around Suyodhana as his army fled in a disorganised retreat, pushing him back with them like a tidal wave.

"Retreat!" Bhishma blew the conch again and the retreat became a stampede.

Horses galloped past Suyodhana, raising a dust storm. Arjuna's army advanced on them like a flash flood. Why were his commanders, Drona and Bhishma, not trying to rescue Karna? He had done a reckless thing and it was inexcusable to break discipline, but he could not leave Karna to his fate. A single man could not stand against such an army, even if he was Karna, the formidable warrior.

He saw Aswathama galloping towards Karna, holding off Arjuna's advance single-handedly. But how long could he last? Drona shouted at Aswathama to come back, but the Guru's son fought his way to Karna's aid.

"You can forget about your friends, Suyodhana. Retreat safely if you want to stay alive to fight again," Shakuni advised his nephew before galloping away, without waiting for an answer.

"Fool! What are you gaping at Suyodhana for? Retreat!"

Suyodhana heard Bhishma's voice near him. What was the Pitamaha still doing here? "I cannot leave them to die," Suyodhana said, not looking at Bhishma.

"I took charge of this army on condition that there would be no unnecessary bloodshed. We have found Arjuna; we have won. I am not responsible if a Suta's bowstring was broken by his foe. We cannot fight because of the frustrated and fragile ego of a Suta."

Suyodhana did not reply. What Karna had done was inexcusable from the point of view of any Commander, yet he could not leave his friend to die. He heard Drona's panicked voice behind him and turned.

"Sir, I seek permission to assist my son." Drona stood impatiently, waiting for his Commander's permission.

"Denied," Bhishma said, looking straight ahead.

"Sir, my son is in grave danger. Give me a few soldiers to bring him back safely," Drona pleaded

"Denied. You are ordered to retreat with your division," Bhishma said and his chariot shot forward. Around them Hastinapura's imperial army was rushing back to safety.

"That Suta will get my son killed," Drona said, his head hung in despair.

Suyodhana was surprised at the depth of Drona's emotion. Why then did father and son argue so much if they loved each other so deeply? "Guru, come with me. I am going to save them," Suyodhana said.

Guru Drona's nostrils flared. "You think war is a joke? The Commander has given the order to retreat. There should be no question about not following it. How dare you go against his order?"

"Sir, it is to save your son," Suyodhana said, surprised at the Guru's vehemence.

"An order is an order in battle. It does not matter whether your son or brother is in danger." Drona's chariot carried away the ramrod straight figure of the Guru.

Suyodhana hesitated a moment and then rushed to Karna's aid. He could hear Bhishma shouting at him to turn back, but he could not have cared less. His friend was in danger and nothing else mattered. Seeing Suyodhana dashing towards Karna, Bhishma and Drona turned their chariots and followed him into the fight with Arjuna.

***

"I failed you. You should have left me to die," Karna's voice cracked as he turned away from Suyodhana, sitting near his bed. From a corner of the room, Aswathama stood staring at them both, a stony expression on his face.

"I did not save you. It was Bhishma and Drona," Suyodhana said. How could he tell Karna that Arjuna had mercifully desisted from killing him when Bhishma had appealed to his nephew?

In fact, Arjuna had spared them all. He had used the *sammohana* missile to stun rather than kill. Perhaps the presence of Bhishma and Drona had restrained him.

It was the worst day in Suyodhana's life. It had been a complete rout at Arjuna's hands. True, they had taken only a small force and planned to find the Pandavas, not fight them, but had it not been for Karna's reckless charge, they would have made an orderly retreat under Bhishma's command, without loss of lives on either side. There had been no need for Karna to act so rashly. They had already blown the Pandavas' cover and the results of the Virata skirmish did not matter. What had Shakuni said to Karna to make him behave so foolishly, so unlike his calm self?

Vrishali stifled a sob and Karna's face darkened. "Prince, we are thankful to you for what you did, we are indebted to you for your kindness." Vrishali stopped when she saw Karna's stern expression.

"Leave us!" Karna's voice was soft but it felt like a whiplash.

The blood drained from Vrishali's face but she looked at Suyodhana, her hands folded in supplication. "I don't want to see him dead," she said, her eyes filled with tears.

"I prefer death to this humiliating defeat to Arjuna. I was reckless and paid the price. I have failed you, Suyodhana. I am of no value to you. I am a parasite." Karna turned to face the wall.

"But what made you do something so rash, Karna?" Aswathama asked. Karna did not answer.

"What did Shakuni say to you?" Suyodhana asked.

"It was my fault, my ego. I cannot blame anyone. He only said that even in women's dress, Arjuna looked every bit a Kshatriya."

Suyodhana and Aswathama exchanged glances. Had Shakuni resumed his devious games of manipulation or was it just an innocent remark that had provoked the sensitive Karna? How could they blame Shakuni? Thus far, his planning had been faultless – whether it was the game of dice or the invasion of Virata.

"Your body armour saved you from certain death, Karna, as also the efforts of Bhishma and Drona. It does not matter. We have won. The Pandavas will have to repeat 13 years of exile. Virata was the last battle with them," Suyodhana said, smiling at his friend.

Aswathama clicked his tongue. Virata, the last battle with the Pandavas? He was not so sure.

***

Shakuni spent the whole day roaming in the jungle to find Dhaumya and his cronies. He had seen them rushing to Virata after the battle and had patiently waited for them to return. He finally found the forlorn group of Brahmins at the edge of the Virata forest. Guru Dhaumya was sitting in the middle of the group with his head buried in his hands. His disciples stood with their gaze fixed on their feet.

Shakuni had wandered long enough to look sufficiently distressed. He removed his headgear and ruffled his hair and beard. He tore his *angavastra*, threw one of his shoes away, and taking his dagger from his waistband, cut himself in a few places. He had to look like he was running from the battlefield. Then he slumped limply over his horse's back and nudged it towards the group.

*****

42 DATES OF DESTINY

"A WARRIOR IS COMING TOWARDS US!" Shakuni heard the excited shout from one of Dhaumya's disciples. He closed his eyes. The horse carried him to the group, where he collapsed to the ground. Dozens of Dhaumya's disciples crowded over him. In a faint voice, Shakuni cried for water.

Water hit his face and he woke artistically, as if from a stupor. His gaze scanned every face and stopped at Dhaumya. "Guru Dhaumya, please...do not kill me."

"Shakuni, you Mlecha... what are you doing here?" Dhaumya cried as his disciples moved away in shock. They had thought the warrior they had given water to was a true Kshatriya. But this was a Mlecha, and his touch would pollute them.

"Everything is lost, Guru," Shakuni cried in abject misery. "Arjuna has destroyed everything. He has defeated my poor nephew and killed Karna. We have lost everything. Have mercy on me when Yudhishtra rules this land. I will go to my own country. Do not punish me."

Dhaumya looked at his disciples in surprise. Was the Mlecha making fun of them? "Stop drivelling, you barbarian. Arjuna did not kill anyone. He spared the lives of all those evil men because he respects Drona and Bhishma," Dhaumya spat in disgust. "It is we who should be crying. The Pandavas have lost the game. They have been found before their time in exile is up."

"So another thirteen years of wilderness for my nephew's enemies?" Shakuni asked slowly, eyeing Dhaumya from the corner of his eye.

"Stop rejoicing, evil Mlecha. We will find a way," Dhaumya said, his voice harsh with loathing.

"What choice do you have, Guru? You follow the solar calendar. In Gandhara, we follow the lunar calendar." Shakuni coughed to add effect. He looked at the Priest humbly, watching to see whether he had taken the hint.

Dhaumya's face lightened. "What are you saying, you Mlecha?"

"Had you people followed the lunar calendar, the days of exile would have ended long ago. But alas..." Shakuni shook his head, trying to get up from the floor.

Dhaumya turned to whisper to his disciples. Shakuni could feel their growing excitement. The Guru had taken the bait. Dhaumya and his cronies hurried away without even casting a glance at him. Shakuni hoped they were going to meet the Pandavas, or better still, Krishna. He sighed with relief. He had given the Pandavas a small leaf to cover the shame of their blatant demand for the throne, despite having lost the bet. Suyodhana would be livid. Shakuni could not repress a smile. The Indians would now fight over calendars. Shakuni felt he was closer to his goal now than at any other time in his life. *Dharmayudha*, a bloody holy war would destroy everything. The priests would justify it, the Kurus would think it was their duty to shoot down their blood relatives, fathers would kill sons, uncles their nephews – the whole country would be damned. 'Gandhara, I will not disappoint you again. Krishna, you think you are an *avatar*, but you are just a *cowri* on my board.'

***

Yudhishtra had a faraway look in his eyes. He felt deeply relieved that there would be no war now, even though it meant another thirteen years in exile. But their failure to remain incognito in the last fortnight of their long exile had been a devastating blow. They had come so close to being free. Everyone blamed him. 'What choice did I have?' he wanted to ask Draupadi, but feared what he would hear in reply. They were sitting in the woods near the Virata palace. All his brothers looked gloomy and irritated. He had failed them again.

"Don't worry about the extended exile. You have suffered enough. Go and ask for your share of the kingdom, Yudhishtra," he heard Krishna say.

Share? What share? Yudhishtra wished Krishna would go away and leave him alone. He heard Draupadi's derisive laughter. What right had he to Suyodhana's empire? He was the bastard son of an ambitious mother. Was that a claim? Had he been in Suyodhana's position, would he have cared to share power with a bastard cousin? Perhaps. After the long years in the forest, Yudhishtra had lost interest in fighting for revenge. Life had been calm and peaceful. He was tired of power games. Then why had he ordered Arjuna to save the cows of Virata when he heard of Suyodhana's adventure? He was all too aware of the terms of their exile, yet he had exposed them all. Yet how could he have remained a mute spectator when holy cows were being hurt? Had power changed Suyodhana so much that the boy who cried over a slain parrot did not hesitate to slaughter cows? Yudhishtra realised now that Suyodhana had never intended to kill the cows; it had been a trap to lure them out of hiding and he had fallen into it.

"No, I cannot do it," he said to Krishna. The Yadava shook his head and walked away.

Dhaumya was waiting near the tree where Krishna had tied his horse. He and his disciples immediately surrounded the Yadava, clamouring for his attention.

"He refuses to fight, saying it is *adharma* to break the conditions of exile. I do not know how to convince him otherwise," Krishna told the Brahmins as he untied his horse.

"There is a way," Dhaumya said, a smug smile on his round face.

Krishna turned around, one hand on the bridle. He saw the eager anticipation on the faces of Dhaumya's disciples as their

Guru whispered his plan. Krishna's eyebrows flew up and a dazzling smile spread over his face.

"Guru, it is brilliant. I did not know you were such a strategist. It is inspired. Genius!" Krishna exclaimed in genuine admiration.

"Anything for the victory of *dharma*, My Lord," Dhaumya said, bowing his head.

"I think I can convince Yudhishtra with this argument." Krishna quickly walked back to the clearing where the Pandavas still sat despondently.

Dhaumya and his disciples followed. When they had disappeared among the trees, Shakuni emerged from the shadowy woodland. He clicked his tongue to turn his horse. It was time for the next move. It was time to tell Suyodhana about Ekalavya's murder. Shakuni's horse galloped through the parched forest towards Hastinapura.

*****

43 MURDER

A GUARD ENTERED TO INFORM Suyodhana that Prince Krishna awaited him. The Crown Prince took leave of Karna and hurried towards the Sabha. Why had Krishna come all the way from Dwaraka to see him? Aswathama ran behind his friend, whispering a quick warning not to be taken in by the charming Yadava. They were about to enter the hall when Shakuni too, appeared. He had been waiting for them in the shadows.

"Later, uncle. Krishna is in the Sabha."

"Suyodhana, I have some terrible news." Shakuni's grave voice made them stop and look at him. "Ekalavya is dead."

"What?" Suyodhana and Aswathama exclaimed in unison.

"Killed! Murdered in cold blood."

"Who killed him?" Aswathama asked.

Shakuni's expression became sombre. "I don't know who did it, but I heard about his murder from a group of tribals. They found his rotting body. Vidhura helped them bury it."

Suyodhana held on to a pillar for support. That was the reason the Nishada had not turned up for his daughter's wedding. How was he going to break the news to Lakshmana?

"How do you know he was killed?" Aswathama asked.

"I can only recount what I heard. His skull was split open, as if he had been hit with a stone or something blunt. There are rumours floating around that Krishna murdered Ekalavya."

"You are just speculating," Aswathama's voice was stiff with disdain.

"How can I know for certain since I was not there?" Shakuni retorted.

"I would rather not meet Krishna today. This news of Ekalavya's death..." Suyodhana said quietly.

"I don't think you have a choice, nephew. Krishna has come with a message from Yudhishtra," Shakuni said.

"I smell trouble," Aswathama stated with finality.

"Come, let us hear what Krishna has to say," suggested Shakuni and turned towards the Sabha.

Krishna stood in the centre of the great hall, a smile on his lips. Suyodhana's grip on his sword tightened. There would be no compromise with his cousins and their extended exile, or with the man who had murdered Ekalavya.

Krishna's eyes glinted at the sight of Shakuni. Bhishma sat grim-faced. King Dhritarashtra waited, twisting the *rudraksha* beads he habitually wore round his wrist. What did the Yadava have to say?

Before Krishna could speak, Suyodhana said in a voice from which all emotion had fled, "Ekalavya is dead." The Sabha froze in shock.

"How did he die?" Dhritarashtra asked, stunned by the news, his fingers frozen on the beads he had been turning.

It was clear from his impassive face that it was not news to Bhishma. Drona looked up, overcome by a sudden sense of guilt and loss. The fearless boy who had chopped off his thumb as his *Gurudakshina*, flashed before his eyes. His heart acknowledged in silence that there had never been an archer to equal Ekalavya.

Suyodhana watched Krishna, his eyes never leaving that handsome face, his eyes quenched of their usual burning fire. The Yadava stood alone in the centre of the Sabha, looking from Shakuni to Suyodhana, weighing his options.

*****

44 THE MESSENGER

"I KILLED THE NISHADA," said Krishna, each word falling into the stillness of the Sabha with the force of thunder.

Suyodhana drew his sword and rushed towards Krishna in speechless rage, but Aswathama restrained him, with both arms around his friend's trembling frame.

"Suyodhana, if I had not killed the Nishada, your daughter would have remained unmarried. I killed him to save my son," Krishna said, drawing an almost imperceptible nod from Bhishma.

Suyodhana did not miss the gesture and his rage exploded into angry words. "I made a great mistake in permitting my daughter to marry your degenerate son, Krishna. It was not Ekalavya who deserved to die, but your son. How dare you come here and declare your guilt before us all?"

"To kill evil is my *dharma*," Krishna said softly.

"You kill whoever you please and then claim your victim is evil. Is that *dharma*?" Suyodhana's voice shook with all the emotion he had buried in his heart since he had watched his beloved daughter being carried home in Karna's arms, battered and deflowered.

"Suyodhana," Bhishma stood up. "Let us hear why Krishna has taken the trouble to visit us. He has come with a request from Yudhishtra, as I surmise," he said in the calm voice of reason.

"There is nothing to discuss, Pitamaha. The Pandavas must extend their exile for another thirteen years. You yourself fixed the terms. I do not wish to talk to this manipulative man."

Aswathama put a hand on Suyodhana's shoulder, urging him to sit down.

"I regret the Crown Prince prefers to place his own emotions before the good of his country," said Krishna calmly.

"You killed my friend..." Suyodhana gazed at Krishna with loathing.

Bhishma intervened again. "This is neither the time nor the place to discuss the Nishada's death. We are here for something important and are duty-bound to hear the respected messenger."

"Pitamaha, Ekalavya was not just any Nishada..."

"Do not drag me into your petty squabbles, Suyodhana. I am here because King Dhritarashtra requested my presence. Now let us hear what Krishna has to say," Bhishma said with utter finality.

"Your Highness, with your gracious permission," Krishna said, bowing to Dhritarashtra, "Prince Yudhishtra has sent me to stake claim to half the empire." There was pindrop silence in the Sabha.

Suyodhana sprang up like a man possessed. "That is preposterous!" he shouted, shoving away Aswathama's restraining hand.

"Suyodhana, it would become you to display some of the dignity attached to your exalted station. The Sabha is here to listen and to respond," Bhishma said in a voice that allowed no argument. He turned to Krishna. "As per the terms of exile, the Pandavas are required to repeat their twelve-year stay in the forest and one year incognito. It is perhaps unfortunate they were discovered just a few days short of their term."

"Revered Lord Bhishma," Krishna said, his charming smile once again lighting up his face, "they were never found during their exile."

"That is absurd!" protested Suyodhana. "We were all there at Virata. We saw them with our own eyes."

"The Pandavas were never found during their period of exile. They came out to fight Suyodhana after it had ended. In fact, Arjuna defeated the Hastinapura forces, which means the entire empire now belongs to Yudhishtra by right."

"Enough!" Suyodhana was on his feet, trembling with rage.

"I request you to hear me out. While I understand Suyodhana's sentiments, the truth cannot remain hidden," Krishna stated calmly.

"Let him speak," Dhritarashtra commanded.

Krishna smiled at Suyodhana and then turned towards Bhishma. "Sir, Suyodhana is right, but the Pandavas are more right."

"Krishna, pray, do not speak in riddles," Bhishma implored, trying to conceal his irritation.

"Your Excellency, allow me to explain. In Bharatavarsha, two calendars are used – the lunar and the solar. When Suyodhana says the Pandavas were found before their period of exile was over, he is referring to the solar calendar. When Yudhishtra says the Pandavas had completed their thirteen years, he is referring to the lunar calendar. Both are right, but the Pandavas are more right."

"Absolute nonsense! Pitamaha, Krishna is up to his usual tricks." Suyodhana's voice shook with fury.

"Revered Lord Bhishma, does the Kuru dynasty trace its lineage from the Moon or the Sun?" Krishna asked humbly.

Angry murmurs rose in the Sabha. The Kurus traced their lineage from the Moon, hence they were known as *Chandravamshis*.

"The Kurus have followed the solar calendar for many generations. The lunar calendar is used only for *ekadashi* fasts and on other auspicious occasions," Bhishma said.

"Since the Kuru dynasty uses the lunar calendar for all auspicious occasions, it is the more important of the two. The

Pandavas are thus more in the right. Let us begin negotiations from that point," Krishna said, as if he was proposing the most logical thing in the world.

"There is nothing to negotiate. We will not be taken in by devious tricks, Krishna." Suyodhana pointed a damning finger at the smiling Yadava.

"I request to be allowed to state the terms," Krishna said, ignoring Suyodhana completely.

Before Suyodhana could protest, Dhritarashtra said, "You have come as a messenger and custom dictates you be allowed to speak without fear. Suyodhana, be seated and listen to what Krishna has to say."

Suyodhana sat down without taking his gaze off Krishna's face. From the corner of his eye he noticed Shakuni. Something was wrong. Had a smile flashed across that face? He turned and looked at his uncle. No, perhaps he had been mistaken; Shakuni's face showed only concern.

"Yudhishtra is prepared to give half the kingdom to Suyodhana," Krishna began. The entire Sabha rose in agitation.

"Respected Krishna," Bhishma's deep voice rose over the din, "please bear in mind that the claim to the throne has yet to be settled. We already have a King sitting on the throne of Hastinapura."

"My apologies, revered Lord Bhishma, it was but a slip of the tongue. I beg your pardon, Your Highness. May I carry a message to Yudhishtra that the King has graciously agreed to divide the empire into two, between his own son and his brother's son?"

"Enough of this drivel!" Suyodhana said in a voice that was as cold as it was clear. "My father is the King and I am his firstborn son. There is no question of dividing the kingdom or sharing it with a gambler."

"Yudhishtra is prepared to make a concession: when he says half the kingdom, he does not include the expanded empire Karna won for Hastinapura. The Pandavas will settle for Indraprastha and the city they themselves built." Krishna's face was impassive.

"Indraprastha! The city built on the bones of slain Nagas? The city Maya and his people were thrown out of, according to the tenets of *varna* and *jati*? The city its ruler gambled away, and where I stood naked and abused? How does Yudhishtra even dare to ask to be its ruler? If he is as righteous as he claims, let him follow the conditions of the dice game as they were laid down, and go into exile for another thirteen years."

"Prince Suyodhana, that is unfair. What you suggest is *adharma*."

"You Yadava should be the last person to preach *dharma*. I know what your *dharma* is and I know what you mean by *adharma*. If you are an *avatar* of Vishnu as you claim, then it is you who dwells in my heart and I follow my heart. That is my *dharma*. Krishna, when have you ever been fair to anyone? Were you fair to Jarasandha, to Sisupala, to Hiranyadhanus, to the thousands who died in Khandivaprastha? Were you fair to Ekalavya?" Suyodhana asked, pointing a shaking finger at Krishna.

The Yadava turned to Bhishma. "I am merely trying to avoid a war, but Suyodhana is intractable. The voice of reason cannot reach deaf ears. The Pandavas will settle for a vassal kingdom and the same rank Karna holds as King of Anga."

"So they can impose their rules? So that Dhaumya and others like him become unquestionable?" Suyodhana thundered.

"Five villages will also do," Krishna added in a soft voice.

"So they can kindle a revolution from there?"

"You are making peace impossible, Suyodhana. Have a care what you do in such unthinking anger and haste," said Krishna, his voice losing some of its calm. "This is the final offer: Yudhishtra will settle for a house."

"Krishna, we gave them a house years ago. In fact, we gave them a palace. All those present in this Sabha will remember what the sons of *dharma* and their pious mother did with it. We were left to deal with the widows of the soldiers they trapped and killed in the palace fire. It might be a minor detail that they also baited a Nishada woman and her five children with food and then burnt them alive. These are perhaps small footnotes in the glorious stories of *dharma*," Suyodhana said, his voice dying into silence. Many heads nodded in agreement.

"Suyodhana, power has gone to your head and you cannot discern between right and wrong," Krishna said succinctly.

"Stop! Not another word from you, you cunning Yadava. Remember, you are standing in the Hastinapura Sabha. You accuse me of being power hungry? What about you? You are using the Pandavas and their gullibility to finish off your enemies. Tell me why I should share my birthright with the bastard sons of my aunts?"

"Suyodhana!" Bhishma stood up, trembling with anger. "Mind what you say. You were not raised in the gutter. Krishna is our guest..."

"What have I said that is untrue, Pitamaha? What right have the Pandavas to claim the throne?"

"Suyodhana, it would have served you better if you had studied the history of the Kuru race more closely instead of absenting yourself from your classes," Krishna said with a mocking smile. "The revered sage, Veda Vyasa, would no doubt have had the answers to your questions. He would perhaps have asked you who the father of respected King Dhritarashtra, revered Pandu and *mahatma* Vidhura was. It may have helped you to understand Yudhishtra's claim."

There was an edgy hush in the Sabha.

"Don't try to corner me with the custom of *niyoga*. Sage Veda Vyasa is our grandfather and we are proud of it. The *niyoga* was done with the blessings of the elders and not surreptitiously in the jungle, as in the case of my aunts, Kunti and Madri. Can

Yudhishtra point to any man and say, 'Here is my father'? It is claimed that Yudhishtra is the son of Yama, the God of Death; Bhima, the son of Vayu, the God of the Winds; Arjuna, the son of Indra, King of the Gods; and Nakula and Sahadeva, the sons of the Gods of Dawn and Dusk. Do you think we are naive enough to believe such bizarre stories? Do you?"

"You have one last opportunity to avoid a bloody war and the total annihilation of your race, Duryodhana," Krishna said, his lips smiling, but his eyes burning with anger.

"Are you threatening me, you cowherd?"

"You do not know who I am."

"I know who you are, and I am not one of those naive women of Vrindavana to fall prey to your charms. You have an agenda and you use words like *dharma* to cloak your evil intent. I am not afraid of war. If that is to be, so be it. Hear this, Yadava, go and tell my aunt's sons that I will not give them even a tiny portion of the earth which legitimately belongs to me, not even the space to jab a needle."

The Sabha erupted into an uproar. War was now certain.

"Arrest the Yadava," Suyodhana said calmly. The din in the Sabha became deafening.

Krishna smiled at the Crown Prince. "Duryodhana, it is time for you to see who I am." There was a blaze of light, as though something had exploded. Krishna said, "King Dhritarashtra, your son will ruin this kingdom and take everyone to their doom. He is leading your people to annihilation. He does not know whom he is speaking to, nor what he is saying. He is walking the path of *adharma*. The war will finish your line. Be warned and beware. He is challenging the will of God. Know that I am Death and I am Life. I am Time and I am Timelessness. I am the Beginning and the End. I am Brahma, Vishnu and Shiva. Behold my glory."

Suyodhana watched impassively as many people in the Sabha fell to their knees and bowed to Krishna. What was it they saw in him that he did not? It was just Krishna up to his usual tricks. Enough of this charade, Suyodhana decided.

"Enough of your street magic, Yadava! You are nothing but a charlatan. Whom are you threatening? If there is a war, so be it. If I die, I will go to a warrior's heaven, like a true Kshatriya. But I will not hand over the kingdom to a gambler."

Suyodhana smiled when he saw that Krishna was at a loss for words. Perhaps the Yadava was wondering why his famed *Vishwaroopa* act had failed to impress. What had he to fear when he had men like Karna and Aswathama beside him? Why claim to be a God and then commit unspeakable acts? It was better to be just a man and die for one's beliefs and convictions with the head held high.

"Duryodhana, you will pay dearly for this. Not just you, but this entire Kuru Sabha and everyone in this country. The voices that remained silent when a woman's honour was dragged through mud in this very chamber, remain silent even now. It is for the best that you did not agree to the terms, since future generations would have said that I compromised with evil. Men of the Sabha, hear my words...this man has brought war upon you and nothing, I repeat, nothing is going to save you. Remember I warned you of what awaits you," Krishna thundered at the dumbstruck Sabha.

"Arrest this charlatan!" Suyodhana barked at the guards.

Jerked from their stupefaction, the guards rushed towards Krishna. He dodged them with ridiculous ease, knocking them down. Smiling at Suyodhana, Krishna walked out of the Hastinapura Sabha as if retiring after a friendly chat with friends.

The Sabha emptied as courtiers dispersed in animated groups to discuss what had transpired. In the hubbub that ensued, Yuyutsu moved towards the stunned Crown Prince, who had yet to come to terms with the realisation that war was inevitable.

"Brother, I have some important things to discuss with you," Yuyutsu said. Suyodhana looked up at the merchant's smiling face and knew his troubles were just beginning.

"What of the deal I had enquired about?" Yuyutsu asked.

"This is neither the time nor the place," Suyodhana said, irritated..

"It is always a good time to talk business. My dues are long pending. This country owes me money, a lot of money, Suyodhana."

"The treasury is almost empty, but you are collecting taxes and tolls. What more do you want?"

Yuyutsu chuckled, "There is nothing much to collect these days, little brother. Your country is poor."

"There is drought. Once the rains come, everything will be alright."

"Before the rains, war will come and then what will happen to my money? It is all the more important that I secure my money now. Do you want me to broker a deal with the Pandavas?" Yuyutsu asked.

"You will be paid after the war."

"Hmm, how sure you are of victory! But I am not so confident, I want my money now!"

"You scoundrel! Have you no sense of gratitude or obligation to your country?" Suyodhana trembled with frustration.

"I am only following my *dharma*. My duty is to trade," Yuyutsu said, rubbing his thumb with his index finger. Overall, Suyodhana was a bad bet since Krishna was supporting the Pandavas. A message from Parashurama was lying safe in his waistband. By siding with the Pandavas, he was taking a huge risk, but Parashurama had promised him the better deal. If he won this gamble, he would not be trading in cloth and spices, but in countries and kingdoms.

"Are you not ashamed to make such demands at this critical time?" Suyodhana towered over Yuyutsu, his fists clenched.

"I am beyond such emotions. I do not concern myself about results. Detachment is my *mantra*, brother." Yuyutsu emphasized the last word and smiled.

"Do not dare address me as your brother."

"Are you afraid, Prince? Do not fret. I am not after your throne. Pay me well, pay me regularly, and I will govern the country for you."

Suyodhana punched Yuyutsu in the face. The fat merchant fell in a heap at his feet. But Yuyutsu only laughed and got back up. With provocative slowness, he wiped the blood from his nose.

"Don't stare at me like I was vermin. It is I who own this palace and most of this country, my dear brother."

"Get out, before I kill you!" Suyodhana said in a menacing voice.

"Yudhishtra is a more business-friendly ruler than you, brother."

"You snake!" Suyodhana advanced threateningly upon Yuyutsu.

"Money can buy all things, brother, even bravery, fame, and your kingdom and its little people."

Suyodhana shouted for the guards to escort Yuyutsu out. His half-brother chuckled. Scores of Yuyutsu's own soldiers appeared, surrounding him in a protective ring.

"Always looking for a fight, my little brother? You have no respect for businessmen. I am now going to the Pandava side. Send word whenever you want me. I am always available to the highest bidder."

Yuyutsu walked out from another business meeting. In one stroke, Suyodhana's armed strength had halved, while the Pandavas' had doubled. He should have been more careful with his words. To hell with it, this was a war he would fight alone if required, he told himself. When he looked around, he was alone. The cavernous oppressiveness of the hall that had seen many intrigues and battles was suffocating. Suyodhana no longer felt sure of the future.

*****

45 WINDS OF WAR

"KRIPI," DRONA CALLED OUT AS HE REACHED HOME. The news from the Sabha had shaken him to the core. He was certain there would now be a war. He would be compelled to choose between his son and his beloved disciple, Arjuna. If only he could make Aswathama see reason and get him to shift allegiance.

Kripi opened the door. Seeing his grave, troubled face, she put a hand on his arm, but Drona merely pushed her away with a grunt and walked to his *puja* room. His sacred thread lay sweat-soaked across his chest. His mind seethed like an ocean in a storm. He prostrated himself before the idol of Shiva. 'Lord of the Universe, show me the right path; show me my *dharma*. Should I fight beside my son or Arjuna?'

If he stood by Aswathama, Drona knew he would have to give his support to Duryodhana, whom he had always despised. If he took Arjuna's side, he would have to fight his own son. 'What is my *dharma*? Have I not been the most pure of Brahmins? Have I not followed all the rituals and conducted all the ceremonial sacrifices expected of a Brahmin of the highest lineage?' Then why was the Lord placing such an impossible choice before him?

Drona heard his son enter the house and mother and son speak in whispers. He could feel his son's eyes burning into his back. Then he heard Aswathama slam shut the door of his room. Drona raised his head, looked at the idol of Shiva, and gasped! Ekalavya! The untouchable was in his prayer room! How was it possible when the Nishada was dead? Hadn't Krishna said he had killed Ekalavya? Then how was the Nishada standing where Shiva's idol should have been?

Drona's throat felt parched, his hands shivered. "Mahadeva, are you testing me? Are you saying Ekalavya is immortal...that there is life beyond death? Forgive this ignorant Brahmin." Drona's lips trembled as he mumbled the Lord's name repeatedly. Gradually peace descended on him like a gentle balm. Drona's decision was made. He knew the side he would be on in the war. He owed it to the Nishada, whose future he had stolen. He owed it to his son. It was his *dharma*.

There was the sound of excited knocking at the door. Dhaumya's voice called to him from the street. Reluctantly, Drona rose from his prostrate position and wiped the dust from his forehead. When he opened the door, Dhaumya entered, grinning like a split watermelon. Drona offered the priest a seat and then sat down on the veranda swing. To buy time, he opened his *paan* box, took out two leaves and started filling them with lime and betel nut.

"Guru Drona, war is now certain," Dhaumya began.

Drona nodded in silence, offering his visitor a *paan* before pushing the other into a corner of his own mouth. He pulled the spittoon closer and then said, "I was at the Sabha when Krishna spoke."

"It is the best thing that could have happened," Dhaumya said, clearly delighted. He looked at the Guru in unabashed glee and then frowned when he saw Drona's lack of enthusiasm. "Duryodhana will be finished..."

"Hmm..."

"All the Kauravas will die."

"Hmm..."

"The Suta will die."

"Hmm..."

"Krishna's Narayana Sena will support the Pandavas. The Southern Confederate will declare their independence and join the Pandava cause." Dhaumya counted them off on his fingers.

"Perhaps." Drona looked into the distance, at the waters of the shimmering river. A crow sat cawing outside.

"*Dharma* will be restored," Dhaumya said with finality.

"Hmm..."

"Of course, you will lead the Pandava army. Arjuna will be delighted to have you as Commander-in-Chief," Dhaumya gushed, trying to keep his voice calm.

Drona finished chewing his *paan* and then brought his gaze back to the priest's face. "What makes you think I will?"

"But, of course! You are the greatest of all Brahmin warriors and will naturally stand on the side of *dharma*." Utter conviction rang in Dhaumya's rather high-pitched voice.

"You are right. I will stand on the side of *dharma*," Drona nodded, picking up another betel leaf from his box.

Dhaumya looked at the Guru. Something in his words made him pause. He ask hesitantly, "But you *will* act as Commander-in-Chief of the Pandava armies, won't you?"

"I am a soldier of *dharma*. I will fight in the Kaurava army." Drona pushed the swing gently. Its creaking as it swayed back and forth accentuated the shocked silence. A lizard clicked *tchak tchak tchak* from the thatched roof above. Drona watched Dhaumya's expression turn from shock to disbelief to anger. He spat vermilion juice into the spittoon. Kripi, who had come in with a few pots of buttermilk, stood frozen in surprise.

"Guru, you are joking at my expense?" Dhaumya finally asked.

"I have never been more serious, Guru Dhaumya."

"Are you mad? You are a Brahmin; you must support *dharma*."

"I am indeed a Brahmin and I know my *dharma*. I will do everything in my power to see the Pandavas defeated," Drona stated.

"You will be alone on the Kaurava side. You will have to fight Bhishma," Dhaumya said desperately, trying to suppress the rising panic and anger in his voice.

"So you think," Drona answered calmly. "Bhishma will lead the Kaurava army. Another *paan*, Guru Dhaumya?"

"You are making a grave mistake, Drona. Your love for your son has made you blind. You will regret this all your life."

"Perhaps..."

"You will fight against Arjuna?"

Drona hesitated an instant. Something caught in his throat. He said in a gruff voice, "If that is what the Lord ordains."

"You are a fallen Brahmin." Dhaumya's lips trembled with anger. "You choose to fight against Krishna, Lord Vishnu himself?"

"It is my destiny."

"You will rot in hell if you defy Krishna."

"So be it."

"You are worse than Kripa! You evil Brahmin...you Rakshasa! With the powers vested in me I hereby excommunicate you and your family from the Brahmin community," Dhaumya proclaimed, his voice shaking with rage.

"Dhaumya, Brahminism is not a caste but a way of thinking. I had become one of the living dead, caught in meaningless rituals and superstitious beliefs. But I now know the *Parabrahmam*; I am twice born – a real *dwija*." Drona closed his eyes. In his mind, Shiva danced in his divine glory.

"May you die an inglorious death," Dhaumya cursed.

Kripi dropped the pots of buttermilk in shock. She rushed to her husband and hugged his feet. Drona sat in meditative silence, the swing creaking ominously as it moved back and forth. Dhaumya stood up and rushed away without another word.

"Do not cry," Drona said to his sobbing wife. He knew she would be thinking of her son, imagining his gouged body and lifeless eyes. He knew he had never treated Kripi as his equal, nor had he ever expressed his love to Aswathama. He had always been the dutiful husband and stern father. Now he looked at his life's faithful companion and said, "I always considered you my Lakshmi, massaging her Lord's feet. But I should have seen you as my Shakti, my Parvati, my equal half, just as Shakti is to Lord Ardhanareeswara."

Kripi's eyes swam with unshed tears. She could not believe the words her husband had spoken, words she had never hoped to hear.

Drona shut his eyes. "It will be a shame if I survive this war."

Kripi tried to protest but Drona placed a hand on her head. "This is my promise to you, wife, your son will not die in this war. Not before me."

Kripi wept for the man she had more feared than loved. She felt guilty that she had worried more about her son's life than her husband's death.

Drona's feet were wet with Kripi's tears as she bent her head in reverence. Drona's face remained serene, his mind still. There were no cries of love or war.

*****

"YOU MEAN THE PANDAVAS SHOULD FORGIVE the shaming of their wife and thirteen years of exile?" Krishna had been arguing with his brother for some time.

"The years of exile were the outcome of the Pandavas gambling away what they had. Duryodhana cannot be blamed for that," Balarama stated unequivocally.

"Duryodhana?" Krishna chuckled. "So a strong man can do anything he pleases? Only by winning the war against Duryodhana can the Pandavas avenge themselves."

"What makes you think the Pandavas will win?"

"Brother, if the Pandavas lose, they will go to the heaven of the brave. Future generations will consider them heroes who died in the cause of *dharma*. If they refuse to fight, the world will see them as cowards. What could be more shameful than that for Kshatriyas?"

"Krishna, thousands will die. The war will make so many women widows, so many children orphans. Can you even imagine the horrors of the famine that is sure to follow?" Tears of frustration and anger welled in Balarama's eyes.

Exasperated, Krishna replied, "Brother, it is the *dharma* of Kshatriyas to fight, to kill evil men and protect the weak..."

"Is it *dharma* to kill? *Ahimsa* is the greatest *dharma*. All God's creatures are divine; to take life is the greatest sin."

"What is life but an illusion?"

"Life is an illusion only for you, Krishna."

"The entire universe is an illusion – *maya*. Life is just a dream."

"The pain of life is real, the joy of living is real, and the myriad emotions that make life worth living are all real."

Krishna smiled, "Brother, the wise do not grieve for the dead, nor love the living. The soul is immortal and pervades the entire universe. He who thinks that his soul is killed when his body is slain, is ignorant. The soul has no birth or death; it is unborn, unchangeable and eternal. Only the body perishes. Just as we throw away old or soiled clothes, the soul discards the body."

"Say that to a mother who has lost her child. Try telling that to one who has lost her beloved. What you say is merely an intellectual exercise, Krishna. It does not solve anything but acts as an excuse for violence." Balarama turned away and walked to the window. He was weary of the world.

Krishna looked at Balarama's bowed shoulders and for a moment pity welled in his heart. He loved his brother but he could not stop now. Too much was at stake. "What is born will die, brother. What dies *will* be reborn. Day gives way to night and night to day. It is the eternal cycle of life. Why mourn the unavoidable?"

Balarama shook his head in dismay but let his brother continue. He told himself not to be swayed by emotion.

"That is the path of *sankya*," Krishna stated.

"Call it by any name you wish, but violence is wrong," Balarama responded so softly that Krishna had to bend forward to hear.

"Unfortunately, war has now become a necessity. If we allow Duryodhana to rule, there will be an intermingling of castes," said Krishna.

"Is that such a bad thing?"

"It will result in the ruin of society as we know it. Lawlessness will ensue. No one will know what his *dharma* is."

Balarama smiled. "Ruin of society, Krishna? Because a few priests will not have their way?"

"Brother, I have created four caste divisions according to the work people do. That is their *dharma*. As long as people know and follow their *dharma*, society will remain strong and stable. When there is *adharma* and people forget their caste and work, chaos ensues."

"Those who benefit accept your system as a divine message. But what of those who are crushed by it? Hunger and disease know no caste or race. Why have no divine beings manifested to destroy these evils?"

"I have never sanctioned the crushing of one caste by another, brother. It happens as an aberration and will be dealt with later. A free society without rules is bound to self-destruct eventually. No creature is superior or inferior to another, but each has its own function in the natural order. So has caste."

"It is a beautiful theory but impossible in practice. Prejudice is born when divisions exist."

"Divisions are natural. The duties prescribed for Brahmins, Kshatriyas, Vaishyas and Shudras are all different. Brahmins are those who seek knowledge, they must be restrained and austere. Kshatriyas must be brave and firm and have the bearing of rulers. Agriculture, the tending of cattle, and trade, are the duties of the Vaishyas. For the Shudras, duty consists in servitude to the other three classes."

"Krishna, there lies the problem."

"Brother, every man who engages in his duty as ordained, attains *moksha*. He should perform his duty without thinking about the fruits of his actions. Doing one's duty as prescribed incurs no sin."

"Who decides what one's duty is?"

"The scriptures are the authority to determine what one should do."

"The scriptures are for man, not the other way round. Krishna, you speak of arbitrary divisions, unnatural ones."

"Unnatural? Nature deludes men into thinking they should live passionately. If everyone follows what is natural, without self-restraint, ruin will result."

The silence between the brothers was like an impenetrable fog. Finally, Krishna moved closer to Balarama. "For a yogi, pain and pleasure are alike. He is self-contained."

"A yogi?"

"When a man gives up desire, he is freed from craving enjoyment. He has no affection or pride and thus attains peace of mind. He maintains equanimity in both pleasure and pain. That is the way of the yogi."

"Krishna, you are giving an impossible prescription for an imaginary illness. It is natural for the mind to be restless, to seek, to strive, to achieve what it can."

"A yogi knows this and anchors his mind on me. He learns to look at a Brahmin, a Chandala, a cow or a dog in the same way. A yogi is indifferent to the results of his actions. He performs *nishkama karma*."

"That is not possible, even in an entire lifetime of trying."

"Brother, who said it happens in one lifetime? The person who strives thus will be born again, and will strive from the point he reached in his previous life. It takes many lives to meet the supreme goal of being one with me."

Balarama smiled, remembering the naughty younger brother who had insisted on following him around. "And if he fails?"

"Those who fail are born again and again, as worms or beasts. They have to work their way up to human form and start striving again."

"I do not understand, Krishna. A man does wrong *karma* and is then born as a beast, say a buffalo, but can we find anything more serene and detached than a water buffalo? It is indifferent to rain, sunshine, dirty water or dry grass. It is the picture of total contentment. Except for physical pain or pleasure, it does not worry about the results of its actions. Does that make the buffalo the supreme yogi? If it does, it should achieve *moksha* and not be reborn." Balarama waited to see what his divine brother would say.

"You are arguing for the sake of argument," Krishna said, a trace of irritation in his voice. "Brother, a man's concern should be about his *karma*, not the fruits of his action. He should be devoted to his work without getting attached to it, and be equally impervious to success and failure."

"Where can you find such a person, Krishna? How will I recognize someone with such a steady mind? How does such an unusual person sit, speak and move?" Balarama asked.

The sarcasm in Balarama's words left Krishna unmoved. "He is called a *stithapranjna*, one whose mind has equanimity. He is not agitated amid calamities, does not crave pleasure, and is free of attachments, fear and wrath."

"How is that possible, Krishna? We are but human and creatures of frailty."

"Just as a tortoise withdraws its limbs into his shell, the yogi withdraws his senses from the objects of desire. Just as the tortoise thus becomes strong, a man also gains strength when he withdraws from desire and steadies his mind in contemplation."

"Krishna, if you have reached that much-desired state, why does it matter to you whether Yudhishtra wins the war or Duryodhana? Why not keep your mind steady in contemplation instead?"

"Brother, I do my *karma* without attachment, free from its results. The destruction of evil is my duty. I do not relish violence, but I do what is necessary."

"A convenient argument, Krishna, and a recipe for a heartless world. It is a *mantra* for a conscienceless society."

"Why do you say that?"

"Krishna, a tyrant can unleash a pogrom and say it is his duty as a ruler to cleanse his kingdom. We can justify any violence in the name of duty and *dharma*. Any war can be justified as both sides consider they are following their *dharma* in butchering each other. Even a bandit can claim that robbing is his *dharma*."

"Brother, he who performs action without worrying about the results is sinless. Those who perform actions with passion should be ready for the bitter or sweet fruits of those actions."

"That is an even more dangerous argument. Is misery the result of the *karma* of the miserable? Then compassion would have no meaning."

"You do not understand, my brother, because your eyes have yet to see the vision of divinity."

"Krishna, such ideas can only create a callous and indifferent society. If someone is wretched, it can be explained away as the result of some past action, if not in this life then in some other birth. Why help the miserable and get entangled in their *karma*?"

"Brother, you have taken my words too literally – it was just an allegory."

"Krishna, allegory is an old trick of philosophers and prophets. Their words are like scattered clouds in the sky, according to one's power of imagination, one can see any shape in the clouds. Allegory is a safe bet for prophets and Gurus. When caught, they can claim that was not the right meaning. If you want to say something, why not say it in plain language, without ambiguity?"

"Hear it then, brother. I allude to men like Duryodhana, who are deluded by their evil desires. Their passionate actions cause misery."

"So desire and passion are the greatest evils of man?"

"Brother, by desiring an object, attachment is born. From attachment, wrath is born. From wrath comes want of discrimination. From want of discrimination arises ruination of intelligence. From loss of intelligence springs loss of understanding, and then man is ruined."

"Krishna, from desire, life is born. From attachment, love. From passion, beauty. From compassion, humanity. Desire is the very foundation of nature."

"Desire is the offspring of a base nature. Duryodhana is the epitome of *tamo guna*. Such men claim life is created from lust. They are deluded by ignorance and tossed about by a million thoughts."

"Thoughts are what make a man, Krishna."

"The right thoughts, brother. Men like Duryodhana can only sink into a foul hell. They are wedded to vanity, power, pride, lust and wrath. In every life, they repeat the same mistakes and their path spirals down and down instead of up and up."

"Krishna, if you are the Supreme Soul hurling these unfortunate men and women into demonic wombs, how are they to blame? By your own admission, *you* have made them that way."

"There are three qualities in nature, brother – *satva*, *rajo* and *tamo*. All three are present in all of us. But it depends which one we nourish. *Satva* is the quality of light, knowledge and equanimity; *rajo* is the quality of bravery, chivalry and power; and *tamo* is passion and desire."

"Show me one person who is not passionate about something."

"Yudhishtra."

"Ah, the man who gambled away his wife. Was it because he was detached about her or the kingdom he wanted to win by dicing?"

"Yudhishtra is a true yogi, a man of knowledge. I have to protect such men, who follow the right path."

"But you have not answered my question, Krishna. I fail to see the Pandavas as detached yogis or seekers of knowledge. They appear to be nothing more than seekers of power."

"Brother, you have chosen to close your eyes to the truth. The Pandavas are my devotees. They have chosen the path of *bhakti*. They regard me as the highest object of attainment and worship me with devotion. I am their deliverer from the ocean of this sad world. I give you this great *mantra* as well, the path of yoga and the imperishable system of devotion. I declared it to Vivaswat eons ago and he declared it to Manu, who passed it to Ishvaku, and so it has reached this age."

"You are talking about Kings of the distant past, but you live today, Krishna. You are even younger than me."

"Many births of mine have passed. Many lifetimes of yours have passed too. I know it, you do not."

"I do not understand your words, Krishna, how will others do so?"

"Then know that I am the Unborn. I am the Lord of all creatures. Whenever there is loss of piety and evil men like Duryodhana rise to power, I am born, again and again, age after age, for the protection of the righteous and the destruction of evil; to establish piety and devotion to God."

"Krishna, you are merely deluding yourself. I have known you since the day of your birth," Balarama said, shaking his head in amusement at the thought of his naughty little brother being the saviour of the world.

Krishna smiled. "Brother, I am offering the human race the chance of redemption from misery. He who knows this truth will achieve *moksha*. He will not be born again but become one with me. Forsaking everything, let my devotees come to me as their sole refuge and I will deliver them from all sin. Surrender to me with complete devotion."

"Krishna," Balarama said, a rare smile tugging at the corners of his mouth, "the world is indifferent to the petty travails of men. The search of an individual for self or God, within or without, is an insignificant event for the universe."

"Brother, many who have believed in me have been freed of attachment and passion. In whatever manner people come to me, I accept them. All paths lead to me. Your path too."

"Why should one seek God and try to escape from this beautiful world? Why exchange a hypothetical *moksha* for the real world? *Jagat satyam, Brahma mithya.*"

Balarama had many questions for his brother but before he could voice any of them, Krishna said, "To those who worship me in any form, I give gifts and preserve what they deserve to have. Even if they revere other Gods and worship me irregularly, I bless them. But since their devotion is incomplete, they take birth again and again, after enjoying a place in heaven. Do everything as an offering to me. That way, you will be detached from your actions and come to me. Brother, know that even if a wicked person worships me alone, he is regarded as good."

"If you are the Supreme Being, indifferent to the results of your actions, why are you so obsessed with whether someone worships you or not? And you say worshipping you will redeem any sin?"

Krishna ignored the incredulity in his brother's voice. "None devoted to me is lost, even if they are sinful. Even women, Vaishyas and Shudras can attain *moksha* if they worship me. In this transient and miserable world, be engaged in my worship. Fix your mind on me, be my devotee, bow to me, take refuge in me and you shall come to me."

"Who are you, Krishna?"

"Brother Balarama, you do not know who you are or who I am. You are infinity, *ananta*. But I am beyond infinity. We are one, yet we are different. The difference lies in realization."

"Whoever you are, Krishna, you are bringing war and death to thousands," Balarama said, his shoulders drooping in defeat.

Krishna's eyes looked at Balarama but gazed beyond him. "Know that I created the universe at the beginning of *kalpa*. As all creatures who take birth, live and die, the universe, too, has a lifespan. This is not the first universe you are living in, nor will it be the last. I will destroy it when the time comes and create a new one. That, too, will be destroyed in due course. This cycle will continue eternally. I only perform my *karma* here, detached. It does not affect me."

"Everyone has to eat the fruits of *karma*, Krishna. It does not matter whether the actions were performed passionately or in a detached fashion. We still have to eat the bitter fruit. Now, brother will fight brother. You have encouraged it. War will come, Krishna, and then none of these fancy words will help. I am afraid of what will come..."

"Brother, you do not know me and my Supreme nature as Lord of all entities. Ignorant people disregard me. I am the Supreme Soul and I have assumed this human body. Only noble souls know me, they glorify and bow to my divinity."

"Is that Duryodhana's sin – that he does not bow to you? If you are indeed the Supreme Soul, why not gift him understanding and devotion? Why bring death and misery to innocents who have nothing to do with either of you? Why not destroy the evil man alone, instead of dragging all of Bharatavarsha into a war?" Balarama asked his brother.

"I am the Father and Mother of the universe, and I am the Creator. I am Immortality. I am Death. I am that by which this universe is held. I am the life force, the source of evolution and dissolution. There is nothing greater than me. I am *Om*."

"Krishna, what has happened to you, my brother?" Balarama cried.

"He who knows me as the Supreme Lord of the worlds, without birth and beginning, is free of all sin. Behold my glory of a thousand splendid suns. Behold my infinite energy. I have no beginning, middle or end. Behold my blazing radiance and many-hued eyes."

Balarama watched in horrified silence.

"I am Death, the destroyer of worlds. Behold the sight of the sons of Dhritarashtra, Bhishma, Drona and the great warriors from both sides entering the mouth of Time. See how their heads are crushed, their limbs torn apart. Behold the future and the spectre of the past. Behold me for I am TIME."

"Krishna..." Balarama's voice shook. "Because of your actions I fear something terrible will befall Dwaraka. That is the law of *karma*, the law of the universe. It does not spare any man, even an *avatar*." Balarama turned away. He had lost the argument. There was nothing left for an ignorant and deluded man like him to argue about. He did not have the intellect to understand the divine song of God. Outside, the ocean had turned blue-black, like the colour of his brother's skin. The waters beat restlessly against the rocks.

"I am TIME..." Krishna's voice echoed in Balarama's ears and fear of the future chilled his heart.

*****

47 THE SONG OF MAN

BALARAMA'S GAZE ALIGHTED ON THE YOKE in one corner of the small room. There was a time when, as a young man, he had carried it over his shoulder every day, to teach his people about agriculture and irrigation. He caressed its woody contours and then placed it on his shoulder, feeling its familiar weight. He would walk through the dusty streets of Bharata, from the Himalayas in the north to the city of Devi, where the three seas met in the south. He yearned to lose himself in the vastness of the land, far from the madness of men and their calls for *dharmayudha*.

Balarama heard someone behind him and turned. Duryodhana's daughter stood in the doorway, tall and graceful. Ever since she had arrived in Dwaraka, following her marriage to Krishna's renegade son, she had been a silent presence in the palace, much like the shadows that graced its walls at night.

Lakshmana spoke softly. "Uncle, why are you leaving us?"

Balarama looked at her sorrowfully. "I do not know, daughter."

"May I accompany you?"

Balarama was tempted to ask what her husband would say. Samba was unpredictable and dangerous.

"My husband will not even notice," Lakshmana said, as if reading his mind.

"Daughter, the path will be too rough for a Princess's soft feet."

"It would be an honour to walk barefoot with you."

"It will be a very long walk, daughter. People may jeer or throw stones at us."

"I am not afraid."

Balarama smiled as he ran his fingers over his now bald head.

"Someone else wants to come with us, too," Lakshmana said.

Valsala, his beautiful daughter, stepped out of the shadows and touched her father's feet. "Take me too, Father."

"But Abhimanyu?" Balarama asked.

"His new bride, Uttara, is beautiful. He has no time for me now."

Balarama's heart ached for his child as she rested her head on his chest. He put his arms around her gently, wishing he could protect her forever.

"I wronged Lakshmana Kumara, Father. Now, I am tasting the fruits of my own *karma*. Uncle Krishna was not to blame. I was blinded by my love for Abhimanyu and we compelled him to help us. That is why it happened. Look at us now. Abhimanyu and I rarely see each other and when we do, silence is the only language we speak."

Lakshmana Kumara's perplexed face rose before Balarama's eyes. Would he ever be able to forgive himself and find peace? He began walking, ignoring the bowing guards and looking straight ahead. He was no longer their King. The two women hurried to keep up.

People on the street paused to watch the curious sight. Then a man joined them, and then a woman. One became two, two became ten and ten became a hundred. Soon, thousands were following the old man and the two young girls, without asking any questions.

A few days later, an untouchable and his blind dog joined the strange procession. Ironically, the songs he sang were about Krishna's love. The crowd sang with him as Balarama walked through the miserable villages of his country, carrying his yoke on his shoulder. The motley crowd stopped at hamlets to serve those forgotten by their rulers and forsaken by God. The Song of Man was composed without words.

Near the banks of the Yamuna, they encountered a group led by Carvaka. The atheist Guru laughed when he saw Balarama. "Where are you going to, Sir?" he asked, gazing at Balarama's entourage.

"In search of God, Carvaka. Perhaps I have found him in you? And where may you be going?" the saint asked the atheist.

"I am searching for Man, Balarama. I think I have found him in you."

The atheist and the saint laughed aloud. The crowd around them joined in the laughter without comprehending a word either had spoken.

"That is a dangerous thing to do, Carvaka, searching for Man in a holy crowd could get you killed," Balarama said, chuckling.

"But you are walking an even more dangerous path, Balarama, if you have begun to see God in an atheist."

Balarama put his arms round the shoulders of his daughter and niece. "Carvaka, I have no great philosophy to offer except that of love. I know no *mantras* except that of peace. I am not an *avatar*, but an old man in a *dhoti*; an insignificant man in a land of dazzling Gods. But I will not give up. I will return in every age to walk with my children. I do not seek *moksha* from that. I have only one simple wish – to return to my country whenever she needs me."

"Balarama, they will come after you. Their intellects may be blunt but their arrows are sharp."

"I will suffer happily for my children, but I will not give up till I teach them the *dharma* of *ahimsa* and love."

The saint and the atheist, seekers both, bowed to each other and went their separate ways.

*****

48 THE GREAT SECRET

"SOME OTHER DAY, JARA," Vidhura said, trying to walk away.

But the beggar blocked his path and pleaded with folded hands, "Please, Swami. Devi Kunti is sick with worry."

Vidhura had been quietly ignoring Kunti's requests to visit her. He could not think of a way to avoid the visit now. Swallowing hard, he turned back and started walking towards the street where he had once lived. Everything looked familiar, yet strange. There were a few new houses and the tree at the corner had grown corpulent with age. Some of the houses needed a new coat of lime and a few street lamps leaned at precarious angles. The smell of garbage permeated the air and a cat peered out of an overflowing dustbin. Nothing much had changed, yet everything had.

"Ma," Jara called.

The door creaked open and Vidhura gasped as he looked at Kunti. She had aged beyond his wildest imagination. The once beautiful face was now a web of wrinkles, the long and glossy black hair, silver. He hoped the meeting would soon be over and he could leave.

"Vidhura, how old you have grown!" Kunti exclaimed, drawing an answering smile from Vidhura.

Vidhura touched his balding pate and said with a courtier's grace, "Time has not been kind, Devi, yet you look untouched by its hands."

"Still the same sweet talker, Vidhura. Come in. I have been desperately trying to reach you for quite some time."

Jara walked away. The dog sniffed at Vidhura's hands and then trotted off behind its master. Vidhura stepped out to the veranda and sat down. His son had once fallen here and they had rushed him to the palace Vaidya late in the evening. For two days the boy had cried in pain...

"There is going to be a war."

Kunti's words brought Vidhura back to the present. "Not if I can do something about it," he replied.

"You should visit me sometimes. No one comes here except Krishna." Kunti dabbed her eyes with the end of her sari.

Vidhura looked at the floor, not wanting to face her. "Devi, things have not been good for me, either," he finally said.

"I called you here for a particular reason. There was a time when I wanted my children to outdo Gandhari's sons in everything. I was afraid to become the poor relation living on their charity. But when I look back now, it all seems so meaningless."

"Devi, the rivalry between the cousins is deep, yet, if you wish, the war can still be avoided."

"I want my son to be King after Dhritarashtra," Kunti said, looking towards the hills in the distance.

"Gandhari wants Suyodhana to be King and you want Yudhishtra." Vidhura sighed. He was wasting his time here.

"I do not speak of Yudhishtra." Kunti turned away from Vidhura and pulled her *pallu* over her head. Her face was in shadow but Vidhura saw the glimmer of tears in her eyes.

"I don't understand." For some reason, his heart began pounding in his chest. Perhaps it was the way she had spoken.

"I speak of Karna."

Had he heard correctly? Vidhura's heart began beating like a frenzied drum. "What has that Sutaputra to do with it?" Vidhura asked, looking at his sister-in-law in astonishment.

"He is not a Sutaputra."

Vidhura remained silent, waiting for Kunti to say something more.

"Karna is my son," Kunti said on a sob. Her unshed tears threatened to choke her.

Vidhura stood up, holding on to the bamboo pole near him. The world had turned upside down. The man who had been ridiculed for his caste by everyone was Kunti's firstborn son?

"But how?" The news was as incredible as it was shocking.

"I had him before my marriage to Pandu. He is my illegitimate son. It would have created a huge scandal for the Princess to have a son before marriage. I was just sixteen. So I gave him to Mother Ganga, in a reed basket, leaving him to live or die. Every day I have prayed for him, his health and happiness."

"Devi, how could you have been so cruel, to him and to yourself?"

"Vidhura, I have borne the pain and guilt every living moment since that day. I saw him when he came to challenge Arjuna on the day of the Princes' graduation. I watched him being humiliated by one and all. Only Duryodhana stood by my son. Now my sons will fight each other and I am afraid."

Vidhura knew not how to respond. He felt both revulsion and pity for the old woman before him. The reasons and justifications could be many but Karna was the real victim in this drama. "Why did you choose to tell me this now?" he finally asked in a low voice.

"I know what you must think of me, yet even now I do not have the courage to tell the world that Karna is my son."

Vidhura waited but Kunti turned away. He wondered if she realized that her secret would drag the whole country into a bloody war. Thousands would die and be left destitute. He wanted to shout at her but when he looked into Kunti's face, he could not bring himself to do it. He would have to find another way.

"Devi, I will tell Lord Bhishma. He will find a way. Perhaps this is our last chance to prevent the war."

Kunti sat with a faraway look in her eyes. Vidhura bowed and took his leave. The future looked frightening. It was going to be a major war and both sides would do anything to win. Vidhura walked the familiar road to the palace. He had to meet the forgotten old man and tell him about Karna. It was his country's last hope.

***

The wheel of *karma* was turning. Suyodhana had been struck with many tragedies but the best time to strike was when the enemy was down. The Southern Confederate had declared its independence from Hastinapura. Parashurama braced for Karna's army to descend upon them. When nothing happened, he grew bolder. The Guru restored *dharma* by reversing Suyodhana's reforms. Though Parashurama longed to be at Kurukshetra, he knew his fighting days were over. He would control his puppets from behind the scenes.

"What is Takshaka's new city called?" Parashurama asked Uthayan.

"Nagapura, the City of Nagas. Takshaka has reversed the caste rules and everyone except Nagas are considered untouchables."

"The rise of *Kali* is imminent." Parashurama spat out red *paan* juice. "Nagapura sits at the centre of Bharatavarsha – an ideal place to instil the laws of *dharma*."

"Guru, the Nagas have forgotten the lessons of Indraprastha but we will remind them. Do we move to Kurukshetra after that?"

"Kurukshetra! It will be the mother of all wars. Are the Kings of the Confederate ready to fight evil?"

"Not Kalinga, Guru. The traitor supports the Suta, saying he has been chosen by the Sun God."

"But Krishna is siding with the Pandavas. Evil will be vanquished."

***

The Confederate army marched towards Kurukshetra, ravaging everything in its path. They captured Nagapura and butchered thousands of Nagas. Takshaka was on the run again. Parashurama felt smug. From the city of the Nagas, he would decide the present and future of Bharatavarsha.

Uthayan travelled further north and led the Kings of the Southern Confederate to the Pandava camp. He bent to touch Krishna and Dhaumya's feet and then bowed to Yudhishtra. "We have come from the distant South to help the cause of *dharma*."

"Ah, we were expecting you," Dhaumya said smoothly. "We would like the Confederate army to arrange for all the food and weapons for the Pandava side."

"But we came to fight Duryodhana," Uthayan protested. He was confused, this was not the treatment he had expected. It was almost insulting. Battles had been fought in the South for far more trivial reasons.

"It is a critical job, King Uthayan. Only you can do it. The country is reeling from drought and there is barely anything for the people to eat, let alone horses and elephants. It needs great administrative talent and your people are famous for that." Dhaumya smiled.

Perhaps what the good priest said was important. Uthayan turned to his soldiers. "Scrounge in every home and force open every granary. There is no time to waste. We must consolidate our supplies before the enemy grabs it." Uthayan began barking orders to his men. In an exemplary display of Southern discipline, the Confederate army spread into the countryside to forage, pilfer and loot.

"Why did you do that, Guru?" Arjuna asked. He felt offended by the lack of respect shown to another warrior.

But Dhaumya merely smiled. "They are not pure Kshatriyas. They have Asura blood. This is not only about winning the war but also who wins it." He let his words sink into the minds of the

Pandavas. The last thing he wanted was Uthayan or any Asura King winning the war for them. It would be best to keep such glory and achievements to the fringes. The carefully built theory of caste purity would collapse if Uthayan turned out to be as skilled as Arjuna. That would make the war meaningless. In matters of *dharma*, it was not worth taking such risks.

Dhaumya noticed a dark-skinned young man standing alone at the edges of the forest. He looked like a Naga. But what was a Naga doing at the Pandava camp? As the Guru watched with growing anger, the young man bowed low. He had to find out who the youngster was. The face looked oddly familiar. Suddenly, Dhaumya stopped. The Naga resembled Arjuna! If he was right, then he would have even more work to do to save *dharma*, the Guru thought.

*****

49 WAR GAMES

BHISHMA STARED AT THE EMACIATED figure standing before him. He had expected Vidhura to age but nothing had prepared him for the frail and hunched man standing before him with bowed head.

"To what do I owe the honour of this visit, Vidhura?" he asked gruffly, trying to hide the distress he felt. His words sounded harsh even to his own ears.

"Sir, forgive me, but I did not have the strength to see you like this," Vidhura answered, looking at the floor.

"I am just a forgotten old man, caged in my room, unwanted by my grand-nephews and my country." Bhishma wished Vidhura, that man of unfaltering reason and intellect, would protest, but his former Prime Minister stood in stricken silence. Bhishma shifted the manuscripts on his table listlessly. Only a few palm leaves containing verses from the *Upanishads* remained. Once there had seemed too few hours in the day to get through what lay on his work-laden table.

Vidhura's heart filled with sorrow. Could any country prosper when it dishonoured the noble and the brave? "Our country is crumbling," he said in a low voice.

"We don't deserve anything better," Bhishma said, slamming his palm on the table.

"Sir, why did you not stop Suyodhana from pawning the country to Yuyutsu?" Vidhura asked the question that had troubled him for a long time.

"One Prince pawns his wife, another pawns his country to a merchant. What is the difference between the fools?" Bhishma asked, standing up. Despite his years, he still had the powerful frame of the warrior.

"There is going to be a war," said Vidhura softly, almost to himself.

"So be it. At its end, there will be one fool left instead of two."

"Drought and famine loom large. People are starving to death," Vidhura said, knowing Bhishma knew it better than anyone else.

"What am I supposed to do about that? There is a King on the throne; there are *mahatmas*, sages and *avatars* living and preaching throughout this land. Ours is a holy land, is it not? We fight bloody wars to uphold *dharma*. Let the common man die. We can offer them *moksha* in the afterlife." Bhishma's lips curved into a bitter smile.

"We must stop the war." Vidhura finally raised his head and looked Bhishma in the eye.

"Do you know a way to do that? For I do not. Both sides are bent on destroying each other. I have done what I could for as long as I could. Enough! Let there be war. Let no fool, including old ones like me, be spared. Let a new Bharata rise from the ashes of our funeral pyres."

"I have met Kunti," Vidhura said in a low voice that was almost lost in the echoing vastness of the chamber.

"Then you had better hurry to meet Gandhari as well, or else it could become another cause for war," Bhishma said with a tired smile.

"She told me something shocking."

Bhishma grunted.

"About Karna."

"I do not wish to hear anything about that Suta."

"Karna is not a Suta, nor the son of a charioteer."

"I always knew he was a bastard. It shows in his arrogance."

"Sir, he is the bastard son of Devi Kunti."

Bhishma became as still as stone. Only the pulse throbbing in his temple suggested he was aware of what had been said. Then he turned away saying, "It is a lie. Kunti is up to something."

"Karna was born before Kunti's marriage to Pandu. His father belonged to the Suryavamsha dynasty of Sri Ramachandra." Vidhura explained the entire sequence of events.

Reluctantly, after many interpolations and questions, Bhishma took a deep breath and said, "This changes everything, Vidhura. I have always been harsh on Karna. Now it seems he is the eldest of my grand-nephews, but that does not make him a Pandava. He is the illegitimate son of a daughter-in-law of the house. Of course, there are *shastras* which sanction that, but the husband is required to acknowledge his wife's children begotten before marriage. That has not happened here."

"Sir, this is the only chance for peace. Make Karna the next heir and no one will be able to question it," Vidhura begged earnestly.

"My son, you do not know Suyodhana or Yudhishtra as I do. Nor do you know Karna. And you have not considered Yuyutsu. He too, is an illegitimate son of Dhritarashtra. His father has accepted him publicly as his son. He could well stake a claim to the throne. But I doubt Karna will be prepared to betray Suyodhana."

"Who will say no to the throne of Hastinapura, Sir? Karna will agree. You only need to suggest it."

"Vidhura, for a wise man, you are being short-sighted. The issue of the inheritance has to be settled once and for all. War is the best way to do that."

"Sir, a war at this time would be a terrible thing. And what of the thousands who will die for no fault of their own?"

"It is the *dharma* of Kshatriyas to fight."

"The rains have failed for the third year."

Bhishma went to stand by the window. "I will lead Suyodhana's army but I will ensure that none of the Pandavas die. We can use the drought and famine conditions to force peace. In three or four days, supplies will start running out. Then we can work out a truce."

"In three or four days thousands will have died, Sir."

"War is not about individuals. People are bound to die, but I will ensure the Kuru dynasty survives," Bhishma insisted, annoyed that Vidhura had failed to see his deeper point.

"There are other enmities that also run deep, Sir. Dhristadyumna, Drupada's son, has vowed to kill Drona."

"Nobody can touch Drona."

"Karna and Arjuna are itching for a fight. Once the war starts, you will be unable to control it," Vidhura said with utter certainty. He could feel the knot of fear in his stomach.

"Hmm, you have a point. Karna has an impulsive nature. I saw it at Virata. We must find a way to keep him off the battlefield."

"Sir, please reconsider... a war will be disastrous for all." Vidhura looked at the old warrior by the window and knew he had lost. As long as Bhishma breathed, there would be no compromise.

"Getting sentimental in your old age, Vidhura? It will be a skirmish, a display of arms to demonstrate to these fools the foolishness of war." Bhishma walked up to Vidhura and placed both hands on his frail shoulders.

Vidhura took both Bhishma's hands in his own and pressed them together. He stood still, praying silently. Bhishma felt sorrow fill his heart as he looked at Vidhura's bent head. He was just a trembling shadow of the fine, upright man he had once been. Bhishma saw his own reflection in Vidhura's eyes. They both looked so insignificant now. Was he starting something they could not control? No...he had years of experience in leading armies. He knew how to pace a war. Only that Suta...perhaps not a Suta...had to be kept away from the battlefield.

Vidhura paused at the door, remembering something important. "Sir, be wary of Shikandi."

"Ha, what can that eunuch do to me?" Bhishma asked with genuine amusement in his still rich voice.

Vidhura hesitated a moment and then walked away with tired steps.

'Poor man, he is far too sincere for these times,' Bhishma thought as he took a sword off the wall and swung it gracefully. His old limbs were still supple. He chuckled to himself. It would be good to be back in action. Bhishma felt alive again.

***

When Suyodhana entered the Sabha, the air was thick with anticipation. Bhishma had called the Sabha to make an important announcement. Suyodhana sat down near Karna. Why was Bhishma avoiding his gaze? His father looked worried.

The murmuring stopped as Bhishma rose to speak. His voice lacked its usual power and he sounded weary. "I have nurtured this country with my blood. Vidhura and I toiled day and night so that our people could sleep peacefully. Alas, now my grand-nephews want to fight each other. Both sides have committed unspeakable atrocities. I have failed as a teacher and grandsire to them."

Suyodhana felt overcome by shame. He should never have behaved as he had with Draupadi, no matter what she deserved. What had revenge gained him? Then sudden resentment swamped his mind. How could Bhishma equate the atrocities of the Pandavas with his foolishness? His action had been directed at one woman, who had shamed him; the Pandavas had killed thousands of innocents.

"Since war has become inevitable, I am forced to take sides. On one hand there is Arjuna, who is dear to me. I admire his humility and skill with arms. There is Yudhishtra, who is saintly in his demeanour. I owe much to Draupadi for not speaking out when Suyodhana shamed her in public."

Suyodhana's heart sank. Bhishma was going to side with the Pandavas. He would have to fight his venerable grandsire. And if Bhishma himself was partial to the Pandavas, there was little question that Drona would side with them also. Aswathama would then go with his father. He had only Karna.

"I have to consider Suyodhana too. He has his faults. His arrogance and temper have earned him many enemies. What he did to Draupadi was unpardonable. Yet I do not judge people on one incident. How is Suyodhana as a ruler? The treasury is almost empty and we are staring at imminent famine. That is not the mark of a great administrator. But his mistakes are those of inexperience. One can gain experience, acquire wisdom and correct mistakes. He has corrected one such mistake by not giving in to Yuyutsu's demands."

Suyodhana watched Bhishma intently. What was he hinting at?

"What cannot be acquired is goodness of heart. Suyodhana has proved himself the better human being through numerous acts, some of which you may perhaps not be aware of. The elevation of the son of a Suta as King of Anga; treating Ekalavya as an equal; his misguided but well-intentioned acts to bring equality to all men and women across the country; his open stand against what he considers unfair, all prove his goodness of heart. If he allows me to do so, I can teach him administration. What I need not teach him is compassion towards the downtrodden and a sense of fairness and justice."

Suyodhana's hands were wet with perspiration. Bhishma's next words fell as gently as winter rain. "Son, will you not compromise with your cousins, since I ask it of you? Will you not share a small part of this kingdom in order to avoid bloodshed?"

Suyodhana wavered. He was at a loss for an answer. Gaining victory in war was not going to be easy. Neither was he sure who would decide to defect to the other side. By compromising, he could keep Hastinapura and most of the country. Finally, he looked at the patriarch and said, "Pitamaha, can you vouch that Dhaumya will not impose his laws in the Pandava part of the kingdom?"

"No one can predict the future, son."

"In that case I would be forsaking half my subjects."

"If you lose the war, you will be forsaking all your subjects."

"I will not lose. *Dharma* is with me."

Bhishma shook his head. Why did people always need to take the hard road to learn life's lessons? Sighing, he pronounced his decision: "I will fight against the Pandavas."

Suyodhana was not sure he had heard correctly. He looked at Bhishma in disbelief and then fell to his knees, touching his forehead to the floor in reverence before the patriarch. He could hear Dhritarashtra's jubilant voice and people shouting in excitement.

Drona stood up. "It will be a great honour if Lord Bhishma would permit me to fight by his side."

It took a few minutes for the Sabha to comprehend the implications of Drona's simple statement. They had expected a sizzling speech from the Guru denouncing Suyodhana. Deafening cheers rose from all sides, drowning a few murmurs of surprise. Aswathama stared at his father in amazement, his heart thudding with happiness.

Before Duryodhana could express his gratitude, a boisterous laugh resounded through the Sabha. Kripa walked in and went straight to his brother-in-law. "A sudden change of heart, Drona?"

The Guru stared at Kripa in distaste and said coldly, "I am merely doing my duty."

"Oh, I thought you were trying to repay an undeserved fee," Kripa chuckled. He turned to Suyodhana. "Will you recruit an old street dog into your army?"

Suyodhana grasped the old master's hands. He suddenly remembered the early days when Kripa had taught the young Kuru Princes, before Drona had come to replace him... How unpredictable the winds of war were! He had come to the Sabha with little hope after Yuyutsu's defection, yet those he had always considered to be Pandava supporters were now flocking to his banner.

"How about the Yadavas?" Kripa asked.

"Yadavas? Krishna hates me. The entire Yadava army will be fighting against us."

"Hmm, you think so?" Kripa said, and then called, "Kritavarma!"

The tall Yadava General entered and bowed to the King and Bhishma. Kritavarma addressed Bhishma in a clear voice. "Sir, the entire Narayana Sena has come to fight for *dharma*. Allow us to serve under you in your army."

Such bizarre things were happening! Suyodhana was at a loss for words. Krishna had lost control over his own army and they had defected to his side? Was there a trap here?

"General Kritavarma, is Krishna aware of your decision?" Bhishma asked.

"Sir, Lord Balarama himself asked me to follow my conscience and Krishna gave the Narayana Sena the option to choose. The majority chose to come with me."

"And Krishna did not object?" Suyodhana asked, still bemused at the turn of events.

"When I informed him of my decision to side with you, all he said was, 'Each one according to his own *dharma*'."

Suyodhana stared at Kritavarma. What was it about Krishna that he could not fathom? Krishna was an enigma.

"Where is Lord Balarama?" Bhishma asked.

"Sir, he is walking as a mendicant through the little-known pathways of our land, heartbroken. He has relinquished the throne."

Why had his Guru not sided with him, wondered Suyodhana. When so many great men had decided to fight on his side, thinking it was the right choice, why had only Balarama remain neutral?

Bhishma cleared his throat. "The kingdoms of Pragjyotisha, Mahishmati, Avanti, Madhaydesa, Bahlikas, Kamboja, Sakas, Trilingas, Tusharas and many others, have offered alliances. The friendship of Anga, Gandhara and Sindhudesa, etc., remain firm; they will always stand by us. The kingdoms of the Southern Confederate, like Chera, Chola and Pandya, are expected to ally themselves with the Pandavas. Magadha also."

"Kalinga?" Kripa asked

Bhishma looked at Karna. "The old King of Kalinga will be on the side of the warrior chosen by the Sun God."

"Karna is the chosen one," Suyodhana said, smiling at his friend.

"It is too early to predict which side Karna will fight on," Bhishma said. There was a murmur of surprise all around. Surely there could be no doubt about that? Karna would stand Suyodhana's friend unto death.

"Sir, you insult me and my friendship with Prince Suyodhana." Karna's bright face darkened as he stood to his imposing height.

"When a Kshatriya speaks, a Sutaputra ought to remain silent," Bhishma replied coldly.

"Pitamaha," Suyodhana said, "why do you alone refuse to respect the great warrior that Karna is? Even the Sun God chose him as his own."

"Prince, you will have to choose between him and me. Wars are for Kshatriyas. This Suta is both immature and reckless. We saw it at Virata. Let him be content with driving a chariot."

Face aflame with rage and humiliation, Karna turned to walk out of the Sabha but Suyodhana grabbed his wrist. "Karna, do not go."

Karna looked into his friend's eyes and asked, "Do you trust me to win the war for you?"

Suyodhana faltered. If he chose Karna, he was sure to lose the support of both Bhishma and Drona. How many others would refuse to fight beside a Suta? Karna saw the hesitation in his friend's face and deliberately prised Suyodhana's grip from his wrist, one finger at a time. He bowed to all the great men in the Sabha and walked away.

Bhishma sighed softly to himself. The deed was done.

*****

50 RELUCTANT WARRIORS

"ULUKA, SEEK YOUR COUSIN'S BLESSINGS. You too, Vrika." Shakuni's voice startled Suyodhana. His uncle was beaming at him.

"Why have you called your sons from Gandhara?" Suyodhana asked as he placed his hands on the bent heads of the young men at his feet.

"Do you think Gandharan Princes hide behind their mother's *pallu* when a war is on?" Shakuni asked, and then added with a smile, "Of course, Lakshmana Kumara is different."

"What do you mean, Uncle?"

"Oh, we all enjoy his poetry. And what a voice he has!"

Suyodhana's face clouded with anger. Shakuni immediately replaced his smile with a look of specious concern. "Suyodhana, do not force the boy to do what he does not wish to. We are all here to bring you victory. The boy is his mother's darling. Allow him to remain here. We can enjoy his verse once we have vanquished the Pandavas."

Shakuni left with his sons. Suyodhana remained standing, his face furrowed with worry.

***

"He is the future ruler, Bhanumati. Why don't you understand?" Suyodhana tried to keep calm. He did not want a discussion with his wife about their son.

"I want to participate in the war, mother," Lakshmana Kumara's voice was low, fearing his father's temper.

Suyodhana sighed. 'What am I going to do with such a boy?'

"This is between your father and me, son," said Bhanumati.

"He is not a baby, Bhanu. He cannot hide in the palace and write poetry when the entire country is at war."

"My son is not going to fight *your* war and die. Let us have no argument about this."

"Do you not understand what is at stake?"

"Mother, I wish to fight beside my father." Kumara's voice was soft but sure.

"I have said no. Leave us. This is for your father and me to decide."

"Stay where you are, Kumara. Bhanu, he is a Kshatriya. Why do you insist on bringing shame upon him and me? Do you really wish to hear him being called a coward?"

"It is better than calling him dead."

"He is the same age as Abhimanyu. Have you not heard the paeans the bards sing about Subhadra and Arjuna's son?"

"So that is it... my son is not as good as hers? I am not as good as..."

"Enough! He is coming with me into battle, like a true Kshatriya."

"You are not going anywhere." Bhanumati turned back to her son.

Kumara shook his head at her gently and then moved to stand beside his father. "I am sorry, mother, but I must go. I cannot let down my father, the family, the country..."

"What do you know about fighting, son? How will you face great warriors like Arjuna?" Bhanumati said, her voice cracking. She went over to her son and put a hand on his shoulder.

"I will do my utmost, mother."

"It will not be good enough. You will die. Do not go! You are the only one left to me."

"Bhanu, stop this!" Suyodhana went to stand in front of his son. But the defiance had gone from Bhaumati's face and she looked vulnerable, like an injured sparrow. Suyodhana lifted her chin and looked into her wet eyes. How beautiful she still was! "Bhanu, don't you trust me? Don't you believe me? Do you think I would allow any harm to befall him? He is my son too, Bhanu."

"I am afraid." Bhanumati pressed her face to her husband's chest.

Suyodhana gently ran his hand over her hair. "So am I, Bhanu. So are all the fathers and mothers of Bharatavarsha. This will be the war to end all wars in our lifetime."

"He is all that we have. Why not give up your claim to the throne and avoid the war, Suyodhana?"

"It is not about the throne or power, Bhanu."

"You are lying to yourself. Power is all that matters to you. You do not care what happens to me or our son."

"What do you want from me, Bhanu? That I allow the sons of my Aunt Kunti to ruin the country? I want people to remember me as the one who fought for them."

"Have you thought about what will happen if you fail?"

"The country will sink into the quagmire of *jati* and *varna*."

"But have you thought about what will happen to you if you fail? You will be painted as the greatest villain who ever lived. Do you want that?"

"Bhanu, fear of posterity cannot prevent me from doing what I know to be right."

"You talk as if you know you will lose."

"No, Bhanu, I will not lose. *Dharma* is on my side. *Dharma* never loses. Besides, Lord Bhishma, Guru Drona, Karna, Aswathama, are all there. How can I not win? Trust me, nothing will happen to our son. He too, must do this."

"My heart is breaking..." Bhanumati broke away from her husband and rushed from the room, weeping.

Suyodhana sighed and turned to his son. He could not remember when he had last been alone with his son since the marriage fiasco. It was difficult to say it but he plunged on with what was on his mind. "Son, I had been harsh on you. I only learnt later that you were trapped. Valsala and Abhimanyu played a cruel joke on you and I believed them."

"Father, that is behind us. Let it remain there."

"Are you still in love with Valsala?" You need not try so hard to keep your emotions hidden from me, son. I know how it feels. Suyodhana wanted to put his hand on his son's shoulder but it felt as heavy as lead. "When the woman you love leaves you, it hurts like the fires of hell. At first you think it will kill you, then time heals the wound. The scar always remains but it is no longer agony."

"Do you still remember her, father?"

"Who?" Suyodhana snapped.

"Abhimanyu's mother, Aunt Subhadra."

"Who told you about that?"

"Has *your* wound healed, Father?"

"Who has been feeding you with such nonsensical tales? I have been married to your mother for more than two decades. Ask her whether I have ever been unfaithful. I do not collect women like Subhadra's husband."

"It was not my mother who told me about your love for Aunt Subhadra."

"Then who?"

"Aunt Subhadra herself."

Suyodhana was dumbfounded. She had no right to do that. His throat became parched and something which he had buried deep within, began to hurt again. He did not trust his face to hide what he felt so he turned away from his son.

"She wants to meet you, Father."

"Any of my subjects can meet me at an appointed time," Suyodhana replied. He hoped his son could not hear the palpitations of his heart.

"She wants to meet you alone. She has something to say that is very important."

"It is improper to meet another man's wife in secret."

"She will be waiting for you by the temple near the river, tonight."

How could a father discuss his first love with his son? 'Subhadra, you never left my heart.' Instead, he smiled and asked, "Are you afraid?"

Kumara knew his father had deliberately changed the subject. "Yes, I am. Only fools feel no fear."

It was certainly not the reply Suyodhana had expected from his son. Perhaps he had not taken the time to know him. "Don't tell me you are doing it for me," he said.

"No. I am a Kuru Prince and we are a race of warriors." Kumara's eyes belied his words.

'I do not deserve such love, my son,' thought Suyodhana as he looked as his son's gentle eyes and calm demeanour. Kumara walked away, leaving Suyodhana's heart heavy with the emotions of both the past and the present.

Subhadra would be waiting for him tonight. Suyodhana wished night would never fall.

***

Iravan was nervous. The smoke from many cooking fires snaked towards the heavens. The idea of sneaking into the Pandava camp seemed more and more crazy as he neared the encampment. His cousin Khatotkacha had proved his worth by foiling the marriage of the young Kaurava Prince. He might even be invited by his father, Bhima, to fight. But did his own father, Arjuna, even know of his son's existence, he wondered?

The sun was a ball of fire above Iravan's head but winter was sneaking into the shade of the trees. There had been no rains this year either and he was hungry more often than not. War would be a quick way to end the misery.

"Halt, Naga! How dare you pollute this holy place?" Dhaumya's bark made Iravan jump.

"I...I am Iravan, son of Arjuna," he managed to say.

"What do you want?" Dhaumya asked tersely.

Words deserted Iravan. Where was his father? His palms were sweating but he resisted the temptation to rub them together. "I have come to join my father," he gulped.

"This is not a hunting ground for savages. This is a Kshatriya war." Dhaumya spat on the ground and instinctively Iravan knew he had walked into trouble.

*****

51 IRAVAN

IRAVAN LIFTED HIS BOW AND DREW AN ARROW from his quiver with shaking fingers. Warriors turned their heads to see what the fraças was about, and some of them ambled over to watch. Iravan's arrow soared high into the sky like an eagle and perched an inch below the fluttering saffron Pandava flag. He shot another arrow and then another, and another. Under the amazed gaze of the priests and Kshatriyas alike, the Naga drew the figure of a serpent with his arrows. Finished, he bowed to Guru Dhaumya.

"Who taught you to shoot like that?" Dhaumya asked. The crowd of onlookers shoved each other to get closer to hear the answer.

"My Guru, Ekalavya."

As whispers ran through the crowd like wind through grass, Iravan wondered where his father was. Had Arjuna seen him?

"Son of Arjuna, do you wish to help your father win the war?"

"I do, Swami," Iravan said. The glimmer of hope made his voice tremble. He felt lightheaded.

"Are you a *brahmachari*?" Dhaumya's voice was as smooth as silk.

"Am I... a what?"

"You are not married?" the Guru snapped, losing patience.

"No, Swami." Iravan's breathing quickened.

"Are you willing to lay down your life for your father, Iravan?"

"I am, Swami." His heart thudded against his ribs.

"Good." Dhaumya turned to his disciples. "Make arrangements for the sacrifice. The most eligible man has offered himself."

There were angry murmurs among the Kshatriya warriors but they became silent when Dhaumya stood up. The priest walked away, keeping as much distance as possible between himself and Iravan's polluting body.

***

Someone poured water over Iravan's head. It was freezing! Ganga water for his purification, someone said. The chanting of holy *mantras* rose on all sides and a priest placed a *tilak* on his forehead. A garland of red flowers was thrust over his head.

"What is happening?"Iravan asked, but the rising crescendo of holy chants drowned out his voice. In some corner of his mind he felt a sense of pride; everyone was bowing to him. But his instincts screamed danger as he struggled to understand what was happening. Why were they dragging him like a goat? Oh no! He was to be sacrificed like a goat! Iravan tried wriggling away but too many people pushed him towards the fierce idol of Kali and strong hands held him down at the sacrificial altar. The stone was slippery with blood. The severed heads of goats mocked him. The smell of blood and goat urine almost made him gag. Iravan felt dizzy and his limbs grew weak. 'Ma Kali, what wrong have I done to these people?' he asked from the depths of his desperation.

"What is happening here?" Iravan's heart missed a beat. He had heard that voice in his dreams. His father had come at last. Iravan struggled to get up and look at Arjuna, but he was shoved down.

"To ensure our victory, this brave man has volunteered to sacrifice himself." Dhaumya's voice seemed to come from a distance, slurred and strained. They were going to sacrifice him! Iravan struggled to free himself. He did not want to die. He was too young to die.

"A human sacrifice? He is just a boy," Arjuna said to Guru Dhaumya.

"He volunteered. Our tradition respects all customs. We are a tolerant people," Dhaumya intoned unctuously and threw saffron powder on Iravan's face. The boy coughed. His tears mixed with the powder, looking like blood.

"Only barbarians such as the Nagas follow such customs."

His father's words hurt Iravan more than the vice-like grip of his captor. His ceased to struggle and went limp. 'He trapped me,' Iravan wanted to scream but the words died in his throat as flowers and rice were pushed into his mouth.

"He is trying to say something," Arjuna said.

Dhaumya placed his ear to Iravan's mouth. "Oh, he is saying his last wish is for us to raise his severed head on a stake. Rather a strange request. The poor fellow believes his head will then witness the great war of *dharma*."

'No! I do not want to die. I came to help my father.' Iravan spat out the rice and flowers. "Father, help me!" The *mantras* were deafening. The coldness of a sword touched the back of his neck, marking its striking spot. 'My Guru Ekalavya only sacrificed a thumb. I should be proud to sacrifice myself,' thought Iravan as he shut his eyes tight.

"Wait! I know this boy, I know his face," Arjuna said, but the sword had already fallen. The decapitated head of his son rolled towards his feet, its eyes staring at him in innocent surprise.

"Guru... it is my son, my son..." Arjuna jumped away from Iravan's head as if it was a viper ready to strike.

"A great sacrifice in the name of *dharma*!" declared the priest.

"Krishna! They have killed my son! Is this *dharma*?" shouted Arjuna, his voice and body trembling.

Krishna ran to where Arjuna stood gazing in shocked horror at his son's decapitated body. He looked at Dhaumya, his eyes glowing like coals in his dark and handsome face.

"It was the Supreme Sacrifice, Lord." Dhaumya bowed.

Krishna did not miss the implication. The wily Guru was alluding to Ekalavya's death. Things were getting out of hand. Dhaumya's fanaticism was frightening. Krishna yearned for a stable society, but looking at the priest's glittering eyes, he wondered what the future would bring.

Arjuna freed himself from Krishna's grip. "I am sick of this. I will not fight anymore."

"Arjuna, listen to me, I will explain." Krishna hurried after his friend, trying to talk Arjuna out of his depression.

Dhaumya picked up the lifeless head of Iravan by its hair. "Raise this thing on a pole and plant it in the middle of the battlefield. May it strike terror in the minds of all low-castes who forget their *dharma*."

Soon, Kurukshetra had a stake pierced into its heart. The lifeless eyes of Iravan bored into the conscience of the warriors on both sides for the next eighteen days. The temple of *dharma* had sacrified its first blood.

*****

52 KSHATRIYA

"CASTE! CASTE! CASTE!" Karna kicked a stone into the water. His toe hurt but it was nothing compared to what he felt inside. He had never expected Bhishma to stoop so low. Years before, Karna had tried to drown himself in the waters of this holy river. It would have been far, far better had Kripa left him to die that day. He had suffered enough for many lifetimes. What pained him the most was the hesitation he had seen in Suyodhana's eyes. His defeat at Arjuna's hands at Virata had shaken the belief of even his closest friend. Arjuna was a lucky bastard. He had everything – caste, lineage, fame; he even had the woman Karna had once loved deeply. 'Draupadi, why do I still yearn for you?' he thought in agony. Could a Suta even lift his eyes to such a woman?

A shadow fell on the water and Karna's warrior instincts became taut and alert. Someone stood behind him. In one fluid movement he had turned, his sword in his hand.

"Krishna!" Karna could not hide his surprise. "Have you come to do to me what you did to Ekalavya?"

Krishna smiled his most charming smile. "Karna, my friend, you are like my brother. Why would I harm you?"

"I am in no mood for small talk, Krishna, leave me alone." Karna sheathed his sword. Krishna was the last person he wanted to talk to. He stepped into the water, his back to the Yadava. The river was turning saffron in the west.

Krishna scooped up some water and washed his face. "I understand your pain, Karna, but like the waters of the holy Ganga, what I say will cleanse your soul."

"Krishna, leave me alone."

"Do you know who you are?"

"The whole world knows who this Suta is."

"What is it that you have always wished for, Karna?"

When Karna remained silent, Krishna said, "To be a Kshatriya."

"I know I am only a lowly Suta. Now go."

"All Bharatavarsha could be yours before you can blink, Karna."

"Krishna, the peddler of impossible dreams. But even Sutas run out of patience sometimes."

"Karna, I met your mother today."

Karna's heart skipped a beat. When had he last been home to see his parents, Athiratha and Radha? Why had Krishna cared to visit a stable-keeper's hut?

"She wants you to be King of Hastinapura."

"All mothers want their sons to be Kings."

"Ah, but *your* mother can make you King of Bharatavarsha. If you agree, no one can stop you. You will be the greatest of all Kshatriyas, the King of Kings."

"If you are done with mocking a poor Suta woman, please go."

"I am not talking about your Suta mother, Karna."

"So even mothers have castes now?"

"Karna, you are not a Suta, but the greatest of Kshatriyas."

"Do not tell me that caste is based only on character and not on birth. I am tired of that excuse. All the high-castes parrot it but I can no longer accept their smug smiles and platitudes, as though their high status was the result of their exalted character and not a mere accident of birth. To them it is just a philosophy, but to us at the bottom, it is life."

"Karna, listen to what I am saying. Radha and Athiratha are your foster parents. You are a Kshatriya by birth."

Karna stared at Krishna in complete bewilderment. What was the Yadava trying to tell him? It did not make any sense. In the distance he could see Vidhura. Beside him stood a veiled woman. She looked oddly familiar. His heart skipped a beat. Could it be...?

"Karna, you are the son of a *Suryavamsha*, a Prince of the exalted Sun dynasty, the same as Lord Rama. And your mother is Devi Kunti."

The world spun around Karna. He felt dizzy. He was the son of Kunti, the mother of the Pandavas? Arjuna, his most hated enemy, was his brother? His heart felt like it would burst through his chest.

"Karna, do not blame your mother. She was unmarried when she had you. You know how it is. An unmarried woman giving birth to..."

"So she decided to throw me away! Mother... is she not ashamed to call herself that?" Anger was a strong shield to hide behind. His emotions threatened to overwhelm Karna. Nothing made sense. "Where did my parents find me? In the garbage?"

"They found you in the lap of Mother Ganga."

Karna quickly pulled his legs out of the river and began climbing the steps of the ghat.

"Karna, I have not finished."

Karna halted. "I must see my mother."

"You are a great man. Devi Kunti will be delighted."

"I meant my real mother, Krishna. I must see her."

"Patience, brother. It is admirable that you love your foster parents, but remember, you are going to be Emperor of Bharatavarsha."

Karna paused. The ache in his heart felt like a physical pain. His head was aflame. He yearned to reach Radha's safe embrace, away from a world gone mad.

"Karna, Yudhishtra would have no objection to handing over the kingdom to an elder brother. Now that you are a Kshatriya, Dhaumya and the other priests too, will have no objection."

"Krishna, there is already an heir to the throne."

"Karna, you are the eldest; the throne is rightfully yours."

"You think Suyodhana would agree with you?"

"If he does not, we will fight him. *Dharma*..."

"Is this the advice of a divine *avatar*? To betray the man who has made me what I am? Is this your *dharma*?"

"The Pandavas are your own blood. Kunti is your mother, Karna."

"I have only a few friends, those who stood by me when the whole world jeered at my caste. No Kshatriya other than Suyodhana came to my rescue; no Brahmin other than Aswathama stepped forward to shield me. Even if you offer me the whole world, I will never betray them."

"You can avoid a war that will kill thousands."

"Accept Suyodhana as King and there will be no war."

"For your mother's sake, if not your own, accept the throne, Karna."

"Radha is my mother, Krishna. I am a Sutaputra."

"Then I will offer you something you will not be able to refuse."

"Do not say another word. Leave me alone, Krishna." Karna guessed what was coming and he did not trust himself.

"Kunti will persuade Draupadi to be your wife, too. As the eldest, you will..."

"Enough! The Pandavas would do anything for power – gamble, cheat and even sell their wife to the enemy."

"Karna, you are throwing away a great destiny."

"Leave this Suta alone!"

"Karna, you will regret it."

"Let *dharma* win, Krishna."

Karna hurried away from the river, his mind in turmoil. Everything he had always believed in had come tumbling down. He felt ashamed that he had almost been tempted by Krishna's offer, particularly the last one. 'Draupadi, you almost made me into a devil.' He hated and loved her with equal ferocity; how was that even possible? But as Karna neared his childhood home, his feelings towards Draupadi turned to pity. How could she bear to live with such husbands?

The hut looked the same. There was the toy bow he had played with, it still hung on a nail on the mud wall of the veranda. The *rangoli* his mother had painted in the courtyard brought a flood of memories rushing back. It was here that he had waited impatiently for his charioteer father to take him to Guru Drona; it was in this hut that Athiratha had comforted him when the Guru had rejected him. He was the luckiest son alive to have had such love.

"Ma!" Karna called. His heart thumped against his ribcage when he heard the familiar rustle of her saree. The door creaked open and the aroma of his mother's cooking wafted out. A stooped figure with greying hair stared at him, her gaze lingering on his dazzling earrings. Radha burst into tears of happiness.

"Who is that?" Karna heard his father ask.

Before his mother could say anything, Karna embraced her and said, "I am hungry".

Radha showered him with kisses and Karna melted in shame, guilt and love. He had returned to where he belonged. Radha hurried off to prepare his favourite dishes. Adhiratha looked up as Karna's tall frame filled the doorway but he did not say a word. Karna smelt the musty sweetness of his home. He would stay here until his friend needed him again. Karna knew in his heart that such ruthless enemies would not fight fairly. His friend would lose, but he, Karna, would ensure it was a glorious defeat and far better than a shame-filled victory. It was the least a Suta could do for his Kshatriya friend.

*****

53 Love Returns

WHEN HIS SON HAD TOLD HIM SUBHADRA would be waiting near the temple, Suyodhana had convinced himself he would not go. Bhanu had cried herself to sleep, grieving for her son. He had held her so that he would not be tempted when the time came. He could not remember when he had last hugged Bhanu that way. His wife purred in her sleep, content with his touch. It almost broke his heart. Yet, at the appointed time, he stood near the temple, the Ganga flowing like dark ink in the background.

"I did not think you would come," she said.

Her voice was just the same as all those years ago, when they had been teenagers lost in love. The breeze ruffled her hair and he wished he could tuck the strands back behind her ears as he used to do. Instead, he folded his arms across his chest.

"Thank you for coming, Suyo. I did not think Lakshmana Kumara would tell you. He is a sweet boy," Subhadra said, her diamond nose stud glittering in the moonlight. "Do you still think of me?"

Thank God, she could not see his face. 'What answer do you want from me, Subhadra? Would it make you happy if I told you the truth, that I have ached for you every moment?' Suyodhana turned away. "Why do you care?" That was not what he had meant to say, a simple no or nothing at all would have been better.

"How is Arjuna?" Suyodhana asked. It was a foolish question and an awkward one. She did not answer but a smile played on her lips. Those full red lips were just the same too, and the memory of their taste came flooding back to him. He wanted nothing more in that moment than to kiss them once again. Suyodhana shook his head and looked up at the night sky.

"It is about Abhimanyu."

"I hope he is looking after Valsala. Oh I forgot, he has married again hasn't he? How is Uttara doing?"

"Suyo, you are still angry about what my boy did to your son?"

'No, Subhadra, I am still mad at what you did to me years ago.' It was almost more than he could bear to be alone with her, so near that he could smell the fragrance of her hair.

"My son is so full of vigour that I sometimes fear for his life. He still loves Valsala, but he is madly in love with Uttara now."

"No doubt he will marry scores of women. He has a long way to go."

"He is such a handsome boy," Subhadra said and then frowned. "I know what you have left unsaid, Suyo – like father, like son. If you think I am unhappy I married Arjuna, you are mistaken. I do not care how many wives he has, he still loves me the most."

"Your vehemence convinces me. My prayers are always with you."

"Sarcasm does not suit you, Suyo. You are still in love with me." Subhadra laughed.

Her still girlish laughter made him feel that spring had come early.

"Was it I who called for this rendezvous or you?"

Subhadra fell silent. Time had not healed the wounds, only kept them hidden. "I have come as a friend," she said, averting her gaze.

Suyodhana walked towards the river. The silver moon lay shattered in the Ganga. He hoped Bhanu had not woken to find him gone.

"Uttara is pregnant."

"Convey my congratulations to Abhimanyu. But you do not look nearly old enough to be a grandmother, Subhadra."

Subhadra's dimples leapt into her cheeks for a brief moment. "Abhimanyu is impatient for war."

"Should I be happy to know your son is itching to kill me?"

"Suyo, he just wants to help his father."

A sharp retort rose to Suyodhana's lips. To his surprise, she began to weep. "I am afraid... he does not listen to me. To his father he is just one among many sons from many wives, but I have only him. He is too young to fight in this war." She moved closer and gripped Suyodhana's *angavastra*, wetting his chest with her tears. Her perfume brought back ghosts of long dead moments and he felt himself going weak at the knees. Even after all these years, he could not bear to see her in tears.

"Please, Suyo, spare my son. He is too young to fight you or Karna or the other great warriors on your side."

Suyodhana's mind felt numb. He could almost hear Bhanu pleading with him about Lakshmana Kumara. Bhanu! What was he doing here with Arjuna's wife? Suyodhana turned away from Subhadra, freeing himself from her grip. "It is war, not child's play. In battle, warriors get hurt and killed."

"Is Abhimanyu just a warrior to you? As a child, he adored you."

"The women's wing of the Dwaraka palace is large. If he is afraid, let him hide there."

"My son is no coward! He is Arjuna's son!"

"Then ask Arjuna to protect him, if he can."

Subhadra's eyes flashed in anger. Suyodhana refused to meet her gaze and stood staring at the river, his hands crossed over his chest.

"You are no longer the Suyodhana I knew."

"The Suyodhana you knew died when you eloped with my cousin."

"I thank my stars and my brother Krishna, for that. You are the most evil man I know."

"Duryodhana is evil, Subhadra; the whole world knows it."

"Your arrogance knows no limits. You have insulted my son, my husband, and me. You will pay the price, Duryodhana. I will tell my son not to flinch if his arrow points at you. I will advise him to be the worthy son of a great father. He will be the storm that will destroy your armies."

"You came to beg me for your son's life and now you are cursing me? You have not changed at all."

"Duryodhana, keep away your Lakshmana Kumara from the battlefield. If the royal poet shows his face to Abhimanyu, you can start making the funeral arrangements for your son."

Suyodhana turned and walked away. He could feel her eyes on his back. He was furious and yet, how he loved her still! He hurried back to the palace, his head bent. When he passed his son's chamber, he paused to listen to Kumara's breathing. He fiddled with the pearl necklace he wore, trying to suppress long-forgotten memories. Then too, the air had smelt of burning incense and smoking torches. Bhanu had been talking to Subhadra, and Abhimanyu had been a soft little bundle in his arms, playing with his pearl necklace. He had bestowed the necklace on Subhadra's son, kissing his curls.

The smoke from the dying torches was making his eyes burn. Suyodhana hoped Subhadra had returned safely. He should not have left her alone at the deserted riverbank. He reminded himself that memories should not blunt the sharpness of his weapons. He was a Kshatriya and war was his *dharma*. Hopefully, Abhimanyu would not be wearing that pearl necklace when he faced him on the battlefield.

*****

54 RULES OF WAR

"PITAMAHA, HOW CAN ANYONE PREDICT what will happen in the course of battle?" Suyodhana asked, bewildered by the words of the document in front of him. He and Yudhishtra had been summoned to the patriach's chambers to agree to the codes of war. Suyodhana looked up impatiently, wondering if this was just another trick by his wily cousin. He felt only pity for Yudhishtra, who wished to impose the old rules of *varna* on his people. And the rules Bhishma was now reading aloud, belonged to an era which should have been finished and buried long ago. Once the war was won, Suyodhana vowed to himself that change would come.

Yudhishtra sat reading the ancient codes and ethics governing warfare from a birch leaf manuscript as the cousins faced each other in Bhishma's chamber. A lone lamp lighted their faces. In the shadows, Vidhura stood with lines of worry creasing his forehead.

"I am ready to take the oath, Pitamaha," Yudhishtra said.

"People who have no intention of following the rules are the first to agree to them," Suyodhana retorted disdainfully.

Bhishma brought his hand down on the table, making the lamp flame flicker. Both cousins bowed their heads. Vidhura picked up the birch leaf and handed it over to Bhishma.

"This is not a casual game of dice, this is war. The two of you have destroyed the peace of this land with your petty rivalry. Even now you cannot stop bickering. This is the ancient code of conduct in war, written by our great rishis and seers. We are not Mlechas."

"I have always believed in *dharma*, Pitamaha," Yudhishtra said, raising his head. Suyodhana's lips curved in a smile of derision.

"Once I have read it aloud, I would like both of you to take the oath by placing a hand over the flame." Bhishma waited for either of his grand-nephews to speak. When there was no response, he began reading.

"Rule 1: All battles shall begin after sunrise and end at sunset precisely. Rule 2: A group of warriors shall not attack a single warrior. Rule 3: In a duel, both warriors shall use the same type of weapon and be mounted or remain on foot alike."

"How is it possible to ensure such a thing in the heat of battle?" Yudhishtra asked, his broad brow creased in confusion.

"What is so difficult, cousin? A warrior on foot fights only another warrior on the ground. A mounted warrior fights only another who is mounted, a chariot fights only another chariot, and an elephant another elephant," Suyodhana said.

Bhishma nodded and continued. "Rule 4: If a warrior surrenders, he shall not be harmed or killed. He shall be extended the respect due to a prisoner of war and his wounds shall be treated by the *Vaidyas* of the capturing side. Are both of you clear about this?"

The cousins nodded. Bhishma adjusted the wick of the lamp and moved closer to the light. "Rule 5: An injured or unarmed warrior shall not be killed. Rule 6: An unconscious warrior shall not be harmed. Rule 7: Water carriers, drummers, *Vaidyas* and their assistants, scribes reporting to their commanders or rulers, who are not warriors but present on the battlefield, shall not be harmed or killed."

"What if they are spies?" Suyodhana asked.

"Either side may ask the other to remove from the battlefield any man suspected of being a spy, and allow a replacement to be made."

"Are such elaborate rules really necessary, or even practical?" Suyodhana asked Bhishma.

"I fear for those under your command, Suyodhana, if you have not yet grasped the scale and complexity of this war. From north to south, armies are marshalling to fight on one side or the other. Before it ends, death and detruction will stalk this land. The world has never seen anything like it and God willing, never will again. There will be at least eighteen *akhshounis* in combat. Do you want to fight without rules?"

Both sides were still trying to assess each other's strength. Alliances were being forged every day. The numbers were overwhelming.

"Rule 8: No warrior shall kill or injure another by striking from behind. Rule 9: No warrior shall attack a woman."

"That is surely ridiculous. Are women even allowed to fight?" Yudhishtra asked with a smile.

Bhishma put down the birch leaf and stared at the Pandava Prince. "You are a scholar, Yudhishtra. I trust you have read history. It will serve you well to remember Durga."

"But she was a Goddess, Pitamaha, not an ordinary woman."

"Do not forget that every woman has the same strength within her. She is not a thing to be pawned." Yudhishtra looked away, ashamed. "Or to be stripped in public," added Bhishma. It was Suyodhana's turn to flush and drop his gaze. "Rule 10: No warrior shall strike a horse or elephant if his life is not threatened."

"Even the animals have rules?" Suyodhana asked.

"Only men break the rules, Suyodhana, not the animals. Every life is precious, be it an ant or a human. So no animal shall be injured unnecessarily. Rule 11: The rules specific to each weapon shall be followed. A warrior shall not be attacked or killed when his bow has broken or he is disarmed. In a mace fight, the warriors shall not hit below the waist."

"Pitamaha, we know these basic rules of combat; they were the first lessons we were taught in warrior training at the age of five," Yudhishtra smiled at the stern-faced patriarch.

"There is no harm in reminding ourselves, Yudhishtra. The final rule is to fight fairly, in the true spirit of *dharma*. Kurukshetra is the temple of *dharma*. History will not forgive or forget those who break the rules of *dharma*. Remember, the battlefield is one of life's great levellers. It does not matter whether you are bareheaded or wear a crown. Neither the Gods nor men can escape the laws of *karma*."

Bhishma put the birch leaf back on the table and looked at his grand-nephews. Both sat with bowed heads. There was no going back now. After a moment's silence, the old man put out his hands over the flame of the lamp saying, "Repeat after me..."

Yudhishtra was the first to put out his hand. Bhishma waited for Suyodhana to follow.

"Pitamaha, if I give my word I must then abide by it. I fear that in the heat of battle I may not always be able to follow my oath."

"Your cousin has agreed and he, too, is a man of honour, I hope. You are my grand-nephews, scions of the Kuru dynasty, inheritors of the legacy of the great Emperor Bharata. Our dynasty has given its name to our holy land. You are all Bharatas. Let your conduct be worthy. Now, repeat after me..."

Suyodhana placed his hand over the naked flame but cringed when his fingers touched those of his cousin. Bhishma's voice filled the room as his grand-nephews repeated his words, the flame of truth their witness.

"*Om*. In the name of Brahma, Vishnu and Maheshwara, in the name of the Goddess Adi Parasakthi, the mother of the universe, in the name of the seven sacred rivers of Bharata, in the name of all the mothers of this holy land, in the name of truth and honour, in the name of *dharma*, I, Gangadutta Devavrata..." Bhishma paused for the cousins to speak their names and then continued, "...do hereby take the oath of honour, and promise to abide by the ancient and sacred rules of *dharmayudha*; that my men and I shall fight according to the teachings of *dharma*. I enter the battlefield with the full knowledge that this war is sacred, as is every particle of sand in holy Bharatavarsha. I shall not contemplate or commit any act not in accordance with *dharma*. I shall strive to uphold what is right and win or lose with honour."

When his grand-nephews had repeated the complete vow, Bhishma sat back with a sigh. The die was cast. Death and glory beckoned the brave. Yudhishtra and Suyodhana bowed and took their leave without looking at each other.

Suyodhana was a worried man. He felt angry at the way Bhishma had manipulated him. The Pitamaha meant well, but he was sure Yudhishtra would not follow the rules he had so blithely agreed to. Even if his cousin was a changed man, as some claimed him to be, Krishna would follow his own rules. Suyodhana knew he faced a ruthless enemy who would stoop to any level to secure victory.

Suyodhana stood still in the corridor outside Bhishma's chambers. Intricately carved pillars stood like sentinels on either side, stretching as far as the eye could see. He saw his cousin quickly walking away. The ancient and noble dynasty of the Kurus had always been known to set the highest standards of rightful conduct by Kshatriyas. He was a Kuru scion and he could not dishonour his forefathers by going back on his given word. 'Yudhishtra, even if you break every rule to win, evil Duryodhana will not, whatever be the provocation,' he murmured to himself.

***

Vidhura put away the precious parchments and looked up at Bhishma to take his leave. Suddenly Bhishma felt a searing pain and slumped forward, clutching his chest. Vidhura rushed forward saying, "Sir, what has happened? Should I summon the Royal Physician?"

Bhishma rose slowly, leaning heavily on the table. Vidhura steadied the shaking lamp. "It is nothing, nothing, my son. My time has not yet come..." A cool breeze was blowing but Bhishma's face shone with perspiration. "Oh, do not fret, Vidhura, it is just lack of exercise. I must start training."

Vidhura assisted the old warrior to his bed and then left reluctantly. Bhishma rested a hand on his chest. The pain refused to go away. There was no cure other than death. But he could not go yet... He had to live to ensure that his grand-nephews did not make a mockery of what he had stood for all his life. He had suffered many heartaches... he would live through this one, too. The great war for *dharma* was about to begin. Death would have to wait.

*****

55 DHARMAKSHETRA

SUYODHANA SURVEYED THE BATTLEFIELD from his chariot. As far as the eye could see, armies stretched on either side. The air was rich with the pungent odour of horse and elephant dung. Soon, the stench of blood and gore would mix with them. Vultures had alighted on the treetops, patiently awaiting their reward. It was the smell of war, of death and devastation. Horses neighed in excitement and the ground reverberated with the tread of elephants. Waves of cheering rose on both sides as captains galloped along the ranks, barking orders to their troops. A dry breeze carried fine sand from the barren lands to the south-west, and Suyodhana shielded his eyes from its sting. He stood tall and twanged his bowstring. His army roared. One way or another, this would be his final role as warrior.

As Suyodhana gauged the men on both sides, so eager to kill and die, he felt a pang of guilt. Was he doing the right thing by imposing such a war on his people, already reeling under the onslaught of drought and famine? But what was the alternative? Should he have given away his birthright to the illegitimate sons of Kunti, allowing them to impose rules that would divide society? If the oppressive *jati* system of the Southern Confederate was the future of Bharatavarsha, then this war was worth fighting. He was not sure he would win, but fight he would to his last breath. He wanted the throne; he had stopped feeling guilty about that long ago. He wanted it for his people as much as for himself. Once, when Karna had asked him why he so blatantly admitted this selfish desire, Suyodhana had said that it made him feel more human. No ambition was purely selfless or selfish, acknowledging it honestly to oneself made life much simpler. To Karna's embarrassment, he had told him that he had acted on impulse, prompted by a sense of justice when he had made him, a Suta, King of Anga. But later, when he had thought about it, he admitted there had also been an element of selfishness in the act. He had wanted Karna to fight for him and be a deterrent to Arjuna. Karna had protested, professing eternal friendship, but Suyodhana had replied that no one could predict the future. The words had been uttered half in jest, but now they proved to be the simple truth. Karna was not by his side when he needed him the most.

Bhishma was about to sound the conch to start the battle when a chariot from the Pandava side rushed into the middle of the vast field. It halted between the battle-ready armies. Bhishma raised his hand to signal a halt. The emblem on the chariot's flag had Hanuman – it was Arjuna's chariot! Why was the Pandavas' most celebrated warrior taking the huge risk of exposing himself, wondered Suyodhana, his brow furrowed under his crested helmet. One arrow from the massed ranks could take Arjuna down. But he had given his word to Bhishma that there would be no transgression of the codes of war. He too lifted his arm to halt his men.

Bhishma's gaze met Arjuna's across the field of battle. He raised a hand in benediction upon his grand-nephew, saying, "*Vijayai Bhava*". Suyodhana saw the gesture and seethed with rage. Where did the old man's loyalty rest, with the army he commanded or the illegitimate sons of Kunti? Had Karna's removal been a deliberate ploy? Suyodhana's troubled gaze travelled to Drona, who was looking at Arjuna and Krishna. Were the Guru's eyes shining with admiration for his favourite disciple? Were they all making a fool of him? Who was there on his side whom he could trust implicitly? Shalya was Nakula and Sahadeva's uncle. Kritavarma was the Commander of Krishna's famed Narayana Sena. And who could predict what Kripa would or would not do? He was unsure of his Uncle Shakuni and his brother-in-law, Jayadratha. Yes, his brothers would stand by him. But the only person he could trust completely in the whole army was Aswathama. How he wished Karna was with him! The war appeared unwinnable, but it was too late to retreat.

As Suyodhana looked at the ordinary foot soldiers who had no agenda other than to serve him, a lump formed in his throat. What had he done to deserve their love? His treasury was almost empty and they had not been paid for two weeks. On the other side, Yuyutsu was tempting everyone with fantastic gifts in this world and Krishna was offering heaven in the next. His opponents had everything – money, the Confederate forces looting the countryside for supplies, an *avatar* who inspired fear of hell and promised *moksha*, and spin masters who portrayed their side as the epitome of *dharma* and him as the devil. Yet, Suyodhana, who had little to offer, still had eleven *akhshounis* against the Pandava's seven. People were still ready to die for their Crown Prince, evil or righteous.

Suyodhana laughed at the irony. His men were daring the priests and philosophers of the land who had made their lives miserable. They had aligned under his leadership, rejecting Yuyutsu's money and Krishna's *moksha*, laughing at the priests who tried to scare them with the promise of hell and an endless cycle of lives as worms, women or untouchables. They had trusted him over the peddlers of *dharma*, ready to fight on half empty stomachs, willing to die so that their children could have a better tomorrow. The responsibility and trust they had reposed in him felt overwhelming. Fight he would, and win. He was a man with human frailties, but his dreams were big. Such dreams should not wither away, else there would be no hope for his country or the world.

Suyodhana gripped his mace and said a prayer. He felt inexplicably powerful. *Dharma* was on his side and *dharma* would win. He was ready to fight. He looked over at Arjuna, expecting to encounter a look of defiant hatred from the Pandava. To his surprise, he saw Arjuna throw down his bow and collapse to the floor of his chariot.

*****

56 THE SCEPTIC

AS ARJUNA GAZED AT THE VAST ARMIES on both sides, ready to drench the earth with blood, he was overcome by despair and despondency. He threw down his bow and sat in his chariot, his head bent, his shoulders stooped.

"Krishna, when I see Pitamaha, my Gurus and my kin standing facing me on the other side, my throat feels parched with sorrow, my heart sinks. What sins am I to commit? They are my kin, after all, these warriors of the Kuru race, and you are asking me to slay them! How can I shoot my Pitamaha, who has always loved me? How can I fight Guru Drona, whose affection for me is greater than his love for his own son? My Uncle Shalya is opposing me, so are so many others I have always loved and respected. Duryodhana may be arrogant and brash, but he is my cousin. Does not the throne belong to him by right? Am I not the bandit trying to steal it from him? I cannot fight, Krishna. It is better they kill me and take everything from us. For if we win, I will not be able to sleep with so much blood on my hands. The kingdom is not worth it. Nothing is worth this bloody war that you are urging me to fight. Leave me alone, Vasudeva. I do not want to fight."

Krishna looked down at his friend and put a hand on Arjuna's shoulder. "Arjuna, you are deluded by false compassion. You are haunted by imaginary fears. Listen to me."

"No, Krishna. You want me to kill my own people, the Kurus. Have you not heard that with the death of the warriors of a *kula*, the customs of that race are lost? When customs are lost, women go astray. They become free without their masters and the intermingling of castes can occur. Their sons are *kulaheen*, without caste, and ineligible to do *pitrukarma* for their ancestors. If their sons do not perform the last rites, the souls of all the Kuru warriors will descend into hell. It is sin, sin, sin. I will not fight my own people. What enmity do I have with the warriors fighting just for their livelihood? No, do not make me commit such a crime."

"Arjuna, do not be effeminate. You are being deluded by false compassion. You are inviting infamy. Future generations will call you a coward for running away from battle."

"Krishna, have you too not run from the battlefield, years before, unable to face the wrath of the great Jarasandha?"

"I retreated as a strategy, not from cowardice. You are being a coward, Arjuna. All this talk of compassion is just an excuse to hide your fear of failure."

"Krishna, how can *bhakti* towards one's Guru be called cowardice? How can you call devotion to Pitamaha illusion? If I can hear the cries of widows and children in my ears, and if my soul tells me there is no need for this war, how am I a coward? It takes more courage to walk away from here than to fight in a war in which I no longer believe," Arjuna retorted, dismay and sorrow filling his heart in equal measure.

Krishna smiled at the anger flaring in Arjuna. Good, his words were awakening the warrior in his friend. "Arjuna, you mourn for those who do not deserve to be mourned. There is nothing worse than false sympathy. You talk like the atheists who believe they are wise but are, in fact, misled souls. Your words may sound right superficially, but that is because you are not using your intellect to delve deeper. Death is just a part of life."

"I do not understand, Krishna."

"Partha, just as boyhood, youth and old age are in one's body and manifest themselves at the appropriate time, so is death. But what dies is born again. That is the eternal law of *karma*. Death and birth are like day and night. Do we mourn the night when we rejoice at the birth of a new day? To the wise, just as day and night are part of nature, so are life and death."

"Krishna, you trivialise death. I can understand death when its time comes, but not murder. You are asking me to kill. It is not *dharma*."

Krishna waved his arms at the vast Kuru and Pandava armies and said, "You think you can kill them or they can kill you? You doubt, because you do not know who you are. You are not the body; you and your body are separate. Understand that the body is just a garment that hides the real *you*; the body is just a covering for the *atman*, the soul. The soul is eternal and unchanging. There is no death for the soul. Just as you change your clothes when they are dirty, soiled or torn, the soul changes bodies. Death is nothing but the casting away of old clothes by the divine *atman*."

"What good would it do to my soul to fight this war and win a kingdom, since it would be my body that would enjoy the pleasures of kingship and feel the pain of killing my kinsmen? Should I fight for the enjoyment of my body, which is just a cloth waiting to be cast aside? If only the *atman* matters, what good would this victory do me? Am I not being foolish to tend to my body, when I should be feeding my soul?"

"Understand that the soul cannot be drowned by water, cleaved by the sword or burned by fire. You cannot destroy it when you kill someone, neither can your enemy destroy your *atman*. *Atman* is the reflection of the *paramatman* which pervades the universe and beyond. Life is just a manifestation of the *paramatman*, as transient as the reflection of the moon on the waves of a lake, and as real. Life is nothing but a flash that happens in the interval between birth and death. Imagine the vast universe and the majesty of time, and you will understand life is as permanent as the flicker of a leaf in the breeze. When you cannot kill the soul, why be obsessed with the thought of hurting others?"

Arjuna shook his head in defeat. "Krishna, despite what you say, I cannot be the cause of so much death and misery."

Krishna replied, "Arjuna, you will bring infamy to all the warriors of Bharatavarsha by refusing to do your *dharma* as a Kshatriya. There is nothing else greater for a Kshatriya than a battle fought fairly. Heaven awaits the Kshatriya who dies in battle. By abandoning the chariot of war, you will bring infamy to the Kurus. Is infamy not equal to death? Do you wish to be called a coward by everyone? Slain, you will attain heaven in another world; victorious, you will enjoy heaven in this world. What have you got to lose by fighting, my dear friend?"

"Oh Krishna, do not make me commit this sin. Iravan's face still haunts me. Abhimanyu is dearer to me than anything in the world. It would be the same for Duryodhana. What will I do if I lose Abhimanyu? I have wronged Duryodhana's son once already; how will I face myself if I kill his son? How will I face my Guru if I kill Aswathama? Karna is my enemy, but now I can understand that we have wronged him as much as he has wronged us. Let this madness end. Let all the infamy be mine."

"My dear friend, you are getting attached to this illusionary world and its meaningless bonds. You are forsaking your duty for you are afraid of the results. You are afraid of your actions, thinking you will get entangled in the bonds of your *karma*. Consider pleasure and pain, victory and defeat, gain and loss, life and death, as equal and insignificant. Fight the battle in the name of duty. Be devoted to your cause and *dharma*; do not worry about the outcome."

'But, Krishna, it is the outcome that matters. If not, why do people strive repeatedly until they succeed? Why succeed at all if the outcome does not matter? I am afraid of the results if I succeed in this war. I fear that death and universal suffering would be the only outcome. Should I not worry about that? Am I an unthinking monster?"

"Do your duty without desiring the fruit of your actions. You will free yourself from the obligation of repeated births and deaths."

"I love life and this is a beautiful world. Why should I kill my brethren in order to reach a place where there is neither happiness nor pain? Why should I strive to become a stone, unmoved by anything, existing just because it happens to be there? That is not life."

"Arjuna, be the man who is unmoved by circumstances and just does his duty. Be like the lotus which, though it blooms in the water, is never wet. Similarly, bloom in your *karma* but never get drenched by it, or overwhelmed by its results. Be a *stithapranja*, devoted to your *dharma* and duty."

"Even if it involves misery for others?"

"Do not get attached to the results of your work. Be devoted to the work alone. Misery is an illusion."

"If work creates misery, why work at all, Krishna? Why not abstain from all duties and take refuge in the forest like the rishis?"

"A man deludes himself if he thinks that by renouncing his duties he can escape the snare of *karma*. No one can live without working. The intelligent man knows not to get attached to the results of one's work and to do it as one's duty, *nishkama karma*."

"But it seems so unnatural to live without passion, Krishna."

"My friend, such thoughts belong to evil souls like your cousin, Duryodhana, who are attached to the world and indulge their passions and senses. That is the mark of *tamo guna*, the quality of darkness, their imperfect knowledge which will cause their ruin."

"But Duryodhana can say the same thing, that he is doing his duty, to protect what he believes is his birthright. Is it not his Kshatriya *dharma* to fight? Why should it be an evil quality in him and noble in me?"

"Duryodhana fights for desire; he is consumed by wrath and jealousy."

"So are we. This war is the result of our desire for vengeance for what he did to Draupadi. We too are filled with passion, wrath and human emotion."

"I advise you to discard all anger and wrath towards Duryodhana, and fight because it is your duty to restore *dharma*. Once you overcome your anger, you will also overcome your false sense of attachment towards your kin."

"If I outgrow the anger I feel about Duryodhana's treatement of Draupadi, then there is no reason left to fight. What would become of me? I would be but a killing machine."

"You would be a yogi who has conquered the senses. The senses are superior to an inert body, the mind is superior to the senses and the intellect is superior to the mind. You must be the man who walks the path of intellect. That is the path of devotion to one's cause. This is a secret I told Vivaswat aeons ago, he declared it to Manu, the first man, and Manu told Ishvaku of *Suryavamsha*, and through many thousand generations it has passed to the sages. Now I am declaring it to my friend, Arjuna."

"You are my friend, we are the same age. Vivaswat was born at the beginning of creation. Manu was the first man. How could you tell them what you have just told me?"

"Many births of mine have passed, as have yours. But my essence knows no deterioration. I take birth in every age, whenever there is a loss of piety and *adharma* arises, to protect the weak and oppressed. I arrive in this world to finish evil men like Duryodhana."

"I am confused, Krishna. If you are omniscient, you should know what *adharma* is. If you are omnipresent, why take birth at all or come to the world, when you yourself are the world? If you are omnipotent, why create evil at all? Why create *adharma* if you have the power of creation and destruction? If *adharma* is a mistake, then you are not omnipotent or omniscient. But if you created *adharma* by design, then you are not the compassionate Supreme Soul, having known the suffering that would ensue.

It reeks of sadism. If *adharma* arose on its own and you have to fight to vanquish it, you are not omnipotent but just like any of us lesser mortals. Krishna, if you are the Supreme Essence of the world, and *adharma* exists in it, it merely shows that the world that is you, is imperfect. If the world is imperfect, then so are you."

Krishna laughed in genuine amusement. "You talk like a wise philosopher, my friend. But suffering also is an illusion. Pain and pleasure are part of the natural rhythm of the world. A lion kills a deer; the lion's *dharma* is to kill to eat, the *dharma* of the deer is to run and escape. One does not exist without the other. I come to the world as the protector of *dharma* when the balance changes towards *adharma*. I am Duryodhana and I am Arjuna. I am Yudhishtra and I am Shakuni. *Dharma* and *adharma* are but different manifestations of the same energy. What is *dharma* today will be *adharma* tomorrow. That is why a yogi does not bother about the results of any action."

"There are many men who have abandoned action and sit in contemplation in the forests."

"They follow the difficult path of knowledge, of *sankhya*. Yoga is the easier path; devotion to one's duty without worrying about results. You will not be bound by the fruits of those actions."

"Then the responsibility will be yours, Krishna? For any sin I commit, for any atrocities?"

"It is your nature that engages in action. I receive no one's sin nor their merit. But I do reside in you and everything animate or inanimate. Listen to yourself and you will know what your duty is. The four *varnas* I have created are not based on birth but the nature of human beings. Those who walk the path of knowledge are Brahmins, those who take the path of action are Kshatriyas, those who travel the path of devotion are Vaishyas, and those who indulge in sensory pleasures are Shudras, destined to serve all others. As long as the world exists, there will be divisions. The strong will try to dominate the weak. I appear when the balance is disturbed, but there is no perfect balance in the world. Perfection is stillness, perfection is death. A wheel that does not move is useless. I am the axle of the wheel of *dharma*. Knowledge is the pin. What is at the top today will be at the bottom tomorrow. The *dharmachakra* moves with time, forward and cyclically."

"Krishna, I am a warrior. Your words are all too difficult for me to understand. I am confused. Is there no meaning to life then? What is the purpose of life? Are we just cogs in the *wheel of dharma*, travelling cyclically without any purpose?"

"Move to the center with knowledge, devotion and contemplation, and be one with me. Though the axle is the main part of wheel, it does not move. Similarly, a devotee who has escaped the cycle of birth and rebirth, from the wheel where *dharma* and *adharma* keep changing places, finds refuge in me as the axle of the *dharmachakra*. When such a person becomes one with me, he can see that the rotation of the wheel is just a rhythm and that *dharma* and *adharma* are parts of the same wheel."

"Most of what you say eludes my understanding. Every time I ponder over what you have said, I find a different meaning. It sounds logical when I hear it, but I am an ordinary man and when confronted with the realities of life, I forget your lessons. I find that instead of striving to become a *stitapranja*, it is easier to cry when I feel sad, to laugh when I feel happy, to shout when I am angry and to embrace when I feel love. I find it far more exhilarating to be part of the wheel, even a tiny dot on it, but always in motion. In my deluded mind, I feel it would be dull being part of the axle. It is more wonderful to keep moving with the wheel than be still with the axle."

Krishna laughed again. He saw that the armed ranks standing on either side were getting restive, but he had one more important lesson to teach his friend who was so passionate about life.

"Arjuna, fight and win the world. Do your duty."

"No, Krishna. My doubts remain uncleared."

Krishna sighed. "I will give you a simple formula – easier than the path of *sankya*, or the path of devotion to duty. Yoga is the path of bhakti – be devoted to me. Perform every act as a prayer to me."

"How can I act when I fear the outcome of my action?"

"Think *Idam na mama*, this action does not belong to me. Do it as an offering to me, as a prayer to Krishna."

"Who are you, Krishna?"

"Arjuna, think of me at all times. Fix your mind and understanding on me and fight the battle. Attain me and be freed from the cycle of birth and death. I pervade space; all entities are in me. Behold my divine power. Worship me, always glorify me, and strive with firm vows. Worship me through your *nishkama karma*, worship me through your *bhakti*, and attain me through your knowledge. I am the Vedic sacrifice, I am the *smrithis*, I am *swadha*, I am the medicament of herbs, I am the *mantra*, I am the fire. I am the offering in sacrifice, I am the father of the universe, I am the mother. I am OM. Through your renuniciation and devotion be released from the cycle of *karma* and come to me. None devoted to me is ever lost."

Arjuna looked at his friend in bewilderment. "Krishna, I have never really known you. Show me the real you."

"Behold me, son of Kunti. Behold the suns of different universes, behold Rudra, the Aswins and Maruts and other demigods. See the entire universe. Behold my sovereign mystic nature. Behold Time."

Arjuna blinked as Krishna lifted his hand. He wondered if he had been hallucinating. He felt he was in a trance. "Yes, I see you... without beginning , middle or end. You are of innumberable arms, and the sun and moon are your eyes. The world is trembling. I see all the sons of Dhritarashtra entering your fierce mouth and all the warriors of our side as well. I see everyone being crushed, everyone rushing to you like moths to a flame. You are the energy of the universe. I see all my foes dead."

"Now wisdom has dawned in your mind. I have already slain all the warriors. You are just an instrument. Do not worry about the outcome. Fight and defeat your foes." Krishna settled back in the charioteer's seat and took up the reins.

Arjuna raised his conch and blew it, signalling the start of the war. For the next eighteen days, he would shoot where Krishna pointed. Though assailed by doubts and moved by his actions, he would strive to kill without worrying about the end result, trusting in his friend's wisdom. But later, when the wheel of *karma* turned, he would forget all the lessons Krishna had instilled in him in the temple of *dharma*.

*****

57 THE FIRST EIGHT DAYS

ELEVEN KAURAVA AKSHAUHINIS faced seven on the Pandava side. Yuyutsu's caravan supplying food and armaments stretched behind the Pandava lines. It would make all the difference. Winter had set in and the sun above was weak. A depressing mist pervaded the battlefield and a cold wind made the warriors shiver as they stamped their feet and clanged their swords and shields. Bhishma's silver chariot stood in the middle. The wind tossed his white mane and played with his banner emblazoned with-the golden palm tree and five stars. When he heard Arjuna's conch, he addressed his troops.

"The heaven of warriors beckons you, bravehearts. Do not worry about the future. It is our duty to fight and die if needed. This war is for our *kula* and *desha*, for *dharma* and Bharatavarsha. *Dharma* will win. Never forget the tenets of war. Fight bravely, fight fairly." His soldiers cheered at his words.

Far away, Karna sat depressed and alone in his camp as the war cries reached him. He was the only warrior kept away from the battle. His bitter mind wished Bhishma a speedy death.

Drona and Kripa led the army from the right and left flanks respectively. Aswathama and Sushasana protected Bhishma's flanks. Shalya, Madri's brother, the maverick warrior who had chosen to side with Suyodhana against his nephews, Nakula and Sahadeva, stood in his chariot, a wicked grin on his face. Fearless and wreckless, Shalya was a warrior who could turn the tide of battle. He was feared for his unpredictable actions and formidable fighting skills. Suyodhana was at the centre, under his banner of two coiling serpents, choosing not to fight under any divine emblems. This war was for the forgotten people of his country. The *nagas* were also a tribute to Ekalavya.

Arjuna arranged his phalanx in the *vajra* formation, suitable for swift, penetrating attacks. Yudhishtra was at the centre, with Bhima and Dhristradyumna guarding his flanks. Yuyutsu's mercenary army had joined the Pandavas, swelling their ranks.

When the sun had lost its blush and the mist reluctantly lifted off the grass, Bhishma's stentorian voice boomed over the battlefield, "Attack!" The days of carnage had begun. The war of *dharma* would have many twists and turns but it gave no thought to the parched countryside reeling under drought.

The first day belonged to the Kauravas. Despite the help of Yuyutsu's mercenary army, Bhishma wiped out an entire Pandava *akhshouni*. Uttara, Prince of Virata, was killed. But on the second day, the King of Kalinga, who had broken away from the Southern Confederate to support Karna, was killed. By the end of the third day, the Pandavas had managed to create disarray in the Kaurava ranks. Bhishma's conservative approach had demoralised the Kaurava ranks and Suyodhana had the first of his many arguments with the Pitamaha.

At the end of the fourth day, Suyodhana stormed into Bhishma's camp accusing him of siding with the Pandavas. Bhishma refused to respond, leaving Suyodhana fuming. It was becoming increasingly evident that the old man was not fighting to win. Ordinary soldiers were dying like flies but no warrior belonging to the Kuru clan had died on either side by the fifth day. Bhishma's undeclared strategy was to make the war unviable for both sides and somehow force a truce. The war dragged on for the sixth and seventh days, with thousands of ordinary soldiers dying; still not a single Kuru on either side was laid low. It seemed that Bhishma's strategy had indeed paid off when Yudhishtra, moved by the sight of so many dead, pleaded with Krishna to stop the war. In the Kaurava camp, Bhishma stood like a wall, unmindful of the desperate pleas of Suyodhana to kill Arjuna or Yudhishtra, and gain victory.

The eighth day was a decisive turning point in the great war. Krishna directed the Pandava Commander, Dhristadyumna, to attack the Gandharan forces. This resulted in the death of many of Shakuni's men, including one of his sons. An infuriated Shakuni led twelve of Suyodhana's brothers deep into Pandava territory but retreated when the attack could not be sustained. While Shakuni himself escaped unscathed, the Pandavas killed the dozen Kaurava Princes, escalating the war to a new level, from which there was no turning back. The fighting had gone beyond Bhishma's power to control. His promise not to spill any royal blood sounded hollow even to his own ears.

Karna attended the funeral of Suyodhana's twelve brothers. He advised his grieving friend to remove Bhishma as Commander before they lost everything. Bereft and enraged, Suyodhana, accompanied by Aswathama, stormed into Bhishma's camp to give the patriarch a final ultimatum.

*****

58 Traitor

BHISHMA DID NOT LOOK AT SUYODAHANA. Perhaps Pitamaha had thought that by allowing his brothers to die, he would force a truce, thought the Crown Prince, his mind ablaze with anger, his heart filled with grief. Suyodhana was convinced that Bhishma was fighting a sham war and not attacking the Pandavas. He had tried to protect the Kaurava brothers too, but now, after Shakuni's disastrous foray into the Pandava lines and the death of twelve of his brothers, Suyodhana was in no mood to forgive.

"Pitamaha, it has been eight days since the war started."-

A physician was dressing Bhishma's wounds. Aswathama stood in the shadows. "And?" Bhishma asked, flexing his arm. The physician requested him not to move his hand until the next day. The patriarch merely looked at him in irritation. The physician clucked his tongue in defeat and hastily walked out after a cursory bow.

"There seems to be no end in sight," Suyodhana said.

"You can always stop it," Bhishma replied, lifting an eyebrow.

"But we are not winning, even with you in command."

"We are not losing either."

"Pitamaha, twelve of my brothers are dead and you tell me we are not losing? We should allow Karna to fight."

Bhishma's eyes turned to his nephew, burning with fury. "What is it that you ask, Suyodhana? That we let a Suta fight our battles for us?"

354

"Pitamaha, we all know you are not allowing the men to go after any of the Pandavas."

"Are you telling me how to conduct the war, Suyodhana? Are you here to perhaps instruct me on strategy?"

"So many have already died."

"Oh, so many have died? What was it you expected when you started this foolishness? You will be sick of death and destruction long before this ends."

"I want the Pandavas dead. You are protecting Arjuna. Unless we take him down, this will never end."

"Are you accusing me of disloyalty?" Bhishma asked softly, taking a step forward to stand inches from Suyodhana. "I am not a slave you won in a gambling game, nephew. I chose to fight on my own terms. If I have not killed any Pandava, I have not allowed you to be killed, either."

"My brothers are dead, Pitamaha, we must win this war and end it quickly. The casualties are mounting and the drought situation has worsened. More people are dying on the streets without food than are being slain in Kurukshetra."

"Would you like a truce?"

"No, not after what they have done; not when I know what they would do to my people if they win."

Bhishma took a deep breath. "Then what is it that you want?"

"Kill Arjuna."

"No, I will not allow any of my grand-nephews to die. All of you are my blood, the sons I never had."

"Were not those who died your grand-nephews, too, Pitamaha? Or were they not important because they were Dhritarashtra's sons and evil Duryodhana's brothers? Allow Karna to fight! He is not related to anyone and he will not have such qualms."

"This is not Karna's war. I do not want a Suta to fight under me."

"Pitamaha, I know that is not your real reason. There are Kiratas, Nagas, Asuras, Rakshasas, and Nishadas fighting in our army. Perhaps you are afraid Karna will achieve what you could not?"

"I have nothing left to prove anymore, Suyodhana. Not to you and certainly not to Karna."

"Pitamaha, the soldiers are saying I do not care for their lives. Any more of this and we will have a mutiny on our hands."

Bhishma stared at Suyodhana and then turned away in silence.

"Pitamaha, give me an answer. Should we summon Karna?"

"No, Karna is impulsive and could change everything."

"If Arjuna goes down, Yudhishtra will sue for peace, demand a truce. Arjuna must be killed before the sun sets tomorrow."

"I will defeat him," Bhishma's words barely reached Suyodhana.

"He has to die, Pitamaha."

Bhishma sat on his spartan bed, waiting for Suyodhana and Aswathama to leave. Finally, they bowed and left the old man alone. The pain in his chest had returned. His hands were shaking. He had lived too long for anyone's good. 'Ma Ganga, your son has become a burden to all.' Tomorrow, he would kill Arjuna and be done with it. If that was the price for saving his country, he would do it. Or perhaps he would sacrifice himself instead.

*****

59 LIABILITY OF CONSCIENCE

THE NINTH DAY BELONGED TO BHISHMA. The grand old Commander was like a natural force – a hurricane, a rampaging elephant, a tidal wave. His commanders executed various attacking formations like *krauncha vyuha*, *garuda vyuha* and *sarpa vyuha* at lightning speed. From opposite flanks, Drona and Kripa attacked the Pandavas and drove Arjuna's *akhshounis* to face the central thrust of Bhishma's attack. Aswathama cut off Bhima's men from the main body, while Kritavarma pinned down Drupada's men.

By afternoon, Bhishma had penetrated deep into Arjuna's *akhshounis*. Twice, Arjuna found himself face to face with his grand-uncle. Both times Bhishma cut off Arjuna's bow with contemptuous ease. He had two opportunities to shoot at a weaponless Arjuna, but the old warrior waited for his opponent to pick up his spare bow. Krishna managed to rescue Arjuna by skilful driving, getting the chariot away from Bhishma both times.

The sun was about to set and Bhishma did not wish to take any more chances. The war had to end. He deployed his *yantramuktha astras* and blasted his way through Arjuna's defences. With needlepoint precision, his *hastamuktha* arrows destroyed Arjuna's cache of weapons. For the third time that day, Arjuna found himself helpless before the old warrior.

"Krishna, I cannot find my *Gandiva*. The moment I touch my bow, Pitamaha's arrow will kill me." Weapons lay scattered on the chariot floor and acrid smoke stung Arjuna's eyes.

Krishna looked at Bhishma, standing poised to shoot his final arrow at Arjuna. The war was almost lost for the Pandavas.

Krishna whipped the horses and the chariot lunged towards Bhishma, taking him by surprise. Bhishma's charioteer veered and Krishna shot past.

Bhishma's chariot turned and gave chase. The two chariots weaved through the fighting men, parting the elephant corps and shattering the ordered ranks of cavalry. Warriors stopped fighting to watch the deadly chase.

With a sudden jerk, Krishna turned his chariot. Bhishma's charioteer pulled at the reins with both hands. The chariots stood facing each other. Bhishma was deep inside the Pandava lines, cut off from his men. The Pandava army closed in. Krishna had trapped Bhishma but the seasoned warrior stood rock steady in his chariot, his face calm, his muscles taut. He shot an arrow, knocking the pin out of one of Arjuna's chariot wheels. The wheel rolled away and the chariot tilted to one side, throwing Arjuna off balance.

Krishna jumped down from his seat and rushed to Arjuna. "Pick up your *Gandiva*, it is behind you," he yelled urgently, pointing at Bhishma. Arjuna's grasping hand found the bow and instantly he was back on his feet, bow at the ready, to shoot back at Bhishma. But Bhishma had put down his bow and was standing unarmed.

"Kill him *now!*" Krishna urged, but Arjuna hesitated to shoot the unarmed Pitamaha.

"Arjuna, the sun has set. I have stopped fighting as per the rules of war. We will meet tomorrow," Bhishma said.

Arjuna put down his *Gandiva* and bowed to his grand-uncle.

"What are you hesitating for? Kill him!" Krishna urged yet again. But Arjuna shook his head and walked back to his broken chariot.

"You have forgotten all your lessons, Arjuna. If you do not kill him, I will," Krishna declared. He raised the fallen wheel of the chariot from the ground and held it above his head, ready to throw it at Bhishma.

Bhishma did not blink. He just gazed back at Krishna, his hands folded. "I am honoured to die at your hands, Krishna. Kill me if you wish, but protect *dharma*."

The wheel fell from Krishna's hands, raising a cloud of dust. He nodded his head and followed Arjuna. Bhishma's chariot turned around. The Pandava army, which had surrounded him, parted to let the Commander of the Kaurava army pass. Bhishma felt content Arjuna had not shot him as he stood unarmed. Neither had Krishna flung the chariot wheel at him. There was still hope for the country. Both sides were fighting according to the traditions of war.

As dusk crept over Kurukshetra, Bhishma passed Iravan's severed head on the pole. Once again, sorrow and doubt seized his soul. The grand old man of Bharata took a deep breath and prayed, 'May *dharma* win.'

That night, in the camp, Suyodhana confronted Bhishma again, questioning his actions, accusing him of disloyalty. Why had he not shot Arjuna when he had had the chance? Bhishma asked whether Suyodhana preferred the dishonour of winning by ignoring the rules of warfare? Suyodhana had no answer.

As Bhishma and Suyodhana argued on about the ethics of war, unknown to them, a ruthless conspiracy was being hatched in the Pandava camp to bring the patriarch down.

*****

60 EUNUCH SHIELD

MIST CRAWLED FROM THE RIVER, giving an eerie feel to the night. The howls of jackals rose and fell. The flapping of vulture wings could be heard as they feasted in the dark. Even the music of Krishna's flute could not transcend the dread in the Pandavas' minds as they sat around the fire warming their hands. Finally, Krishna put away his flute and chided Arjuna for not killing Bhishma when he had the chance.

Arjuna merely shook his head. The war was nearly lost. Duryodhana stood on the verge of victory. "I see no way to stop Pitamaha. The way he is leading the army sends shivers down my spine. What is the use? Even if Pitamaha goes, there are Drona, Kripa, Karna, Aswathama and Duryodhana to reckon with. The list is endless."

"Patience, Arjuna. One person at a time. Let us deal with Bhishma first. We must trap him into using his own vows." Krishna tapped the flute at his waist, a smile on his lips, waiting for the Pandavas to speak.

"How do we do that?" asked Dharmaputra Yudhishtra.

"He would never fight a woman..."

"I will fight him then. I cannot forget his silence when the Kauravas tried to strip me in the Sabha," said Draupadi. No one could doubt her courage or willingness to fight.

"Oh, Draupadi, the real man among the Pandavas. But it cannot be you, my dear. We cannot field a woman against Pitamaha."

"You are contradicting yourself, Krishna," Yudhishtra pointed out.

"Oh future King of Hastinapura, calm your mind. Why do you worry when I am with you?" Krishna put a hand on Yudhishtra's shoulder. Then he turned and called, "Shikandi!"

The eunuch walked in and the Pandavas gasped. "It would be demeaning for Bhishma to fight Shikandi. We can also claim he is not a woman, so we have not broken the rules of war. Arjuna could stand behind and..."

"No!" Arjuna shouted, revolted by the very idea of such subterfuge.

"Arjuna, there is no other way. *Dharma* must triumph."

"No, not like this! Not against the man who has always been fair to everyone. Not by hiding like a coward behind this creature."

"Then let Duryodhana become King and you can go into exile for another thirteen years."

"Krishna, let me fight! Bhishma will not see tomorrow's sunset. Let me fight Drona, who professed love for Arjuna, yet when the time came, sided with evil. Let me fight that unscrupulous son of the Guru and claim the precious stone he wears. Let me fight Kripa, let me fight all the men who remained silent when I was being shamed," Draupadi said fiercely, her long hair blowing wildly in the wind.

Krishna took Shikandi's arm and walked out. Draupadi would take care of the others. It was unfortunate but there was no other way to stop Duryodhana from winning.

"For decades, one dream has possessed me – to kill Bhishma and avenge my mother's death. I am grateful for this opportunity, Lord Krishna. I am your humble servant," Shikandi said.

"Good, but you must be at your feminine best tomorrow."

"I will charm the old man, just wait and watch," Shikandi replied with a coy look.

An owl hooted in the dark and another answered. Their hooting went on and on until the eastern horizon grew grey with weariness.

***

Even Draupadi could not make Arjuna change his mind. The next day, his *vyagra vyuha* formation, which remained in waiting, struck back whenever the enemy least expected it, alternating lightning strikes with a languid pace, which confused the Kaurava army. For the first time in nine days, the battle turned against the Kauravas. Arjuna effectively used the *yantra muktha* missiles to strike deep into the enemy ranks. By afternoon, he had slain seven more of Dhritarashtra's sons.

By late afternoon, Bhishma struck back. By killing the Kaurava Princes, Arjuna had crossed an invisible line and there was nothing now to hold back the veteran general. *Vyali vyuha*, the dragon formation, was Bhishma's answer to Arjuna. He moved around his chariots holding the *yantramuktha* missiles, spitting fire into the enemy ranks while the elephant corps wreaked devastation. He followed it by a quick cavalry attack, like the lash of the dragon's tail. Bhishma was within hailing distance from Arjuna when dusk spread its mantle over the battlefield.

When Pitamaha's first arrow struck Arjuna's shoulder, he was shocked. "Krishna, Pitamaha has reached me again." Another arrow missed Arjuna's throat by a hair's breadth.

"Die a fair death and leave your wives at Duryodhana's mercy," Krishna suggested in a flat tone.

"Call that creature!" Arjuna shouted as another arrow knocked off his headgear. He knew they were warning shots. The next one would pierce his throat.

"Shikandi!" Krishna called and the eunuch jumped into the chariot.

They turned and rushed towards Bhishma. Something exploded behind them – another of Bhishma's powerful weapons. Time was running out. Bhagadatta, King of Kamarupa, cut across their path on his war elephant, trying to block them. Krishna wove the chariot past, lashing the elephant with his whip as he rushed past. The elephant trumpeted in pain and grabbed at them with its trunk. They barely escaped its maddened fury.

Arjuna saw Bhishma standing in his chariot, his bow drawn. His arrow tip caught the setting sun and looked like it was on fire. Shikandi moved to stand in front of Arjuna. The smell of the jasmine flowers the eunuch wore made him want to vomit. Shikandi began making lewd gestures at Bhishma. The Pitamaha's blazing eyes said it all. He put down his bow and stood staring at them. Shakuni hurled the choicest and the most obscene abuse as their chariot halted a few feet away from Bhishma. Arjuna flinched when he looked into his granduncle's eyes. The look of disappointment and sorrow in those eyes would remain with Arjuna till the end of his days.

"Shoot!" Krishna ordered. Looking away, Arjuna shot Bhishma. The eunuch's shrill laughter echoed round him. Still hiding behind the eunuch, Arjuna shot the next arrow. He was so close he could hear his arrow pierce Bhishma's body. He shut his eyes and shot another arrow. Shikandi kept screaming obscenities. Not a cry of pain, not an accusation, not a reproach, not even a word of advice escaped Bhishma's lips. Scores of arrows pierced his body, yet the grand old man of Bharata, the son of Ganga, refused to fall and die. And he refused to raise his weapon against a perceived woman.

Arjuna recoiled in disgust when Shikhandi's lips kissed his cheeks. He knew what it meant. Pitamaha had fallen. Bhishma lay on a bed of arrows – his arrows. More than fifty arrows had pierced his body. Shikandi danced round the fallen figure in wild abandon, howling with laughter and making bawdy gestures.

'Oh, Krishna, what have you made me do?' Arjuna cried in silent anguish, his heart filled with grief. But his friend was watching Shikandi's bizarre dance with a slight smile. Arjuna rushed to Bhishma and fell at his feet. "Forgive me, Pitamaha..."

"My son..." Bhishma turned his head away.

The celebrations continued around the fallen Commander. The victorious warrior sat sobbing at Bhishma's feet, trying to find solace in Krishna's advice that the soul was immortal and nobody could kill anyone. Then why did he not feel detached from his actions? If *dharma* had prevailed, why did his heart drown in sorrow? "Forgive me..." Arjuna wept, kneeling beside Bhishma who lay on his bed of arrows.

When Suyodhana heard the news, the darkness blotted out his vision. Had his constant accusations caused the Pitamaha to fall? The throne they were fighting over belonged to Bhishma. Suyodhana felt he was as much responsible for Bhishma's death as his cousin, Arjuna. His words had been sharper than any of Arjuna's arrows.

As darkness fell over Kurukshetra, Suyodhana knew it was time to recall Karna. His friend was not bound by any false sense of duty to the Pandavas. He had risked the wrath of the priests and earned infamy for Karna, whom he loved more than any of his brothers. The Suta he had made into a Kshatriya, would win him the war. Suyodhana called a guard and asked him to fetch Karna.

As the messenger galloped off to fetch Karna, Suyodhana could hear the loud celebrations from the Pandava camp. Iravan watched with all-seeing eyes, awaiting the arrival of the Suta who had been summoned to pay his dues.

*****

61 SURYAPUTRA

KARNA WAITED FOR ARJUNA TO LEAVE Bhishma's side. It was almost dawn but Arjuna refused to move. Karna was afraid the old warrior would die before he could speak to him. He had many questions to ask. Why had Bhishma always been unfair to him? It was cruel to ask a dying man such questions but Karna knew he must if he were to ever find peace. Just when he had decided he would have to confront Bhishma despite Arjuna's presence, Yudhishtra arrived and took him away.

'Tears are cheap once deceit has done its work,' thought Karna as he walked towards Bhishma and stood over him. No sound escaped Bhishma's lips. Not even on his deathbed did he let others know he was in pain.

Bhishma sensed someone's presence. "Who is that?" the rich voice was a travesty of itself and a lump formed in Karna's throat.

"It is I – Sutaputra." Karna moved to kneel beside the fallen warrior.

"Karna, my son, there is something you must know. You are Kunti's son, the eldest of all," Bhishma whispered.

"No, Sir, I am Radha's son."

"Karna, don't you recognize who you are?"

"Sir, I am a Suta of low caste, who refused to be intimidated by the accident of my birth."

"Do not be cruel to your mother, Kunti, Karna. The blood of Lord Ramachandra flows in your veins. You belong to the *Suryavamsha*."

"My mother is Radha and my father is Athiratha, the charioteer. I have no divine lineage."

"You are punishing us all, Karna. You alone can stop this war."

"Sir, have your oft-stated objections to me melted away because you no longer think I am of low caste but a Kshatriya? You have never treated me fairly."

"Do not carry harsh thoughts about a dying man. I only wished to keep you away from this madness, Karna."

"How can I stay away when Suyodhana is in danger? I will fight until my friend is King."

"The throne belongs to you, my son."

Karna withdrew his hand from Bhishma and stood up. "What wrong have I ever done to you?"

"Karna, I did my duty to my country. When the Confederate demanded your head, a war for your sake was a risk not worth taking. It was not in the interests of the kingdom."

"Would you have given them Suyodhana or Yudhishtra's head had they asked for it? Would you have allowed any of the Kuru Princes to suffer the humiliation I have suffered all my life?"

"I have no answers to your questions. Perhaps things would have been different had I known you were Kunti's son."

"Even for the great Bhishma, it is all about caste?"

"Karna, you are my grand-nephew, like Suyodhana or Yudhishtra."

"Yet I was treated like a dog. You could have changed that."

"Will you not allow an old man to die in peace, Karna? You want me to bare my heart to you? Then hear what I have to say. I was afraid of you, and jealous."

"The great Bhishma afraid and jealous of a charioteer's son? Sir, you mock me yet again."

"I knew that if I allowed you to fight, there would no Pandavas left. You have no equal, Karna. I merely chose to save my clan and country. Do not fight in this war. Persuade Suyodhana to stop. We have already paid a terrible price. Only you can do this. Accept Krishna's offer..."

"And betray Suyodhana? Betray the man who did not think twice about making a Suta King of Anga? Betray friendship for a worthless throne? Sir, I would rather die."

"You make this old man proud, son. You are indeed the best of the Kurus. I have no regrets but sometimes I wonder if I did the right thing by abdicating the throne. I lived for this country, yet here I lie on my deathbed, a bed of arrows shot by one of my grand-nephews hiding behind a eunuch. Here I await the Lord of Death to claim me once the sun has crossed the sky into *Sankranti*, while my countrymen butcher each other around me."

Karna's hard resolve broke at Bhishma's words. He bent down beside the prone figure and gently took Bhishma's hand between both his own. "Forgive my harsh words, Pitamaha. Bless this Suta."

"Blessed you are, Karna, by the Gods and by the love of the people. Remain so forever – unflinching in adversity, selfless in giving and brave hearted in battle."

"You did not bless me with victory, Pitamaha."

"No victory will be greater than yours, my son. Your name will be remembered till the sun burns in the sky." Bhishma raised a hand to touch Karna's head in benediction.

Choking back his tears, Karna touched the patriach's feet. How deeply he had craved acknowledgement from this man! Abruptly, Karna stood up. He had his answers but they only made him feel sad. He had to win this war at any cost but he vowed in his heart to seek out Arjuna and make him beg for his life, for the cowardly way in which he had brought down this great man. Karna walked to the river and stepped into its freezing waters. The sun was an orange ball in the east. He began to recite the *Suryagayatri*.

"My son..."

Karna cringed, his eyes still shut in prayer. He recognized the voice. A shiver ran through his body when she touched his arm. Karna completed his *mantras* and dipped his head into the rippling water. He prayed she would leave him in peace. He yearned to stay in the water and die there. When he came up, she was weeping. He wanted to hate this woman but he felt only weariness. As he stepped out of the river, she stood in his way.

"Devi Kunti, allow this Suta to pass. Let not my polluted shadow fall on you."

"My son, will you not forgive your mother?"

There was nothing to say. Karna stared into the distance, his arms folded across his powerful chest. He wished he were somewhere else, far away from the woman before him. Finally he said, "Who am I to forgive the Rajamata of Hastinapura, the mother of the noble Pandavas? I am but a water weed taken from the Ganga by a Suta."

"You are nevertheless my son, Karna," Kunti raised her head, her eyes blazing with a hint of their old fire.

"Where were you when my father pawned his only possessions to give me an education? Where were you when the world laughed at my ambitions? Where were you when I was being insulted about my caste at every turn?"

"Son, you must find it in your heart to forgive me. Stop this war!"

"The war will end with the death of your five sons." Karna's skin flushed. The Ganga glowed in the golden rays of the sun.

Kunti tried to fall at his feet but Karna pulled her up. Anger throbbed in his deep voice. "Devi, you forget your exalted station."

"Spare my sons. They are all I have. We have suffered enough. Do not kill them." Kunti stood before him with folded hands.

"This is a war, Devi. If they are fearful, you can stop the conflict by asking them to accept Suyodhana's rightful claim to the throne."

"My sons are not afraid, Karna; it is a mother's heart that speaks."

"I will kill them all, have no doubt about that."

"They are your brothers, Karna. Be generous and spare them."

"You have too many expectations from the son you never wanted."

"Forgive them, Karna, even if you cannot forgive your mother."

"Forgive Arjuna for all that he has done? Tell your noble son I am not a great man like Bhishma. He is in for a nasty surprise if he tries such tricks with me."

Kunti dried her tears with her *pallu* and looked up at Karna calmly. "I know how to stop this war and still win. I will announce to the world that you are my son. Your evil friend will have to step aside for you. Then, my son – and not Gandhari's – will sit on the throne."

"So this is all a part of your political game? You came to me because you wanted to win a petty point over Maharani Gandhari?"

"Call it what you will. No one can prevent me, not even you, my son. I will do it."

Karna was taken aback. His first thought was for his friend. Suyodhana must never know. "If you do so, I will kill myself with my own sword. Suyodhana will be the rightful heir again. Rest assured that I will ensure you do not win."

"Karna, spare a thought for your mother. Spare my five sons."

"Five sons? Five including the twins of your co-wife Madri, but not six, including the son you threw out like trash?"

"Do not misunderstand me, Karna. Allow me to explain. I do not wish you to die. You are my firstborn, my flesh and blood. I carried you for nine months and bore you in pain..."

"What about Draupadi?" Karna asked, his eyes cold and unforgiving, his lips curved in a derisive smile.

"She will be your wife, too. Being the eldest, you will have first right."

"You would do anything for power? Even this?" Karna's eyes mocked as he let out a bitter laugh.

Kunti looked away from the condemnation written on her son's face. "I did not mean..."

"I will spare the lives of four of your five sons – all except Arjuna. That is my promise to you."

"Oh no...son, do not harm your own brother. It is a great sin."

"You will have five sons after the war, Devi, not six. Either it will be Arjuna or me, though I am ashamed to call myself your son. Please leave before I regret my decision."

Kunti reached out her hand in blessing but Karna evaded her touch. He turned back to say, "I must thank you for throwing me away, else I would never have known what a real mother's love is. Accept the gratitude of this Radheya, Devi Kunti." Karna bowed and walked away with steady steps.

'I thought he would agree to the kingship if I asked, if I admitted I was his mother. Oh, what have I done?' Kunti cried silently.

Krishna stepped out from behind a tree and walked towards his aunt smiling. "Every man has his destiny and Karna has chosen his." He put a comforting arm around her shoulders.

"You are wrong, Krishna. I am not being manipulative. It was not a game to me. He is my son," Kunti declared coldly, shaking off Krishna's arm.

"And a great son, too! A son you can be proud of." Krishna's smile broadened. "Nevertheless, it was a valuable promise to extract from him, Aunt."

*****

62 GANGADATTA

BHISHMA COULD HEAR THE WAILING OF WOMEN. He could smell the blood from the battlefield. If only they would stop this carnage. The work of a lifetime was being destroyed before his eyes. "Oh death, why you have forsaken me?" the grand old man of Bharata moaned in pain. He wished Karna had stayed for a little longer. He wished his nephews would come and stay with him until he took his last breath. What had he achieved after a life lived for others – a bed of arrows shot by Arjuna or the abuse Suyodhana had bestowed upon him? No one needed him now. All his efforts had been in vain.

Shakuni's anger he could understand. He was a Mlecha. But how he had loved him as a boy! Bhishma knew he had wronged Shakuni – shattered his kingdom, killed his father, and made his sister marry blind Dhritarashtra. He should have killed the little boy when he had found him cowering under his sister's bed. It had been a grave mistake, but he knew he would have taken the same decision again. What he could not understand was Krishna's ruthlessness and single-minded determination to win the war. True, he had come with an offer of truce, but why was he meddling in the affairs of the Kurus?

Krishna's obsession with *dharma* as he defined it, was the reason for all this carnage. How much more blood would flow for an idea nobody understood and each person defined in his own fashion? Both sides passionately believed they had *dharma* on their side. The tragedy was that no one was going to win, not even Krishna. They would all be losers in this war. Women and children would be the worst affected. His countrymen, already affected by the drought, would surely lose the most. They had always lost, irrespective of who ruled them. This war had no winners.

Bhishma wanted to cry aloud to the Gods in heaven, 'Have you no mercy that you afflict this poor earth and its people with so much misery?' Then, in a moment of shocking clarity, he saw that the war *would* have winners, waiting in the wings like vultures, for the warriors on both sides to die. They would inherit this holy land, make a hell out of it and call it eternal *dharma*. His life had been futile.

Bhishma was glad he would not live to see it. He wished death would come. He was unwanted, even by the beasts feasting on the dead in the temple of *dharma*. He was condemned to wait and witness the rise of *Kaliyuga*. 'Ma Ganga, forgive your son, Gangadutta, for I have failed you,' the great warrior of the Kurus cried alone.

Far away, in the camps on either side, preparations went forward for the next day's battle. They had already forgotten Bhishma. He was the past.

*****

63 END OF A POEM

DRONA ELABORATED ON HIS BATTLE PLAN for the next day. After Bhishma's fall, despite his friend's pleas, Karna had declined the post of Commander-in-Chief and Suyodhana had been compelled to appoint Drona as Commander of the Kaurava forces.

"Father, Mother has given me her blessing."

Suyodhana turned to see his young son standing behind him. Kumara looked glorious in his battle attire. Suyodhana embraced his son. Was he doing the right thing by talking this untested boy into fighting such a ruthless war?

"And here, Kumara's forces will meet Abhimanyu's battalion head on. If Arjuna's son tries to launch an attack on Kripa's *akhshouni*..."

Drona's voice hammered in Suyodhana's brain. He wanted to protest but his pride silenced him. He knew Lakshmana Kumara was not Abhimanyu's equal in battle, but how could he say so without hurting the boy's pride and his own? Suyodhana's mind was a knot of worries as the Guru outlined his war strategy to his generals. If something went wrong, how would he face Bhanu? How would he face himself? But surely, nothing would go wrong?

***

"This is a stupid war." Shakuni sat in his tent, his hands restless. His eyes gleamed in the golden light of a burning torch. His son sat close by, listening. A moth buzzed around the torch and dived into the flame. An acrid smell filled the air.

"This war is the most gruesome fighting I have seen, Father," Uluka remarked, shaking his head.

"This is a sham war. It is neither gruesome enough, nor bloody enough. Nothing is happening. These Indians stick to some ancient rules which make battles a joke." Shakuni rattled his dice together and threw them on the floor. "What we need is raw emotion, wounds that will never heal. These Indians must carry the scars for centuries."

"What do you suggest, Father?" Uluka asked.

"Important people must die, not just foot soldiers," Shakuni said softly, looking at his sons. "Sleep well, for tomorrow we change everything." He took the torch and thrust it head first into the sand. The flame broke into a thousand sparks and died with a hiss, drowning them in darkness. Shakuni lay awake long after his sons had fallen asleep.

***

"Prince Kumara, it is your father...you must help him! Hurry, Abhimanyu has trapped him," Shakuni shouted from his chariot.

Kumara looked around, trying to locate his father's chariot and banner. Where was the white flag with the coiled serpents? Through the cloud of smoke and dust he finally he saw it at a distance. Abhimanyu's forces had encircled his father's chariot. Guru Drona had warned him of such a move. How foolish he had been to stop for the wounded men around him! His father would die because of him.

"Take me there," Kumara screamed to his charioteer, pointing to the fluttering white flag. He braced himself as the chariot rumbled on at great speed. Arrows rained around him and a couple pierced his armour. "Faster, faster..." he yelled. The bow he held was heavy and his armour was suffocating him. Kumara had no clear idea of what he had to do, only that he had to save his father somehow.

When he reached the spot, his father was nowhere to be seen. Instead, Uluka, Shakuni's son, was fighting Abhimanyu from his chariot. Uluka's had a similar flag, with one coiled serpent, but it also had the small emblem of Gandhara in its left corner.

"Hey, you coward! Why are you running away?" Abhimanyu yelled at the fast vanishing Uluka.

Kumara realized he had made a grave error and placed himself in harm's way.

"Prince, see who we have here," a soldier said, jumping into Kumara's chariot.

Abhimanyu turned and his eyes grew wide with surprise. "What are you doing here, Kumara?" he asked as he threw down his bow and unsheathed his sword.

Another soldier jumped into Kumara's chariot. With a force he had never imagined he possessed, Kumara kicked the first soldier. The second one charged at him but Kumara cut him down with his sword. Clutching his lacerated stomach, the man collapsed onto the chariot floor. Kumara looked at the river of blood in a daze. He threw down his sword, saying in horror, "I have killed a man!"

Kumara's charioteer tried to leap down and escape but Abhimanyu cut off his head with a slash of his sword. Then he advanced towards his childhood friend and grabbed Kumara by the hair.

"Abhimanyu, are you going to kill me?" Kumara asked softly,

"This is war, my friend. I am sorry, Kumara. The world will miss a poet." With one clean sweep of his sword, Abhimanyu severed Kumara's head. It dropped to the ground and rolled away. Arjuna's son thrust his sword into the head and raised it for the world to see. "Behold! I have killed Duryodhana's son and heir!"

All around him, conches sounded and drums boomed to mark his feat. His father and uncles arrived to congratulate him. He had made them proud. Abhimanyu stood in the middle of the battlefield with Kumara's head raised on the tip of his sword. He felt a twinge of pity for the friend he had killed, but the exhilarating victory and pride in his father's eyes soon swept away such feelings.

He was about to walk away when he saw something strange. What was wrong with Iravan's severed head? He blinked. The head had somehow changed into Kumara's, then some Rakshasa's, before changing back to Iravan. The head kept changing its features. Abhimanyu's throat went dry. He stared in utter horror and disbelief. He was looking at his own severed head on the spike.

***

"I want him dead," Bhanumati said fiercely, her eyes and lips red and swollen from crying.

Suyodhana did not raise his head. He yearned for the release of tears but they refused to come.

"You killed him! You told me you would protect him; that no harm would befall him. I want to see your Subhadra weep like me. Go! Get me Abhimanyu's head! Give me your word as a man that you will kill him."

"Bhanu, it is a war... your son died like a warrior."

"I don't want words, I want Abhimanyu's head. Kill him mercilessly, just as he killed my son."

"Devi Bhanumati, it was I, as Commander, who failed to protect your son." Drona came forward with head bowed.

"Guru, do not protect my husband. It was not your fault but his. He failed to protect his only son. But we are nothing to him. How does it matter that our son is dead? My Kumara never wanted to fight anyone, never wanted to be a warrior. He was a gentle soul. But he went to make his father proud. Now he is dead. My son did not want the throne. For whose sake does my husband fight but his own?

"Abhimanyu will not see tomorrow's sunset, Devi. This is Drona's word. They have broken yet another rule of war – not to attack a disarmed man. We will not rest until we have vanquished the amoral Pandavas."

"What good will that do my son, Guru? My Kumara is never going to come back."

"His sacrifice will not have been in vain. Place your trust in me."

"Guru, you are too kind, but why does my husband remain silent?"

"Bhanu, we must go after Arjuna and Yudhishtra first."

"Oh, so it pains you to think of killing Subhadra's son? I do not care whether you or Yudhishtra wins, but I want the man who killed my son dead." Bhanumati turned away, sobbing.

Suyodhana caught her by her wrist and drew her to him. "Bhanu, Abhimanyu will not see the end of tomorrow."

"You have turned me into a monster, Suyodhana. Poor Subhadra. I feel pity for her. I feel pity for all the mothers who will lose their sons in this horrible war." Bhanu wept on his chest.

Suyodhana ran his fingers through her dishevelled hair. "Abhimanyu will die tomorrow. Never fear, our son will be avenged," he whispered in her ear.

Bhanumati's tears fell like winter rain.

***

64 WHEEL OF DEATH

HIS ARMY STRETCHED TO THE HORIZON. Suyodhana looked at the elephant corps, alternating with the cavalry, infantry and chariots, moving in concentric circles. Mounted archers, in perfect synchronization, like the spokes of a chariot wheel, darted off to attack enemy battalions. He had only heard of the famed *chakravyuha* formation. It was as beautiful and sinister as a King Cobra uncoiling. Drona, as Commander-in-Chief, had made all the difference to the war. It was no longer fought by a patriarch to teach his successors the lessons of war, but by a ruthless strategist who did not care about expending lives. The war had taken a deadly turn.

Karna's chariot went past Suyodhana like lightning, tilted at a crazy angle on its right wheels. Karna yelled a warning but his charioteer merely smiled and told him to watch his target. It would have been unthinkable for any ordinary charioteer to talk back to the King of Anga, but Shalya was no ordinary man. He was King of Madra and the best charioteer in all of Bharatavarsha. He had volunteered to drive Karna, and Suyodhana had overruled Drona to allow it. It had not helped that Shalya was Madri's brother and hence the Pandava twins' uncle. Shalya considered himself a better charioteer than even Krishna. Suyodhana smiled at Shalya's skill and the irony of a Kshatriya charioteer for a Suta.

"Brace and thrust!" Drona's voice boomed and the circle shifted into an egg shape in a trice.

No man in his right senses dared to attack a full-blown *chakravyuha* formation. The best strategy for the opposing Commander was to wait for the storm to pass. Like typhoons, *chakravyuhas* lost energy after the initial thrust. It was a difficult task to keep such a huge formation perfectly synchronized. If someone managed to break in, all hell could break loose. The change of shape now was a sign that someone was trying to break in. Only a reckless or foolish Commander would order a frontal attack on the *chakravyuha*. Arjuna was no fool, neither was he reckless, so what was happening?

"Disperse." Drona's voice was calm but it sent shivers through the Kaurava ranks. Disperse? Break the *chakravyuha*? Was the Guru in his right mind?

"Guru Drona!" Suyodhana shouted but the Guru's face was set in granite. Suyodhana turned and saw Abhimanyu's chariot rushing towards them at great speed. An arrow came flying towards Suyodhana. He deflected it with his mace. The *chakravyuha* had been breached! Behind Abhimanyu, the Pandava cavalry charged at full gallop, sending the *chakravyuha* into disarray.

On Suyodhana's left, Karna's chariot came rushing to a halt in a cloud of dust. A finger length more and it would have crashed onto his. Shalya grinned. Karna's face was creased with worry. On Suyodhana's right, Aswathama's chariot raced up. Karna jumped into Suyodhana's chariot and shot an arrow with a single, fluid movement. It lodged in Abhimanyu's shoulder, drawing blood, but the young man did not bother to pull it out. His murderous stare was fixed on Suyodhana's face and his arrow whistled past the Crown Prince's head. Karna's next arrow caught Abhimanyu's other shoulder but Arjuna's son did not even flinch. He aimed at Suyodhana's throat.

"Formation!" Drona's unruffled voice rose above the din and the *chakravyuha* formation closed. What was Drona doing? "Cut and close!"

One of the spokes of the formation detached itself and wound around the Pandava attacking cavalry and cut off Abhimanyu from his troops. A perfect trap! Abhimanyu had not seen the danger, his eyes fixed on Suyodhana. With a loud crack, the wheels of Abhimanyu's chariot broke loose and fell, throwing him to the ground. Abhimanyu looked stunned. The force of the fall had broken his bow in two. The wheel pin lay on the ground with Drona's arrow through it.

"He is all yours, Prince," Drona said in a flat voice to Suyodhana.

Abhimanyu leapt up, drew his sword and stood in combat position. His face betrayed not a flicker of emotion as he stood calmly, his eyes coldly sweeping the Kaurava ranks. He stood alone in the Kaurava *chakravyuha*, there was no going back. Suyodhana jumped from his chariot and walked towards him. Karna, Aswathama and Jayadratha followed, swords drawn. Suyodhana could not but admire the raw courage the young man showed. How he wished Abhimanyu had been his son. The thought of his own dead son snapped Suyodhana back to reality. Abhimanyu deserved no mercy.

"Halt if you value your life," Abhimanyu said, his voice clear and unafraid. "Four against one – is this *dharma*?"

Suyodhana's laughter held a bitter ring. "Righteousness died when your father hid behind a eunuch and shot Pitamaha. *Dharma* was buried when you murdered an unarmed Kumara. He was your friend, Abhimanyu. You betrayed him in life and in death."

"Uncle Suyodhana, stop this whining and fight like a man!"

Jayadratha rushed at Abhimanyu, but the youngster moved away from the arc of Jayadratha's sword and pushed him away with his shield. Jayadratha lost his balance and fell. Abhimanyu laughed. Suyodhana felt pity stir in his heart as Aswathama swung his sword. Abhimanyu tried to dodge it but the wily Brahmin warrior had anticipated it. At the last moment, he changed his swing to a thrust, cutting deeply into Abhimanyu's shoulder. Blood eagerly followed his blade.

Abhimanyu grunted in pain. "Cowards! Fighting four to one. Shameless beasts!" he yelled, swinging his sword at Karna.

Karna blocked the blow with his shield and swung his sword at Abhimanyu. The youngster blocked it with his own sword and angry sparks flew over them. In a moment, the sword had been dislodged from Karna's hand. Abhimanyu attacked like a whirlwind and Karna struggled to block his thrusts and blows with his shield.

It was all happening very quickly. Jayadratha had managed to walk away, his face contorted with rage and shame. Beaten by a mere boy! The King of Sindh gritted his teeth and tried to rush towards Abhimanyu, but Suyodhana restrained him. The boy was for Karna. The next moment, Suyodhana saw something wriggling in Karna's hand. The *urumi*, the rope-like sword of the South, which Karna wore like a belt, shimmered in the sun. It rose high into the sky and then coiled itself around Abhimanyu's sword. The boy looked stunned as Karna prised the weapon from his hand. Before he knew it, he had lost his shield as well.

Abhimanyu bent and picked up the broken chariot wheel, blood flowing from the wound in his shoulder. Karna and Aswathama walked towards him, but Abhimanyu's gaze was fixed on Suyodhana. With a roar, he threw the chariot wheel at him. Suyodhana swung his mace and hit the flying wheel, smashing it to pieces.

"Hurry," Drona's voice urged. "Arjuna is trying to break in."

"Kill me if you dare, you cowards," Abhimanyu said, his chest heaving with exertion and pain.

"Arjuna has arrived. It is now or never," Drona said from his chariot.

Karna and Aswathama moved another step closer and Abhimanyu took a step backwards. Karna turned to Suyodhana, a silent question hung in the air between them. It seemed so wrong, so ignoble to hack a boy to death like this. Subhadra's pleading face came to Suyodhana's mind. His eyes locked on the pearl necklace Abhimanyu always wore. He remembered gifting it to him when he had first held the infant Abhimanyu in his arms. This could have been his Kumara. 'No! He killed my son without mercy. He put his head on a pole for everyone to jeer at...'

"Finish him!" Suyodhana ordered.

Jayadratha, who had moved behind Abhimanyu, acted in a flash. He grabbed Abhimanyu's hair and slit his throat with his sword.

"No!" Arjuna's yell made them all look up. He and Krishna had managed to break the *chakravyuha* but he was too late. Jumping from his chariot and throwing down his bow, Arjuna rushed to his son's lifeless body. "Guru, why did you do this?" he asked, his eyes full of tears.

Drona looked at Arjuna, pity in his heart, but he had given Bhanumati his word. The war was far from over.

Suyodhana knew what it felt like to lose a son. "You deserve nothing better, Arjuna. Your son killed mine without giving him a chance to defend himself." Karna, Aswathama and Jayadratha moved to stand beside Suyodhana.

"You evil men, you killed my son! Four against one. Cowards!" Arjuna spat on the ground in contempt. "You call yourself warriors?"

Jayadratha laughed and said Abhimanyu had got what he deserved.

Arjuna gently put down his son's lifeless body. "Jayadratha, it was a terrible mistake to spare your life. You are worthless and I should have killed you the day you sneaked into Draupadi's tent. But you will not see tomorrow's sunset. If you do, I will jump into a pyre and burn myself in its flames. This is my oath before God."

Drums rolled and horns blared, making the vow known to the world. Jayadratha turned pale. He could almost see the finger of death pointing at him.

"Arjuna, bent on suicide instead of facing a Suta?" Karna mocked.

Without a word Arjuna picked up the body of his son and walked to his chariot. Suyodhana felt his throat choke with pain. Of course Arjuna would tell her how they had killed her son. 'Subhadra, what have I done to your son? Oh God, what have I done? No! There are no wrongs in this bloody war.' He had kept his word to his wife by killing Subhadra's son. With it, everything to do with Subhadra had died a violent death. He could now face Bhanu with a clean heart, he told himself, trying to pacify his tortured mind.

The Guru blew his conch, signalling the end of battle for the day. Instead of elation, the weariness of war blanketed Suyodhana's mind as they walked back to their camp in silence. He coud not bring himself to join in the celebrations of his excited men. Subhadra's face refused to leave his troubled mind. 'I have become Duryodhana, but did I have any choice?' he asked himself.

Silence shrouded the Pandava camp. Tomorrow it would be their turn to avenge blood with blood.

*****

65 WARRIOR'S HONOUR

UTHAYAN WAS ECSTATIC. Finally Guru Dhaumya had requested the help of the Southern Confederate. They were no longer part players who scoured the countryside for food and supplies for the Pandava army. It was demeaning to act like bandits and terrorize poor villagers. Yet he had done his duty well. It was not going to be an easy task to break the defences set by Drona and kill Jayadratha. No wonder Arjuna was considered a hero. In comparison, his life looked dull and boring. Uthayan had to do something he could be proud of.

"In the name of Lord Vishnu , I vow to kill Karna tomorrow. If the Suta lives to see tomorrow's sunset, I, Uthayan Cheralathan will jump into a pyre and give up my worthless life." Uthayan felt elated as loud cheering rose around him. Drummers beat a frenzied rhythm and bards blared their horns. His vassal Kings bowed before his courage. Priests applied sandal paste on his forehead and garlanded him with red flowers. The bards began singing paeans about him and his illustrious dynasty. A vow of such magnitude could only be heard with awe and respect.

***

Suyodhana knew Jayadratha's safety was more chimeric than real. In his mind he clearly understood Arjuna's anguish and rage over Abhimanyu's death. He had felt the same emotions seething like a cauldron in his soul when Kumara had been killed.

A strange mist had rolled in from the rushes of the Ganga. Visibility was down to a few feet. "*Shakatavyuha*!" Drona's command brought Suyodhana back to the gruesome battlefield. All around him cavalry and elephants were assembling in a box cart formation. Where was Arjuna's chariot? By promising to kill Jayadratha before sunset, surely Arjuna had overreached himself? There was no way Arjuna could pierce the *shakatavyuha*. It was a formation designed for defence, with a hundred circles of cavalry, chariots and elephants. Jayadratha stood beside Suyodhana in the centre of the formation, pale with fear and tension. 'Hold on, friend. In a short while, we will watch Arjuna commit suicide,' Suyodhana said silently to himself. There was yet another challenger who had made a rash promise to immolate himself. But Karna could take care of himself. Uthayan was no match for him.

***

Screams, challenges, dust, blood, arrows flying thick and fast – it was a scene from hell. At any moment now, Drona would sound his conch to mark the end of the battle for the day. Despite ferocious fighting, the Southern Confederate armies had not been able to penetrate the *shakatavyuha*. The casualties on both sides were heavy but the Southern forces continued to come on, like moths attracted to a flame, caring nothing about certain death. But Karna continued to hold them off. The time for celebration was fast approaching.

A bloodcurdling scream made Suyodhana turn, his heart skipping a beat. Karna! Uthayan was in Karna's chariot, but where was Karna? He saw the Asura King's sword lifted high, ready to strike. How had the Confederate Commander pierced the formidable box-cart formation?

"Quick! Take me to Karna," Suyodhana prodded his charioteer.

The sun had set and his soldiers were already celebrating their victory. Arjuna had lost. But Suyodhana felt numb. Was Karna alive? What meaning had victory without Karna? Crores of armoured elephants blocked his path, hiding Karna's chariot from his sight. He could hear Drona's victory call and his troops taunting Arjuna.

"Go around the elephants," Suyodhana urged his charioteer. Why was the fool taking so much time?

When the last of the elephants had moved, he saw Karna standing in his chariot. What had happened to Uthayan?

"Move! The King is wounded. Let him pass," Karna shouted to his troops.

A wounded man staggered through the ranks, a deep gash in his back oozing blood onto his mahogany skin. Karna's soldiers parted for Uthayan to walk to safety. The Southern Confederate leader had lost his final war. He dragged himself to his camp.

Suyodhana reached Karna's chariot. How had Uthayan hurt his back? Surely Karna would never do such a dishonourable thing, even in self-defence?

"No Suyodhana, banish the thought," Karna said, guessing the question in his friend's eyes. "It was a fair fight. Unfortunately, he turned his back at the last moment, when the blade was already descending. It was not fitting. He was a brave adversary."

"The wound is not deep enough to kill him. Tomorrow, I am sure you will give him a death befitting the brave warrior he is."

"No, he is already dead. See what is happening."

Uthayan had arrived in his own ranks. A Confederate soldier spat on his face. Like a ritual, the other soldiers spat on their King's face, calling him a coward. The man who had once been their Supreme Overlord, stood with his head hung in shame, covered in spittle.

"What is this, Karna?"

"He has betrayed the pride of their race by turning his back during a fight. The wound on his back has branded him a coward. His body may still be alive but his soul is dead."

"Karna, is this how they treat a leader who was courageous enough to penetrate the *shakatavyuha* and take you by surprise?"

"It is the custom in their part of the country."

"What a war!"

"It is terrible, but we won today, Suyodhana. I only regret I could not make this Arjuna's last day on earth."

"Such a rash promise!" said his friend, a rare smile on his lined face.

"Why is the camp suddenly so silent?"

"Where...is Jayadratha?" A knot formed in Suyodhana's gut. "Turn back the chariot. Hurry!" he urged his charioteer.

Why were his men standing with their heads hanging? What had happened? Some soldiers were lighting torches. What was that crowd doing in the middle? And why was the enemy camp cheering? Suyodhana jumped down from his chariot before it could come to a halt and rushed into the crowd. "Where is Jayadratha? What has happened?" he yelled.

One of the men pointed to the ground. He knew what he would see. No, it could not be. It was already dark. The sun had set. Battle had ceased. Surely Arjuna would never do it. He was not so dishonourable. But Jayadratha's headless body lay on the ground, Arjuna's arrow embedded in his chest. 'Oh, Sushala! What can your brother say to you?'

"I taught him better. Today I feel ashamed to say Arjuna was my disciple." Drona's voice was calm but he could not hide the pain he felt. "Suyodhana, I could not save Jayadratha."

"Guru, it was not your fault. They cheated to win, just as they did with Pitamaha Bhishma," Karna said.

Drona put his hands on Suyodhana's shoulders. "Do you know what Krishna said when I confronted him? That there had been no sunset, only a solar eclipse, which he had created with his powers of illusion. They had the nerve to argue that they killed Jayadratha a fraction of a moment before the sun set."

"A convenient excuse for Arjuna to break the rules of war," Aswathama hissed.

"Carry Jayadratha's body to be cremated with full honours due to a King. Where is his head?"

"While the Guru was arguing with Arjuna, Dhristadyumna carried it away like a trophy."

"This war sickens me," Suyodhana turned away, his heart heavy.

"No, Suyodhana. This is not the time for despondency. They will do anything for victory and it is our *dharma* to vanquish such unscrupulous devils," said Karna, his eyes fixed on his friend's face.

Drona blew his conch to assemble the troops. Then he announced, "Thrice have they broken the ancient rules of war. They use blatant lies to justify their shameless acts. Our enemy will stoop to any level. For our country, our future, for humanity and *dharma*, we must win. From now on we will not end the battle at sunset. The war will end when we kill the last Pandava. *Garudvyuha*!"

The soldiers rushed to take their positions in the eagle-shaped formation. At Drona's command, they rushed with terrifying speed and swooped down on the Pandavas. Iravan's dead eyes watched the dreadful slaughter that followed without emotion, indifferent and unmoving like a *stithapranjna*.

***

In another part of Kurukshetra, a strange ritual was unfolding. Uthayan had failed to kill Karna by sunset. He had turned his back when it had mattered the most. His life was not worth living anymore. He had no philosopher-friend to explain the mysteries of *dharma* and dissuade him from keeping his word. One last time he asked his ancestors' pardon for being a coward. The bards lamented his shame, a shame shared by all his men, which they would carry for generations. Dressed in a loincloth, his face blackened with ash, Uthayan entered his funeral pyre. In his last moments, Uthayan prayed history would judge him kindly.

But he need not have bothered. His history and that of his people did not matter to Bharatavarsha. They belonged to the wrong side of the Vindhya mountains.

*****

66 HALF DHARMA

SUYODHANA SAT WITH HIS SISTER, SUSHALA. She had not
spoken a word nor shed a tear since her husband's headless body
had been carried into the palace. Dhristadyumna had run off
with Jayadratha's head and deposited it in Jayadratha's father's
lap. The erstwhile King of Sindh had become a mendicant
upon relinquishing his kingdom to his son. He had been deep
in meditation in the jungle near Kurukshetra, when his son's
severed head had been flung into his lap. This act of savage
cruelty caused life to flee the sage's frail body. The Pandavas
justified it by saying that Jayadratha himself had claimed there
would be total destruction of the world, should his head ever be
allowed to touch the ground after he died.

Gandhari arrived with Dhritarashtra to be with their daughter
and share her grief. But Suyodhana did not have the courage to
look at his mother. He tried to speak to his grim-faced father,
to condole him on the loss of his many sons in the war, but
Dhritarashtra cut him off saying such talk did not become a
Kshatriya. His mother refused to listen. Suyodhana felt bitter.
His parents had always instilled in him the importance for a
Kshatriya to be prepared for war, yet when events turned ugly,
they turned away from him. Sons, brothers, fathers, thousands
of men – the losses kept mounting. There had been a time when
even the death of a sparrow would affect him. But life had
numbed his heart and mind. Death held no meaning anymore.

Suratha sat shivering behind his mother. Arjuna had killed his
father. He would be expected to avenge his father's death one day.
His mother had said so. He sat looking at his father's headless
body until it was time to perform the final rites. As he lit his

father's funeral pyre, he looked towards his mother. Sushala's eyes were dry. They burned with rage but held no grief. Suratha feared Arjuna, but he feared his mother's wrath more.

***

"There is nothing to hold us back now," declared Drona.

"Guru, your talk of the noble values of war only served to get Jayadratha killed," retorted Shakuni. "You insisted on sticking to ancient rules when the other side had no compunction in breaking them at will."

"Take care, Mlecha! Do not presume to teach me how to command."

"You can silence me, Guru, but can you gag all our soldiers?"

Drona struggled to hold his temper in check. This was not the time and place to take on the foreigner. "Enough of mourning like women! Suyodhana, convene the war council." Without waiting for a response, Drona walked away.

Suyodhana felt his grief turn to anger. Shakuni was right. Guru Drona had not done anything to ensure victory. He would speak his mind at the war council. If the Guru disliked his straight talk, he would just have to bear it. As Crown Prince, he had the right to demand results from his employees.

***

The battle raged day and night for the next three days. The Pandavas lost four *akshahounis*. The night formations designed by Drona confused and terrified them with their brilliant use of light and shadow, deceitful moves, surprise attacks, explosives and chemical weapons. The mood in the Pandava camp was sombre.

Despair hung heavily on Yudhishtra as he paced his tent. "Krishna, what do we do now? Shall we sue for peace? So many have died. I do not wish to rule a kingdom of widows. It is enough."

Dhaumya banged his staff on the ground, saying, "Prince, these are not the words of a Kshatriya. Do you not wish to avenge your wife's shame?"

"We have tried everything. Death and more death has been our only reward," Yudhishtra cried, his heart heavy, his mind weary and his body exhausted.

A flame-tipped arrow landed in the neighbouring tent, setting it on fire. Soldiers ran with pitchers of water, shouting to each other.

"Guru Drona is attacking at night. He has become ruthless. The Asuras know how to fight at night, but the soldiers of the Southern Confederate now refuse to help. They say Arjuna did not keep his word and killed Jayadratha by deceit. They have started questioning our claim of being on the side of *dharma*. I, too, feel they are right. They want to return home to the South. We should have accepted their help when they offered. We have lost. We cannot stop Drona. It is a sin to fight the Guru."

"Yudhishtra, be calm. Nothing is lost. Everything depends on you." Krishna placed a hand on the eldest Pandava's shoulder.

"How can you say that, Krishna? What can I do? Even Arjuna is unable to get near Drona. The Guru is fighting like a man possessed. He is like Rudra...Shiva. No one can touch him."

"You can, Yudhishtra," Krishna's said softly. His words fell like a pebble into a pool, spreading its ripples wider and wider.

"Do not mock me, Krishna. Perhaps you can defeat him, but you have taken a vow not to touch any weapon in this war. Why don't you lead us and fight Drona?"

"I cannot help those who will not help themselves," replied Krishna.

"What should I do?"

"Tomorrow, I will ask you to do something. Do it without questioning."

"I am prepared to do anything you say, Krishna, for Hastinapura. Anything to stop this bloodshed. Help us!"

"Be patient. Tomorrow we will turn the tables on the Kauravas."

Another flame-tipped arrow landed close to them, throwing debris and sand into their tent.

"I feel sad for Drona. What a warrior!" Krishna said smiling.

"Only you could smile when defeat is staring us in the face, Krishna," Arjuna said heavily.

"Tomorrow you too, will smile, my friend," Krishna replied, "provided your righteous brother does what I say and you remember the lessons I imparted to you before the fighting began."

"Do not ask me to do what I did to Bhishma Pitamaha, Krishna. His eyes haunt me. I do not want such a victory."

"Where there is *dharma*, there will be victory, my friend," Krishna replied.

As if in answer, another flame-tipped arrow fell dangerously close to them and an explosion boomed death into the night. Krishna did not even bat an eye; nor did the smile leave his lips.

***

Drona felt elated. In fourteen days he had almost ended the war. He had answered Suyodhana's rude allegations about siding with the Pandavas, with his flaming arrows. How dared Suyodhana speak to him like that? Drona had his faults but treachery was not one of them. That despicable Mlecha Shakuni had planted such ideas in the Crown Prince's mind. Well, the Pandavas had lost two-thirds of their army. He had even killed his old friend, Drupada. But he had yet to get Arjuna. He rarely missed a target but Krishna had managed to swerve the chariot every time. For one evil moment, Drona considered shooting Krishna. But his sense of fairness won the battle of conscience. No, he would not stoop to the level of shooting an unarmed charioteer. He was a

Brahmin after all, and he would fight as per *dharma*, unlike the shameless Kshatriyas, who would do anything to win.

"Sir! Terrible news…" A runner arrived, panting.

"What is it?" Drona could not hear clearly over the din of battle.

"Sir, it is the most terrible news…"

Drona's heart sank. There could only be one thing that terrible. "Where is Aswathama?" Drona's lips trembled and his eyes blurred. 'Oh Kripi, I have failed in my promise to you. What has happened to our son?' He shook the trembling messenger. "You fool! Tell me where my son is!"

The runner bowed his head. Drona held on to the wheel of his chariot. "Is he wounded or…?"

The runner remained silent, not daring to raise his head. He could not face the Guru.

"No…no one can touch my son – not Arjuna, nor any of the Pandavas. He is the greatest warrior in all Bharatavarsha. My son, my son…"

The runner turned and vanished among the soldiers. "Take me to Yudhishtra," Drona barked to his charioteer.

"Sir, it is too dangerous. He is deep within enemy territory."

"Fool! Take me to him!"

The chariot rushed to the Pandava side. Drona's arrows mercilessly cut down anyone who dared stand in his way. The opposition soon thinned, till there was no one left fighting him. Instead, the Pandava soldiers stood bowing in respect, joining him in his mourning.

'No, no…my Aswathama cannot be dead. This is a ploy, a trick,' Drona's mind screamed.

Drona halted beside Yudhishtra's chariot. When he saw the eldest Pandava's face, he understood that everything had indeed been lost. Nevertheless, he had to hear the truth from Yudhishtra. He had been Drona's favourite student, after Arjuna. Except for these last few days of conflict, he had always favoured Yudhishtra over Suyodhana. No, Yudhishtra would not lie to him. Arjuna would not lie to him. They were like his sons. He was their Guru. If they turned away from him now, life would not be worth living. His favourite disciples would never do that to him.

In a voice that shook despite his efforts to remain stoic, the Guru asked the man who was known never to tell a lie, "Yudhishtra, my son, what has happened to Aswathama?"

Yudhishtra could not face Drona. His gaze fell to his feet.

"Son, I know you will never lie to me. Tell your Guru what has happened."

Yudhishtra hesitated. Despite the cold, his forehead was beaded with perspiration. He closed his eyes but his Guru's pleading face refused to leave his mind. He swallowed, his throat dry. Yudhishtra gripped his spear and prayed for courage.

*****

67 LIES

"ASWATHAMA IS DEAD!" The clangour of war stilled on both sides as Yudhisthtra's words fell softly into the silence.

Drona clutched his chest and collapsed to the floor of his chariot, hitting his head as he fell. The Guru had already lost consciousness when Yudhishtra mumbled, "But it was an elephant."

Yudhishtra climbed down from his chariot and walked away, not waiting to see what would happen next. *Dharma* tasted like bitter poison in his mouth.

Krishna looked at Arjuna, but his friend flung down his bow. "No, Krishna, I cannot kill him. Not like this, not after making him believe we have killed his son, when what we did was rename an elephant Aswathama and kill the poor beast. It is a lie. I cannot live this lie anymore. He had always been my benefactor; he always stood by me. Do not ask me to commit another dishonourable act."

Krishna looked at Dhristadyumna, their nominal Commander. Draupadi's brother jumped down from his chariot with his sword drawn. "Krishna, I thank you for this. From the day he ordered Arjuna to drag my father and me to Hastinapura in chains, I have loathed this fake Guru. He killed my father yesterday. I want nothing more than to cut off his head."

Dhristadyumna jumped into Drona's chariot and caught hold of the unconscious Guru's hair. Like a watermelon, he slit the throat of the man who had nearly defeated the Pandava army single-handedly, holding aloft the dripping head. "Behold! The Commander of the Kauravas! This is my tribute to my dead father, Drupada. This is my offering to Guru Dhaumya. See what a gory end has befallen this Brahmin, who chose the side of *adharma*."

Shikhandi came running and hugged his brother, dancing in Drona's chariot. The eunuch shouted, "*Yadho dharma, thatho Jaya.*" Where there is *dharma*, there will be victory. Dhristadyumna laughed aloud. The Guru has paid for his *karma*.

Yells of jubilation rose from the Pandava ranks. Krishna did not wait to watch Dhristadyumna's celebrations. The chariot in which Arjuna sat grief-stricken, turned to follow Yudhishtra.

A cry of agony rose from the Kaurava ranks and the Pandavas paused to listen. It was Aswathama. Filled with murderous rage, he rushed screaming towards the Pandava side, while Karna tried to restrain him. With Drona's fall, command had shifted to Karna's shoulders as he was the second-in-command. Aswathama began cutting down anyone in his path but Karna's conch sounded the end of battle, shocking the Guru's son.

"How dare you stop the fighting?" Aswathama shouted at Karna.

"This is a *dharmayudha*. The sun has set. I will not allow any transgressions of *dharma*," Karna replied in a flat tone, looking away from his friend.

Aswathama turned to Suyodhana, waiting for him to overrule Karna, but Suyodhana too, did not look at him. Aswathama's heart hammered in his chest. The Suta was not allowing him to even avenge his father, the man who had saved Karna from Arjuna's arrows in Virata. But what hurt most was Suyodhana's silence.

Aswathama stood paralysed with grief and frustration as he watched Dhristadyumna's men turn away jubiliantly. They would talk about Karna's chivalry for years, but Aswathama knew Karna was just using *dharma* as a cloak. This was his petty revenge for the treatment Drona had meted out to him when the Suta came seeking knowledge. Karna was using the same *dharma* as revenge. *Dharma* or *adharma*, he would get back at Dhristadyumna, he would make the Pandavas pay a bitter price, the son of Drona vowed. He shouted at the vanishing figures of the Pandava warriors, "Evil men, the fruits of *karma* are bitter. You are ecstatic about killing the most formidable warrior through deceit? Do you think the sin of *Brahmahatya* will not haunt you? Then the talk of the body shedding soiled clothes will not be of any solace, and the wisdom of being detached will sound like a hollow drum. I will get you, you evil Pandavas!"

Aswathama fell to his knees as soldiers carried away his father's lifeless body.

*****

68 DHANAVEERA

THEY SAT BY THE RIVER, listening to the distant cries of the *chandalas* as they hauled off the dead to the cremation ground. The breeze carried the lingering odour of burning flesh. The ghostly light of the flaming pyres lit the southern sky. The river looked sinister and the water that sloshed at their feet was thick with blood.

Aswathama looked at his reflection and cringed when the precious stone shone in the moonlight. It had brought him so much bad luck. He had been inconsolable since his father's death. "He died because of me. I was a worthless son, never able to rise to his expectations," he murmured yet again.

"Aswathama, why are you punishing yourself like this? Guru Drona was proud of you. He was a great man," Karna said to the Guru's son. This was not the time to remember that Drona had always treated him as a lowly Suta, thought Karna.

"I should not spoil your great day, Karna. Congratulations on becoming Commander of the Kaurava army, none deserves it more," Aswathama said without turning his head.

Karna looked at his friend. What was wrong? Was it that Aswathama had still to come to terms with the shock of his father's death or was it something else? "I owe everything to Suyodhana; Aswathama, you know it as well as I do."

"It was long overdue, Karna. No one is more qualified than you to command. Bring us victory. Spare none of the Pandavas."

Karna sighed. He was thankful for the darkness that hid his face.

"Why are you so silent, Karna?"

"I will not spare Arjuna, that I promise you."

"Not just Arjuna. None of the Pandavas must be spared!"

"I have given my word…"

"Word?" Aswathama's breathing quickened. He squinted at Karna. What was his friend up to?

"I will not kill any of the Pandavas except Arjuna. I have given my word to Kunti Devi."

"Karna, are you crazy?"

"I could not refuse. She begged for the lives of all her sons."

"You are a traitor! You should be tried for treason and hanged," yelled Aswathama, grabbing Karna roughly. "You cunning rascal! Let us see what Suyodhana has to say about this. The Suta has shown his true colours."

Aswathama jumped up and would have run towards the camp had Karna not held him back. "Listen to me, Aswathama! I have vowed to kill Arjuna and defeat the Pandavas." How could he tell his friend that he was the eldest of all the Kurus and not a lowly Suta? How could he say the throne was his for the asking, that he could end the war if he agreed to become King? That would be the greatest act of disloyalty to Suyodhana. "Trust me, Aswathama. I will win this war and see Suyodhana crowned King."

Aswathama looked at his friend. "I don't want to create a rift in the camp, Karna, but Suyodhana will be heartbroken if he hears this. How could you do it? Suta, you are no longer my friend. I will be watching your conduct on the battlefield. If I find the slightest hesitation in you, the arrow in your throat will be mine. A traitor as our Commander-in-Chief! There is no bigger fool than Suyodhana!" Shrugging off Karna's grip, Aswathama walked away.

"Aswathama, stop!" Karna called out but the Brahmin had vanished into the shadows of night. *Traitor!* The word pierced Karna's conscience. Was he indeed a traitor to the man who had done everything for him? He had no answer. But there was no question of going back on his word, either. There was only one thing left to do – fight until he won or die in the attempt. 'Forgive me Suyodhana…Aswathama…I never deserved your friendship.'

"Karna!" The voice startled Karna from his reverie and his hand went instinctively to his sword. He relaxed when he saw an old Brahmin standing near him. The face seemed oddly familiar. "I have come to seek alms."

Karna knew he had heard that voice before. He looked at the stooping figure with suspicion. Who was that standing behind the mendicant in the dark, almost hidden by the bushes?

"Promise you will give me what I ask."

"I know you from somewhere, Swami," Karna replied, peering at the figure before him.

"No one knows me. I am a nonentity. Give me your word and keep your reputation as the man who never denies anyone anything."

Karna sensed a trap. The man standing before him was no ordinary Brahmin. Feeling helpless in the face of a request for alms, he said, "Ask and it shall be yours."

"Give me your armour, forged by the great smiths of the Surya temple."

Karna was shocked. "What did a Brahmin want with a warrior's armour?"

"Karna, deny me and I will go away without complaint. I understand. It is your only protection against Arjuna's arrows. Without it, you will not last for more than a few minutes before my son."

"What did you say? Your *son*? Who are you? Indra? Has the Lord of the Devas stooped to this level to protect his son?"

How dared Indra even suggest he could not face Arjuna without his armour? Karna undid the armour and waited for the Brahmin to extend his hand. "Take it. Know that my *dharma* is my protection. If your son thinks he has to strip me to beat me, then go and tell him that Karna stands naked. With or without armour, this Suta *will* defeat him."

Indra looked at Karna with admiration in his old eyes. "Son, I have no words for your chivalry and bravery. If there is any fairness left in this world, you will win. We are both cast-offs – you by your mother and I by my son. But I am still his father and this my gift to him."

"Every moment I feel I am betraying Suyodhana. Sir, you have got what you came for. Now please leave me alone."

"Karna, I am a fair man. Allow me to repay your generosity. Else, I will not be able to sleep with a clear conscience."

Karna looked at the old man in surprise. Was he trying to pull another trick? Indra turned and signalled. A dark figure emerged from behind a bush. In the dull moonlight, the man's eyes glittered liked diamonds in his dark face.

"Karna, this is my son, Mayasura, the greatest sculptor to have walked this earth – the man who created Indraprastha, the city named after me. Yes, life is full of irony is it not? Maya, bow to the great Karna. You will see none like him in this world or the next."

Karna looked at the coal black Asura in surprise.

"Give it to him," Indra ordered and Mayasura placed a thick arrow in Karna's hands. It was sharp, sturdy and beautifully forged.

"*Yantra muktha*?" Karna asked, running his fingers along the smooth contours of the missile.

"Yes, with the power of the *vajra*. It is called *Shakti*, after the Mother Goddess. Truthfully, I was planning to give it to Arjuna. I was cynical about your reputation and wanted to test it. But now, how I wish *you* were my son, Karna. This is my gift to you.

It can only be used once, but it has unimaginable power. Perhaps you will use it against my son. No one can accuse Indra of being unfair. I may be poor and broken today, but I am still King of the Devas."

"I humbly accept your offering, Lord Indra," Karna said, placing the missile in his quiver. Then he took Mayasura's coarse hands in his. "If we win this war, be assured that these hands will once again build beautiful gardens and temples. I am honoured to have met you."

"My son has not been of sound mind since we were evicted from Indraprastha. Forgive him if he has not treated you with proper respect." Indra took Mayasura's arm and walked away with Karna's priceless armour.

Karna looked at the disappearing figures, pondering over life's ironies. He scanned the battleground and saw the silhouette of Iravan's head. A wasted life, he thought. Why did the Nagas and Rakshasas even bother to fight this war? This was a Kshatriya war. The knowledge that he too was a Kshatriya was more of a relief than he would admit. He would prove that he was a better Kshatriya than anyone who fought on either side. He would be generous in his gifts and noble in abiding by the laws of warfare. That was the Kshatriya code of honour. That was what set them apart from other men.

But in the dead of the night, when silence reigned, except for the moans of dying men and beasts, a sense of deep guilt assaulted Karna. Aswathama's words came to haunt him. By keeping his word to Kunti and giving his armour to Indra, he might earn eternal fame, but was it not a betrayal of the trust Suyodhana had placed in him? He had no answer. The time had come to fight Arjuna, man to man, without the protection of his armour. Let destiny decide who the better warrior was and who the better man.

*****

69 RAKSHASA

KHATOTKACHA WAS GETTING IMPATIENT. "Mother, Lord Krishna himself sent a messenger to fetch me. He says only I can save my father from that Suta warrior."

"You are just a boy, Khatotkacha. If your father cannot stop Karna, how can you?"

"The messenger says my father is asking for me. I am his only hope."

"You are the only one I have, my son. It is not our war."

"My father needs me, Mother. I must go."

"Father! Now he remembers his son? The last time we saw him, he would not even look at me. You are a Rakshasa, a forest dweller, the son of a Rakshasi."

There was no point arguing with her. Khatotkacha touched her feet but Hidumbi did not move. He turned to go.

"Go and die! You know how they treated Iravan. Oh Shiva, I will have no one to care for me in my old age."

Khatotkacha stopped at the door and turned back. "Is this your final blessing, mother? Maybe you will only see my dead face."

"Oh, no, no…I did not mean it, son. Don't go!" Hidumbi came running after him, but her son did not look back.

An owl flew past Khatotkacha. An owl in the daytime? A bad omen. A strange fear gripped the superstitious Rakshasa. Then he shrugged and picked up his stone mace from the corner of the mud veranda. A few of his Nishada and Naga friends were waiting for him, armed with bows, poisoned arrows, spears, crude swords and stone maces. Khatotkacha nodded to them. "Come, let us go to Kurukshetra and teach that Suta a lesson!"

Shrieking and screaming, the Rakshasa and his savage friends started running. They had to save the Pandavas from a humiliating defeat at the hands of Karna. The owl that had perched on the roof hooted ominously thrice and then flew away into the jungle.

***

"Son, no rules apply to you. Rakshasas are experts in night warfare. Wreak havoc in the Kaurava ranks," Krishna instructed.

Khatotkacha sneaked a peek at his impassive father. Bhima sat polishing his huge mace. He had not spoken to his son since his arrival at the Pandava camp.

"Go talk to your father." Krishna patted Khatotkacha's shoulder.

The Rakshasa moved towards his father with hesitant steps, afraid he would be snubbed. He just stood there, awkward and tongue-tied. Finally, Bhima looked up and smiled at his son. Khatotkacha dropped to the ground and bowed his head. Would his touch pollute the Kshatriya?

Bhima's strong arms lifted him up. "How you have grown!" he said and abruptly walked away.

Was that all? Khatotkacha had imagined this reunion so many times. Bhima had not even inquired about his mother.

***

The next morning was colder than usual. Kurukshetra stretched far and wide. Khatotkacha felt a shiver of anticipation. He was going to fight Kshatriyas. In doing so, his father was bestowing a great honour on his Rakshasa son. Soon, he would face mighty warriors like Karna, Suyodhana, Kripa, Aswathama, and others. Katotkacha was nervous. He had to make his father proud. He looked again at the vast battlefield and shuddered. This time it was not the chill that made him shiver. The gory face of Iravan stared back at him. The Rakshasa gripped his stone mace and prayed, "Oh Shiva, give me the courage to face the mighty."

***

The war took an ugly turn after the Nishadas and Rakshasas under Khatotkacha joined the Pandava side. The forest dwellers jumped from elephant to elephant and darted through the cavalry. Their wild cries made the beasts run wild. They climbed chariots with monkey-like agility, shot their poison-tipped arrows and vanished like magic. Their recklessness shattered Karna's classical war formations.

Seeing Shakuni once again near his friend, Aswathama rushed to Suyodhana. "It seems your friend is not fighting with his heart," the Gandharan was saying.

"If Karna does not fight for me, no one ever will," Suyodhana retorted with complete conviction.

Shakuni eyed Aswathama and suppressed a smile. "Your trust in the Suta is touching but he is not worried about you; he is after glory."

Suyodhana turned to his uncle in irritation. "Can you not see how Karna is struggling to save us from that Rakshasa?"

"Oh certainly, but ask him why he spared Yudhishtra and Bhima today. He cut off their bows and mace, yet he didn't kill them."

Aswathama saw a frown crease Suyodhana's face as he prodded his charioteer towards Karna. Aswathama was shocked to learn that the Pandavas had been spared. Could there be a greater traitor than Karna? He had to warn Suyodhana. When he reached his friends, they were arguing.

"No more arguments, Karna. I want the Rakshasa dead," Suyodhana said, finishing his tirade.

"Suyodhana, I will not lie. I spared Yudhishtra and Bhima's lives today. My fight is with Arjuna, and I will kill him."

Karna's charioteer howled with laughter. "The Suta had the chance to kill the twins too, but he did not. What a fool I carry in my chariot!"

Suyodhana ignored Shalya and turned to Karna. "This war is not about your personal vendetta. We are fighting for a cause. Why did you give your armour away? Why are you not using the so-called magical weapon Indra gave you?"

"Suyodhana, I have kept the *Shakti* for Arjuna."

Shalya smirked. "This Suta will die still hugging that stupid *astra*. No one has even heard of it. I am afraid it will burst behind my back at any moment. Dream on, Suta, but if you want to win this war, use the *ageneya astra* and finish off all the Pandavas. Throw away that stupid thing given to you by that Asura."

"Sir, I must ask for your silence," Suyodhana said to Shalya.

"Alright, if you do not value my advice, I will not give it. Once a Suta, always a Suta." Shalya cracked his whip and laughed.

Suyodhana felt like smashing his mace on Shalya's head but controlled himself. He said to Karna, "That Rakshasa will have finished us all long before you reach Arjuna. I am disappointed in you, Karna."

Suyodhana moved away in his chariot, leaving behind a devastated Karna. Did Suyodhana suspect his loyalty after all he had done?

Aswathama watched Karna lift the *Shakti* and put it into the *yantra* to launch. "Traitor!" he hissed.

"The Brahmin said it right. You are a coward and a traitor." Shalya whipped the horses and the chariot hurtled towards Khatotkacha at breakneck speed. Karna cranked the *yantra*, tightening it to launch the *Shakti astra*.

"Watch out Suta, it is going to burst in your face," Shalya shouted into the wind over the rattle of the chariot.

Karna looked for Khatotkacha and pointed the *yantra* at him. He was throwing flaming torches at the Kaurava cavalry with both hands. The Rakshasa would never know what hit him, thought Karna, tightening the tension another notch.

Khatotkacha saw a ball of fire coming towards him at great speed. People screamed and ran in all directions but he stood paralyzed as the *astra* whistled through the air towards him. He knew this was the end and his mind was strangely calm. The earth shook with a loud explosion and he was thrown into the air.

When Khatotkacha opened his eyes, the severed limbs of men and beasts were still raining down around him. He did not feel any pain. He tried to get up, but it felt as if he had no body. When the soot and smoke cleared, he saw many faces peering down at him. They all appeared to be standing at a great height. Where the *Shakti* had touched the ground, a huge crater had formed and Khatotkacha was lying in it. The look of horror in their eyes confirmed his worst fears. He saw Bhima staring down at him from the edge of the crater and tried to get up to greet his father, but he could not feel his arms.

"He has no limbs left," someone said. Khatotkacha blinked and waited for his father to come down and talk to him. He could hear the Kauravas celebrating his fall. He heard other voices and saw his uncles join his father. They looked somehow relieved.

"Karna used the *Shakti* on Khatotkacha. Now he has nothing, Arjuna" remarked Yudhishtra.

"All Rakshasas have to be killed one day or the other, Bhima. It is good he is dying for *dharma*," Krishna said and Bhima blinked.

'You would have killed me because I am a Rakshasa, Father? I don't know what *dharma* is, I am just a forest dweller. I did my best for you.' Gradually, Bhima's face faded away. The sounds of celebrations died. His mother had been right – this was not their war.

As the celebrations continued on both sides of the great field of Kurukshetra, darkness cloaked the Rakshasa in silence.

***

Suyodhana lay awake in his tent, wondering if Karna had betrayed him. What right had he to give away his armour, to make promises that could lose them the war? Was not his friendship enough? Suyodhana felt bitter for having placed all his trust and hope in Karna. Bhanumati had been right, the Suta had ditched him when it mattered the most. His mother was right; he had been a fool. Who else would cheat him? He wondered if he should order Karna's arrest and try him for treason. No... surely his Karna could never betray him? Had he not used the *Shakti* on the Rakshasa boy? Was he not inviting his own death by giving away his armour? There had to be some reason for Karna's strange behaviour.

Battered on all sides by accusations of evil doing, Suyodhana had sometime wondered about their truth, following the madness of trying to disrobe Draupadi. He had often drawn strength from his own noble action of making a Suta a King. It had defined him. It had convinced him that he was not the evil man hungry for power that his opponents made him out to be. Suyodhana needed to believe in Karna's sincerity in order to find meaning in his life. No, he could not believe Karna did anything for selfish reasons. He would win the war for them. They all shared a common dream of a better tomorrow for Bharatavarsha – he, Aswathama and Karna. If one of them betrayed another, life would not be worth living anymore. He had to bury all doubts. If Karna proved to be a self serving man, what then was the point of winning?

*****

70 Death of a Mlecha

THE NIGHT WAS DAMP WITH THE PROMISE of much awaited rain. It was the seventeenth day of carnage in the temple of *dharma*. Among the thousands crying over the loss of loved ones, one heart-wrenching cry stood apart in its poignancy. Krishna, four of the Pandavas and Draupadi, stood huddled near the fire, too numb to speak, while Bhima sat in the darkness, his howls of grief rising above the howling wind, almost primeval in their intensity.

"Bhima, please understand that he was a Rakshasa. This is a war and warriors die. It is hard, but that is how life is," Krishna said. Bhima let out another howl.

Bhima had been silent until they brought up Khatotkacha's inert body from the crater. But all hell had broken loose when he was asked to light his son's funeral pyre. Since then, the second Pandava had not ceased his wordless crying, an agonised howling that went on and on. With words, they tried to reason with him. With pain, he answered them back.

"It is useless to talk to him," Krishna said in a tired voice, sitting down near Arjuna.

"Watching him before, one would never have thought he cared for his Rakshasa son. He did not even speak two words to the boy. But the agony of a silent man is the most painful to watch," Arjuna said. Bhima's wails rose again and they all shuddered. "Krishna, is the war worth all this? *Dharma* has given us only misery. I am not even sure who is righteous and who is evil." Arjuna shook his head. Far away, smoke from the funeral pyres snaked towards heaven.

"I explained everything to you before the war. If you do not have the answers even now, I have nothing more to say," Krishna replied.

"Krishna, I admire your wisdom. Great men will praise those words. Alas, men like Bhima and I do not possess the intelligence to understand your meaning. We are neither rishis nor scholars. I wish I could have cried as he is doing, when I lost Abhimanyu. It is hard to be detached about what I do, Krishna. Why should we fight our own cousins and lose everything?"

"It is your duty to fight, Arjuna. Don't worry about the results."

"The outcome scares me, Krishna. When all that gives meaning to life is lost, what use is victory? Tomorrow will be terrible. I am not afraid Krishna, but Karna will be a tough opponent, with or without his armour."

"Arjuna, just do your duty, the rest will take care of itself. You must take advantage of the slightest opportunity that presents itself."

"Karna may be a Suta, but he is a great warrior. Krishna, I wish to win fairly against him, unlike what we did to Pitamaha or Guru...."

"How naive you still are, Arjuna my friend," Krishna said with a smile. "Once you win, everything will be considered fair."

***

Suyodhana had instructed the Brahmin never to leave Karna alone, even for a moment, and to support him in finding Arjuna. But he had other plans. Karna was capable of looking after himself. There was a bigger enemy Aswathama had to take on – one within their own ranks. He should have done it long ago.

Aswathama rode towards Shakuni. The Gandharan was watching something with unwavering concentration. He had to get the wily foreigner alone. Aswathama assessed his chances of shooting Shakuni, as if by accident. No, Suyodhana would see through it. Besides, the Gandharan wore heavy armour and was a formidable warrior. He ruled out special *astras* since the casualties on his own side would be huge. That was something the Kauravas could not afford. No, he would not shed the blood of innocents for the sake of one Mlecha.

"Hiding in the rear, coward?" Aswathama taunted, hoping to provoke Shakuni.

"Ah, my favourite Brahmin boy!" Shakuni turned around smiling.

"Sahadeva is looking for you, Mlecha. Remember, the youngest Pandava has vowed to kill you. It's just as well you are hiding here at the rear to save your thick skin."

"Hmm, but what is that you are doing here instead of supporting the Suta? Today is the day he is taking on Arjuna. Don't you want to watch Karna die?" Shakuni chuckled.

"You scoundrel! Traitor! You are not even fit to speak his name. What has the Gandharan army done for the Kauravas other than to stuff their stomachs?"

"Grand words, Brahmin, but see what is happening to your Suta friend. Krishna has laid a trap and Karna has fallen right into it. Can you see where they are going?" Shakuni asked, shielding his eyes with his hand and gazing into the distance.

Aswathama followed Shakuni's gaze and saw two chariots racing away. One flew the flag of Hanuman and the other chasing it had the emblem of Surya. Was Karna chasing Arjuna or was Krishna leading Karna into the swamps of the Ganga? Something was wrong, terribly wrong. Aswathama jumped into Shakuni's chariot.

"Hey, what do you think you are doing?" Shakuni cried in surprise.

Aswathama lunged and grabbed the whip from Shakuni's charioteer. In one swift movement he lashed at Shakuni. The whip caught the Gandharan's nose and split it open. Caught unawares, Shakuni staggered and fell to the chariot floor. Aswathama pushed Shakuni's charioteer out and whipped the horses. The chariot flew forward, leaving the fallen charioteer's cries far behind.

Shakuni rose and drew his sword. Aswathama whirled the chariot round on one wheel, catching Shakuni off balance and cracked his whip at the Gandharan again. Sudden searing pain shot through Aswathama's arms. An arrow had hit him. Another zipped past his throat. Who was shooting at him?

Shakuni leapt at Aswathama again but the Brahmin cracked his whip and tripped him. Another arrow hit Aswathama's arm, making him scowl in pain. Then he saw who was shooting at him – Uluka. Shakuni's son was riding parallel to his chariot. 'Good,' thought Aswathama, if his plan worked, he could take out both father and son together. His plan was crazy, reckless and brave. He was tempted to fight them in a straight duel but the last thing he wanted was for the remnants of the Kaurava army to begin fighting each other. No, it had to appear as though the Pandavas had killed the Mlecha.

Aswathama jumped back into the chariot from the charioteer's seat and kicked Shakuni. The chariot raced on towards the Pandava side. Shakuni swung his sword and wounded Aswathama on the thigh. The Brahmin fell and rolled over. With a maniacal grin, Shakuni thrust again. But Aswathama had feigned his fall and was waiting for his moment. He rolled away from the fast-descending sword and was on his feet in a flash, while Shakuni struggled to free his sword which had plunged two feet into the wooden floor of the chariot.

Aswathama coiled the whip around Shakuni's throat and whispered in his ear, "Game over, Mlecha!"

"Shoot, Uluka, shoot!" Shakuni yelled to his son, galloping beside them. Uluka hesitated. What if he hit and killed his father? "Shoot!" Shakuni cried desperately, but the boy merely stared back in an agony of indecision.

They were only a few feet away from the Pandava lines and Aswathama could see the surprise and shock in the eyes of the Pandava soldiers. A shower of arrows welcomed them as both chariots broke into the Pandava formation. Soldiers tried to stop them, thinking it to be a surprise attack on their Commander, Sahadeva. The chariots ran over men, crashed into others, but did not halt. Aswathama did not know how many arrows hit him. He held on to the throat of the Mlecha, ignoring his own pain and trying not to think of impending death. The chariot floor was wet with blood – his and the Mlecha's.

Finally, Uluka fell with an arrow to his throat. Aswathama hissed into Shakuni's ear, "There goes the Gandharan heir."

Shakuni uttered a cry of agony as his son died before his eyes. Aswathama felt the Gandharan going limp in his hands. "You are next, Mlecha," he hissed.

Their chariot crashed into Sahadeva's, throwing the youngest Pandava off balance. Aswathama shoved Shakuni out of the chariot and the Gandharan fell face down. But he scrambled up, holding on to Sahadeva's chariot for support. Sahadeva aimed an arrow at Aswathama but his bow broke into two before he could shoot.

"Kid, take your time with the Mlecha. I have a friend to save from your brother," Aswathama said, slinging his bow back over his shoulder and taking the whip in his hand.

Stunned by such an extraordinary feat of archery, Sahadeva looked at the Brahmin warrior covered with blood. Before he could react, Aswathama's chariot had vanished behind a cloud of dust.

Shakuni eyed Sahadeva, surrounded by scores of Pandava soldiers. He knew he had only a few moments to live. He should have killed that bloody Brahmin in Gandhara when he had had the chance. Nevertheless, Shakuni had achieved what he had lived for – India was dying before his eyes. He had won. He took out his dice and smashed them on Sahadeva's chariot wheels, laughing.

Someone hit him across the jaw. Fists punched him in the stomach. A boot kicked him in the groin and a sword swiped across his cheek. He heard Sahadeva say, "Not so quick, my friends, not such an easy death for the Mlecha."

"Too late, you bloody Indians...much too late..." Shakuni said before blackness overwhelmed him completely.

*****

71 WHEEL OF DHARMA

A LIGHT DRIZZLE WAS FALLING when the battle started in earnest. Karna had spent a sleepless night tossing on his hard bed. Bhima's howls of grief, which the breeze carried to the Kaurava camp, had made him restless and angry. It came as a surprise to him that Bhima cared so much for his Rakshasa son. It somehow made his own act all the more cruel, as if he had wounded an animal. Karna had decided on the *vajra* formation for a quick thrust into the Pandava ranks. He did not intend to drag out the war.

Where had Aswathama disappeared to? He was supposed to be here supporting him. The Brahmin had been behaving strangely of late. Karna wished he could tell his friend why he had spared the other Pandavas, but... "Take me to Arjuna," he said calmly to his charioteer.

Shalya grunted in reply and the chariot began weaving its way through the Pandava army at great speed. For a change, Shalya was silent. Perhaps Bhima's agonizing cries had affected him too.

"Hurry, Shalya. To Arjuna..."

"Suta, do you think this is a pleasure trip and I am your guide? Take me to Arjuna; take me to Arjuna, as if he were the lover you are dying to meet." Shalya laughed at his own joke and veered off the path, cutting diagonally across from where they had intended to go.

"Stop blabbering and..." Before Karna could complete his sentence, an arrow whizzed past him. Shalya had swerved from its path with matchless dexterity.

"Watch out, Suta. Without me, you are a dead Suta," laughed Shalya.

"Stop talking nonsense and take me to Arjuna!"

"Brace yourself, Suta, we are going to catch up with my old friend, Krishna. Let us see who is the better charioteer." Shalya whipped his horses, laughing in glee.

At breakneck speed, Karna's chariot pierced the Pandava ranks. Karna began shooting down everyone in his path, spreading panic. Krishna moved away from him, weaving a complex path to keep the chariot away from his arrows. Both sides had suffered huge losses but with adequate supplies arranged by the Confederate forces, the Pandavas were better able to drag out the war. For the Kauravas, supplies had run out and if Karna was unable to kill Arjuna this day, the writing was clear on the wall.

"Faster, faster..." Karna urged.

"You wish to die of a broken neck?" asked Shalya, his face alight with the thrill of the chase. He whipped the horses savagely and the chariot veered to one side, almost toppling over. Shalya slid to the other side to regain his balance, grinning at Karna. "You almost had your wish. Want to see any more stunts?"

It was no use talking to this maniac, thought Karna. He should have taken a less skilled but sane charioteer, but no one was as good as this reckless genius. Only he could match Krishna's skill with the reins. The chariot was weaving its way through the Pandava elephant corps. Shalya leaned over and whipped one of the elephants.

"What are you doing?" Karna yelled as the elephants began to stampede.

"Just watch the fun," Shalya laughed, weaving through the wall of pounding elephant legs around them. As if by magic, a path opened up while the elephants ran in all directions, destroying everything in their way. Shalya killed more Pandava soldiers by his dexterous handling of the chariot than Karna had done in the entire day.

"There they are!" Shalya pointed to the fast-vanishing rear of a chariot. The Hanuman flag fluttered in the wind.

The skies opened all of a sudden and rain started falling in a heavy downpour. Some mounted archers cut in from their right and tried to slow down Karna. He shot them down with ease but Arjuna had gained on him considerably. Where was the coward running to?

Shalya halted the chariot abruptly. "Let us go back."

"Are you crazy?"

"It is you who are crazy, you ignorant Suta! Krishna is up to his usual tricks. The ground is slippery here and the wheels may sink. Let us catch them when the ground is dry."

"Don't order me around, Shalya. You are my charioteer and I the Commander-in-Chief of the Kauravas. Take me to Arjuna!"

"Your wish is my command, most revered, most respected Chief." Shalya spat on the ground and muttered, "Bloody Suta!" The chariot raced on, chasing the Hanuman flag.

The river was flowing swiftly, swelled by the downpour. Krishna drove his chariot perilously close to the surging waters. Shalya managed to catch up with him and for some time the horses galloped on neck to neck. Krishna was calm and composed, as if he was riding through the streets of Hastinapura instead of on slippery ground. Shalya hooted, taunting Krishna and abusing Arjuna and Karna in equal measure. The two warriors began shooting at each other. With the wind screaming in his ears and the rain lashing his face, Karna managed to wound Arjuna twice. Arjuna scarred Karna's forehead. It was difficult to keep their bows steady in the wind and rain. The chariots jerked and rolled in the slushy mud. The roar of the river frightened the neighing horses.

Inch by inch, Krishna started gaining on Shalya. With a jerk, Arjuna's chariot zoomed past. Shalya was slowing down again. What was wrong with the man? Karna was livid. Was he fighting for him or the Pandavas?

"He will turn now and face you. Brace for Arjuna's arrow," Shalya said, his voice quiet and sombre for once.

As predicted, Krishna executed a sharp turn, with inches to spare from the river, as mud spattered into the water. Shalya veered left and Karna thought they would fall. A flaming arrow whistled past, a hair's breadth away from the chariot. Karna shot back but missed Arjuna. Krishna had handled his chariot with remarkable skill. He and Shalya were fighting their own battle.

Krishna's chariot tilted at a crazy angle. Arjuna's figure loomed large and Karna could see the unflinching concentration in his face. Another arrow came hissing at him but Karna ducked it. He instantly shot back at Arjuna but missed. Krishna's prowess in steering the chariot was remarkable.

"Use your *ageneya* now, Suta. Aim at his chest or waist. You will miss if you go for the throat," Shalya advised.

"Are you now my archery Guru?" Karna snapped.

Shalya hooted with laughter and wished Karna death. Cursing, Karna began loading the *ageneya* in the *yantra*, winding it up. The rain had become fierce and the wind pushed them back. The chariots circled each other at speed, churning mud. Karna feared his chariot would fall apart. His maverick charioteer was driving the horses crazy with his shrieks, whip and stunts. Shalya ducked from arrows or hung out of his seat with one hand. He prodded the horses with kicks, jumping out to run alongside and then climbing back to do more terrifying stunts. His unceasing jeers and chatter began to affect Karna's concentration.

"I will turn the chariot to face him. Use your *ageneya*." Shalya veered to the right at the most unexpected moment, catching Krishna by surprise. Shalya circled Krishna's chariot and cut across unexpectedly. Karna could see the frothing river as Shalya drove straight towards it. "Turn and shoot at his chest, or you will miss," Shalya screamed against the wind, standing up in his seat to crack his whip.

Karna let loose the *ageneya*. The fiery *astra* shot towards Arjuna's throat. Karna felt elated. There was no way Arjuna could escape.

"Fool! Fool! Fool!" Shalya screamed as he pulled at the reins to turn the chariot.

When Karna looked back, he was horrified. Krishna had driven his chariot into a ditch to evade the *astra*'s path. His horses were neighing in fear, their front legs thrashing in the air. Arjuna's chariot wheels were stuck deep in the mud. Shalya had been right. He would not have missed had he aimed for Arjuna's chest. He heard the muted explosion of the *ageneya* in the distance.

"We have them trapped. Use your *nagastra* fast," Shalya urged.

"No. It is against *dharma* to shoot when their chariot is stuck."

"What? What did you blabber, Suta? You kill him now or you will die at Arjuna's hands."

"It would be dishonourable."

"Is this the time to turn noble? I refuse to risk my life for an idiot." Shalya jumped out of the chariot and began walking away.

"Hey! Where are you going? You cannot leave me like this at such a crucial moment!"

Shalya walked on without a word, not bothering to turn to look at Karna. Lightning cracked open the sky and struck a tree. The river had started climbing up its banks. It was as if the rain God was trying to make up for his years of absence in a single day.

Karna took the reins. He knew he could not match Krishna's charioting skills and Arjuna's archery skills by himself. His unlucky stars were haunting him again. He had a choice. To shoot Arjuna before Krishna could extract the chariot from the mud would have been child's play. He toyed with the idea. Then the image of his other great foe, Uthayan, waiting for him to extract his stuck chariot wheels on the banks of the Narmada flashed into his mind. No, he could not do it. No honourable warrior could. He waited.

Krishna managed to extricate the chariot. It was getting dark. The roar of the Ganga had become deafening. Karna could see the Kaurava army rushing to rescue him. Krishna had trapped him by moving away from the battlefield and like a fool, he had given chase. Arjuna's face became clearer as his chariot approached at great speed. Karna saw hesitation in those eyes. Karna had no charioteer and according to the ethics of war, Krishna had to get down to make things equal. It seemed that Arjuna was arguing with Krishna.

Karna pulled at the reins with one hand, holding his arrow in place with his teeth. The chariot pitched and jerked in the mud. When he felt he was in position, he shot at Arjuna. Karna saw Krishna's face light up with a smile. The arrow had struck Arjuna's shoulder. That ended Arjuna's dilemma. Karna had indicated his willingness to fight without a charioteer. He would not ask for any favours from Arjuna, not after a lifetime of insults and jeers, and never from the man who had taken the woman he had loved. No, this Suta was more Kshatriya than anyone else.

Karna took aim but as he did so, his chariot stopped – the wheels had become stuck in the mud. There was no other way but to get down and extricate them, just as Krishna had done a while before. Swallowing, Karna called out, "Halt there, Arjuna! My wheel is stuck. I ask you to wait till I get my chariot out."

Arjuna's raised bow came down and Karna jumped into the slush. Putting his shoulder to the wheel, he started pushing.

"What are you waiting for? Shoot the Suta!" Krishna said, pointing.

"No, Krishna. He is unarmed. It would not be fair."

"Would not be fair? Does the man deserve fairness? Have you forgotten how he insulted Draupadi in the Sabha? Have you forgotten how he killed Abhimanyu? Shoot him now!"

"Krishna...I cannot. It would be dishonourable."

"This is your last chance. Look to your right. The Kaurava army has arrived. Kill him and we stand a chance of escaping in the confusion that will follow."

Arjuna raised his bow and aimed at Karna's throat. Karna looked up. Surely Arjuna was just posturing? No warrior possessed of even a modicum of honour would shoot a man like this. Karna put his entire weight against the chariot, raising it little by little.

Arjuna's arrow pierced Karna's throat, pinning him to the chariot wheel. Karna knew it was over. Shalya had been right, he should have taken the opportunity when it had come. But then he would have been like Arjuna, another puppet, another Kaunteya. He was Karna, son of a poor Suta, a proud Radheya, and he would die that way. He saw Suyodhana jump down from his chariot, lose his balance, fall, get up again and rush towards him. The entire Kaurava army was running towards their fallen Commander. In the confusion, Karna saw Krishna turn his chariot and vanish from the scene. Arjuna never looked back.

Karna could feel Suyodhana's arms around him but darkness was falling fast. The rain on his unarmoured skin felt like needles of fire. He could faintly hear his friend talking to him. Karna wanted to thank him for everything he had done, for standing up for him when no one else would, for the many things, big and small, that only a friend would understand.

Karna felt Aswathama's hand grip his own. He heard Suyodhana accusing him of not being there to support Karna when it had mattered. "I thought Karna would be safe. Look at me, Suyodhana, I am bleeding from a hundred cuts. I....I am sorry I was late," the Brahmin cried, guilt struggling with denial at what he saw.

Had his friend not called him a traitor? 'But I am not a traitor, Aswathama, and neither are you, my friend,' thought Karna wearily. 'Suyodhana, do not blame Aswathama. He had his own reasons for not being there. Look at his body – every inch covered with wounds. Aswathama do not go away! I forgive you, my friend, and you must forgive Suyodhana for his harsh words. Do not leave me now. Stay with me for a few moments more,' Karna wanted to cry out to Aswathama who was dragging himself away, but he could not speak; he was drowning in his own blood.

'My friend, I do not want the empire Krishna offered me. If anyone deserves it, it is you, Suyodhana. You gave your unconditional love without asking about my caste when the whole world shunned me. I could not win the war for you, dear friend.' Garbled words came from Karna's mouth, meaningless and useless. But no words were necessary. Their friendship went far beyond words. An arrow shot at an unarmed man could not destroy it. Suyodhana pressed his friend to his bosom, his tears washed away by the tears of heaven.

Karna, the man whose life the Gods were fond of playing dice with; the man who had chosen to remain a low-class Suta when an empire was offered to him on a platter, died in his friend's arms. The war lost all meaning for Suyodhana.

*****

72 THE KILL

WHEN HE LEARNED AFTER KARNA'S DEATH that Shalya had abandoned his friend at the most critical juncture, Suyodhana ordered Shalya hunted down and killed. In the small hours of the eighteenth day of the war, as Suyodhana lay tossing in his bed, he sensed a presence in his tent. He sprang up, his warrior instincts alert to the presence of an intruder in his camp.

A figure stood in the shadows, head bent. "Suyodhana, it is I, Shalya. Forgive me for what I have done."

Grabbing his sword, Suyodhana rushed at the traitor, but Shalya said, "You have every right to kill me. I was a traitor in your camp for I hated the Suta. My ego was hurt when you made me the Suta's charioteer. I wanted Karna to fail, and discouraged him with my harsh words. All night I hid in the jungles beyond Kurukshetra, thinking about the rights and wrongs of the war. I know I was responsible for the death of the noblest of men. It did not matter that he was a Suta. What I did is hurting me like a dagger in my heart. I came to beg for your forgiveness, a chance to redeem myself. I am a *maharathi* and a better warrior than all the Pandavas. I shall defeat them for you, for the man I cheated. I shall kill Krishna and Arjuna today if you will let me fight for you. But if you prefer to hang me for treason, I am ready for that, too."

Suyodhana shouted for the guards to tie up Shalya. The maverick had surrendered without protest. Suyodhana was unable to decide whether to trust the blackguard or not. Finally, when dawn was breaking, he walked to Kripa's camp and sought his advice. The Acharya said they were at a stage when they should accept anyone willing to help them. The

422

situation was desperate. Only a few warriors remained. If he was to make good of the situation, it was best to make Shalya the Commander-in-Chief. Suyodhana consulted Aswathama and Sushasana and they, too, were of the opinion that none was equal to the maverick Shalya in warfare and strategy, provided he bent his sharp mind to it.

Just before battle resumed on the eighteenth day, Suyodhana freed Shalya and appointed him Commander-in-Chief of the Kaurava armies. Shalya bowed to Suyodhana and assumed charge. Kripa watched, an amused smile on his face, as the new Commander called for a strategy meeting. The first thing he did was to ensure there was no hand-to-hand combat or individual duels. They had to attack as a united front; they would break the rules and form unconventional formations that weren't in any book on warfare. Only winning counted, winning was *dharma*, the new Commander exhorted his troops. Suyodhana felt uneasy, but he had no choice.

The first half of the eighteenth day saw the bloodiest slaughter. Shalya attacked aggressively, defeating Bhima, Nakula and Sahadeva, causing them to retreat hastily with their troops. His aim was to corner Krishna and then kill both him and Arjuna. By the time the sun was a hot ball of fire over their heads and the shadows were short dwarfs running under their feet. Shalya had demolished the last of the Pandava resistance. He tied spikes and lances to the wheels of the chariots and raced through the enemy battalions, cutting down horses, making elephants panic and using lethal powders. Poisonous arrows and oil pots flew fast and furious, creating orbs of fire. The Pandava situation was becoming hopeless. Yudhishtra was overcome by despair.

Krishna manoeuvered his chariot to reach Yudhishtra and told him that he would create a diversion but that Yudhishtra would have to act quickly. He would tempt Shalya to follow him in his chariot and Yudhishtra would then use his lance to strike him down from behind.

Horrified, Yudhishtra protested that he would do no such thing. He had not killed anyone in the war; others had done the butchering for him. "Krishna, I cannot take anyone's life, even my enemy's. Life has taught me many things and ..."

"Brother, you want us to kill for you while you yourself will not lift your little finger? Talk of *ahimsa* on the battlefield are the words of a coward. Do as Krishna says, or else we are doomed. You are a Kshatriya. We are fighting to make you King," Arjuna snapped.

"But Shalya is our uncle, the brother of our step-mother, Madri."

"He is our enemy now. I killed Pitamaha; I killed our beloved Guru for you. Everyone we are fighting is kin, including Duryodhana. This is war, brother. Do your duty, or else *adharma* will triumph," Arjuna said, his eyes never leaving his brother's face. Krishna smiled.

Before Yudhishtra could react, Krishna's chariot had vanished into the thick of battle, rushing headlong towards the Kaurava Commander. Yudhishtra waited with a heavy heart for it to return, with Shalya in chase. The lance felt heavy in his hand.

Soon, an uproar was heard and dust rose to cloud the sun. Men and chariots came rushing towards Yudhishtra. Krishna's chariot flew past him in a blur and he heard Krishna shout, "Now!" Yudhishtra closed his eyes and threw his lance with full force at the chariot chasing Krishna and Arjuna. He opened his eyes when he heard the shouts of jubilation around him. '*Maharaja Yudhishtra Vijaya!*' his soldiers were shouting.

In the chariot that had toppled over, Shalya lay dead, a lance through his heart. His accusing gaze pierced Yudhishtra's heart, sharper than the lance he had hurled at his uncle. Yudhishtra collapsed in his chariot, his hands shivering. He had killed his uncle, that too, by attacking from the rear. He had thrown his lance at the back of the Kaurava Commander...like a coward... a man with no honour. It was amoral, adharmic... Suddenly he remembered the Nishada woman and her five children in

Varanavata. His mother had told him they had to do it to save themselves. Now he was a man in his prime and life had taught him that nothing good could come from violence. But he felt as helpless as a twig caught in a flood. He could smell the blood on his hands, the blood of his kin, the blood of men he had once respected and loved.

"I will go and finish Dushasana and Duryodhana," he heard Bhima say.

Victory was at hand, but it failed to cheer the son of *dharma*.

*****

73 THE LAKE

HE HAD FAILED THEM ALL. He was a despicable creature.
He had kept hope alive till Shalya fell. Now there was nothing
left. Suyodhana's teeth chattered as he lay submerged in the icy
Samanthapanchaka lake. It was bone-chilling cold but nothing
could soothe the burning inside him. He had stayed in the lake
the whole night, trying to shake off the smiling image of Karna.
Kumara's innocent face haunted him. No, he could not give up.
This was a strategic retreat. He needed time to think. He had to
live somehow to fight another day. If he dug deep into himself,
surely he would find the courage? The Pandavas had broken
every rule of war, yet they had won. No, the war was not over
yet, and never would be, until *dharma* was restored. It would
continue with or without him.

Who was that? Suyodhana heard a twig snap. Had they found
him? His mace lay half-buried on the slushy shore. He was not
sure he even had the strength to lift it, let alone fight with it.

"Get out of there, you fool! They will find and kill you."

Acharya Kripa! Suyodhana lifted his head from the water. Two
figures stood behind Kripa. One was the Yadava Commander,
Kritavarma, and the other was...

"Suyodhana, I have failed you. I failed Karna," said Aswathama.
Suyodhana did not want to face him. "Suyodhana, Bhima killed
Sushasana a short while ago. Your brother fought to the last.
Bhima downed him with a kick to the groin. He tore Sushasana's
arm from his shoulder. When Sushasana raised his other arm in
defiance, Bhima cut off both his hands. Still, Sushasana did not
utter a cry of pain. He spat in Bhima's face and laughed at him.

Can you believe that? Enraged, Bhima tore open Sushasana's chest and drank his blood. Then Draupadi, too, came to drink Sushasana's blood. The rage that woman carried within her! She finally bound her hair after thirteen years, having first dipped it in your brother's blood. She could not stop laughing."

"Enough, Aswathama!" snapped Kripa.

"They killed Karna when he was helpless. They killed my father with a lie. They killed Bhishma through deceit. They killed Sushasana with a foul kick... should we allow them to win after all this? If they win, no one will ever believe in *dharma* again."

"Aswathama, my friend, get away from here. Run as fast as your legs will carry you. Save yourself to fight another day. Carry the flag for all of us," Suyodhana said, looking into the distance where the sky dissolved into the lake. "Can't you hear the victory celebrations from their camp? Bhishma still waits for death on his bed of arrows, but they do not care. Mercifully, everything will be over soon."

"Kritavarma and Aswathama want revenge. I have been trying to talk sense into them. Nothing good will come of such foolishness," Kripa said with utter certainty.

"The celebrations in the Pandava camp will not last long," vowed Aswathama, gritting his teeth.

"Suyodhana, this rash fool will not listen to me," Kripa said.

"Aswathama, they will not treat you harshly. You are a Brahmin and they know what they did to your father. I have to fight to the end but you must survive, for all of us, for *dharma* to win," Suyodhana said to his friend.

"So you think I should become their *Rajaguru*, like my father? You think they will spare me because I am a Brahmin? Do you really think I want to lead such a life after what they have done to you, to Karna, to countless others?"

Suyodhana wanted to tell Aswathama to leave the past behind, but the bitterness in his heart refused to go away. It was through a travesty of justice that the Pandavas had won the war and he was hiding like a water rat. Suyodhana scooped up some water and looked at Aswathama. His friend waded into the water and stood before him. The image of the wispy Brahmin boy whom he had saved from Bhima years before rushed to his mind, choking him with tears.

Perhaps Aswathama was remembering the same thing for he said with a crooked smile, "That mango you gave me years ago..."

"You never got to eat it, though. Ekalavya snatched it from you." They laughed. The mention of Ekalavya brought back bitter memories. No, it was not justice that the Pandavas had won everything. Suyodhana poured the water over Aswathama saying, "I appoint you Commander-in-Chief of the Kaurava army. *Vijayi Bhava!*"

Kripa snorted. "A Commander-in-Chief of an army of three!"

Aswathama hugged Suyodhana. "Don't hate me when you hear what I have done."

"I will be dead by then, my friend. But you still have a chance to go back and claim the exalted life of a *Rajaguru*."

Aswathama dunked under the water and stayed there for some time. When he emerged, the sun was rising out of the blood-red lake. The Brahmin took water in his trembling palms and recited the holy *Gayatri mantra*. Mist rolled down from the distant hills and countless birds swooped around in the rushes by the lake. It was a beautiful day. A good day to die.

Suyodhana closed his eyes as Aswathama touched his shoulder. He heard the splash of water as his friend climbed out onto dry land. A cold breeze carrying the stench of blood and decaying flesh from the battlefield caressed him. He thought of the patriarch still lying on his tortuous bed of arrows, waiting for the spring solstice, waiting to die. 'Forgive me, Pitamaha, I never knew your worth when it mattered,' thought Suyodhana. In his mind, he was still the little boy who had sat on Pitamaha's lap, embarrassed to kiss the old man in public. The bristle of his beard, the smell of the sandalwood paste on Bhishma's forehead – a thousand memories...priceless...useless.

"There he is!"

Suyodhana prayed for courage. They had found him. He opened his eyes to see Krishna sitting in his charioteer's seat, caressing his whip and smiling at him. How he wished he could have wiped that smirk off the Yadava's face. Behind him stood his enemies, smug in victory. No, not all of them. A shade of distress clouded Yudhishtra's eyes and Arjuna's brow was furrowed with worry. Why did he not get down from his chariot? Suyodhana could hear people rushing in from all sides. Drummers came running, preparing for a bloody show. Overcome by sorrow and pain, Suyodhana watched his subjects jostle and push each other to watch him die. Some looked sad but most of them seemed excited to be present at the kill. Nothing was more entertaining than the fall of a great man.

The crowd parted for Dhaumya. "Come out of the water, you coward!" Dhaumya drove his staff into the slushy earth and the crowd cheered.

Suyodhana raised his head, his eyes blazing with their old fire. Dhaumya took a step back, trying to free his staff from the mud. Suyodhana came out of the water, tying his hair into a topknot. He shook the water from his body and slapped his thighs. Dhaumya disappeared into the crowd, leaving his staff of office behind. As Suyodhana bent to touch the ground and say a silent prayer, the crowd fell silent. He picked up his mace from the mud, wiped it clean and placing it on his shoulder, walked up to drier ground. On the way, he crushed Dhaumya's staff like a twig.

Thunder clapped overhead and dark clouds swirled from the southern horizon. The wind howled, snapping the gnarled branches off dried trees. Huge waves from the lake smashed against the rocks on shore and shattered like dreams. A surge of water rushed ashore, hugged Suyodhana's legs and then returned to its cold abode in the lake. Like the tears of heavens, drops of rain began to fall. The parched earth, drunk with blood for eighteen days, drank the cleansing rain like a thirsty beast.

The panicked cry of an owl filled the air. Suyodhana looked up and saw a group of crows chasing it. Bad omens! But he had arrived at a point where he no longer cared about omens, good or bad...or anything else. Suyodhana stood with his heavy mace on his shoulder, waiting for any of the Pandavas to make the first move.

*****

74 OORUBHANGA

"WHY NOT SURRENDER, DURYODHANA?" Krishna asked.

Suyodhana neither looked at Krishna nor responded to him.

"Surrender, and we shall spare your life. We may even give you a vassal state to rule. You surely know your time is done."

Suyodhana ignored Krishna and stood staring at Yudhishtra. "Who is first? I can also take on all five of you together." If his cousin had expected him to plead for peace and accept his suzerainty, he was living in his own fantasy. An owl fluttered above, blinded by daylight, struggling to reach the darkness of the forest. Somewhere, a dog howled.

"Choose one among us. If you win, the throne of Hastinapura is yours," Yudhishtra said. The son of *dharma* had gambled again.

Suyodhana could not help smiling when he saw the expression on Krishna's face. Destiny was giving him one more chance. He walked up to Yudhishtra and gazed at him from head to toe. It would have been a simple matter to pick Yudhishtra for a duel with maces and smash his head to pieces. He moved on to Arjuna's chariot and said clearly, "Karna...Drona...Bhishma..." Arjuna turned away, ashamed. The twins, Nakul and Sahadeva, blessed with perpetual boyish good looks, stood straight as arrows under Suyodhana's gaze. 'Men who refused to grow up, ' he thought as he turned away. 'Tchaw!'

"I choose Bhima," Suyodhana said. The tension eased out of Krishna's face. It was a duel Suyodhana had always yearned to fight, a childhood dream nourished from the time he had hidden under his blind father's bed, quivering in fear of his hefty cousin.

'Bhanu, Karna, Aswathama... strengthen my arms.' The crowd parted as Suyodhana moved to the centre. It was silent except for the chirping of birds.

Bhima picked up his mace and walked forward to face Suyodhana. "Kill him, Bhima! Kill the devil!" Draupadi's voice rose into the air like a shrill chant. The crowd roared with excitement and the drums began to beat.

Bhima charged like an elephant. Suyodhana ducked at the last moment and Bhima lost his balance. Suyodhana's mace connected with Bhima's shoulder, drawing admiration from the crowd. Bhima spun around and hit back. Suyodhana blocked him. The power of Bhima's mace was shocking. Suyodhana countered Bhima's brute strength with agility. Bhima brought down his mace again and again, smashing the ground. Suyodhana dodged and danced back, landing powerful hits on Bhima's shoulders and chest. In excitement, the frenzied crowd began calling each warrior's name in turn, urging each one to kill the other...smash the head, crush the chest and batter the face. The drumming rose to a deafening pitch.

In time, both warriors began to show signs of fatigue but neither gave up. Suyodhana's hits started to affect Bhima. There was no doubt in the spectators' minds about who was the more skilful and who the stronger. Skill against power, agility against force, the duel raged on as though there was no end.

The chance came when Bhima stumbled. Suyodhana rushed in to smash Bhima's head. From the corner of his eye, he saw Krishna tapping his thigh with his flute. What trick did the Yadava hide behind his smile? The answer came as binding pain shot through his thigh. Suyodhana staggered and fell. Bhima had hit him below the waist, against all rules of duelling, and shattered his thigh. Suyodhana collapsed onto the ground in pain and anger. Treachery! Deceit! Bastard!

An uneasy silence fell on the crowd. They had all seen the dastardly act committed by the big Pandava. Yudhishtra closed his eyes in anguish and Arjun jumped down from the chariot, his heart pounding, his face grim. Where had honour fled?

Suyodhana tried to get up on his other leg but fell back helplessly. Bhima's legs were so near. With a swing of the mace he could bring down his opponent and pay him back in the same coin. But he could not do that, he was a Kaurava, *ajaya*, unconquerable. Suyodhana grunted in pain. The leg had swollen. 'Hold on, hold on...' he thought silently, willing himself to find the courage to go on. Painfully, Suyodhana raised himself using his mace and stood on one leg. Suddenly, he landed a powerful blow on Bhima's face, smashing his front teeth. Suyodhana looked at Krishna and laughed.

"Bhima, smash his other thigh!" Dhaumya shouted from the safety of the crowd.

Bhima swung his mace again and brought it down on Suyodhana's other leg. Suyodhana refused to fall, refused to cry in pain. He stood with his head held high as Bhima swung his mace again and cracked his thighbone. Slowly, like a giant tree being axed, Suyodhana fell to the ground. His head hit the ground, splashing earth all around. Bhima's face leered above him as the noises blurred and darkness claimed the eldest Kaurava.

Dhaumya and his group of priests cried out at the top of their voices, 'Dharma has won!' The Guru raised his arms and his disciples danced around the unconscious Suyodhana, singing, "We have vanquished evil. *Dharma* has won."

Suyodhana opened his eyes with great effort. The pain shooting from his thighs was excruciating. *Dharma* had won? Suyodhana could stand the pain but not such a blatant untruth. Where was that Yadava who had brought this upon him? Where was Krishna, who had pointed out his thigh to Bhima? Suyodhana turned his head and saw Krishna standing with his arms crossed over his chest, a smile on his face. Speaking was an effort but speak he would to the Yadava who had brought death and destruction to his country and people. Like a cobra whose tail has been smashed, but which retains life in its head, Suyodhana raised himself on his powerful arms and glared at Krishna. "Satisfied now, Yadava? Until the world lasts, people will remember your deceit and cruelty. Is there one rule your side has not broken or one warrior the Pandavas killed fairly?"

Suyodhana turned his head to towards Yudhishtra and laughed wearily. "Yudhishtra, you think you have won? How will you sleep in peace hereafter? Your father...no, not your father, for you do not know who your father is, but your mother's husband cheated my blind father of his birthright for many years. Now you have done the same to me. Yet you claim to believe in *dharma*?"

Suyodhana faced Krishna. "You have more tongues than Ananta when you speak of one's duty. You preach *dharma*, but you do not follow it. I was born a Kshatriya, lived as a Kshatriya and I will die a Kshatriya. I was an ordinary man, no *avatar*, but as a ruler, I cared for all, never discriminating against anyone. I never had to roam the forests like the man who claims to be *dharmaputra*. No one ever dared to raise a finger against my wife or brothers. You had to beg for my mercy to save your wayward son, Krishna, but my son died in battle for me. I had the great Bhishma, Guru Drona, Karna, and many others, give their lives for me. Now I follow them like a true Kshatriya. I kept my word to Pitamaha and never broke any of the rules of war. Warriors were willing to die for me despite your threats of hell. You could not even convince your own Narayana Sena to fight against me. They died for me, Krishna, for they believed *dharma* was on my side. Your people died for me, Yadava. Think about that and then consider the *dharma* that you preach."

Suyodhana paused, willing the darkness that threatened to overcome him to hold its curtain for a few more moments. "I made one grave mistake, but I do not repent it. If this is punishment for that mistake, I shudder to think what punishments lie in store for the Pandavas and you, Krishna. I have only one regret, that my pious parents will have no sons to perform their last rites. I go to where Karna has gone before me. If your *Gita* is true, Krishna, then I have lived and will die according to the Kshatriya *dharma*. The heaven rishis speak of, for men who die doing their duty, will be mine. I have had a good life for I feared no God or *avatar*, but lived as my heart told me to. No priests dictated what was right and wrong to me. I lived like a man and will die as one. My thighs were broken by foul play but I still hold my head high. I am blessed. Time will tell who was right and who was wrong. You will remember my words, Krishna, when death stares you in the face one day. The laws of *karma* are beyond even your control. Now, go and leave me to die in peace. I do not wish your faces to be the last thing I see on this beautiful earth. Leave me alone to ascend to the abode of Mahadeva."

Krishna's eyes looked away from the dying Kuru Prince. Suyodhana's words remained coiled in the recesses of his mind, ready to strike on the day he would be lying with an arrow embedded in his leg. He turned to his friends and said, "It is over. *Dharma* has won."

Like a song halted midway, the rain stopped and the heavens were silent once again. In the woods, a Brahmin buried his face in his arms and vowed silently, 'It is not over. It is never over.'

*****

THE VICTORIOUS PANDAVA ARMY rushed to the Kaurava camp, looting and burning everything in sight. Yudhishtra felt dazed, like a man who had drunk too much *soma*. He waited for the exhilaration of victory to sweep over him, but all he felt was a dreadful emptiness that crushed his ribs and choked his breath. The earth lay desecrated with blood and mangled flesh. Vultures circled high above before landing on carrion. Dogs fought each other for the bones of warriors, while ravens cawed, announcing their feast of *dharma*.

Krishna pulled at the reins, stopping his chariot near Yudhishtra's lonely figure.

"Why do I feel no elation, Krishna? No joy?"

"You are merely exhausted, King of Hastinapura," Krishna replied.

"How will I face my uncle and aunt? Suyodhana's words haunt me. We did not spare a single son of Dhritarashtra."

"No, we spared the noblest of them all. Have you forgotten Yuyutsu, who sided with us, with his fabulous warriors, when we needed him? Do not indulge in morbid thoughts. You have won and the people will soon forget the rest. What we did was for *dharma* and the fact that we won proves *dharma* was indeed with us."

"My mind is troubled, Vasudeva. Go to my Uncle Dhritarashtra and Aunt Gandhari and prepare them for the terrible news of their sons' deaths."

"If you wish it so. I will convince them their sons deserved to die."

"Krishna, I have always trusted you. Respect their grief."

Krishna smiled. "Rejoice in your victory, Yudhishtra, for Bharatavarsha has a new Emperor who will respect the scriptures and follow *dharma*."

***

Dhaumya arrived to announce that the riches of Suyodhana's camp had been secured. By law, whatever the vanquished enemy had owned belonged to the victor. Arjuna hesitated, his mind filled with a stange unease that he could not quell.

"It is as the good priest says, Partha. Enjoy what you have earned with your prowess and skill. Now get down from the chariot, your brother has given me an errand to perform," said Krishna.

Arjuna sighed and descended from the chariot that had carried him through eighteen days of warfare. Bhima arrived, pulling Draupadi with him. Nakula and Sahadeva followed behind.

"All Suyodhana's wealth is now mine. How sweet victory is!" Draupadi said. Yudhishtra shook his head, dismayed and troubled.

"The saint is worried. Brother, forget your cares and laugh with us," Bhima said, thowing an arm over Yudhishtra's shoulder.

"If only we had the gem Aswathama wears," Draupadi sighed.

"Beware what you wish for, Draupadi. Fate has a nasty habit of fulfilling wishes in a way you never wished for."

"Playing with words as usual, Krishna? Come down from that chariot. How can I thank you for all that you have done?" Draupadi laughed as Krishna jumped down with a smile. At that moment, lightning struck the chariot, stunning everyone. It burst into flames, the horses neighing desperately in the throes of death.

"Krishna, an ill omen! I am afraid the Gods are angry with us for killing all the *maharathis* of the Kauravas. Have mercy on us."

"Yudhishtra, you are no longer the mendicant banished to the forest. You are the Lord of Bharatavarsha. Do not worry about the chariot. It was already burnt when Bhishma's arrow struck it on the first day of the war. I kept it intact. Now, since the war is over, it has exploded."

"*Hare Krishna!* Behold the glory and miracle of the great Lord," Dhaumya cried. The crowd broke into a frenzied chanting of the Lord's name. Krishna raised his right hand in benediction, smiling at the faithful in all his divine glory.

"I wish to bathe in scented water and sleep in a soft bed again after thirteen long years. I am going to the palace at Upapiplava," said Draupadi, looking at her husbands.

"Queen Draupadi," Krishna said in a teasing tone, "take your sons with you to the palace."

"My sons are with my brother, to celebrate the great victory. The boys deserve it," Draupadi said and then called for the servants to bring her palanquin.

Bhima whispered in Yudhishtra's ear, "Draupadi adores that gem Aswathama wears. Where has the cursed Brahmin gone? I will slay him and bring it to her."

Yudhishtra turned to look at Bhima. Did the same blood run in their veins? "Has your thirst for blood not been quenched even after such carnage, my brother? Let us not add the sin of *Brahmahatya*. Leave Aswathama alone."

"We already have the sin of *Brahmahatya* on us. Remember, your own words caused Guru Drona's fall."

There was no refuting Bhima's words. Yudhishtra looked away, ashamed.

"Brother, forgive my harsh words. We are going to Duryodhana's camp; there are many men and women there who are now our slaves. Guru Dhaumya has declared that all the Shudras will be our *dasas* as in the days of old. We will restore our great traditions."

Yudhishtra remained silent. Bhima bowed and was about to leave, but hesitated before climbing into his chariot. "Brother, something tells me that the Brahmin is dangerous. He is like a wounded tiger. He will strike back. Give me permission to hunt him down."

"No, Bhima, I will allow no more killing. How I wish Lord Balarama was here!"

Bhima shook his head and ordered his charioteer to drive him to Duryodhana's camp. The spoils of war awaited him. How good it would feel to sleep in Duryodhana's bed, how poetic and sweet would be the revenge of drinking *soma* from his crystal cup. Bhima turned and saw Yudhishtra walking towards the spot where Bhishma lay dying. His brother was unpredictable. What good would it do him to visit the dying old man when the Goddess of victory had become their consort?

****

An owl swooped down into a tree and the crows there cawed in fear. "Night has made the bird stronger. Do you understand, Uncle?" Aswathama asked Kripa. The gem he wore in his headcloth glittered as lightning flashed though the forest, turning night into day. Darkness immediately rushed back, cloaking the world in shadow.

"Sneaking into the Pandava camp at night is downright crazy, Aswathama," Kripa replied, squatting beside the lake, not far from where Suyodhana lay dying.

Kritavarma stood nearby, deep in thought. "Kripa, Bhima hit Suyodhana below the waist. He is worse than any Mlecha!"

Aswathama's patience snapped. "I owe it to Suyodhana."

"How will the three of you do it when there are over five thousand warriors in their camp?" Kripa asked, annoyed by his nephew's lack of common sense.

"I don't know how, Uncle, but I must do it if I am to ever find peace again."

"We can surrender and then gradually incite the people. We can have a revolution soon and..."

"No, Kritavarma, this must be done tonight. Shiva, give me courage, give me power."

"Pray, and perhaps the Lord will clear your muddled mind from such foolish thoughts," snapped Kripa.

Like a man possessed, Aswathama ran into the forest. Kripa and Kritavarma looked at each other in astonishment. Kripa uttered a curse and began running behind Aswathama. Kritavarma followed. The sky cracked open with lightning and a drizzle began. They could hear Aswathama running through the forest, stumbling on roots, crashing into bushes and chanting the name of Shiva. Birds awoke in screeching panic above them and hares scurried away in alarm.

Kripa and Kritavarma lost Aswathama for some time and when they found him again, he was lying prostrate before the idol of Rudra, the fiercest form of Shiva. Thunder clapped and lightning flashed, lighting up another statue nearby – Drona stared at them in stone. With a shock, they realised they were standing in Ekalavya's practice ground. What forces had led their feet to this place, hidden deep in the forest? The storm raged around them. Was Rudra welcoming them with his thousand arms or sending them a warning?

Aswathama's voice rose over the thunder. "Oh Shiva, Lord of the Universe, Lord of all beasts, humans and demigods, Lord of Kailasa, be one with me in my fight for *dharma*. Be the strength in my arms, the fire in my eyes, the power in my bow and the sharpness in my sword. I go to do what no warrior should, knowing I will be despised for attacking my enemy while they sleep. I do it for my country, for the future of Bharatavarsha, and for my friend. If loving my motherland is a crime, let me be called a criminal. If friendship is a sin, let me be a sinner. Let all the blame be mine, but give me the courage for this one night. Be with me, All-merciful, All-knowing, All-powerful

Parmeshwara. Oh Destroyer of the Universe, be the sword in my hand tonight."

Kripa and Kritavarma stood watching Aswathama as the idol of Shiva shone in the lightning. A cobra traced its way up to the throat of the idol, spread its hood and hissed at them. Aswathama raised his head and the gem in his headcloth sparkled. The cobra slid down the statue and vanished back into the bushes.

"Can we help you, Mahabrahmana?" a voice whispered, startling the three men.

Kripa unsheathed his sword and stood in combat position. Wind rushed past their ears as Kritavarma took a tentative step towards the prostrate Aswathama. Who had spoken? Kritavarma stared at the idol of Shiva in disbelief. Suddenly, as lightning flashed and the earth rumbled to the sound of thunder, an old man stepped forward. He stood leaning on his staff, his white hair flying in the wind like the mane of a fleeing horse.

"Vasuki!" Kripa said, astonished.

Aswathama scrambled to his feet and Vasuki bowed to him. "Mahabrahmana, we, the Nagas, are with you in your divine mission. If we do not do something tonight, our lives will be as stormy and dark as this evil night. You are Rudra, the destroyer of foes and we are your *bhutas*. The cobra was an omen. Our people are at your service."

Vasuki gave a low whistle and men slithered down from the trees around them. Armed with maces, bows and poisoned arrows, the Nagas surrounded the three warriors. Vasuki leaned on his staff and proclaimed, "Today is the day for revenge, for Ekalavya, Iravan, Khatotkacha, and the countless others who died in Khandivaprastha. We shall avenge our brothers. Just as Krishna and Arjuna trapped us in Khandiva, we shall trap them in their dwelling. The wheel of *dharma* belongs to no man. *Dharma* is time and time is Mahadeva, the Lord of destruction. The wheel is turning, my friends, and it will crush those who are now riding high. Hail Kalabhairava, Lord of Time!"

Thunder crashed overhead but hundreds of Nagas raised their maces and tridents and roared in unison, *"Har Har Mahadeva!"*, as if challenging the very heavens.

Aswathama prised the sword from the hands of the Rudra idol and bowed before his father's statue. "Bless me, Father. Forgive me for what I do," he whispered. He paused for a moment to look at the angry skies. The gem sparkled like a star. Then he began running to where the Pandavas slept, smug in their victory. Kripa and Kritavarma followed. Like the *bhutas* of Shiva, the Nagas ran after Aswathama, as stealthy as a cobra stalking its prey.

Vasuki watched them disappear into the forest and then fell on his knees before the idol of Shiva. "Forgive me, Lord, for what I have done to the only Brahmin who was compassionate to our people. But I had no other choice. Be merciful." He waited for a sign that his Lord had forgiven him but all he heard was the roar of the storm. Nor did he see the cobra slithering towards him.

***

Krishna stood uneasily before Dhritarashtra and Gandhari. The old King sat with bowed head, his strong arms tense.

"You did not have the kindness to spare at least one son, Krishna?" Gandhari asked in a cold voice from which all emotion had fled.

Krishna did not reply. Dhritarashtra's body shook and he wept like a distraught child. Gandhari put a comforting hand on her husband's shoulder. Finally, Dhritarashtra said in a hoarse voice, "I heard how Bhima killed Suyodhana. Sanjaya told me. I bow to your sense of *dharma*. May you and your tribe increase, my Lord."

"Your son had perpetuated evil in this land. He stole what was Yudhishtra's and refused to return it. I tried for peace and he insulted me. I had warned you of this that day, revered Kuru King," Krishna said in a soft voice.

"The kingship belongs to me, Vasudeva Krishna. Fate made me blind but that does not mean my firstborn had to be unlucky, too. You stole what belonged to me and gave it to others – my kingdom, my sons, everything. The seers should have known that the one who stole butter in his childhood would steal kingdoms when he grew up."

"My Lord, sorrow has blunted your wisdom. Your son tried to strip his cousin's wife, and he paid the price. So did the great Bhishma, Drona and all the others – they paid with their lives for their silence. That is the law of *dharma*. I am just a *dharmapurusha*, an agent. *Dharma* is eternal, unchanging, omnipotent."

Dhritarashtra had nothing more to say. His tears had dried. He lay down on his bed and turned his face to the wall. Krishna waited nearby, fidgeting with his flute.

Gandhari said, "The King needs to rest." Krishna bowed and was about to leave when Gandhari's soft words pierced his heart. "Prabhu, what was my Vikarna's fault? He was the only one who spoke up in the Sabha. We shall meet tomorrow at my son's funeral, tell me then so that a mother's heart can be soothed by *dharma*."

Krishna bowed again and gently closed the door of the royal chamber. He sighed as he stood in the veranda of the Hastinapura palace. The massive stone building was eerily silent except for the sobs coming from its unlit rooms. The thunderstorm had not passed. As his eyes scanned the south, his heart began to hammer. His sharp ears had picked up the sound of marching men. He leapt from the balcony and jumped into the saddle of his waiting horse. He knew what was happening. The Brahmin they had let go was returning. He prayed he was not too late.

***

Three dark figures stood with bated breath before the Pandava camp. The eyes in Iravan's head gleamed in the moonlight and a strange fear gripped them. The Nagas were restless as they waited for instructions. They shuffled their feet and whispered to each other in hushed voices. It was grotesque, the irony of the laughter they had heard, the cruelty of the merriment in the Pandava camp. Now the camp lay crouched like a sleepy beast, slumbering in drunkenness, careless in victory. Rain had made the ground slushy.

A deep moan sounded, it came from Kurukshetra. Was it Bhishma or Suyodhana? Aswathama gritted his teeth. "You two stand at the gate and do not allow anyone to escape. I am going in with them," Aswathama said to Kripa and Kritavarma, gesturing to his Naga companions. He turned and rushed at the guards at the gate. Before they knew what was happening he had plunged his sword into their hearts. The Nagas lit their torches, illuminating their painted faces and hair tied to resemble cobra hoods. Their ash-smeared bodies and tridents made them look like creatures from another world. Howling and ululating war cries as old as humanity, they broke into the Pandava camp, slaughtering everyone in sight.

Aswathama ran from cottage to cottage, searching for the Pandavas. He stumbled upon half-naked men, tottering out on drunken legs and quickly dispatched them to the abode of Yama. The Nagas were setting fire to the camp and letting loose the elephants and horses from their stables. The beasts ran amok. Many of the Pandava warriors were crushed under the stampeding feet of the elephants before they even knew what was happening. Others were terrified by the sight of the Nagas aiming tridents at them. "Rakshasas are attacking! Shiva *gunas* are attacking!" they screamed, not sure if what they were seeing was real or the effects of the *soma* they had consumed. Panic gripped the Pandava camp and they began indiscriminately firing arrows, swinging swords and bludgeoning with their maces whoever they found. The few who managed to escape, fell into the waiting hands of Kripa and Kritavarma, who showed no mercy. The fire that had lit Khandiva years before and killed thousands of Nagas had come back to destroy Arjuna's camp. The wheel of *dharma* kept turning.

Aswathama kicked open the door of a luxurious-looking camp and saw a man looking out of his window. "Time to go, friend," he said in a calm voice. Dhristadyumna looked at Aswathama and froze in fear. Before he could scream, Aswathama had kicked him in the groin. He doubled up on the floor, writhing in pain. Grabbing hold of Dhristadyumna's hair, Aswathama dragged him out and kicked him in the ribs.

"It is wrong to kick me when I am down and unarmed," pleaded the Commander of the Pandava army.

"Yes it is, and it is all you deserve, you scoundrel!" Aswathama pressed his knees on Dhristadyumna's chest, pinning him to the ground. "It would appear that a prostitute has begun preaching the virtue of chastity." Aswathama smashed his opponent's face with the hilt of his sword.

Dhristadyumna clutched at his broken nose, blood spurting through his fingers. Aswathama grabbed his arm and started hacking off his fingers, one by one. "Mercy, mercy..." Dhristadyumna begged.

"Mercy, mercy..." Aswathama mimicked, pressing the edge of his sword to Dhristadyumna's throat. "You cut off my father's head when he was bowed with grief and now you squeal like a pig?"

"Kill me if you must, but do not torture me..."

"Bhishma is lying there out in the cold, waiting for death. Suyodhana is lying with his thighs broken. You are a lucky bastard to die so easily. Have you ever killed a chicken?" Aswathama asked as he threw down his sword and cracked his knuckles.

When realisation dawned, Dhristadyumna begged, "No, oh no... that is so disgraceful. I am a Kshatriya. Give me a death befitting a warrior. Kill me with your sword."

"Bare hands give more satisfaction." Aswathama gripped Dhristadyumna's throat with both hands. "I want to see the fear in your face, to see your eyes popping out as you run out of breath, like this, this, this and..." He peered into Dhristadyumna's eyes. "And the final snap of your throat. Farewell!" He kicked Dhristadyumna's inert body away and let out an animal howl. He had much more work to do.

In the shadows, the eunuch waited for him. Shikandi swung his sword and hit Aswathama's head. The Brahmin's instincts saved him as he deflected the blow with his sword, but the eunuch managed to inflict a gash on his forehead. Aswathama knocked him down and plunged his sword deep into Shikandi's heart. He kept stabbing until he was sure the eunuch was dead.

Around him, tents were on fire. Kripa and Kritavarma had entered the camp and were running around, holding flaming torches in one hand and swords in the other, setting the tents alight. Men and women were running in panic, screaming and falling over each other.

Where were the Pandavas? An arrow hit the gem on Aswathama's forehead and fell at his feet. He touched his forehead. The gem was still there but his forehead was bleeding. Aswathama turned to see where the arrow had come from. Another swished past him, a finger's breadth from his throat. He ran to the hut from where the arrow had come and smashed open the door with a kick. He saw five men in the dancing light of the fire that was devouring the huts nearby. They were all choking, coughing and panting in the smoke. The heat was unbearable. Aswathama caught hold of one of the men. In the glow of the flames, there was no mistaking his face. "Here goes the gambler." Aswathama cut off the head with a swift swing of his sword. His laughter rose above the crackling of the fire and the terrified screams outside. Then he caught the biggest of the remaining men and thrust his sword through his heart. "This is for shattering Suyodhana's thighs, Bhima. May you rot in hell!"

"Where is that shameless cheat who shot Karna when he was down? Ah, Arjuna, why are you hiding behind the pillar? First you hide behind a eunuch, then you crouch like a lizard in the cracks of the wall! What a warrior you are, my friend! Aswathama cut off the man's head.

Aswathama advanced on the last two. A burning pole fell behind them. With a swing, Aswathama cut off both their heads. Then he ran out screaming, "Suyodhana, we have won the war! *Dharma* has won! I have won the war for you. The Pandavas are dead! I killed them. Where there is *dharma*, there will be victory."

An owl sat pecking out the eyes from Iravan's head. As Aswathama ran towards Suyodhana, screaming victory, it gave a hoot and vanished into the night.

Kripa ran into the hut that and looked at the five slain bodies. "Oh, Shiva! He has made a terrible mistake," he whispered, horrified by what he saw. He ran into the fiery night calling for Aswathama. Kritavarma turned the bodies over to examine them and felt panic and guilt overcome him. They would now be hunted like mad dogs and slain. He was sure of it. He ran out and mounted a horse that had strayed and galloped off towards Dwaraka. The Nagas stayed back to butcher the last of the men and women in the camp. Drunk on blood-lust and euphoria, they danced as the fire blazed around them.

Kripa caught up with Aswathama ar. grabbed his shoulder to stop him. "Uncle, I must see Suyodhana and break the good news."

'Fool! You have not killed the Pandavas, but Draupadi's sons! They will come after you. Run for your life if you want to live to fight again. I am going to Hastinapura, to hide in the slums. Run to Vyasa's *ashram*. Only he can save you." Without waiting for a response, Kripa vanished into the night.

Surely Kripa was wrong? But Aswathama remembered their faces, how he had killed them so easily. They were teenaged boys, not seasoned warriors. He had known it when he killed them, but had tried to convince himself that he had killed the Pandavas, not their sons. Now, when Kripa had said the words, the magnitude of his crime hit him like a thunderbolt. 'Oh, Shiva! What a heinous crime I have committed!' Aswathama fell to the ground, his knees buckling under the burden of his guilt.

But the sound of a galloping horse caused his warrior instincts to become alert once more, wary of danger. No, he told himself, he had killed the Pandavas. Kripa was wrong.

Aswathama saw a warrior galloping towards the blazing camp. As the horseman neared, he saw Krishna's grief-stricken face. Aswathama got up and ran on, stumbling over rocks and bruising his knees as he staggered through the dark. He had to meet Vyasa but he had to see Suyodhana as well. Aswathama stood panting under a tree. Night grew old around him and the greyness of a dreaded day crept in from the east. He was afraid of what the new day would bring. He hoped his friend was not dead. He had to hurry to the cold swamps of Samanthapanchaka lake. Perhaps it was unnecessary to say anything at all to his friend. It was best to let him go in peace.

***

When Krishna reached the Pandava camp, the Nagas had gone, leaving the ground littered with the lifeless bodies of men, women and beasts. Krishna surveyed the carnage as the sun rose behind him. He sighed. The nineteenth day was dawning and the earth was as blood red as the eastern sky. The war, which he had won with so much guile, looked so meaningless now. He saw a man sitting by the river, his head buried in his hands. Krishna walked towards Yudhishtra in silence. For the first time in his life, he had no words.

*****

76 THE CURSED

THE LAKE HAD TURNED CRIMSON when Aswathama reached its banks. He dragged himself through ankle-deep mud, frightening the Sarus cranes in the rushes; into flying away with wide, flapping wings. He panted in exhaustion, stopping every few feet. He was not sure where he was bleeding from or where he was hurt. He called his friend's name frantically, desperately swishing his sword left and right to cut down the swamp grass. Any moment they would come for him. Where had Suyodhana dragged himself to die?

Aswathama saw him half-buried in the sludge, lying on his back, his eyes closed, his mouth slightly open. Flies buzzed over Suyodhana's face. When Aswathama reached him, he slowed down, afraid of the finality of everything. A trickle of blood had dried at the corners of the Prince's mouth. As he approached with tentative steps, mice scurried away. The Brahmin collapsed to his knees near the man he had loved so dearly, the friend of his childhood and the brother he had never had.

"Suyodhana, wake up! I have killed them all!" Aswathama shook his friend's cold body, afraid it was too late. He put his ear to the broad chest. Was there a flicker of life?

"Karna...Karna, you defeated them?" Suyodhana whispered. His swollen thighs had turned black; gangrene had begun to set in and his body burned with fever.

Aswathama was overwhelmed with emotion, Suyodhana was not dead. Then bitterness washed over hm. "Suyodhana, Karna did not win the war, I did. He had the opportunity to kill Yudhishtra, Bhima and the twins, but he did not, because he gave his word to the mother of the Pandavas. He gave away his armour so people would think he was a great man. He betrayed you for his own glory and still you speak only his name?"

"Who...are you?"

"Suyodhana, it is I, Aswathama. I have won the war for you, not Karna. Open your eyes. I have forsaken glory to do what no Brahmin or warrior should. I set fire to their tents and killed them in their sleep – a shameful thing, but I did it for you, my friend, and for my father." He was not sure the men he had killed were the Pandavas or their sons, but Suyodhana need not know that in his final moments. But the weight of the lie lay heavy on Aswathama's heart.

"Ah, Aswathama, where...is Karna?" Suyodhana opened his eyes

"Karna is dead, killed by Arjuna. You gave him everything, but he betrayed you."

"Karna could never betray me, or you..."

"Oh, Suyodhana, do not die now when we have won. Tell me what I did was right."

"You have betrayed...*dharma*, Aswathama."

"Suyodhana, I did it for you...to avenge you... "

"Aswathama...no..." Suyodhana was delirious and in pain, struggling to form words as his life ebbed away.

"I have lived for you, Suyodhana. I have lived for our country. Do not call me a traitor." Aswathama threw his arms across Suyodhana's inert body, trying hard to fight back his tears. "Don't go, my friend. We have a country to rule, with justice, equality and prosperity for all. We have a dream to live. Do not go and leave me alone."

"You are still my friend..." Suyodhana's words were barely a whisper. Aswathama bent his ear to Suyodhana's lips to hear. "Aswathama, you are my dearest friend...after Karna"

"After Karna, Suyodhana?" Aswathama looked up. The eyes that had once burned with passion, were closed forever. He gently placed Suyodhana's head on the wet ground. The Crown Prince of Hastinapura had reached the end of his star-crossed life. A plentitude of gifts and sorrow had been his in equal measure. How fearlessly he had believed in justice for all, how fiercely he had fought against caste, yet he was powerless before the frailties of human pride. There was no man Aswathama had loved more, yet his friend's last words hurt him more than all the arrows of Kurukshetra.

"After Karna..." Karna the glorious, Karna the *Dharmaveera*, Karna the man who died for his friend. Poets would sing of the friendship between the Suta and the Prince. And the poor Brahmin would be a forgotten footnote in the history of great men. Aswathama, the despised, the cursed, the man who killed his enemies in their sleep. The Brahmin bit his lip, clutching his hair. His dream had ended in a curse. No one wanted him, neither his dead friend nor the country for which he had dared the cold heights of Gandhara. Neither past nor future belonged to him. He looked at the man for whom he had lived, lying dead at his feet, and broke into sobs. A noble Prince should not be lying in the mud like this. It did not matter that Suyodhana had considered Karna a better friend; for Aswathama, there was no one left. He lifted Suyodhana's head onto his lap and hugged his friend's cold body.

***

Far away, Bhishma still lay on his bed of arrows. Soon, the sighs of the patriarch of the Kurus were drowned by the wailing of thousands of women dragging themselves to the battlefield. Some were old, shrivelled with age and despair; some were young, at the prime of their lives, and for some, life had been about to blossom before the war had cruelly crushed them. Some carried babies in their arms; some had young children sobbing behind them. They were searching for the bodies of their dear ones. Shrieks of shock rent the air as mothers identified sons, widows found husbands, and sisters saw brothers lying headless, limbless, crushed by the wheels of *dharma*. As the lament of the women rose to the heedless sky, vultures feeding on carrion flapped their wings in anger and left. They perched on the leafless branches of trees and watched, impatience in their glowing eyes. Jackals scurried away carrying chunks of meat and flesh they had torn from the corpses.

Aswathama watched the scene with indifference. Life and death held no meaning for him now.

"There he is! Kill him!" Dhaumya's voice was shrill with relief.

They had found him and the end was near. Aswathama's warrior instincts made him alert. No, he would not give up. Kripa had said it right. It was better to surrender and work again patiently towards their goal. If they caught him now, they would kill him before he could negotiate a surrender. He had to reach Vyasa's *ashram* quickly.

"Suyodhana, I have to leave you but I will not give up. Aswathama will prove I was always the better friend to you, not Karna." Aswathama whispered to Suyodhana's cold body. Gently laying the Prince's head on the ground, he rose and took to his heels.

Dhaumya stood in his path. Aswathama swung his sword at the old Brahmin without breaking his stride, turning to ensure that Dhaumya lay writhing on the ground. He cursed when he saw the old man sitting dazed in the slush, surrounded by his disciples. The priest had escaped his sword by a hair's breadth. Soldiers ran towards him, lances at the ready. Aswathama fled into the woods, his heart pounding against his ribs like a rabbit trapped in a snare.

***

Draupadi sat without shedding a tear. Yudhishtra tried to console her but felt overwhelmed himself by the loss of his son; his words lacked coherence and meaning. The five bodies were placed before Draupadi, unrecognisable and ghastly in death. Her sons seemed to accuse her, their eyes staring at her from blackened faces.

"Krishna Madhava, what is the use of winning this war when we have lost our sons? They have followed Abhimanyu to the abode of Yama. Is this our punishment for killing our sires and grandsires, Gurus and kin, through deceit? No, do not tell me about the inevitability of death and the immortality of the soul, Krishna. When one's own sons are dead, such words offer no solace. They are consoling words to be uttered to others. Death is as real as life," Yudhishtra lamented, hammering his forehead with his fist.

Krishna stood nearby, unable to find words to console the man who had become Emperor of Bharatavarsha just the previous day. Priests and other well-wishers stood in a huddle, not knowing what to do or say to console their Lord and the woman who had lost all her five sons in one night. The Pandava brothers stood alone, crushed by the weight of the tragedy.

Finally Yudhishtra stood up and called for his mother. Kunti arrived. She felt old and tired. She averted her eyes, not wanting to look at the charred visages of her once-handsome and vital grandsons. Dead. There was nothing left except death.

In a voice bereft of emotion, Yudhishtra asked his mother, "Who are these who lie stricken here by death, Mother?"

"Why do you torture me like this, Son?" Kunti asked, trying to suppress her rising sobs.

"Why were your grandsons, who had done no one any harm, punished like this, Mother?"

"It was their fate, Son...destiny..."

With a viciousness that startled the people around him, Yudhishtra shouted, "Fate? No, do not blame fate for this, Mother. Remember the night at Varanavata when we trapped five Nishadas and their mother and left them to the fire? They were innocent, like our sons, yet we sacrificed them quoting *karma* and *dharma*. Well, our *karma* has caught up with us. The flames that took the Nishadas have taken our sons, too."

The priests coughed and cleared their throats. Dhaumya did not know what to say to Yudhishtra. All he had wanted was a King who would be putty in his hands, whom he could mould like a potter uses his wheel to shape a pot. He wondered whether he had instead got brittle wood that crumbled at the first touch. "*Dharma* is..." he began.

Draupadi stood up. "Forgive me, Guru, for interrupting your wise words." She gave a bow that was an affront in its elaborate humility.

Turning away from the fulminating Guru, Draupadi said to her husbands," I want the man who killed my sons to be brought before me, dead or alive. I will not allow the funeral of my sons to take place until the cursed Brahmin has been dragged here."

Yudhishtra tried to speak, but Draupadi raised her hands. "Indulge me, King, one last time. This is a mother's request."

Arjuna and Bhima did not wait. They ran through the crowd that had come to offer condolences and gawk at the misery of the royal household. A chariot halted before them. Bhima took over the reins, from the charioteer. Arjuna jumped in just as Nakula and Sahadeva came running, carrying Arjuna's weapons, and climbed into the chariot as well. The four brothers were ready to hunt down the killer of their sons. The chariot sped past the endless line of carts, horses, donkeys and bullocks carrying the dead and maimed. Hundreds of foot soldiers dragged themselves alongside the wounded. Bhima yelled at the bedraggled survivors of the great war to make way.

The chariot turned off onto a rough forest path. As they swerved and swayed along the winding path that led to the hills, Bhima wondered why there had been no fuss when his eldest son,

Khatotkacha, had been killed, or why Arjuna had not chased after the priests who had sacrificed Iravan. Then he shrugged his shoulders and whipped the horses. It was not for him to think, his duty was to do. He would find that Brahmin and crush his skull with his bare hands for killing his son; more importantly, for causing Draupadi pain. Aswathama was cursed and would pay a heavy price.

*****

77 JAYA

WHEN ASWATHAMA REACHED VYASA'S *ashram*, the morning dew still clung to the blades of grass. The air felt fresh after the previous day's rain and the world looked as beautiful as a woman after a bath. A gentle breeze carried the sound of chanting and the aroma of a sacrificial fire. Smoke rose over the *ashram*, dancing in the wind and rising to heaven, carrying the offerings of mortal men to the immortals who had no needs. Aswathama reached the place where deer lived in harmony with tigers, and snakes with mice, covered in blood, reeking of murder and sin. Vyasa eyed Drona's son without pausing his chanting of the Vedic *mantras*. Aswathama collapsed near the sacrificial fire. Once the morning *homa* was completed, Vyasa asked his disciples to fetch herbs and water to clean the Brahmin.

When Aswathama awoke, he was lying on a reed mat. For a moment he was confused, uncertain where he was. Vyasa's gentle eyes were looking at him. Aswathama tried to sit upright but the sage gently pushed him down again, saying, "Rest, my son."

"No, I am a sinner. I killed sleeping men. I have committed a great sin," cried Aswathama. "The blood of innocents is on my hands."

"Know that you are neither the slayer nor the slain. You are just an instrument of destiny. Their time had come."

Vyasa's words did not console Aswathama. He touched the gem on his headcloth and wept. His father had been right; the accursed gem had turned him into a sinner. For a fleeting moment, he was amused by the thought. How could a gem be blamed for his folly and sin? He heard someone moving outside his hut; his warrior instincts surfaced and made him search for his sword. It had vanished.

"This is a place made sacred by thought and sacrifice, son. Here, there is no room for weapons. Your weapons have been taken far from the *ashram*," said Vyasa, watching Aswathama.

The Brahmin felt vulnerable without his weapons. When had he ever been without them since his boyhood days? He was tempted to argue that his enemies were at his heels, but one look at Vyasa's dark and lined face silenced the words on his lips. Aswathama drifted into the sleep of the damned. When the sun had baked the earth and was leaving the sky, Aswathama woke to the distant sound of an approaching chariot.

Vyasa sat cross-legged, singing verses in a melodious voice. His chief disciples, Vaishampyana and Jaimini, sat before him, scribbling whatever the sage sang on palm leaves. The verses were not from the Vedas, Aranyakas or Upanishads, but they nevertheless sounded familiar. Then it struck Aswathama that Vyasa was singing the story of the Kuru dynasty. He was singing of Drona, his father, and how he arrived at the palace of Hastinapura with his wife and little son. As Aswathama listened, a sadness beyond words descended on him. How different it could all have been, he thought. Through misty eyes, he looked at the sage and then blinked unbelievingly. Who was sitting near Vyasa, scribbling faster than his two disciples? He had an elephant face and pot belly. Was it Ganesha, son of Mahadeva? The God of wisdom and auspicious beginnings? Aswathama blinked again and the vision disappeared. Perhaps it was only the hallucinations of a tired mind. There were no beginnings left, auspicious or otherwise, for Aswathama. He awaited his end.

It came sooner than he expected. The rumbling of the chariot grew louder, breaking the serene silence of the ashram and scaring the pigeons that were pecking the ground for grain. Four men jumped out of the chariot carrying glistening swords, spiked maces and tall bows. They were messengers of death.

"Worthy men, do not defile this *ashram* with instruments of violence. Step in leaving your thoughts of revenge, malice and wrath at the entrance, along with your dusty shoes," Jaimini,

Vyasa's disciple said with hands folded in *pranam*. The Pandavas hesitated. They could hear Vyasa singing his *slokas* and only the sound of a writing stencil scratching on a palm leaf broke the silence of the *ashram*.

Aswathama looked at Vyasa in desperation. Why had he not intervened to broker peace? What was more important than a Brahmin's life? But there was no break in the sage's flow of words. Aswathama desperately searched for some weapon. He would not go down without a fight. His gaze rested on the long, sharp Kusha grass piled in a corner. It was as sharp as any sword. His father had made him practise with it before he graduated to real swords. He grabbed a pile of Kusha grass and quickly shoved it into the sacrificial fire. Their tips blazed into flames. Aswathama withdrew one burning blade and threw it at Arjuna, piercing his hand like a dart.

"Don't move, or I will finish you all. This is a Brahmastra and I know the secret chants that will make it destroy the world." The words sounded ridiculous even to his own ears.

Arjuna laughed and drew his bowstring taut. Aswathama saw death staring at him from the tip of Arjuna's arrow. He threw another blade of flaming grass.

Vyasa stopped chanting and rose to stand facing Arjuna. Arjuna lowered his bow, ashamed that he had thought of murder in the holy precincts of the *ashram*. He would get the Brahmin once he stepped out. There would be no mercy for the accursed man.

Aswathama fell to his knees before Vyasa, sobbing. The flaming Kusha leaves hissed in protest as they turned to ash.

"Son, go with them. Surrender and accept your punishment with grace. Let the madness end with you. The world has suffered enough. Be your father's son."

The sage's words broke Aswathama. He had never lived up to his father's expectations. Instead, he had brought eternal shame to Drona's name. He felt Bhima's rough hands on his neck and the anger in Arjuna as he pushed him into the chariot and tied him up like a goat for sacrifice. As the chariot left the *ashram* and swayed its way to Kurukshetra, he saw thick curls of smoke blacken the skies. The funeral pyres were burning on the banks of the holy Ganga, following eighteen days of carnage in the name of *dharma*. He wished he had cremated Suyodhana.

***

Dhritarashtra led the procession of mourners from the palace. He did not ride in a chariot or palanquin, instead he walked, his cane tapping a sharp rhythm on the ground. Beside him walked Gandhari, her arm in his. For once, the old King was leading her. Behind them, thousands of women of noble birth walked, vacant looks in their dry eyes. They did not belong to the first wave of mourners, the wives and mothers of the common soldiers whose deaths meant poverty and starvation for their families. These women of noble birth had never ventured out of the palace without being carried in palanquins and guarded by servants; they had never set foot outside except to visit various shrines in temples. For them, life had been a series of days where they competed with each other to parade their resplendent clothes and ornaments. They could not comprehend the reality of the dreary life of widows they were now compelled to lead. With the death of their husbands, they had become inauspicious, ill omens to be shunned on all happy occasions. They were required to shave the beautiful tresses they had spent hours grooming, and shun silk clothes for coarse cotton. They would be given a fistful of rice every day, which they would cook themselves, as an act of charity by their sons or brothers. No bangles would jingle on their slender wrists or soft sandals grace their lotus feet. They were beggars in their own homes. Of course, there was a choice. They could choose to be *satis* by jumping into the funeral pyres of their husbands and be worshipped thereafter. Many preferred to embrace this inhumane custom rather than spend the rest of their lives in the dark corners of their mansions, crouching like spiders, despised by all, praying for release from their misery. They had loved life and lived it with zest. Now they were outcasts.

Sanjaya, the scribe, helped Dhritarashtra and Gandhari to where their dead sons lay. Gandhari did not weep when he identified for her each of her sons by name. The Pandavas walked behind their Uncle and Aunt, unable to speak a word. The horror of what they had done slowly sank into their minds. Dhritarashtra touched each son's face, sometimes smiling as his fingers found the taut firmness of muscles in his dead sons' limbs. When they reached Sushasana, Sanjaya could not speak. Suyodhana's younger brother was lying with his broad chest slashed open, yet the look of defiance had not left his handsome, dissolute face. Finally, Sanjaya whispered, "Sushasana."

"Bhima," Dhritarashtra said in a barely audible voice. The giant Pandava came forward and bowed, saying, "Here I am, Uncle."

The old King leaned forward, gripping the lion-headed gold handle of his cane. He quietly said to the man who had killed most of his sons, "Nephew, to kill an opponent in war is Kshatriya *dharma*, but to drink his blood?"

Bhima shuffled his feet and looked at his brothers for help. He was a man of action, never comfortable with words. He did not know why he had done it, except to please Draupadi, who never treated him like a grown man. When he saw that even Yudhishtra, who knew all about *dharma*, would not come to his aid, he stuttered, "Uncle, I did not drink it. I...I just wet my lips..."

Bhima looked around and saw the horror on people's faces. He wondered what he had said that was so wrong. Dhritarashtra put a hand on Bhima's bowed head and then walked away. The other Pandavas would not even look at him. He had won them the war by killing all the Kauravas with his brute strength, but everyone praised Arjuna. He was happy with a full stomach and a place to sleep, but when Draupadi had not spoken a word of praise for what he had done, it had hurt. He wondered why no one remembered the death of his son, Khatotkacha. For a moment he wondered where Hidumbi was and felt a pang of guilt. Perhaps Yudhishtra would allow him to go and see here once in a while, now that he had won the kingdom. They won the war because *dharma* was on their side. Krishna had said he was just an instrument when he had asked about the fairness of hitting Suyodhana below the waist after the duel that felled his cousin. There was no need to feel any guilt, he assured himself. If only Draupadi would acknowledge his devotion.

"Bhima, you seem to be thinking a lot," Krishna said as he hurried past him.

Bhima smiled amiably at his friend and wondered again why his brothers had looked so horrified when he had said he had only tasted Sushasana's blood, not drunk it. Why couldn't people say clearly what they wanted from him? He saw six guards carrying along a life-sized iron statue on their shoulders, staggering under its weight. Bhima blinked in disbelief. The statute resembled him. Where had Krishna found it?

Dhritarashtra stood near Suyodhana's body. Bhima saw a tear wet the bandage over the eyes of his usually composed Aunt, and felt uneasy. The soldiers quietly placed the statue behind Dhritarashtra, wiping the sweat from their faces. Krishna gestured for silence. Dhritarashtra turned sharply and asked, "Who is it behind me? Is it Bhima?"

Krishna gesticulated towards Bhima to answer. "Yes, Uncle, it is I."

"I am proud of you, my son. You are the only one equal to me in strength of limb. I hold no grudge against you for what you have done. You are a real Kshatriya. Come, hug me. Let me feel your strong hands and shoulders that are as hard as stone."

Dhritarashtra spread his arms wide. The cane fell to the ground. Bhima felt elated. For the first time in his life someone other than the Sutas and Magadhas, who were paid mercenaries, was praising him. He stepped forward but Krishna put out a restraining hand, puzzling him. Krishna gestured to the soldiers to move the statute so that Dhritarashtra could touch it.

Dhritarashtra tightly hugged the iron statue. The old King's hands became taut and the nerves in his neck vibrated with effort as he grit his teeth. With a crack, the statue that had taken six soldiers to carry, snapped like a twig. All around, people watched in stunned silence as the statue fell and Dhritarashtra let out a roar of rage. "Pandu, see who should have been King! I have killed your son with my bare hands. I have killed the one who smashed my Suyodhana's thighs and drank my Sushasana's blood."

Iron pieces had pierced Dhritarashtra's chest and he was bleeding profusely. Sanjaya rushed to wipe away the blood, but Dhritarashtra pushed him away. "I am a Kshatriya, not an old maid. Do not dare to fuss over me. It feels good to have Bhima's blood on me."

Someone smothered a laugh and soon the soldiers, the priests and all those standing around, were laughing at the blind man's plight.

"It was not Bhima you crushed in your powerful arms, Kuru King, but the statue you kept in your room," Krishna said, a smile tugging at his lips.

Dhritarashtra's smile faded and he fell to the ground like a limp rag. He had lost his last gamble to gain respect as a Kshatriya. They had outwitted him, making him appear a spiteful old fool. He touched Suyodhana's cold body and wept.

Bhima went to sit beside the old man who had wanted to crush him to death a few moments before. As usual he could not find any words but he could feel his uncle's pain. As a warrior, he admired the strength in his uncle's arms. He took Dhritarashtra's wrinkled hand in his own and placed it on his head.

"Who is it? Bhima?" Dhritarashtra asked, touching the Pandava's face. Bhima grunted in reply. Dhritarashtra put his hands on Bhima's head and caressed it.

Bhima knew Dhritarashtra was asking for forgiveness. He said in a low voice which only the two of them heard, "It was war, Uncle."

"I know you were just the mace in the hands of others. I hold nothing against you. We are so alike."

Bhima blinked, not understanding what his blind uncle was saying, but somehow it made more sense than whatever Yudhishtra had said.

"Krishna!" Gandhari, who had not spoken a word, nor shed a tear since her arrival on the battlefield, called the Yadava.

Krishna moved forward and bowed. "*Pranam*, Devi Gandhari."

"Have you got the answer to my question? Why was not even my Vikarna spared?"

"Yes, he spoke up against Duryodhana at the dice game, but when war came, he did not side with *dharma*."

"That is your answer, Krishna? Was he not doing his duty, by supporting his elder brother in the war?"

Krishna did not reply. He shuffled his feet restlessly, wishing this meeting would end.

"Yadava, your *dharma* brought misery, war and death to Bharatavarsha. Your *dharma* made brother fight brother, cousin fight cousin; it pitted nephew against uncle and father against son. Can you not hear the wailing of the widows and the weeping of children? The Grand Sire of the Kurus lies on his deathbed of arrows, shot by his favourite great-nephew, Arjuna. You did not have the heart to spare us even one son, not even Vikarna?"

"And what did your *dharma* earn the Pandavas? Their sons are dead and you have gifted them consciences riddled with guilt for killing their kin in the most unfair manner. Will Yudhishtra sleep peacefully and not be haunted by his deceitful words that killed his Guru? Will Bhima ever stop thinking about his Rakshasa son? How miserable you have made Arjuna's life for what he did to Karna! I pity Kunti. My sons are martyrs, but her sons are merely puppets who will be cursed in this life and thereafter. I could have forgiven you everything, even the unfair killing of Suyodhana, if you had shown some kindness to my blind husband. But, for making a man sunk in grief at the death of his sons look a fool; for making his grief and blindness the object of ridicule, you deserve the worst."

Gandhari's face had lost its dignified beauty. No one dared to look at her. Her sharp words pierced the shocked silence as she uttered a terrible curse. "Yadava, for making a mockery of all that is fair and true, for bloodshed and misery, for the violence you have unleashed, for confusing people about *dharma* and *adharma*, I curse you. As a mother who has lost all her sons, for the sake of all mothers who have lost their sons in your war of *dharma*, for the widows who have lost their husbands, and the children who have lost their fathers, I curse you. May your tribe butcher each other to death and cousins turn on each other. May your city be destroyed and buried. Your devotees claim you have come to save the world, but when the time comes, you will not be able to save even your city. You will not be able to save your wives. You will not even be able to save yourself. May you die an inglorious death, hunted like an animal!"

The priests broke into an uproar but Krishna raised his hand to silence them. "Mother, I accept your curse with folded hands. I am not an exception to the laws of *karma*. I claim no divinity other than the realization that divinity rests in me, as it does in all beings. I know it, others do not. The wheel of *dharma* will turn; it is the wheel of time. Like the *ritus*, it too, will change. What is *dharma* today may be considered *adharma* tomorrow. This war would have happened without me, but it would have stretched on, bringing even more misery. I have broken rules, like guards who chase thieves through a busy market place; they break a few wares here and there, topple an innocent vendor's cart and jeopardise his livelihood by chasing the thief. Those who do not know what the thief stole, may conclude that the guards were heartless to the innocent pedestrians they pushed out of their way, or to the vegetable vendor whose cart they upturned in their chase.

Yet, catching the thief is their duty. Without the guards, the city would collapse into chaos. I am the guard who has broken the rules to restore order. I am the Preserver. Time is the King and he may turn against me. I accept it as part of my duty. I am neither angered nor happy. That is the nature of the universe, which I am. But the laws of *karma* bind me too. I accept your curses or your blessings with humility. Mother, forgive me for what I have done. But I would do it all again, without pleasure or pain, for that is my *dharma*."

Gandhari turned away from Krishna. She was past caring what he meant by those words. Her world lay shattered and all hope had died. A lifetime of struggle had led her from disaster to tragedy, making her bitter. She suddenly thought of Bhishma lying on his bed of arrows, waiting to die. She shuddered. He had been responsible for shattering her sheltered life in Gandhara and bringing her here to marry a blind man. How different life would have been had Bhishma's invasion never happened. She would have married a Gandharan noble and lived in the hills. Instead, here she stood in the temple of *dharma*, where her sons lay dead and her husband was mocked at for his blindness. She put a hand on her husband's arm and whispered, "It is time for the cremation. Please give the order."

Dhritarashtra stood up and said to Gandhari, "Just for one day, why not open your blindfold? Do you not wish to see your sons?"

Despite herself, the silk cloth which hid Gandhari's eyes from the horrors of the world became wet with tears. "I do not wish to see them as they are now. Every day I have seen them in my mind's eye, so handsome and strong. Let that picture remain forever with me. Nor do I wish to see anything that is denied to you."

"Gandhari, you are crying? You, the strongest of us all? If you cry, what is left? This day will pass."

Gandhari found solace in her husband's strength, their usual roles reversed. His strong hands on hers were comforting. She leaned on him and wept, not caring who stared at them or who whispered. They were no longer the royal couple but just two sightless people standing there with their dead sons at their feet.

Gandhari regained her composure. She sensed Bhima's presence near them. Hatred threatened to overcome her. Taking a deep breath she said to the man who had killed her sons, "Bhima, go to your wife. Comfort her. She has lost all her sons."

Bhima touched their feet. Dhritarashtra put a hand on his nephew's head and said, "*Ayushman Bhava.*"

Bhima retreated silently, leaving them to deal with their misery. Khatotkacha's face flashed through his mind again. As he walked towards his grieving wife, he saw Aswathama, tied and kneeling on the ground. Nakula and Sahadeva stood with their swords pressed to the Brahmin's neck. Aswathama raised his head to look at Bhima, his eyes devoid of emotion. The gem on his headcloth sparkled shone in the sun. Draupadi had coveted it once. Bhima rushed to Aswathama and kicked his face. When the Brahmin fell over, Bhima pulled away the gem and ran towards Draupadi.

"Draupadi, here it is! This is what you wanted," he said, showing her the glittering gem.

Draupadi looked at him, pity in her eyes. "Give it to Yudhishtra, Bhima. It will look well in his crown."

Bhima did not understand why she sounded so bitter when she had said 'crown'. Then his gaze fell on his slain son's body, being carried by bearers to the cremation pyre. He blinked to hold back his tears. He had never been close to his son but when he saw the finality of everything, the horror of war struck him with overwhelming force. Draupadi began wailing like any common woman; his beautiful Draupadi, who had always loved Arjuna more than any of them but sometimes murmured Karna's name in her sleep; his Draupadi, whom he could never please, no matter what he did, whether it was facing the perils of the forest and hordes of Rakshasas to get her Sougandika flowers just to see her smile, or carrying her on his strong shoulders through the rough forest paths while she laughed and shared secrets with Arjuna walking beside them.

Bhima looked at the gem he had taken from Aswathama. He did not know what to do with it. Yudhishtra was standing with Dhaumya, arguing about something. The bearers were bringing the bodies to cremate. He stood alone on the battlefield. The gem in his hands sparkled, but looked as useless as a pebble. Finally, he walked over to Yudhishtra and thrust it into his hand.

"What is this?" Yudhishtra asked, irritated at being interrupted when he was trying to seek the meaning of so much disaster from Guru Dhaumya.

"Draupadi says it will look good in your crown," Bhima said and walked away.

Suddenly, Dhritarashtra's voice rose over the anguished whispers and wailing. "No! Not as per their caste, not as per their position." The blind King stood leaning on his cane, but his voice was clear with authority.

Sanjaya whispered something in his ear and Dhitarashtra shouted in rage, "This is an order from the King of Hastinapura. There will be no separate cremation rituals as per caste. Death is the final truth, and truth has no caste, you fool! Tell Dhaumya that this blind man will take on all the sin for this decision. Let me rot in *naraka* for cremating together the Brahmins, the Kshatriyas, the Shudras, and countless others who lost their lives in this war. They fought together and they will go to the next world together. I do not care whether they belonged to the Southern Confederate, the Pandavas or Rakshasas. They will all burn with my Suyodhana."

Sanjaya whispered something, bowing in deference. "If they do not have enough firewood, tear down the palace. Cut the silk curtains, take out the soft carpets and feather beds. No one will be buried like swine. All the rituals for the dead will be done as per the Vedas. If you do not know their fathers' names to speak in the ritual of the dead, tell the Brahmins to say my name as the Pitru of the dead, for they are all my sons.

"The King turned to Yudhishtra. "You may have killed my sons and won, Yudhishtra, but I am still the King. I was always the King and I will be till I choose not to be, or till death claims me. If you wish to overrule me, you will have to fight this old man and kill me...""

"King, it will be as you command. Your wishes will be honoured." Yudhishtra bowed to his uncle before Dhaumya could say anything.

As soldiers ran to execute the royal order, Dhaumya burned with anger. If Yudhishtra was going to behave like this in the future, transgressing all caste rules and flouting every tradition, why had they brought down Suyodhana? This country always had nasty surprises. When would they get the perfect King who would follow the *shastras* as he taught them? His work was so incomplete.

The priests waited for the Pandavas near the river. The five pyres were ready. Draupadi leaned on Arjuna as they walked.

"Brother, shall we kill this sinner?" Nakula asked Arjuna.

Before Arjuna could answer, Kunti said in a weary voice "Stop the killing, my sons. Release the Brahmin."

Draupadi stood up straight, the flames in her heart alight once more. "Don't kill Aswathama, Mother?" she said to Kunti in disbelief. "I have lost all my sons and you speak of mercy? Mother, it is different for you, you have not lost any of your sons. You will never understand what a mother feels when she..loses...her sons."

Kunti tried to hug her daughter-in-law, tears choking her throat. "Daughter, they were my grandsons."

"No, don't come near me. You poisoned your sons' minds and created this war. You made me marry your five sons and ruined me."

"Draupadi," Yudhishtra said gently, "we have all lost. You must not speak to our mother in that way. Sahadeva, free the Brahmin."

Sahadeva reluctantly cut the cords that bound Aswathama, but the Brahmin did not move.

"Let her speak, Son. I do understand what it feels like to lose a son."

Arjuna was startled at these words but before he could react, Krishna moved forward. "Yudhishtra, the priests are ready. The cremation must be done before sunset."

"Son, before you light the pyres of my grandsons, you must pray for my dead son, too," Kunti said, gazing into the distance.

"What did you say, Mother?" Arjuna cried, rushing towards Kunti.

Draupadi raised her head and stared at her mother-in-law.

"Son, make arrangements for the funeral of my eldest son, Karna."

An uneasy silence descended.

"Mother, are you saying Karna was your son, the eldest? Then why did we fight this war? If he was your eldest son, Karna should have been King. Suyodhana would not have objected."

"Karna would never have been King, Yudhishtra, for he was born before I was married. I have carried the secret, killing myself with guilt, dying every time someone insulted him for his caste. On the day of your graduation, I recognised him as the son I had abandoned. Only Suyodhana stood up for him. I fainted when I realised my firstborn would always be the enemy of my other five sons. Before the war, I went to beg him to leave Suyodhana, I even offered him the empire. I tried to persuade him to come to our side so that my sons would not fight each other. But, for Karna, no empire was greater than his friendship with Suyodhana. When I saw he would not relent, I begged him for your lives. He promised me he would spare everyone, except Arjuna. He said he would never stray from the path of *dharma*, even if it cost him his life."

"I am ashamed to call you mother," Yudhishtra said in a voice that made Kunti shudder. "Your secret has destroyed so many lives. I would have given up my claim, had I known Karna was your firstborn. The man whose thighs we so shamelessly broke would have given up his claim. Why did we fight the war? Can you not hear the cries of the widows? How will we escape their curses?"

Yudhishtra turned to Krishna, "What *dharma* is this, my Lord? I fought a reluctant war against my kin and killed lakhs of people for a war without meaning. I, who never spoke an untruth in my life, lied for the sake of this *dharma* and killed Guru Drona. At every turn of the war, we acted in a despicable manner. I consoled myself that it was all for the sake of *dharma*. But what *dharma* is this that brings tears, death and poverty to millions? What *dharma* was I fighting for? I do not want this kingdom. I have stolen it from Karna or perhaps from Suyodhana. I have stolen it from my uncle, Dhritarashtra. Bhishma Pitamaha was himself cheated by his father. We Kurus are all *kulaheena*. We have always been and shall always be, mere puppets."

Krishna tried to placate Yudhishtra but his wrath had already turned towards his mother. "All these things happened only because this woman kept her terrible secret to herself. Let no woman be capable of keeping a secret to herself for so long."

"Now I understand why Karna spared our lives. To think we killed our own brother through deceit!" Arjuna cried, anguished. Even as declared foes he had always respected Karna as a warrior. His own final act of dishonour seared his soul. "Krishna, I think of all those I have killed...my Guru, my Pitamaha, my brother. All my doubts about the war before we began battle, have returned to cloud my mind. I was dazzled then by your wisdom, moved by your *Gita*, and so I aimed and shot where you pointed. But now, how will I close my eyes in peaceful sleep, my Lord? I am but a fool, I do not understand *dharma*. It is beyond my grasp. Your wisdom eludes me and only the lamentations of widows assail my ears. Oh, what have I done?"

Aswathama struggled to rise but fell to his knees in pain. Had he heard Yudhishtra right, that Karna was Kunti's eldest son? Karna could have been Emperor, yet he had chosen to die fighting for his friend. He never betrayed Suyodhana. How could he have even imagined that such a thought could live in Karna's great heart? 'Oh Shiva, what have I done? There is no sinner more deserving of punishment than I.'

Aswathama crawled to where Suyodhana lay, finally at peace. "Suyodhana, the kingdom belonged to Karna, yet he died for you. You were right about him." There was no answer. His friend lay in eternal rest, his body as cold as the icy waters of the lake he had hidden in.

Draupadi wailed for her dead sons. No longer was she the wrathful woman who wished to drink the blood of her opponents. She was just a mother, like countless others who had sacrificed their sons in the war that had no winners. The Pandavas surrounded her, shielding her grief from the public gaze. Krishna stood nearby, trying to console them all, but for once his words gave them no solace.

"Father!" A young woman pushed Aswathama away and fell on Suyodhana's still body. Lakshmana, Suyodhana's daughter, had come with Balarama and Bhanumati, but they were too late. Bhanumati stood frozen and dry-eyed, gazing down at the man she had loved more than life itself. 'Why, Suyo? What was it all for in the end? You are gone...Kumara is gone...Hastinapura is gone!' Her heart filled with unutterable pain.

Balarama looked down at the man he had loved as a son. His gaze travelled to the broken thighs and blackened legs. Suddenly, he remembered the youngster who had yearned to wield the mace, to whom he had taught the art of weaponry. He turned to his silent brother. "Krishna, what is this? How could you let Bhima hit below the waist to kill Suyodhana? How could you allow Arjuna to kill an unarmed Karna? And Drona...and Bhishma? Oh my brother, *adharma* is the only victor in this war. So many people dead for no reason."

"*Dharma* has its own reasons, brother."

Balarama bent down, trying to console Bhanumati and Lakshmana. They did not see Aswathama drag himself away. More and more people assembled in a circle to gawk at the grief of the royals. An old man came forward. He looked at the dead Crown Prince and then at the grieving women." Is *dharma* a war fought without ethics and then glorified?" he asked.

"Carvaka, the Maharishi," someone whispered, half afraid, half horrified by the well-known atheist's words.

"Blasphemy! Tie him up!" shouted Dhaumya, enraged. Finally he had found a target he could direct his frustration at and reassert his slipping authority. He looked towards where Krishna stood at a distance, preoccupied with consoling the Pandavas. He had to act before the Yadava turned his attention to the ruckus the atheist was causing. Who could predict what Krishna would say? He might just smile and accept Carvaka's accusations with humility and walk away. Then what would happen to the careful stories Dhaumya had spread? Soldiers had caught hold of Carvaka. Dhaumya ordered, "Burn him alive!"

Oil was poured over Carvaka and lit. The priests chanted *mantras* as they burnt the man who had spent a lifetime tirelessly working among the people. Finally, Krishna turned his head. His eyes widened in horror at what was happening. He rushed to save the Maharishi but stopped short when he heard Dhaumya say, "Carvaka was a Rakshasa, he burned in the fire of Brahmin wrath."

Krishna whipped out his *Sudharshana*, his eyes blazing at the Guru. But Dhaumya whispered in his ear, "Fire purifies. The Rakshasa is lucky, unlike the Nishada you killed with a stone. Carvaka has achieved *moksha*." Ekalavya's face flashed in Krishna's mind. If only he had killed Samba instead of committing such a heinous crime. He stood paralysed, looking down at Carvaka's charred body. The Maharishi's fists were still closed in defiance.

"*Hare Krishna!* The Lord has restored *dharma* and killed evil. Bow to the Lord, *avatar* of Vishnu. Pray to him for your *moksha*," Dhaumya shouted, prostrating himself at Krishna's feet. There were murmurs as the dazed crowd watched the group of priests prostrate themselves at Krishna's feet. Then, one by one, they too, fell to their knees and shouts of '*Hare Krishna*' filled the air.

Aswathama could see the future of his country unfolding before him. He stood up warily. His friend was dead and he had achieved nothing. Their dreams had vanished, leaving only blood and tears.

"Did he mention me before he died, Aswathama?" The Brahmin blinked away his tears, unable to answer Bhanumati. How could he tell her that Suyodhana had spoken only of Karna... and him. "Tell me, Aswathama. Did he say anything at all?" Bhanumati gazed into Aswathama's face, then her shoulders drooped. "No...no... of course, he did not. It was always Karna... only Karna. The day the Suta entered Suyodhana's life, he was cursed." Lakshmana's sobs mingled with those of Draupadi mourning her sons, but Bhanumati stood in silence. She had no more tears left to shed. There was no meaning left to anything.

Aswathama began to laugh. The priests stopped their chanting to stare at him. The Brahmin laughed as if he would die of mirth. "You fools! You poor, stupid fools!" he gasped, clapping his hands to get everyone's attention. "Suyodhana was a fool, Karna was a fool, and all you Pandavas are fools. You, Krishna, you too are a fool, as am I. Can you not see, as clear as the sun in the sky, that all of us have lost? If you have any sense left, think... who has won?"

"He has gone insane," Yudhishtra said in a shocked voice.

Aswathama faced Dhaumya. "Wise man... you are the only wise man here. You have won, Guru. May the likes of you multiply and bless this country." Aswathama bowed and then turned to the others. "Fools, all of us! Think who has won this war of *dharma*... Think and think again until you understand. Oh my poor foolish countrymen!" He stood beside Suyodhana's body and whispered in despair, "Oh, you King of fools!" Aswathama wept.

Yudhishtra walked to the stricken Brahmin and reached out a hand to touch him, but Aswathama turned and fled into the forest. His words and mocking laughter would echo over time.

*****

78 Taste of Dharma

BHANUMATI LEFT THE HASTINAPURA PALACE for her childhood home immediately, once the funeral rites for her husband were over. Gandhari and Kunti's repeated pleas to remain had no effect on her.

Bhishma died on the day *Uttarayana* began. He remained conscious to the end and tried to warn Yudhishtra about Dhritarashtra. He also advised him how to rule without fear or favour. On the day of *Sankranti*, Gangadutta Devavrata Bhishma departed his earthly body. Yudhishtra performed the last rites for the Pitamaha of the Kurus.

On the night of the funeral, Kripa came to pay his respects, risking capture. Yudhishtra asked his forgiveness for the war, surprising the maverick Guru. The usually cynical Kripa broke down at this gesture from a man whose son he had helped murder. Yudhishtra requested Kripa to accept the position of *Rajaguru*, to guide him in the days ahead. Kripa bowed his head in acquiescence, humbled at last.

They found Vidhura sitting heartbroken near Bhishma's funeral pyre. Yudhishtra lifted up his uncle and took him to live in the palace.

While immersing the ashes of Pitamaha in the Ganga on the third day after his death, Yudhishtra was overcome by grief and guilt. In his despair he attempted suicide, but Bhima and Arjuna restrained him. It took Krishna the better part of the day to focus his mind on the nuances of *dharma* and rule according to the tenets of the *smritis*. But the next day dawned with the shocking news that Yudhishtra would not assume the kingship. Instead, he went to see Vrishali, Karna's grieving widow. Yudhishtra asked her for Karna's eight-year-old son, Vrishaketu, the only survivor in the next generation of Kurus, as the next successor. But the priests decreed that Vrishaketu was ineligible as the son of a Suta mother. Heartbroken, Yudhishtra brought Vrishaketu to live with him, instructing Arjuna to turn him into a great warrior, as befitted the son of Karna. By evening, Yudhishtra had announced that Dhritarashtra would remain King.

Later that night, an anguished Gandhari asked Dhritarashtra why he had accepted his nephew's generous offer. How could he rule in peace when Suyodhana was dead? The old King gave a bitter laugh that frightened Gandhari. The nobility he had displayed at their sons' cremation had vanished, in its place stood an angry old man with Shakuni's cunning and Suyodhana's determination.

The next day he called for Dhaumya, to discuss matters of state. The Guru was sceptical when he arrived to see the King. Everything had gone wrong for the Guru after the war. Instead of a furious rebel-like Suyodhana, who it was easy to accuse of *adharma*, he found Yudhishtra, the man he had nurtured and announced as the epitome of *dharma*.

"Guru Dhaumya, I wish to make amends for the conduct of my dead sons. I do not wish their souls to reside in the netherworld because they have been cursed by Brahmins. I wish to give gifts to one lakh Brahmins and would like your advice, Guru."

Dhaumya could not believe what he heard. Why was the King behaving in such an uncharacteristic fashion? Was this the same man who had insisted that all the dead be cremated together, irrespective of caste? Since he was offering gifts, it would be prudent not to refuse. "The light of *dharma* has shone on you, my King. May Sakra and the other Gods in heaven bless you."

The King bent to touch the Brahmin's feet. Then he summoned Yudhishtra and announced his decision, saying it was required to ensure the peace of the departed souls. Yudhishtra merely bowed and walked back to his chamber, depression clouding his mind.

When Dhritarashtra returned to his own chambers, he laughed aloud and told Gandhari, "I will empty the treasury. They have taken me for a fool but I will defeat Krishna and the others at their own game. Only *my* son will rule this land! Your brother Shakuni was a genius, Gandhari. I sometimes hear him speaking to me."

"You will bring disaster again to the Kuru race," Gandhari said grimly. Her husband laughed mirthlessly in answer.

***

Soon, the treasury was empty as thousands of cows, horses and gold coins were gifted to the Brahmins who came from far and wide to accept the hospitality and generosity of the Kurus. When Yudhishtra spoke to the King about the reports of starvation, deaths and rioting in the distant parts of the country, Dhritarashtra called the astrologers and showed great concern when they predicted grim times for Bharatavarsha. He ordered more gifting of cows and wealth to the Brahmins, basking in their praise and secretly laughing at the men he was making fools of. The priests and astrologers advised a *Aswamedha Yagna*. Sacrificing a horse was the only way to ensure prosperity. Dhritarashtra called his son, the merchant Yuyutsu, and asked him to fund the *yagna* as his patriotic duty. Yuyutsu replied that he was ever on the side of *dharma* and advanced a huge sum, accepting the assets of the country as collateral.

The horse ran through the war-ravaged vassal states of Bharatavarsha. The imperial army followed, crushing those who refused to surrender, and taking huge ransoms from the rest. Arjuna led the war of conquest, bringing death and destruction once again to an already devastated country. Vrishaketu accompanied his uncle in his journey of plunder. The King ensured that whatever was brought back was immediately distributed among the Brahmins, so that the treasury remained empty. Hastinapura fell into greater and greater debt to his son Yuyutsu.

Vidhura left for the forest, disgusted. Kripa, the pragmatist, bided his time, amused at the turn of events. His sister, Kripi,

Drona's sorrowing wife, died. It was left to him to perform the rituals, as his nephew Aswathama had long vanished. No one knew where the accursed Brahmin had gone.

Events took a turn for the worse when the sacrificial horse entered the borders of Sindh. Sushala had been grooming her son, Surutha, to take revenge for Jayadratha's death. Despite the best efforts of the many Gurus who came from every corner of Bharata, Surutha had remained a weakling. The relentless pressure from his mother turned him into a nervous boy who worried perpetually about failure. When Arjuna's imperial army entered Sindh, the Pandava wished for a truce. He had no wish to plunder his cousin's land, and Arjuna hoped to convince Sushala to return to Hastinapura with him.

But disaster awaited the great warrior. As the Hastinapura army entered the city gates, Sushala chided the cowering boy for hiding in his room and not fighting Arjuna like a Kshatriya. Surutha reluctantly left his chamber and mounted his horse. He made a dash towards the imperial army as Sushala watched with pride from the palace. Arjuna blew his conch to welcome his nephew. The horse carrying Surutha panicked and the boy was thrown from his saddle. He broke his neck as soon as his body hit the ground, dying instantly. Arjuna had unintentionally brought disaster to his cousin's family again. The warrior retreated with a heavy heart, more confused than ever about the Great War, when he had killed so many of his kin. The *Gita* made less and less sense to him as life unfolded.

Gandhari's words came true. Dhritarashtra's wily manoeuvring had brought disaster to the Kuru clan. Finally, shattering his last dream of only his son sitting on the throne of Hastinapura, a son was born to Uttara, Abhimanyu's young widow. Bitter and angry, he pined for Suyodhana, locked in his chamber. He emerged to create more havoc by emptying the treasury, giving away more and more gifts and performing rituals with pomp. Uttara and Abhimanyu's son, Parikshat, grew up not knowing what the future held.

When Dhritarashtra finally decided to relinquish the throne, he ensured Yudhishtra would not succeed him by naming Parikshat as his heir. He spoke to Yudhishtra at length on the merits of going to the Himalayas in search of inner peace. He also discussed with Dhaumya the virtues of taking Kunti with them when he and Gandhari left for *vanaprastha*. Dhaumya was delighted. He was getting a boy of barely sixteen as King, who could be easily manipulated. He could then impose his rules without check. The priest listened to Dhritarashtra, well aware of the King's inner motivations, and said unctuously that he would attempt to prevail upon Yudhishtra to undertake a pilgrimage for peace and on Kunti Devi to relinquish court life.

When Dhaumya left, Dhritarashtra sat alone for a long time, contemplating the final blow he had dealt Pandu's sons. The revenge he was taking in the name of his slain sons could not have tasted sweeter. Not all battles were fought on the battlefield with swords and maces. When Gandhari tried to talk to him that night, he turned away and feigned sleep.

*****

79 Vanaprastha

KUNTI COULD NOT BELIEVE IT. After all the years of struggle, this was the last thing she had expected. True, the scriptures said that after the birth of a great-grandson, one should proceed to the forest for *vanaprastha*, yet she had lingered. Parikshat was just sixteen. Could her sons not wait till Abhimanyu's son was married?

"Rajamata, the decision is final. I will leave everything to Parikshat and take asylum in the Himalayas. You, too, must leave with Uncle Dhritarashtra and Aunt Gandhari," Yudhishtra stated in a flat tone.

Even if Dhaumya had said so, why did her son have to listen to such talk? Yudhishtra had behaved irrationally ever since he had learned about Karna. He kept saying they could have avoided the war, that she was responsible for it. Would it really have solved all problems? Would Suyodhana have abdicated in favour of Karna? No, it was Draupadi who was responsible for the war, not her. Kunti pulled her sari *pallu* over her head and turned her face away. She did not want her sons to see her tears. Without a word of blessing or farewell, she walked out of the palace, pausing just for a second in the vain hope that one of her sons would call her back.

"Kunti!"

The dowager's heart skipped a beat when she heard the familiar voice. Once it had filled her with hatred and anger, but there was nothing left to like or dislike any more in life. "Gandhari..." Kunti said, turning her head. She hated herself for the tears that sprang to her eyes when she heard the proud Gandhari sobbing. Kunti took Gandhari's hands in her own.

Dhritarashtra stood gazing at the sky with unseeing eyes. He was content. He, whom they considered blind and incompetent, had outlived and outwitted them all. He heard the two women crying and shook his head contemptuously. They had fought so bitterly over so many years, and now stood together weeping over their lost youth, their lost sons and grandsons, and for the life they had forgotten to live in their pursuit for power. They were old and weary now; burdens to the family. In a palace where hundreds lived comfortably, they were three people too many.

"If Suyodhana was alive, would this have happened?" Dhritarashtra asked softly.

The words pierced Kunti's heart like a knife. She felt angered by the insensitive comment of her brother-in-law but she knew it to be true. Without a word she began walking, holding Gandhari's arm. The sound of Dhritarashtra's stick tapping the ground kept rhythm with her own pace. Kunti walked with her head held high. She could hear people commenting on their plight. She could bear that. But the odd words of sympathy from the very people she had always ignored, pierced her heart. She did not raise her eyes to look at the shabby figures that lined the road. They had come to bid farewell to the royals or to gawk, each as their nature dictated. The war had long been over, but the ravages were still apparent to all.

"Maharaja Dhritarashtra!"

"Vidhura, my brother..." Dhritarashtra 's voice was a shadow of itself.

Kunti watched Vidhura touch his brother and sister-in-law's feet respectfully. When he came to her, she turned away saying, "Why have you come, Vidhura? We are beggars now. We have nothing to give and no place to go."

"Devi, have you forgotten that you have my hut in the forest?"

"We will be a burden to you, Vidhura. I am both old and blind," Dhritarashtra sighed.

"Your Highness, it will be an honour. Of course, it does not have the luxuries of the palace, for it is a Shudra home."

"Brother, I see your words have not lost their barb."

"We cannot change the truth, Your Highness. I may be your brother-in-law, but I am still a Shudra. If a Shudra's hut is not beneath your dignity, I would be honoured to have you all come and live with me."

"There is nothing beneath us, Vidhura," Kunti replied wearily. "We are walking on the street as you can see." And this was her reward for a lifetime spent fighting shadow wars, time wasted on intrigue and strategy, just so that her son could ascend the throne of Hastinapura.

"The war of *dharma* has made most of us beggars. Please come and light up my lonely life."

Kunti did not resist when Vidhura led the way. Together, they walked to his forest home – the hut he had taken almost a lifetime to build. The rest of their lives to be spent in the contemplation of truth, immersed in spiritual matters. That was what they thought.

But the wheel of Kunti's *karma* kept turning. Takshaka and his revolutionary army returned to set the forest ablaze. The fire consumed them all. There was no escaping the bitter fruits of *karma*.

*****

80 LONG LIVE THE REVOLUTION

"LONG LIVE THE REVOLUTION!" Takshaka yelled. He and a few followers had set fire to Vidhura's hut early that morning. They had watched Kunti, Dhritarashtra, Gandhari and Vidhura die in agony. The four old people sat huddled together crying for mercy as the fire engulfed them.

Yuyutsu had driven thousands of Nagas and other low-castes out of their miserable farms and slums. These disenfranchised people had nothing more to lose and they swelled the ranks of Takshaka's army. Then why were they so silent when their Great Leader announced such a victory?

"This is a great day for the revolution!" Takshaka shouted again. The people stared silently at the ageing Naga leader. "Long live the revolution!" he cried in a hoarse voice, punching the air. "This is just the beginning..." Takshaka scowled at the people who had started drifting away. "We will seize power from our enemies; we will lynch men like Yuyutsu." No one was listening. "Long live the revolution!" Takshaka screamed again. Silence was the only response. The people had turned away from him as from a leper. 'An entire lifetime spent uplifting these thankless people and this is how they treat me,' thought Takshaka bitterly as he trudged out of the village.

Finally he arrived at the place where Vidhura's hut had stood. Rain had washed away much of the debris, leaving only a few charred bones in the rubble. He had to do something grand to change the history of Bharatavarsha, thought Takshaka. When he had found Vasuki lying dead at the feet of the idol of Shiva in the forest, years before, he had thought the last challenge to his leadership of the Nagas had ended. There was some poetic justice in Vasuki being killed by cobra bite. However, until now, the revolution he had dreamed of had not taken place. He had thought that killing Dhritarashtra, the old King of Hastinapura, would trigger events but not even his own people considered it worth mentioning. He was desperate for something big to happen. He was getting older and time was running out.

An idea started forming in Takshaka's mind. Parikshat! He had heard the Pandavas would soon be leaving for the Himalayas and the boy would be crowned as the new King. A smile spread across his face as he thought about Parikshat. He would not need an army of idiots with him to do what he planned. He could do it alone. He would kill Parikshat and start the ball of revolution rolling again.

***

A messenger dashed through the dry bed of the river Sarswati to reach Hastinapura. He carried terrifying news. In Dwaraka, a civil war had broken out between the followers of Kritavarma and those of Krishna's son, Samba. The entire city was aflame. Hearing the news, the Pandavas rushed to save the city of their dear friend, who had helped them win the great war. They were shocked to find Krishna's wives, protected only by a handful of guards, walking through the desert in a forlorn procession. Krishna was nowhere to be seen. An old Yadava soldier gave Arjuna the message that the Lord had left the safety of his wives and servants in his hands. Yudhishtra, Nakula and Sahadeva rushed towards Dwaraka while Arjuna started his journey back to Hastinapura with the wives of his beloved friend. His heart was heavy with dread.

On the way, they were attacked by the Durjayas and Nagas. Arjuna found he was no match for the combined attack. Durjaya jumped into Arjuna's chariot, grabbed the *Gandiva* and hit Arjuna on the head with the great bow. It broke into two and Arjuna lost consciousness. When he awoke, he was all alone in the desert. His chariot, his horses and all the valuable ornaments he had been wearing had vanished. More shockingly, Krishna's wives were nowhere to be seen. He, the famed warrior, the greatest archer in the world, the man who had vanquished Karna, Drona, Bhishma and countless others in the war, had lost to a minor dacoit and failed to save his friend's wives.

Arjuna began walking towards Dwaraka, not knowing how to break the news to Krishna and his brothers. On the outskirts of Prabhasa, he met Sage Vyasa. Arjuna fell at the seer's feet, sobbing, "Swami, a dacoit defeated me and took away Krishna's wives. If he is an *avatar*, why could he not save his wives? Why was I unable to defeat Durjaya? I have done my duty and lived according to the scriptures. My mind no longer knows what is right and what is wrong."

The sage lifted Arjuna up and said, "Arjuna, time is God, time is *dharma*. Fame, victory, wealth, infamy, defeat, poverty – all are but manifestations of time. *Kalapurusha* acts with *prakruti*, nature, to set the rhythm of life. Just as seasons come and go, like winter follows the rainy season, which follows summer, which follows spring, time brings different stages. Your time as a warrior has ended. Your *karma* will catch up with you. Krishna's time will end soon; even he is not free of his *karma*. *Prakruti* and *Kalapurusha*, the God of Time, together bring change."

Arjuna bowed. Though the sage had not answered his questions directly, he felt less troubled as he walked on towards Dwaraka.

*****

81 FRUITS OF KARMA

WHAT WAS WRONG? WHY WERE THE BIRDS SO SILENT? It had been raining without pause but even the downpour did little to quench the fires raging through Dwaraka. Balarama was a shattered man. Where had the glorious future he had envisaged for his country vanished? Someone screamed from the street, a blood-chilling cry. His people were hacking each other to death and he was powerless to do anything. Samba and his gang of ruffians were busy looting the city and killing people. Even Krishna's wives had not been safe from the violence of his crazed son.

It had all started with a drunken brawl, which had become a daily feature of late. Balarama had tried banning liquor from his kingdom but somehow it found its way back into the city. When Prince Samba himself was an alcoholic, prohibition had little meaning. Drunk or otherwise, Samba had no business insulting visiting savants. The venerable Kritavarma had tried to keep his men under control but it had been hard for soldiers to watch in silence while Samba slapped their respected Commander. When Kritavarma tried to pacify his agitated soldiers, Samba stabbed him in the back. Dwaraka was in flames before the embers of Kritavarma's pyre had died down. A full-fledged civil war raged between Samba's thugs and Kritavarma's loyal soldiers.

Balarama walked through the burning streets trying to talk sense into those he met. The rioters hid their missiles while he passed, but their eyes and ears were shut to his prayers and pleading. They resumed hacking each other to death the moment he turned the corner. Balarama lost all hope.

The sea had receded as far as the eye could see. Balarama stared at the vast expanse of sand. It did not look like the usual ebbing tide. He turned back to look at the palace. It was in flames and smoke rose like a black python, curling to the skies. His mind felt numb. Krishna had gone to the desert, taking all the women in the palace. Despite Krishna's pleading, Balarama's wife Revathi, his daughter Valsala, and his daughter-in-law, Lakshmana, had refused to leave him. They would be in the palace, waiting for him to come back. Oh God, keep them safe, Balarama prayed as he walked along the forlorn beach.

Where had the sea gone? There was no water as far as the eye could see. Fish lay flapping on the sand and in the shallow pools left by the receding waters. Turtles and monster crabs were leaving the safety of the water and crawling back to shore.

Balarama collapsed on the beach. Perhaps he could finally shut out the stench of burning flesh coming from his city and smell the salty air of the sea instead. 'Krishna, where have you run off to with your countless wives when your people need you the most? Gandhari's curse is coming to haunt us, brother. The fruits of your *karma* will not pass us by. You could have saved us with your divine powers. I am just an ordinary man, but I cannot leave those who trust me in their time of despair. Where have you run to, brother?'

Balarama pulled himself to his knees and stared at the bleak sky. What was that sound? There was an almost inaudible hum. He stood up to see. The vast expanse of nothingness in front of him was frightening. He looked at his wrinkled hands and the salt crystals sticking to his palms. He felt as insignificant as a tiny particle of sand. Then he saw it. The sea had receded to grow into a monster in the sky. A wave that almost touched the clouds stood still in the far horizon to the west.

Balarama knew in a flash what was coming towards him and his city. He bent to pick up a fistful of sand and then stood up, his spine erect, his expression calm. The breeze had picked up and his *dhoti* flapped against his thighs. He raised the fistful of sand saying,"I promise to return whenever my compatriots forget the lessons of *ahimsa*. Not as a prophet or *avatar*, but as a man, with all the glorious failings of human nature." The wind howled back, mocking him. "Laugh now, but I will be born here, in your lap, again and again, until the last of my countrymen learn the lessons of peace. I will come back whenever my people forget the lessons of love. Give me no *moksha*; this is my *mukti*, my enlightenment."

The massive wave had grown even higher and was rushing towards Dwaraka like a fearsome beast. The wind paused, as though to listen to Balarama's last words. "I am Ananta. I am Infinite. I am Immortal. I will return when my people need me most." Balarama hurled the fistful of sand into the gigantic wall of water a fraction of a *nimisha* before it hit him.

Like a giant fist, the wave flattened Dwaraka and rushed inland, burying the great city of Balarama under a mountain of water. Not a single Yadava was spared. It was not the end, but the beginning.

*****

82 THE HUNTER

JARA COULD NOT BELIEVE HIS EYES. There he was, his Lord, his beloved. He had spent years trying to catch a glimpse of him and now Krishna sat all alone under the banyan tree. Could he risk moving closer to his Lord? There was no sign of the smile that made him look so divine. It was the face of a man weary of life.

"Prabhu!" Jara called and prostrated himself on the ground.

Krishna opened his eyes. "Jara...come..." he said in a tired voice.

"Prabhu, I am an untouchable." Jara's joy knew no bounds. His Lord was speaking to him; he knew his name.

"Come to me," Krishna said again.

Jara did not think twice. Pushing back the fear that someone might see him, he rushed to his Lord.

"Can you do me a small favour?" Krishna asked with his eyes closed.

Jara smelt the perfume of the wilted garland around Krishna's neck. His heart almost stopped beating in his chest. "Command me Prabhu!" Jara said eagerly. He waited for a wave of joy to wash over him but he felt nothing.

"There is a bow and quiver behind this tree. Can you get it?" Krishna's voice was a whisper.

Jara walked around the tree to fetch them. As his hand touched the weapons, the suspicion that Krishna would ask him to do something he could not do began to gnaw at his mind. He placed the bow and arrows at Krishna's feet and stole a touch of the divine feet before standing back at a respectable distance. His dog sat down near him.

Krishna tested the sharpness of the arrow and smiled at Jara, who bowed again with hands folded. "Jara, take this bow and arrow."

Jara faltered but took the weapons as if they were floral offerings.

"Now move back a few feet or else you will not be able to aim."

"Prabhu, what do you want me to do?"

"Shoot me, Jara. Kill me!"

Jara threw himself at Krishna's feet and began wailing. "You are my God! You are the God of the Universe. How can I commit such a sin?"

"Jara, it is your innocence of heart and faith that sees God in me. I thought I was helping society but I fear I was being used. I have unleashed powers over which I have no control."

"Prabhu, you are never wrong. Whatever you have done, is right."

"I fear my people will fall prey to the wolves who are bound to use my name. To what horrible fate am I leaving my people?"

"Whatever you did was *maya*, your divine play. We are your children and we should be amused by your pranks," Jara said between sobs.

"Gandhari cursed me, saying I would die uncared for, and my people would perish fighting each other. She predicted that our deaths would be quite unlike those of her warrior sons. See how her curse is coming true. I saved my unworthy son from a Nishada and that son has ensured the destruction of the entire Yadava clan. The long arm of my *karma* is catching up with me. Dwaraka is gone. I came to save the world but I could not even save my own people. I hope Arjuna will protect my wives after I am gone."

"Prabhu, don't tell me these things. Do not try to shake my faith. You are our only hope. Don't take that away from us."

"Shoot me, Jara! No one deserves to kill me more than you."

"I cannot, Prabhu. I have never killed even an ant. How can I kill the person I love the most?"

"You must." Krishna looked at Jara with a calm gaze that brought the beggar to his knees in obeisance.

With trembling hands, Jara took the bow. The blind dog growled. Jara hated himself for doing it but he could not refuse his Lord. There was something so pitiful in Krishna's voice that it sliced through Jara's heart. For his Prabhu, he would even commit the sin of killing. Without looking at Krishna, Jara let fly the arrow, just as Ekalavya had taught him to do so long ago. He heard Krishna's cry of pain and closed his eyes in anguish. The bow fell from his hands and he collapsed to the ground.

"Jara..." Krishna's voice was calling him! He was not dead! Jara opened his eyes. To his horror, he saw that the arrow had pierced Krishna's foot instead of his heart. He rushed to take it out but Krishna stopped him. "Let it be, Jara. My time has come."

"Prabhu, I am a sinner. I have killed you."

"No, you have not. In another life I hid behind a tree and shot you when you were fighting your brother. This is the fruit of my action."

"I don't understand, Prabhu."

"In another life, which you do not remember but I do, you were the Great King Bali, of the Vanara race, and I, Rama. My death at your hands was predestined."

"People call me mongoose, not monkey, Prabhu. You are telling me things beyond my understanding."

"You are blessed, Jara, for it is the size of your heart that counts, not your brain."

"Prabhu, don't leave me. Take me with you to your abode, to Vaikunta," Jara begged, taking another arrow from the quiver, ready to plunge it into his own heart.

"No!" The Lord stared into the eyes of his devotee.

"I know I deserve hell. I cannot go to Vaikunta. However, I will die. I cannot live with the guilt of having killed you."

"Jara, Vaikunta does not deserve you. Stay here and spread the message of love. Do not sing about my deeds on earth but about the Krishna you see in your clean heart. Sing about my idyllic childhood and the innocent women who loved me. Sing about those beautiful days and magical nights where the only language was love. Sing about me as the ideal son every mother desires, the ideal lover every woman dreams of."

"You are all that and more, Prabhu. I have heard Brahmins talking about your wonderful *Gita*..."

"Jara, what your heart sings is more important than any divine song. Let them debate about what I said and what I meant. Kali is rising. The Dark Age is dawning, when a few will rule over many and the wicked will win over the righteous. I should have aimed my *chakra* at Dhaumya's throat, but alas, I pointed at Suyodhana's thigh for Bhima to break, and to Bhishma's throat for Arjuna to shoot at. Perhaps the next time I come, I will preach the peace and tranquility of *dharma*, and the refuge of *sanga*, where everyone will be equal and journey together towards enlightenment. If that does not work, I will destroy the whole world as Kalki and start over."

"It is all *maya*, Prabhu."

"Jara, what is done cannot be undone. Be the Krishna I wanted to be. In my death, allow me to be resurrected as the Krishna of love and compassion. Be here as the light of hope in this miserable world ruled by darkness. Dwell in those eyes that look upon misery with compassion."

"Prabhu, do not leave me alone."

"Jara, a new Krishna will appear – one who melts in the love of your heart and who will always live in the minds of people like you."

Jara put Krishna's head on his lap and tried to sing, but sobs choked his voice. Krishna handed his flute to the beggar. Peace descended on him and the smile Jara loved so much returned to his handsome face. Jara watched through his tears as life ebbed away from Krishna's mortal body. Soon night cast her dark mantle over the Lord and his disciple. Jara sat with Krishna's head on his lap until the eastern horizon began to turn saffron. When he saw some priests coming his way, he kissed his Lord on the forehead and ran away.

Deep in the forest, Jara took out Krishna's flute. The birds stopped chirping to listen, as once again Krishna's enchanting music spread like a gentle mist over the world.

*****

83 HEAVEN CALLS

THE PANDAVAS STOOD WATCHING the giant waves pummel the once glorious city of Dwaraka. Only the tall towers of Balarama's palace remained visible. Soon they too would be swallowed by the raging sea.

Yudhishtra turned away, closing his eyes. "I cannot watch this. Why should it end in this way? We have always been told that good wins over evil and that the righteous are blessed with bliss. Why then is reality so different? We fought Suyodhana and killed thousands, thinking it to be our *dharma*. Now, nothing remains. I have felt no peace since the war and now to think of Krishna's city being destroyed like this! Why has good not triumphed over evil? Or were we evil and this is Suyodhana's revenge? Is Aunt Gandhari's curse coming true? I have always followed *dharma*. If what the seers say is true and *dharma* alone wins, then I have lost. Was I then the man of *adharma*, and Suyodhana the man of *dharma*? Or is life beyond the rules laid down by man? Did my story end with Suyodhana's death and my victory in the war? How nice and appropriate it would have been to say that *dharma* had won and Krishna had led us to a victory of *dharma* over *adharma*. Then the bloody battleground of Kurukshetra would have been truly *dharmakshetra*. Now it is just a place where lakhs of people were slain. My life has been wasted in pursuit of pleasing others. I wish I had lived like Suyodhana, listening to my heart."

Yudhishtra felt his head throbbing. Questions, doubts, the evils of reason and logical thought, were driving him insane. Why could Krishna not have stopped the civil war between his own people? If the giant wave had not wiped out the port city of Dwaraka, the civil war between the Yadavas would have done

it. Or was it all a part of a greater plan? No, it had ended as it
was meant to be. Krishna, in his divinity, knew everything. It
was easier to believe that. The most terrible thing was the fate
of Krishna's wives. Fate? How else could he explain Arjuna's
failure to hold out against a robber like Durjaya? In the terrible
battle in the desert, Durjaya had defeated Arjuna and taken away
Krishna's wives. The *avatar*, who came to save the world, could
save neither his city nor his wives. There was no explanation for
these things other than to believe it was all Krishna's *maya*.

Yudhishtra was tired of questions and even more tired of seeking
the answers. The time had come to take a journey, the last one.
He was going to the Himalayas to contemplate on life. It would
not be easy but it would perhaps soothe his burning conscience.
He was tired of ruling. Let Dhaumya and Yuyutsu take care of
it. He was leaving everything to Arjuna's grandson, Parikshat.
The boy was still too young to be King, but his kingship would
just be titular. The real King would be Yuyutsu. Parikshat had
been compelled to marry, despite his young age, to ensure the
next generation.

***

Once they reached Hastinapura, Yudhishtra made arrangements
to ceremoniously anoint Parikshat. On the day after the coronation,
even before the flowers that decorated the streets had wilted,
Yudhishtra, his four brothers, and Draupadi, walked out of the
palace, leaving the throne for which they had killed so many
people. Seeing his brothers and wife dressed in their simple clothes,
Yudhishtra wished yet again that he was going alone on this journey.
But he had not the will to argue with them. Yudhishtra sighed and
began walking, leaving the palace of Hastinapura behind. There
were hundreds of people on the streets to watch their departure.
No one cheered, no one cried. They knew nothing would really
change for them. Dhaumya, the Guru, mumbled some *mantras* in
blessing, and the final parting was made.

Yudhishtra walked quickly, in order to get away. He could hear
the footsteps of his brothers and Draupadi hurrying behind him.

As he left Hastinapura, he paused for one last look at the city he had fought so hard to prise away from his cousin, using every means, fair and foul. He could almost hear Shakuni's laughter and the dice rolling on the floor. No, it had been destiny, fate, *karma*, he told himself. Everything that happened was for the good, Krishna had often said. Another question arose in Yudhishtra's mind. Everything was for the good, but for whose good? The question terrified him. It was time to go to the Himalayas, away from the real world of illusion.

A beggar was sleeping on a dirty pavement strewn with garbage. He looked as content as a baby. Yudhishtra paused. He knew the beggar. What was his name? Ah, Jara. His gaze stopped on the flute the beggar had tucked into his waistband. Krishna's flute! Where had he got it? Jara's body shivered as a cold breeze nudged him. On impulse, Yudhishtra took off the shawl he was wearing and covered Jara. He paused. He did not want the beggar to owe him anything; he would take something from him for the shawl he had covered him with. Yudhishtra picked up Jara's tattered blanket. It stank of poverty. Yudhishtra smiled. His penance was assuming more meaning.

As Yudhishtra moved on, Jara's dog stirred. It was old, blind and close to death. Many people had kicked and tortured it, yet somehow it had managed to stay alive on the streets of Bharatavarsha, thanks to the kindness of a few. Dharma sniffed the air and caught the fast-vanishing smell of his master's blanket. The blind dog began following Yudhishtra on its tottering legs.

***

In the upper reaches of the Himalayas, Draupadi was the first to fall from exhaustion. Her cries for help were like shards of glass in Yudhishtra's heart and he almost lost his will. But he braced himself. It was a test of the self-control and detachment he had cultivated. He knew she had always loved Arjuna the most. But she did not call out the name of any of her five husbands. As her lips turned blue and death came to claim her, she spoke Karna's name. Closing his eyes, Yudhishtra turned away. Bhima lingered, trying to talk to the now-silent Draupadi. His brothers were far ahead. He called to Yudhishtra, but the eldest Pandava did not stop. Bhima felt his heart would break if he stayed to watch his beloved Draupadi die. Suddenly, Hidumbi's face flashed into his mind, the Rakshasi he had not seen since he had left her, who had starved to death, the mother of Khatotkacha, who had died unlamented. Now Draupadi, born a princess, lay dying like the Rakshasi, uncared for, in this snowy wilderness. Death was the great equaliser, it did not differentiate between a princess and an untouchable. Bhima blinked his eyes, hardened his heart and followed his brothers.

Sahadeva slipped into a gorge but Yudhishtra did not stop. He could hear his brother's screams as he fell. The other Pandavas wavered, undecided whether to follow Yudhishtra or try to save the youngest.

"Attachment, even to a brother, is a sin. He is paying for his *karma*," Yudhishtra said and he continued walking. The wind howled through the mountain passes, but its chill was nothing compared to Yudhishtra's words.

He was far ahead with the dog, Dharma, when Nakula fell. Bhima cried out to Yudhishtra to stop, but his steps only became firmer as he climbed higher.

Before Arjuna fell, he asked Yudhishtra, "What was my sin other than to follow Krishna's orders?" His brother had no answer except to say he must have committed some sin in this or a previous life.

When Bhima collapsed starving and dehydrated, Yudhishtra was tempted to stop. This innocent brother had earned the reputation of being a brute for his sake. He had been a fool to do what others had asked him to, crushing those pointed out to him. He had even dishonoured himself by smashing his cousin's thighs for Yudhishtra's sake. If anyone had sinned without attachment, it was Bhima. Yet, he too, had to die a miserable and lonely death in the cold mountains.

***

The air had become thin and Yudhishtra's limbs had become numb from the cold. Snow fell around him and he wheezed as he climbed higher. The tattered blanket was of little use in this weather. Yudhishtra had triumphed in the race of virtue. He was the son of *dharma*. He had survived. If he waited patiently in the snowy heights, the chariot from heaven would surely come to get him. The lack of air was playing tricks with his brain. Had something zoomed past him? Was it a cloud or Indra's chariot come to take him to heaven? Or had he already reached his heavenly abode? Ah, the chariot had indeed come...

"You have come to take me to heaven," Yudhishtra smiled and whispered into the oppressive emptiness around him. "I am coming, but I bring Dharma with me." His voice was swallowed by the snow-clad mountains. "Heaven, receive your servant," he cried and stepped into the abyss, taking the dog with him.

Silence descended as he vanished into the eternal snows. Nothing stirred for some time, then a tiny paw came over the edge of the cliff, then a muzzle. The blind dog hoisted itself up to safety. It sniffed the cold air and then, with renewed vigour, started on its journey back to where it belonged.

*****

84 GRAND ALLIANCE

TAKSHAKA ANNOUNCED THAT HE WAS going to assassinate King Parikshat. To make his act more daring, and to increase his popularity among the Nagas and others struggling under Dhaumya and Yuyutsu's rule, he spread the news and even gave out the time of the assassination. He claimed *dharma* was with the Nagas. Where there was *dharma*, there would be victory.

As the day of reckoning approached, the security around the palace was tightened and guards roamed the streets, arresting suspicious-looking persons. The palace garden was dug to create a lake and the King lived in a hastily-built tower in its centre, from where the guards could see any approaching assassins. Only a group of priests were allowed inside the tower. They entertained the young King with stories of Krishna's childhood. For seven days, they talked of the glory of Vaikunta and the mercy of the Lord.

Unknown to the young King, whose wife was pregnant, a wicked conspiracy had been hatched. Takshaka was desperate for a victory and one of Yuyutsu's men became the mediator between the dreaded Naga and the *Rajaguru* of the Kurus. Parikshat's death would serve as a God-given opportunity for Dhaumya and Yuyutsu to take control of Bharatavarsha. If a boy was born to Parikshat's wife, they could place the infant on the throne instead of Parikshat, who had been spoilt by Kripa. If it was a girl, it would be even better. Soon, it became a necessity to Dhaumya, even more than to Takshaka, that Parikshat die.

Takshaka entered Parikshat's tower on the seventh day, disguised as a Brahmin, walking in with the group of priests who came to tell the King amazing tales about Krishna. At the end of a story that told of Krishna's seven days of miracles, the *saptaha*, Takshaka shot a poisoned arrow into Parikshat's heart. As the innocent King lay writhing in pain, Takshaka was allowed to escape into the forest.

Some days after Parikshat's cremation, his wife bore him a posthumous son. By then, Yuyutsu, the Vaishya son of Dhritarashtra, had been declared the Grand Regent of the Kurus. He allowed the coronation of the baby, Janamejaya, as the last King of the Kurus, but he retained control and ruled Bharatavarsha in consultation with *Rajaguru* Dhaumya. Where the great Kshatriya, Bhishma, had once sat in splendour, the great Vaishya merchant now sat. The wheel of *dharma* had turned full circle.

***

"What shall we do with this senile man?" the priest asked Dhaumya, pointing at Parashurama.

Dhaumya looked at the man who had once held the entire South under his sway. He was muttering Karna's name. "Take him back to the South. At the Krishna River, you know what to do. He will become immortal."

"What do we do with Vrishaketu, Karna's son?"

"His mother is a Suta; he has no right to stay in the palace. Send him to the stables. Let him take the position his grandfather, Athiratha, once held."

The priest bowed and Dhaumya turned away. He had far more important things to attend to than to listen to the mutterings of an old Guru or worry about a Suta. He wondered again where Kripa could be. They had not been able to find him since the day of Parikshat's death. He had vanished. But Dhaumya felt sure that one day he would find the maverick Brahmin. He knocked on the door of his closest ally. "Grand Regent Yuyutsu, we need your help. Now that Takshaka has struck as he promised, he has given us a new opportunity to strike back. The fool had walked into our trap. What is your opinion on a *Sarpasatra*?"

"It would be a good thing," Yuyutsu said, swirling the exotic *soma* in his bejewelled glass.

"Yuyutsu, we can always count on you."

"I am just a Vaishya, Guru. I keep away from politics. I wear the title of Grand Regent like a crown of thorns."

Dhaumya paused, licking his lips. "I am aware you are only doing your duty, but you will have to take on more responsibility now since King Janamejaya is just a baby."

"As you say, Guru, as you say. We must perform the *Sarpasatra* and sacrifice the Nagas. We can eliminate them once and for all."

"Yuyutsu, there will be those who will say that such killings are against *dharma*."

"Oh, we can call them terrorists or Rakshasas. We will brand them as traitors and blasphemers."

"You are a genius, Yuyutsu."

"I am just a merchant, Guru."

"Yes, but a merchant who can see which side will win. That is an invaluable gift."

"It is merely the difference between being an ordinary merchant and a great merchant. I am a true Vaishya, just like you are a true Brahmin, Guru. Together, we can rule this country well. *Dharma* and *commerce* will both be served." Yuyutsu took another sip of his *soma*.

"People need Gods and *avatars*. They want magic."

"We will give them magic. In return, they will give us their freedom. They will get what they deserve and we will get what we want. To the *Sarpasatra*, the grand sacrifice of Nagas." Yuyutsu raised his glass to Dhaumya.

Takshaka had every reason to worry. He had competition.

***

Far to the south, in a small village called Malanada, a little girl stood watching the King's men demolish a temple. Her grandmother's grip on her wrist became painful when the last brick fell. The villagers did not dare to even murmur. The soldiers threw the idols into the lake.

Long after the last idol came to rest on the muddy lake bottom, while cicadas chirped and frogs croaked, the girl asked the old woman why the men had destroyed the village temple. It was raining outside and she lay with her head in her grandmother's lap.

The old lady's eyes glistened with tears. "It means that the only men who cared for us are dead."

The little girl stared up at her without understanding. Her grandmother ruffled her hair. A wild beast howled in the forest beyond the village. "I am afraid, Grandma," the child said, gripping the old woman's sari.

"Pray, my child. It will ease your mind."

"But there are no temples or Gods left to pray to," the girl said, confused.

An image of the Prince who had relished the pot of toddy from her hands flashed through the old woman's mind. She smiled at her grandchild. "Some gods do not need temples or priests. Just pray they will be born again among us, within us."

The rain drummed on the thatch roof. 'I hope she wakes to a better tomorrow,' the old woman sighed.

A cold wind blew in from the lake, extinguished the lamp and plunged them in darkness. The symphony of the rain continued outside, unceasing, uncaring.

***

85 RISE OF KALI

'HAIL KING JANAMEJAYA!' THE CROWD CRIED. The procession was spectacular and the crowd watching it was delirious with joy. Behind the baby King stood Dhaumya, looking regal with his flowing white beard and dazzling ornaments. Behind the Raj Guru stood Yuyutsu, the merchant. He was sponsoring the great expedition. Patriotic songs could be heard from the onlookers.

"Janamejaya's *Sarpasatra!*" Dhaumya raised his staff of office. The crowd roared back.

The boy King blinked, terrified of the commotion. He did not know they were going into battle. He would rather have been playing with his new toy cart.

"The war of *dharma* has not ended," Dhaumya cried, and heads nodded in agreement. "The Nagas have killed King Parikshat. Our brave new King, Janamejaya, a true Kshatriya, has declared war on the Nagas."

All eyes focused on the little boy in admiration. He wanted to cry but Dhaumya had warned him against doing so in public. He was terrified of the old man with the white beard, and of the fat merchant. Abhimanyu's grandson clutched his toy cart and bit his lip to hold back his tears.

"We will not spare a single Naga. This is the *Sarpasatra* of the great King Janamejaya. Hail son of Parikshat, grandson of Abhimanyu, great-grandson of Arjuna!" The crowd roared in approval.

Yuyutsu smiled as he saw many rushing to join the ranks. They were eager to fight for *dharma* and kill as many Nagas as possible.

It was going to be another great war. He had made a large profit on the last one but it had ended too soon, in just eighteen days. A long-drawn conflict spanning the next few decades was what he wanted. Who knew, if his successors were lucky, it could even simmer perpetually. Yuyutsu could almost hear the jingle of gold coins falling into his lap.

"Hail *dharma*!" Yuyutsu cried, and the crowd thundered back. It was all great fun but he reminded himself to execute Takshaka's order for arms and weapons as early as possible. Like any good merchant, he was hedging his bets by supplying men to Dhaumya and arms to Takshaka. He would win, irrespective of which side did. How he loved this *dharma* business! He would build a few temples and throw in two or three charitable houses to feed Brahmins free. Gratitude...a merchant should always be grateful.

Takshaka and his men were hiding in the kingdom of the invalid King Indra. They would drag the Nagas here, have some fun, and terrify anyone who dared question the *varna* system. Yuyutsu knew he would have to ensure Takshaka was freed in the end, so the anger would continue to simmer. He could inflame it whenever he wanted, whenever profits slumped. He had wasted his youth travelling to many countries in search of opportunities when it was right here, staring him in the face. His country was progressing and opportunities abounded. Good times were coming.

***

Around the corner from where the procession was passing, a group of teenagers shouted at a madman prattling to himself. People usually ignored him; they had better things to do than stop and listen to the ramblings of the crazy one. The man tried to shake off the kids following him by shouting at them, but it only made them laugh louder. They knew the man was harmless and never hurt anyone, especially children. He still had the broad shoulders and long arms of the warrior he had once been. Perhaps he had even fought in some war. Nobody knew his history and nobody cared. He was one of the many milling around in the dusty streets of Hastinapura. He was a madman who did not strike back even when they pelted him with stones. Now just to entertain themselves, the teenagers pretended they were interested in hearing what he had to say. It would be fun to laugh at his ramblings.

"Fools!" the man said, addressing no one in particular. The teenagers snickered. "Where are you running off to, you boys? Listen to me, for I have a story to tell. Do not go away. Let me tell you the story of a few friends who wanted to change the world. One was a Brahmin, one a Suta, another a Nishada; but the best among them was a Kshatriya."

The teenagers laughed. They knew the best part was coming.

"Listen to the story of Suyodhana, the best among men." The crazy one ignored the laughter and continued, "Hear the story of Karna, the man who gave away everything, even his life, so the world would know the true meaning of friendship. Hear the story of the Nishada whose thumb was cut off so he would never challenge the Kshatriyas who considered themselves to be the greatest by accident of birth. Hear the story of Ekalavya, the Nishada who challenged the Gods and his destiny, only to give his life for a woman's honour. Hear the story of Suyodhana, who staked his inheritance and empire for what he believed to be true, who stood by his friends and fought for all of you. Hear the story of the man who looked into the eyes of Krishna and said that he was wrong, who did not even flinch when his thighs were broken. And if you have time, hear my story – of a poor Brahmin who defied his father and led his men to the cold heights of Gandhara for the sake of his country; hear about Aswathama's life."

A stone hit Aswathama's forehead and the teenagers howled in merriment. Wiping away the trickle of blood with the back of his hand, he said, "Before throwing stones, read what the great sage Vedavyasa has written. Read it before they take away your ability to read at all. Read your scriptures before they change everything, keeping you ignorant. Why did the great sage call his epic 'Jaya'? Could there be anything more

ironic than calling it 'Victory'? Who won the Great War – the
great, bloody, Mahabharata war? Did the Pandavas win? If
they did, why did they leave everything to a merchant and a
priest and run away? Did Krishna and his *dharma* win? If so,
where is Dwaraka, today? Gone! So who won? Shakuni, the
Mlecha? Read again what the great sage has written. Fools!
Think who won... Was it *dharma* or Dhaumya? Was it Krishna
or Yuyutsu? What has become of Krishna's people? The
Yadavas butchered each other to death but he could not save
them. Neither could the great warrior Arjuna save Krishna's
wives from the marauding tribes of Durjaya. Read *Jaya* again,
you dirty urchins, before they take the last book from you.
Who won the war? Ask yourself."

The teenagers looked at each other. Aswathama kicked over an
overflowing garbage bin and tried to balance himself on it, drawing
more laughter. "Do not laugh, you fools! For I am Aswathama,
the Brahmin cursed with immortality. I am cursed, for I murdered
the Pandavas' five sons in their sleep. It was a sin graver than
annihilating Khandivaprastha. Those who died in Khandiva do not
matter, for they were just some Nagas, terrorists and untouchables...
some beasts and birds. Trapping Nishada children and their mother
in a house and setting them on fire is not *adharma*. Lying to your
Guru and cutting his throat when he collapses, believing your lie, is
of course *dharma*! Oh, what some men sacrifice for *dharma*!"

Aswathama clapped his hands thrice and called out to the
pedestrians hurrying past. Some looked at him, fear in their
eyes, others with contempt. "Ask whether it was right to bring
Shikandi, who was neither a man nor a woman, to face Bhishma.
Ask whether a great warrior like Arjuna, using an eunuch as a
shield and to shoot Bhishma, was *dharma*? And what is the answer
you get? 'Oh, but the fall of Bhishma was necessary for *dharma*
to win.' Tchaw! The war was not necessary. We had blown the
cover of the Pandavas during the last days of their exile. But then,
dharma for you means changing the calendar itself to win."

One of the boys laughed. Aswathama glared at him. "Don't
grin like a monkey, fool! Your future is doomed. Your country is

ruined. You dare laugh at the fall of Suyodhana and all the noble men like Bhishma, my father, Karna, and the others who fought for him? Read *Jaya* to know how Karna rejected the temptation to become Emperor and instead chose to stand by the man who had given him everything when he had nothing. Read how Karna was trapped by own nobility, how impossible promises were extracted from him; know how he was shot while extracting the wheel of his chariot that was stuck in the mud. Know that Arjuna did not keep his word, as any honourable warrior would have done, when he failed to kill Jayadratha before sunset, hiding behind the lame excuse that the sunset had been *maya*, an illusion created by an *avatar*. Sleep in your beds peacefully by all means, if your conscience still allows you to do so, you lucky devils."

There were murmurings among the sparse crowd of men and boys who had gathered to hear Aswathama.

"I am ashamed for what we did to Draupadi. We deserved punishment for what we did to a helpless woman. We were drunk with power and victory and we tried to strip her in the Sabha. We did an evil thing that day. But does one act make us evil for all time? It is said that noble men like Bhishma and Drona were killed for staying silent when a woman was being dishonoured. But then why does no one talk of Lakshmana and her shame? Was she not a woman, too? Why does no one speak of the Nishada woman who was burned with her children? Was she not a woman? Some blame Draupadi's mocking of Suyodhana and Karna for the war. How convenient to put the blame for the madness of men on a woman! Why do you think the war was only about the Kauravas? Let us talk about Khatotkacha, the Rakshasa son of Bhima, of Iravan. He was Arjuna's son, but because he was of low caste, he was sacrificed. What if Iravan had proved himself a greater warrior than all the Kshatriyas? Then what would have happened to your ideas about caste? It was better to sacrifice the boy before the war started. Does all this sound like *dharma* to you?"

The crowd was dangerously silent.

"The next time you hear the immortal story of Bharata, pause to think whether it was *dharma* to break the thighs of a man who had always played fair, a man who could have easily chosen any of the Pandava brothers to duel with instead of Bhima, but he chose fairly even when he knew everything was lost."

"Stop all this nonsensical talk!" someone shouted at Aswathama.

"You can shut my mouth but can you shut my thoughts or the doubts that confuse anyone with a fair mind? The next time you read the great story of our country, read about the sinner, Aswathama. What I did was ignoble, I should never have killed the Pandava boys. I have been cursed with a conscience. I would have escaped my fate had I too had a friend who could justify my black deed with scriptures. Alas, my friend was a mere mortal, an ignorant and evil man who knew no *dharma*. Even when he was dying, he did not condone my act. He said I should have fought fair and won or died as he was doing. I carry his sadness as a curse on my head just as I carry my conscience. I have no cloak of *dharma* to hide my shame. My body is full of sores but I don't even deserve death."

"Kill this sinner! Kill this liar!" shouted a few priests who had assembled, drawn by rumours about a tirade against *dharma*.

"Liar? I am the liar? Ha! The next time you read Vyasa's great epic, read with your eyes open. I shall be there with you whenever the story is told. I will be standing near you, whispering to your conscience to read between the lines. When you watch plays glorifying the Pandavas and their *dharma*, you will feel the gnawing of doubt in your mind. Know that I am that doubt. When you pray, you will see the lamp flicker; I am the breeze that makes it dance. Do not say I have not warned you. As long as the great epic is read, Aswathama will live, the Brahmin cursed with immortality will be there, looking over your shoulder. You will not see me, but I will possess your mind. I am everlasting doubt as well as the eternal logic of the reasoning mind. I am Aswathama, the cursed."

The crowd stood still, shocked by the madman's words. Insanity was a dangerous thing. The first stone caught Aswathama on the bridge of his nose. He gasped as the next one hit his mouth, shattering a tooth. Before he could run for cover a hailstorm of stones hit him and the crowd rushed at him to stomp him out. They beat him with sticks and stones, anything they could lay their hands on. Still he refused to die, Aswathama, the immortal. He was saved by the sound of a conch. His tormentors turned towards the sound and a cheer rose when they saw the golden chariot with the baby King and the army marching behind.

As the procession moved on, Yuyutsu saw a Brahmin lying near an overturned garbage bin, bleeding. 'Must be drunk,' he thought. He turned his attention back to building up the enthusiasm of the crowd. The juggernaut rolled on. Nevertheless, the sacred thread across the man's shoulder was an insult to *dharma* and he ordered a guard to break it. The man rushed over to the prone figure and tugged at the sacred thread until it snapped. Then he hurried back, almost stumbling over a dog that had somehow slipped through the procession. It yelped at him but a kick in its ribs was enough to scare it away.

Yuyutsu looked at the fallen Brahmin one last time and was surprised to see an untouchable sitting near him, a dog with him. 'Good,' he thought, the sinner was going to die with an untouchable polluting him at the time of death. God was meting out deserving punishment to all sinners. God was great.

***

Jara tried to wake Aswathama. "Swami, Swami," he cried as he fumbled for the pot of water he carried. It was dry. He was afraid to touch the Brahmin, the loss of his sacred thread notwithstanding. How could he wake the Brahmin without touching him? Jara remembered the flute Krishna had given him and he pulled it out of his bundle. He nudged the prone figure on the ground with it and slowly, Aswathama stirred. The dog wagged his tail.

"Swami, wake up. Open your eyes. Look... my Dharma is back."

Aswathama's eyes flared with anger when he heard *dharma* mentioned. With surprising swiftness he sat up, a scowl on his bleeding face. When he understood the beggar had meant his blind dog, Aswathama's face finally broke into a smile. The procession was thundering past near them, raising clouds of dust to the heavens. He coughed, vomited blood, and then fell back. Jara did not hesitate, he lifted the Brahmin, trying to drag him away from the road, away from the march of *dharma*. Jara knew the Brahmin had not fainted because of the injuries he had received during the lynching; he had seen the look of hunger in Aswathama's eyes. No one knew more about hunger than he did. Jara fumbled with his bundle and brought out the cooked rice he had collected the previous day. He spread a banana leaf on the dusty pavement and then shook Aswathama awake.

The procession had gathered speed and the slogans were deafening, shaking the ground. Thunder sounded, cracking open the secret vault of heaven. Rain lashed the streets. The crowd roared in excitement. It was a sign from the Gods that this was a righteous war. The wind howled. The last chariot passed the fallen Brahmin and the beggar, splashing dirty water over them both. Dharma stood up, thereby preventing the little food they had from getting soiled. When the procession had become a dot in the distance, the dog shook himself dry and then went to sit beside its master, eager to be fed.

"Krishna," Jara prayed and Aswathama's eyes flashed with anger. He tried to get up but fell back weakly. "Krishna, you have come before us as food, as this Brahmin. You are love. You are compassion. I offer this rice to you. *Itham na mama.*"

The untouchable began to feed the Brahmin as Dharma the blind dog waited patiently.

Ithi mama Mahabharata Katha

Sambhavami Yuge Yuge

This is the story of my Great Bharata.

It happens in all ages.

*****

Afterword
DHARMA ~
A SUBTLE CONCEPT

THERE IS NOTHING IN INDIA that has sparked more debate than the concept of *dharma*. It is a word that stands alone. Before the Bhakti movement rewrote the *Ramayana* and *Mahabharata* as stories where *dharma* wins over *adharma*, the very concept of *dharma* used to be debated vigorously. The *Mahabharata* is an example of each side believing they had *dharma* with them and they fought for that. Kurukshetra is thus considered to be *dharmakshetra*, a place where two definitions of *dharma* faced each other.

Duryodhana famously asks Krishna that if following *swadharma* or *dharma* as defined by one's heart is the greatest *dharma*, was he not doing his Kshatriya duty by trying to protect his inheritance? The conventional argument from traditionalists is that *dharma* is based on the Vedas. Krishna answers Arjuna's scepticism about *dharma* and *adharma* by saying that the scriptures are the authority for deciding this. Narada, the divine saint, also says to Yudhishtra that *dharma* has three cornerstones or *thrayi mula*: the Rig, Yajur and Sama Vedas. The Vedas are the roots of *dharma*. However, the counter argument to this is given in the *Mahabharata* itself, when Bhishma says *dharma* is the root of the Vedas. Once we accept this argument, then *dharma* becomes a dynamic concept that evolves over time, depending on the needs of the people. So the *dharma* of the Vedas served the needs of the people of the time, but the *dharma* of today may be different. Krishna also says that *dharma* changes with time and place, though he is quick to add that the scriptures are the final authority.

In the *Anusashasana Parva*, Bhishma says to Yudhishtra that only Kala, the Lord of Death (or Yama, the God of Yamam, a measure of time), can decide what *dharma* or *adharma* is, mere mortals cannot understand it. It is Time that decides how humans are punished or rewarded for their *karma* or actions. Everything happens due to some cause. Only time can reveal whether one has acted as per *dharma* or not. This law, though logical, offers no solace to anyone. Every action becomes a shot in the dark as we cannot tell what the results will be. Krishna offers an antidote to this confusion by advising *nishkama karma* or acting without worrying over the outcome, as acts of devotion. This serves those who are confused about what action to take when faced with a dilemma, but it can be a dangerous tool in the hands of others. In British India, thugs often argued that they were dacoits by *jati* and looting was their *kula dharma*. All wars and violence can be justified using the argument of *dharma*.

In contrast, Balarama says *ahimsa* is the greatest *dharma*. His argument becomes relevant when we consider the lives of the women in the *Mahabharata*. It's a man's world, where women get abducted, pawned, stripped, widowed and raped. All the Pandava and Kaurava progeny are male, except for the sole exception of Dushala, as are Karna's children. How can one account for this improbable imbalance? It is ironic that except in the case of Draupadi, no other acts of violence against women are debated within the fine definitions of *dharma*. The Nishada woman and her children are quickly forgotten, the thousands of women and children who die in Khandivaprastha are never mentioned again. Even the fate of Gandhari, abducted and forcibly married to a blind man, is not spoken of except to praise her for being a *pativrata* who denied herself the sight her husband did not have. When Krishna's wives are abducted by dacoits or when Sushala loses her only son, it is they who suffer. Some things never seem to change, even in the twenty-first century.

The counter argument to Balarama's *ahimsa* is: can a ruler be non-violent? How can he then chastise wrongdoers? Another argument which frequently surfaces is the breaking of *dharma* when faced with danger, called *apad dharma*. When one needs to protect one's kin, is it not right to use violence? The epic keeps throwing up questions and from every answer more questions sprout up. There is no absolute right or wrong in Vyasa's *Mahabharata*, echoed in Shakespeare's line from Hamlet: *There is nothing either good or bad but thinking makes it so.*

Yudhishtra dealt with this confusion by following tradition, by acting in the time-tested way. He says to Drupada that he does not understand *dharma* as it is very subtle. He chooses to follow the path of his forefathers and strives to speak only the truth. It is thus natural that such a staunch traditionalist comes into conflict with Suyodhana, who wanted to change everything. He was willing to make a Suta a king, befriend a Nishada, and allow a Brahmin to wield the bow. Briefly, he makes Aswathama King of Uttara Panchala. It is evident he follows his heart. He is a creature of passion, not a man of logic. He admits this many times in the epic. Suyodhana is a man of extremes; he loves his friends unconditionally and hates his enemies with heartfelt passion. For such a man there is no confusion about what is right or wrong. His heart guides him.

Confusion comes to those like Arjuna, Karna, Aswathama and Yudhishtra, who struggle with their conscience. Was it not Karna's *dharma* to protect his friend and refuse to give his word not to kill all the Pandavas to Kunti? On the other hand, was it not Karna's *dharma* to side with his brothers when Kunti revealed he was her son? And Yudhishtra says that had he known Karna was his brother he would not have claimed the throne. The enigmatic question thus remains, had Suyodhana known Karna was his eldest cousin, how would he have reacted? Krishna rejects the claim that Karna was never a Pandava, as he was born before Kunti's marriage, thus making Karna's sacrifice meaningless. Moreover, was Aswathama right in killing Draupadi's sons in revenge? Was he right in trying to prove his loyalty to his friend by committing such a condemnable act? Was he or the Pandavas who killed the Nishadas, *dharmic*? Additionally, Yuyutsu, Dhritarashtra's Vaishya son's emergence as the ultimate victor is yet another irony of the epic.

The greatness of Vedavyasa's work is in the questions it evokes every time we read it, rather than in the answers given by preachers who reduce it to a simplistic tale of good versus evil. Such explanations do great injustice to the genius of Vyasa. I believe such explanations are the result of non-Indian influences on our psyche, the after-product of a wounded civilisation. It may be noted that the rise of the Bhakti movement coincided with the Islamic conquest of India. The open-minded rationalism of Indian thought went into hiding and blind devotion took its place. The blurred lines of *dharma* and *adharma* and the speculative philosophy that thrived in debate and delighted generations of a confident civilisation, slowly gave way to absolute definitions of good and evil, which are almost a Semitic concept and the hallmark of religious beliefs in the Middle East.

Ironically, it is in the villages of India that the willingness to think from all angles and points of view still thrives. In the course of my travels to remote villages, I once met a *sadhu* who refused to tell me his name. I met him near the Gokarna temple and we had an interesting chat. When he asked me what I did, I said I reinterpreted the epics from the loser's point of view. He laughed and asked me why I wrote. He also asked who the loser was in any of our *Puranas* and who the winner? When I said that Ravana and Duryodhana were the losers, he laughed and asked me to read the epics again and again until I understood them. There were no victors or vanquished, just people and their lives, he said. I mentioned that I felt an empathy for the vanquished and wished to present their side as well.

In reply, true to the best traditions of our country, he told me an old Kannada folktale. It was about Barbarika, the son of Khatotkacha, who comes to fight alongside the Pandavas against the Kauravas. He was a formidable warrior and could win the war single handedly, but he has a great weakness. He was so compassionate that he could not stand to see anyone defeated. He was always the champion of the underdog. He supported the Pandavas because the Kauravas had more men fighting on their side; the Pandavas were the underdogs when the war began. But with his help, the Pandavas start winning against the Kauravas.

When Barbarika sees the fallen faces of the Kauravas, he feels pity and changes sides to fight against the Pandavas.

Then it is the Pandavas' turn to lose. Barbarika feels pity stir for the Pandavas and changes sides once again. This continues, causing frustration on both sides. The war could never end if Barbarika kept supporting the losing side. Fed up with Barbarika's actions, the warriors approached Krishna to solve the impasse. Krishna called Barbarika and asked him why he was acting in such a bizarre fashion. Barbarika says he is unable to see anyone vanquished. Krishna takes him to a higher plane and shows him the larger picture. From this vantage point, Barbarika sees that both sides are right and both sides wrong, that both are victors and vanquished, *dharmic* and *adharmic*. Confused, he asks Krishna what he is then fighting for. Krishna answers that what he sees is *maya*, the illusion of life, at once fascinating and confusing. No one can decide what is *dharma* and what is *adharma*, who is the victor and who is the vanquished. Mortals are but tiny specks in the vast universe, blips in the great ocean of time. Disgusted, Barbarika asks Krishna to behead him and raise his head on a pole so that he can watch the fools who kill each other and laugh at them and at the illusion of life. Krishna asks Bhima to do so. Barbarika's head thus witnesses the rest of the war, laughing ceaselessly at the folly of the men on both sides.

The *sadhu* smiled at me and said, "Son, if those who passionately argue for one side or another, care to pause in their arguments, they will hear Barbarika laughing and mocking them."

It was a revelation to me, another of the wonderful stories that never fail to surprise me. The fact that the story was very similar to that of Iravan, which is another popular tale in Tamil Nadu and Kerala, may be incidental. In Tamil Nadu, the cult of Iravan is the most prominent of all village cults. The idol of Iravan, locally known as Aravan, often 10 to 15 feet tall, stands guard at the entrance of many Tamil villages. People unfamiliar with Tamil culture often mistake the statue of Aravan for Ravana. Aravan is considered a guardian God, the God of Koothu, the village dance form, and the protector of women. He is also a God of harvest. In some parts of Tamil Nadu, he is associated with transgenders.

In Kerala, Iravan is linked to death and he is the bird locally known as Kalankozhi (Mottled Wood Owl). Kalankozhi or the bird of death, is considered to be none other than the son of Arjuna, who was sacrificed before the great Mahabharata war. The bird is a harbinger of death. I still remember lying trembling in my bed, listening to the haunting cries of the Kalankozhi, afraid that the morning would bring news of some death. Now the groves that nestled such birds have vanished, swept away by rural development and a generation disdainful of tradition. Along with the sacred groves and the birds of death, the water too has vanished from the village wells. Although the state receives more rain than most parts of the world, drought is a harsh reality now. In modern India, where there are only absolutes of right and wrong, and everything has become 'us versus them' rather than the accommodative culture of our ancestors, the old traditions are slowly vanishing with the Kalankozhi.

But everyone and every faith has a place in the great mosaic of our culture. Nothing is absolutely right or wrong. We may perhaps need the head of Barbarika to see the bigger picture. My attempt here has been to show that another side exists to our stories, as important and as relevant as the conventional tale. Stories, I believe, should be about questions, never about answers. Every answer should give birth to a hundred questions. That is the mark of a confident civilisation and that is how we, the sons and daughters of Bharatavarsha, have always celebrated our stories – with debate, argument and counterargument. Certainly not by accepting without dissent.

Perhaps Barbarika is laughing at all of us. Let us celebrate that laughter.

*****

Suggested Reading

1. Sarva Daman Singh. *Polyandry in Ancient India.* Motilal Banarsidass New Delhi, 1988

2. John Dowson. *Classical History of Hindu Myth and Religion.* Munshiram Manoharlal Publishers, New Delhi, 2000

3. A.L. Ahuja. *Women in Indian Mythology.* Rupa & Co. New Delhi, 2011

4. Ram Sharan Sharma. *Aspects of Political Ideas and Institutions in Ancient India.* Motilal Banarsidass, New Delhi, 2012

5. Vettam Mani. *Puranic Encyclopedia.* Motilal Banarsidass, New Delhi 2010; Malayalam ed: DC Books, Kottayam 2013 [Ed: Perhaps the most comprehensive book on various Puranic characters; written as short notes, alphabetically arranged. A good reference source for anyone interested in Hindu mythology.]

6. The Mahabharata of Krishna Dwaipayana Vyasa- Translated from original Sanskrit to English by Kisari Mohan Ganguly, (1883-1896), e book converted by sacred-books.com

7. 18 Puranas, unabridged version, DC books, 2014 (a collection of 18 Puranas in Malayalam, published by DC books, Kottayam)

*****

SELECT GLOSSARY

Aarti – Worship with lamps

Acharya – Guru, teacher

Achuyuta – Another name for Krishna

Aghoris – Ascetic worshippers of Shiva who do not believe in caste or the taboos of Hinduism; known for extreme and even outlandish penance

Ajaya – Unconquerable

Andha – Blind

Anga – Ancient Indian kingdom; present-day Eastern Bihar and parts of Bengal

Angavasthra – Shawl worn by nobles

Ashwini Twins – Gods of sunrise and sunset

Astra – Arrow/shaft; described by the epics as having divine powers

Asura – Hindu mythology portrays Asuras as demons of darkness – the antithesis to Devas, the Gods; here, they are one among many tribes

Atharva – The fourth *Veda*, which speaks of magic, spells, etc.

Atma – Soul

Avarna – A person who does not belong to the first three castes; literally one without colour (*varna*); opposite of *savarna* (person with a good colour)

Ayurveda – Ancient Indian system of medicine

Bindi – Red dot worn on the forehead by Hindu women

Brahmacharya – Self-imposed vow of celibacy; a period of life as a student when a man observes *brahmacharya*; to seek or follow God

Brahman – The Supreme Power responsible for Creation and the Universe

Brahmin – The highest Hindu caste and *varna* – Priests and scholars; Hindu society was divided into four *varnas* (refer Varna for details), and further subdivided into *jati*s (castes); these varied from region to region (eg. a Brahmin from Kashmir in the north and one from Andhra in the south, belonged to the same *varna* but did not intermarry as they belonged to different castes)

Chaitra – Indian calendar month when spring begins

Chandagyo – One of the most important of the *Upanishad*s

Chandalas – One of the lowest of the Untouchable castes; keepers of graveyards; those who carried the dead

Chaturvarnas – The four *varna*s (refer Varna for details)

Chenda – A south Indian drum beaten with a curved stick; known even today as the *Asura Vadhya* or 'musical instrument of the Asuras' and used during festivals in Kerala and parts of south Karnataka and Tamil Nadu

Chera – Ancient kingdom in south India, with Muzaris as its capital

Chettis – Merchant caste of south India (corruption of the term *shresti*)

Crore – One hundred lakhs; ten million

Dakshinajanapada – Land south of the Vindhyas; south India

Darshan – Literally 'view'; it was customary for Indian monarchs to appear at a balcony and hear petitions from their subjects

Dasa – Servant or slave

Dasi – Female servant/slave

Devi - a polite way to address a woman. Also means goddess. 'Bhavathi' was a later day usage.

Dhanurveda – Science of arms and weapon-making

Dharma – Rough translation: duty, righteousness etc; but *dharma* encompasses more – it is the code of life; antonym: *adharma*

Dharmaveera – Warrior or hero of *dharma*

Dharmayudha – Ancient code of battle

Dhoti – Traditional lower garment for men, made from an unstitched length of cloth; also worn in different styles by lower-class women in ancient India

Gandhara – Present-day Kandahar in Afghanistan

Gandharvas – Singers in the courts of the Gods; considered to be supernatural beings pining for love; messengers between the Gods and men; here, they are simply another aboriginal tribe

Ganga – Ganges

Gangotri – Glacier from where the Ganga originates

Gayatri – Sacred Hindu *mantra* from the *Rig Veda*; when the caste system was at its zenith, many texts forbade Shudras from even listening to it; some texts advocated pouring molten lead into the ears of Shudras who heard the *Gayatri* even accidently – though it is doubtful if it was really practised

Ghat – A broad flight of steps leading down to a river

Gobar – Cow dung

Har Har Mahadev – Hail Shiva, the Greatest God

Hari – Another name for Lord Vishnu

Hastinapura – City of Elephants, capital of the Kuru kingdom

Indra – King of the Gods; used here as a generic name of the tribe who are the nominal rulers of the Devas; Indra, their last King, lives in penury; he is also the biological father of Arjuna

Indraprastha – Ancient capital of the Pandavas; present-day New Delhi

Jambu Dweepa – Ancient Indian name for Asia

Jaya – Victory

Kala – Time; also God of Time and Death, commonly known as Yama (derived from the unit for measuring time – *yamam*)

Kalaripayattu – Traditional martial art form of Kerala

Kalinga – Present-day Odisha (roughly)

Kaliya Mardana – Kaliya: a poisonous snake (*naga*), in the original *Mahabharata*; Mardana: punishment, suppression etc. Kaliya Mardana is one telling of the legend of Lord Krishna punishing the *naga* for his evil deeds.

Kamarupa – Ancient name for present-day Assam

Karma – Action or deed

Kashi – Another name for the holy city of Varanasi or Benaras

Kauravas – Scions of the Kuru dynasty

Khandiva – Present-day Delhi

Kingara – Servants; soldier-slaves

Kinnaras – In Hindu mythology, these are celestial musicians, half-horse and half-human; ere, they are treated as just another tribe

Kirata – A wild tribe

Kshatriyas – The warrior caste; often kings and rulers

Kuravan, Malayans, Vannans, Velans – Tribes from the Western Ghats (Sahyas) of India. They were Priests before the Brahmins became prominent; even today, many rituals in the Malabar region are conducted by these people

Kurta – Indian shirt

Lakh – One hundred thousand

Lathi –-Baton, usually used by the police to control crowds

Leela – Divine play or drama

Lord Vishwanatha – Lord of the Universe; another name for Shiva

Ma – Mother

Madhava – Another name for Krishna

Mahadeva – Great God; another name for Shiva

Maheswara – Great God; another name for Shiva

Mahout – Elephant handler

Mata – Mother

Maya – Illusion

Mela – Gathering

Milavu, Timila, Maddallam & Mrudangam – Percussion instruments

Mlecha – Barbaric/uncivilized people; term usually used for foreigners like the Greeks or Chinese, in ancient India

Moksha – Salvation; *nirvana* in Buddhism

Muzaris – Ancient port city on the South-Western coast of India, 50 kms north of modern-day Cochin, in Kerala

Nagas – An ancient tribe; literally 'serpents'; here they represent a warring tribe who that rises against caste oppression

Namaskara – 'I bow to the goodness in thee' – a form of greeting; also *Namaste*

Nishada – A hunter tribe

Onam – The only Indian festival celebrated in honour of an Asura King – Mahabali; State festival of Kerala; people still believe the reign of this Asura King (cheated of his kingdom by Lord Vishnu in his Vamana *avatar*), is the ideal, and every human being was considered equal

Pallavas – Ancient south-Indian kingdom; its capital was Kanchipuram/Kanchi

Pallu – The loose end of a sari draped over the head or over one shoulder

Panchayat – Indian village Council, usually with 5 members

Pandavas – Sons of Pandu

Pandya – Ancient kingdom in south India with Madurai as its capital

Parameswara – Literally 'Supreme God'; another name for Shiva, one of the Trinity of Hindu Gods (the other two being Brahma and Vishnu)

Parashuramakshetra – Place of Parashurama – the ancient kingdom of Cheras (Gokarna to Kanyakumari, between the Sahyas and the sea). It is believed Parashurama reclaimed this land from the sea and gifted it to the Brahmins

Pariah – Lowest caste, and the most discriminated against

Parvati – Lord Shiva's consort

Pasupathi – Literally 'Lord of the Beasts'; usually applied to Shiva

Patala – Netherworld; here, capital of the Asuras in exile

Poorna – River in Kerala; also known as Periyar

Prabhasa – A city in present-day Gujarat

Prabhu – Sir, an honorific; also used to mean a rich man

Puja – Religious ritual

Purendra – Indra, King of the Gods; also known as 'destroyer of cities'

Ragas – Scales in Indian classical music

Raja Dharma – Code of ethics for rulers

Rajasuya – Sacrifice performed by Indian Kings in ancient times, who considered themselves powerful enough to be Emperors

Rakshasa – Mythological evil being

Sabha – Court or assembly

Sahya – Mountains running parallel to the Western seaboard of India

Samhita – A collection of holy hymns/science/knowledge

Sanathana – Eternal; Hinduism is often considered to be an eternal religion without beginning or end

Sarpasatra – a sacrifice of serpents. This perhaps refers to an ancient pogrom when the Naga race was eliminated

Sari – Traditional attire of Indian women, made from six yards of unstitched cloth

Sarpanch – Village Chief/Head of the Panchayat

Sarswati – A mighty river which once flowed between the Indus and Ganges, which has now vanished

Shastras – Rules, codes, tradition, science, specialised knowledge

Shiva – The Destroyer, one of the Hindu Trinity of Gods who at the end of each eon, destroys the Universe, after which Brahma the Creator, re-creates it

Shivalinga – Phallic symbol of Lord Shiva

Shravan – Fifth month of the Hindu calendar; considered to be a holy month

Shri – Honorific for gentlemen; equivalent to Mister; also spelt *Sri, Shree* etc.

Shudra – Lowest of the four Varnas, the other three being (in order of precedence): Brahmana, Khshatriya, and Vaishya

Sindhu – River Indus; also the land around it; here, Indus is ruled by Jayadratha, Duryodhana's brother-in-law

Smritis – 'That which is remembered'; Hindu laws written by different sages; including *Manu Smriti*, the code for society in ancient India

Soma – Important ritual drink during Vedic times; also the moon

Somanatha – Celebrated temple of Lord Shiva – Lord of Somas (life energy)

Stithapranja – A rough translation is 'one who maintains equanimity in joy and sorrow'; however, the word has a deeper meaning and is said to encapsulate the essence of the Gita

Suta – Charioteer caste; also famous as storytellers. Kings often used them to propagate tales of their valour in battle

Swami – Sir, an honorific used to address a social superior

Swayamvara – Ancient Indian custom wherein a girl chose her groom from a gathering of suitors, sometimes through competition

Tapsya – Penance

Timila – Percussion instrument of Asura origin

Trimurti – Trinity of Gods: Brahma the Creator, Vishnu the Preserver, and Shiva the Destroyer

Tulsi – Holy Basil; a plant revered in Hinduism, especially in the worship of Krishna or Vishnu

Upanishads – Collection of holy books; along with the commentaries (called *Brahmanas*), forming the basis of Indian philosophical thought

Urumi – Sinuous, belt-like sword used in Kalaripayattu, an ancient martial art form of south India

Uttariya – Shawl, worn as a shoulder cloth

Vaikunta – Abode of Lord Vishnu and the heaven reserved for his devotees

Vaishya – Merchant caste

Vana – Grove or forest

Vanara – Monkey; here they are a tribe of mixed descent, living in southern India

Vanga – Present-day Bengal, including Bangladesh

Varna – Literally 'colour'; also meaning 'social groups'; Hindu society was divided into 4 basic *varnas*: Brahmana or Brahmins (Priests and teachers), at the top; Kshatriyas or warriors second; Vaishya or merchants third; and Shudras (farmers, craftsmen, foot soldiers, petty traders, dancers, musicians, etc) at the bottom of the caste hierarchy; below these were the poorest of the poor, the Untouchables

Varnashrama – In the ancient Hindu way of life, the ideal lifespan of an individual maintaining *dharma*, was divided into 4 stages: student, householder, retiree; and renunciation

Vatapi – Present-day Badami, a city in north-central Karnataka

Vayu – God of Winds

Vedas – The four holy books (*Rig, Yajur, Sama* and *Atharva*), of the Hindus; considered to possess all the wisdom of the world

Vijaya – Victory

Vindhyas – Mountain ranges which separate northern and southern India

Vishnu – The Preserver, second of the Hindu Trinity of Gods, who protects the rhythm of the Universe

Yadava – Tribe of cowherds

Yajna – Ritual sacrifice of herbal preparations into the fire with Vedic *mantras*

Yaksha – Supernatural beings, sometimes the patron Gods of trees and forests in Hindu mythology, believed to guard hidden treasures. The female of the species (Yakshi), are notorious for charming unsuspecting travellers into the forest and drinking their blood or eating them; here, they are simply a tribe

Yavana Desa – Greece

Yavana – Greek

ACKNOWLEDGEMENTS

My thanks go to my readers, without whose support, encouragement and criticism of my novels, Asura, Tale of the Vanquished and the first book of the Ajaya – epic of the Kaurava clan, Roll of the dice, I would not have dared to write the second part of *Ajaya – Rise of Kali* – within a year. I thank each of my readers who were kind enough to write to me with their feedback. I also thank the readers of the translated versions of Asura in Hindi, Tamil, Telugu, Marathi, Kannada, Malayalam and Gujarati languages.

To Swarup Nanda, for being friend and guide for *Asura* and *Ajaya*.

To my Editor, Chandralekha Maitra, for guiding me in making my writing better while giving me enough creative freedom, and then suffering my draft manuscripts with patience.

To my Publisher, Leadstart Publishing, for showing confidence in me by publishing my third book, Ajaya, Rise of Kali.

My sincere gratitude to the other team members: Daniel, Indur, Preeti, Iftikar, Rajesh, Ramu, Salam and many others, who have worked with dedication to make my previous books a great success and showing the same enthusiasm for this one.

To my father, the Late L. Neelakantan, and mother, the Late D. Chellamal, for introducing me to the world of mythology.

To my Aparna, for your unstinting support in my endeavours and for the love l often wonder if I deserve.

To my daughter Ananya and son Abhinav, for keeping the storyteller in me alive, by demanding more and more stories every night and being the kind of critics any author dreads.

To my sister Chandrika and my brother-in-law Parameswaran, my brothers Lokanathan, Rajendran and my sisters-in-law Meena and Radhika; also my nephew Dileep, and nieces Rakhi and Deepa, as well as my extended family members, for all those wonderful days.

To my pet Jacky, the blackie, who keeps me glued to my laptop by barking at the slightest show of laziness and demanding I take him for a walk as punishment the moment I lift my fingers from the keyboard.

To Santosh Prabhu, Sujith Krishnan, and Rajesh Rajan, for the evenings spent together discussing Indian philosophy and the *Mahabharata*, years ago, which sowed the seeds of this novel in me.

To Premjeet, for his maverick ideas, to Ashish Bhatnagar for reading and criticising my first drafts. To Essarpee (S R Prashanth) and D Sivaprasad, for their support in my online campaigns.

To my country and my people, for tolerating different points of view and for the richness of our history and mythology.

To the rich traditions of my hometown, Thripoonithura, and the history of Cochin.

To Vedavyasa, the patron of all Indian writers; the greatest writer to have walked this earth.

To the masters of writing in all our Indian languages, with sincere apologies for daring to attempt something that has already been so skillfully essayed by you over the centuries.

I owe much to all of you, as well as to the others who I may have not have named here.

*****

1 BESTSELLER

Tomorrow is my funeral. I do not know if they will bury me like a mangy dog or I will have a funeral fit for an Emperor – an erstwhile Emperor. But it does not really matter. I can hear the scuffing sounds made by the jackals. They are busy eating my friends and family. Something scurried over my feet. What was it? I haven't the strength to raise my head. Bandicoots. Big, dark, hairy rats. They conquer the battlefields after foolish men have finished their business of killing each other. It is a feast day for them today, just as it has been for the past eleven days. The stench is overpowering with the stink of putrefying flesh, pus, blood, urine and death. The enemy's and ours. It does not matter. Nothing matters now. I will pass out soon. The pain is excruciating. His fatal arrow struck my lower abdomen. But I am not afraid of death. I have been thinking of it for some time now. Thousands have been slain over the last few days.

Somewhere in the depths of the sea, my brother Kumbha lies dead, half-eaten by sharks. I lit my son Meghanada's funeral pyre yesterday. Or was it the day before? I've lost all sense of time. I have lost the sense of many things. A lonely star is shimmering in the depths of the universe. Like the eye of God. Very much like the third eye of Shiva, an all-consuming, all-destroying third eye. My beloved Lanka is being destroyed. I can still see the dying embers in what was once a fine city. My capital Trikota was the greatest city in the world. That was before the monkey-man came and set it on fire. Trikota burned for days. Shops, homes, palaces, men, women, and babies, everything burned. But we restored it. Almost every able man joined in rebuilding Trikota. Then the monkey-men came with their masters and destroyed everything again. Hanuman did that to us. The monkey-man brought us death, destruction and defeat.

I do not want to dwell on that. I should have killed him when my son captured him. Instead, I listened to my younger brother, who then plotted against me. But treason and betrayal is nothing new to the Asuras. I was naïve. I foolishly believed I would always be loved by my brothers and my people. I never imagined I would be betrayed. I feel like laughing now. But it is not easy to laugh when one's guts lie spread around like a wreath. Sounds of joy float down to me from my city. The enemy is celebrating their victory. The monkey-men will be busy plundering Trikota. My temples will be looted; the granaries torched, and schools and hospitals burnt. That is how victory parties are. We have done the same and worse to many Deva villages, when the Goddess of victory was my consort. Some ugly monkeys must have entered my harem. I hope my Queen has the sense to jump from a cliff before anything happens. I cannot control anything now. I can feel the hot breath of death on my face.

The jackals have come. Which part of my body will they eat first? Perhaps my guts, as they are still bleeding. What if a part of my breastplate chokes a jackal? I chuckle at the thought. A jackal sinks his teeth into my cheek and rips off a chunk of flesh. That is it. I've lost that bet too. They have started on my face. Rats are nibbling at my toes. I, Ravana, have come a long way. Now I do not have anything left to fight for, except this battle with the jackals. Tomorrow, there will be a procession through the streets. They will raise my head on a pole and parade it through

the same roads that saw me racing by in my royal chariot.
My people will throng to watch the spectacle with horror and
perverse pleasure. I know my people well. It will be a big show.
I do not understand why Rama came and stood over me when
I fell. He stood there as if bestowing his blessings upon me. He
said to his brother that I was the most learned man in the world
and a great King, and one could learn the art of governance
from me. I almost laughed out loud. I had governed so well
that my empire lay shattered all around me. I could smell the
burning corpses of my soldiers. I could feel my Meghanada's
cold and lifeless body in my arms even now. The acrid air of a
smouldering Trikota smothered my senses. I could not save my
people from these two warriors and their monkey-men. And he
was saying I was a great ruler? I could appreciate the irony of it.
I wanted to laugh at my enemy; laugh at the foolish men who
trusted me, who were now lying all around, headless, limbless
and lifeless. I wanted to laugh at the utopian dreams of equality
for all men on which I had built an empire. It was laughable
indeed. But laughing was no way for an Emperor to die. I have
worked hard and fought with the Gods and their chosen men. I
doubt if heaven has a place for people who die of laughter.

Then just as suddenly as it had started, the rats and jackals
scurried away. A shadow, darker than the dark night, fell upon
me. A dark head with curly hair blocked the lonely star from
my view. *Is it Kala, the God of Death, who has come to take me away?*
I struggled to open my eyes wider. But dried blood held my
eyelids together. *Is it one of Rama's lowly servants come to sever
my head and take it back as a trophy?* I want to look him in the
face. I want to look into his eyes, unwavering and unflinching
in my last moments. Something about that head and curly hair
reminded me of my past. *Do I know him?* He leaned down to
look at my face.

Ah! It is Bhadra. My friend, perhaps the only friend left, but I
do not know if I can call him my friend. He was my servant, a
foot soldier to start with. Then he got lost somewhere along the
way. He strolled in and out of my life, was sometimes missing
for years together. Bhadra had access to my private camp when I

was the head of a troop that resembled a wayside gang of robbers rather than a revolutionary army. Then, he had had access to my private chambers when I was the King of a small island. Finally, he had access to my bedroom when I was ruling India. More than that, Bhadra had access to the dark corners of my mind, a part that I hid from my brothers, my wife, my lover, my people, and even from myself.

What is Bhadra doing here? But why am I surprised? This is just the place for people like him, who move about in the shadows. I can hear him sobbing. Bhadra getting emotional? He was never angry, sad or happy. He acted as if he was very emotional now. But I knew he had no emotions. And Bhadra was aware I knew. *Bhadra, carry me away from here. Take me away to...* My strength fails me. I do not know whether the words were spoken or died a silent death somewhere in my throat. Bhadra shakes his head. I am cold, extremely cold. My life is ebbing out of me. Then Bhadra hugs my head to his bosom. I can smell his sweat. Pain shoots through me from every angle and spreads its poisonous tentacles into my veins. I groan. Bhadra lays me back on the wet earth – wet from my blood, the blood of my people, the blood of my dreams, and the blood of my life. It is over. A sense of sadness and emptiness descends upon me.

"I will complete your work, Your Highness. Go in peace. I will do it for our race. My methods may be different, even ignoble, compared to yours. I too was once a warrior but I have grown old. Arms frighten me now. I am terrified of war. I cannot even hurt a child. Nevertheless, my methods are deadly. I will avenge you, me, and our blighted race. Rama will not go free for what he has done to us. Believe me and go in peace."

I did not hear most of what Bhadra said. Strangely however, I was soothed and slipped away from this foul-smelling Asura and drifted back to my childhood. A thousand images rushed to me. My early struggles, the pangs of love and abandonment, separation, battles and wars, music and art, they flashed through my mind in no particular order, making no sense. Meaningless, like life itself.

I sensed Bhadra bowing down to touch my feet, then walking away. I wanted to call him back and take me to a doctor who would put my intestines back, fit my dangling left eye back into its socket and somehow blow life into my body. I wanted to withdraw to the Sahyas forests in the mainland and start a guerilla war, as Mahabali had done years ago. I wanted to start again. I wanted to make the same mistakes, love the same people, fight the same enemies, befriend the same friends, marry the same wives and sire the same sons. I wanted to live the same life again. I did not want the seat Rama has reserved for me in his heaven. I only wanted this beautiful earth.

I knew it was not going to happen. I was sixty, not sixteen. If I lived, I would be a one-eyed, dirty, old beggar in some wayside temple, wearing stinking and tattered clothes – a long way from what I once was. I wanted to die now. I wanted this to end. I wanted to go away. Let the burning cities take care of themselves. Let the Asuras fight their own wars and be damned along with the Devas. I only wanted to return to my childhood and start over again, every single damn thing, again and again, and again...

*****